CRIMSON SKIES

FALLEN FAE GODS 2

JAYMIN EVE

ZAHAK

The beast clawed beneath my skin.

It had been decades since I'd last lost control, but the moment a tiny human wandered into my life, I'd been on the edge of destroying everything I'd built over the last few hundred years.

"What was that?" she gasped, swiveling her head so rapidly that I worried she'd hurt herself.

Her fear was palpable in the air, scenting it darker with a hint of floral and feminine undertones.

Her fear was understandable though.

We were deep in the trench that ran between the lands of Eastern Risest, thrown there by my mother, who had, not even an hour ago, invaded our world. The last thing I saw before her energy blasted us here had been dozens of other dragon shifters drifting down near the Fae Academy.

I had no idea where my brothers had ended up. It was just Morgan and me in this tunnel. We had to get out of here as quickly as possible and put an end to whatever plan my mother had in mind when she brought in the forces.

"You're safe, *la moyar*," I murmured, hands clenched at my sides so I didn't reach for her.

Ever since the night of the fertility ritual, when I'd holed up in my cavern to avoid the aphroditic energies, my dragon had been shifting uneasily. I hadn't truly understood why, when we'd always been content to sleep through the previous ones, until my cock had hardened and the knot throbbed at the base.

My knot for my mate.

A mate who was falsely *bonded to my fucking brother*.

At first, I'd questioned my sanity, until they arrived in Risest. That was when I understood exactly what had happened.

I should have killed Drager years ago and saved us all the trouble of dealing with him.

"Are you sure?" She turned the full force of her focus in my direction and I marveled at the soft beauty of her face. I wasn't used to soft, not in the centuries I'd roamed the worlds. We were human and dragon shifter, incompatible in all ways—my sheer size alone could destroy her.

But I couldn't walk away.

I hadn't been able to walk away from sending Astra to scout around Lancourt to find her essence. My sabre had informed me that my brother was all but keeping her prisoner, which had brought me to his floating land for the first time. Drager had challenged me, already laying his claim to Morgan.

My rage and confusion were beyond scope, but eventually I calmed, and with that came clarity, and a sense of why this was happening. Drager and I were born of the same pod, and we were bonded—whether I liked it or not. I sensed that he felt a confused connection to the human because of our bond. I was still debating if I should kill the fucker and just forget about the rest.

"I promise you're safe," I rumbled, focusing once more. "My dragon is aware of everything in our vicinity. There's only Astra and a few small *eonis* bugs against the wall."

She rubbed her hands over her arms, and fire burned in my gut as she shivered. There was no way she was cold when I naturally threw off enough heat to warm a large room, but she was afraid. A fear that wouldn't ease until we'd left the trench.

"I have an eerie feeling trailing down my spine," she admitted, voice strong despite her worries. "I felt a similar fear when I was near Cal, who's a *yonter*. Possibly it's just being in this trench, you know? Sometimes it's just human instinct that there's danger, not necessarily right in front of you but somewhere out there."

I'd lived in silence for so many years that I'd have expected her brand of nervous chatter would drive me insane. Only, it didn't. I wanted to hear more. I wanted to hear everything about her. Fuck, I would listen to her recite the scriptures if it meant she'd just keep talking.

"The trench is built on the blood of thousands of fae," I said, keeping my voice low. The urge to lie to ease her fears was strong, but as fate had decided to join my bloodstained soul to hers, I wouldn't start our bonding in that way—with falsehoods. "Both of the nightmare variety, and those they lured to their deaths. It's not a place of peace, but we'll get through it just fine. I'm not the god of this land for nothing. I've tamed the nightmares once, and I'll do it again."

I couldn't shift in these narrow tunnels without risking her safety, but even on two legs I was formidable. My reputation here would also be an asset, but with my vulnerable mate to protect, I wouldn't be overconfident. I had to stay two steps ahead at all times.

We continued walking in silence, which was... comfortable. As strange as it seemed.

"How long have you thought we were mates?" she asked, her voice a whisper.

Amusement danced through me, and I almost laughed out loud. "There's no *thought* about it, sweetheart. I've known from the moment you fucked my brother."

She choked on her breath. "A sentence I never expected to hear anyone say. Ever." My mate was resilient, which she'd need to survive in my world.

There was another brief pause. "You're angry about that? About Drager and me? You didn't try and steal me away and it has been weeks. Why?"

Angry? No, I wasn't *angry*. I was the burning rage of a thousand dragons.

From the moment I'd felt her presence in this world, it had taken everything inside *not to steal her away* like the beasts of old and keep her in my cave until she submitted to me. I'd kill Drager first, of course, and then I'd hoard my treasure.

That had been the plan, too, that day in Lancourt, until I'd seen her wide-eyed and fearful stare. That was the moment I realized I didn't want her to fear me. Everyone else could whisper my name in the darkness, like a demon of the night, but Morgan... she was the one living creature in this world, outside of Astra, who needed to find comfort in my presence.

For that, I held my instinct at bay, and decided patience was the key.

"The plan was to destroy my brother and claim my mate that day in Lancourt," I admitted to her, hoping this wasn't when she ran screaming from me. "That was also the day I discovered that you were human. Human and afraid of me. I realized two truths as you stared up at me as if I were a monster. One: you never had the energy of a beast to guide you, and no doubt knew nothing about mates. Two: I wanted you to choose me and not have it be demanded by our nature."

She was just staring at me, her eyes wide and shiny, and I fucking hoped she didn't cry because I would lose my shit.

"I blame Drager for taking what wasn't his to take, even if it was through confusion due to our pod bond, and a sliver of the true mate energy seeping through. You're an innocent in all of this, and I will murder anyone who says otherwise."

I'd already wiped out one family for her, and wouldn't hesitate to do it again.

"I've had enough bouquets of heads for now, thank you," she replied drily. "And I have two truths for you as well. One: I was afraid of you that day, but I was also completely in awe. I couldn't stop thinking about your beast and was desperate to see the man behind it. And two: you shouldn't blame Drager completely. If this is true, what you say—" She cleared her throat. "—then my bond with you had him very confused. He couldn't figure out why I was drawn to him, and he had no choice but to continuously reinforce our bond due to the energy of this world near destroying me."

"Which is the sole reason he's still breathing," I huffed. But if he touched her again, now that these truths were out there, I would lay waste to him and his entire land. "What are your feelings for my brother?"

My beast wouldn't settle until we knew, because in the end it mattered very little how Drager felt about my tiny mate. It only mattered how she felt.

Morgan slowed, turning to face me, her eyes wide and shiny once more. She didn't answer immediately, and I liked that she was considering her answer. "Most of the time I hate him," she finally said, clearing her throat. "He's inconsiderate, dresses me in clothes I can't stand, and doesn't really care about my frailties as a human. But there's just… we do have a bond." She pressed her hands against her stomach, and then her chest. "I can feel him here. Not all the time, but it's there, and I don't know what to do or think about any of this. Is our bond really all because of you? Or is there a genuine connection with Drager as well?"

My dragon's rumbles built in my chest, and I briefly closed my eyes against my fury. "The connection is from me," I bit out, "but the bonding has been manually achieved through his infusion of energy. I have no idea if it's permanent or not at this stage, but trust me, if he's never knotted you again, or been able to feel your mind, then he's not your mate."

Barely able to stop myself from reaching out and dragging her body against mine, I turned away and started marching along the tunnel again, only slowing my steps when I noticed that she was having to jog to keep up. "How come you aren't in my mind all the time?" she asked breathlessly, her curiosity rearing up again. She looked less nervous as we talked, and I calmed as she did.

"Drager," I answered with a snarl; the one topic to have my fury rising again. "His energy is working as a block around yours. I've only been able to push through a few times."

She pressed her lips firmly together, and I heard the deep sigh that tried to escape her. "I can't read your mind," I told her, wondering if that was bothering her. "That won't happen until we're fully bonded, and even then you'll learn how to keep me out—if that's your desire. My brothers and I have a similar connection, able to contact each other over great distances, but most of the time we block those pathways."

My connection to Drager was more difficult to completely shut off, but we rarely bothered to chat mentally. We lost our reliance on one another many years ago, and none of us felt any need to rekindle it. Our animosity had weakened us, as Tylan had said in the clearing before we were attacked. It bothered me that we'd let our petty differences get in the way of building an alliance so strong no one could ever stand against us.

We were the cause of our own downfall. Our only hope was to repair our bonds and form a singular unit of strength before our world was destroyed.

"I don't know how to feel about all of this," she admitted. "On Earth, we don't have true mates. Half the time we don't even have true love. We have the right place and the right time situations, and eventually the magic fails and we get beaten, ignored, or cheated on. Then we divorce and start again. Hence why I mostly fall in love with fictional characters."

Before my brain caught up with my actions, I was wrapping my hands around her tiny shoulders and hauling her up closer to me. She let out a low squeak, pupils dilating as she breathed fast and hard. "What?" she squeaked again. "Are we under attack?"

My beast calmed when we realized that her first instinct hadn't been to expect an attack from me... she thought I was saving her. My sweet human.

"Who hurt you?" I rasped around the beat of my beast. "Give me their names."

I would kill them.

I'd destroy their entire bloodline so that there would never be the taint of their sin in the world again.

She blinked rapidly, before a soft smile tilted up her lips. "There's been no human men who hurt me, Z," she said in her reassuring way. "Don't worry. But I've seen enough in the world and heard enough to know how it usually is."

Leaning in closer, I breathed in her scent. Her fear was fading, replaced by a light muskiness which had my dragon raging inside me. She stiffened just enough that I understood I was pushing her too fast, so I released her gently.

"We need to keep moving," she choked out. "I'm starting to get thirsty and hungry, and… I need to pee." The last four words were rushed and mumbled, her cheeks tinged pink, and my beast was pleased that our mate needed us to take care of her.

"I think there's an area that will satisfy at least two of those needs coming up," I told her.

Her cheeks grew even pinker, but my brother's fucking energy stopped me from receiving the thoughts that went along with her embarrassment.

By the time we were out of the trench, I needed him cleansed from her essence.

No exceptions.

CHAPTER 2

MORGAN

His presence was unnerving.

Drager had never been a huge conversationalist, but Zahak was even less so. Weirdly, though, despite having spent less than a day with him in total, and having spoken only a dozen or so sentences, there was a familiarity I couldn't explain.

Yes, I was aware that he believed we were true mates, and while I wasn't dismissing it outright—too many of our interactions supported said belief— I was biding my time in exploring this possibility.

We were in a dangerous situation, and as such there was no real time for romance or mate bonds or untangling the tangled webs of Drager and Zahak.

It was insane to think that not even two months ago I'd been in my home in Biddeford, Maine, with my best friend Lexie, blissfully unaware that there was an entire supernatural world connected to the library where we worked. I'd also been unaware that Lexie herself was a fae who came from this supernatural world, and that a lot of what I'd built my life around was not, in fact… well, human.

Since then, I'd participated in a thirty-day fertility ritual with one of their fae gods, Drager, who happened to be a dragon shifter. He was one of five brothers: the Fallen Five. That ritual had changed my entire life. Not only did I get incredible sex, but I'd been pulled from my mundane existence into a fantastical experience that I still found difficult to believe.

In addition to the sex, I'd also found myself trapped on a floating land—Drager was still a fucker for that—carried to the ground by a murderous bird and almost died—multiple times; discovered more about this world; attended Fae Academy; learned about the land of Eastern Risest and the Fallen gods they worshipped; and finally figured out who the traitor was.

Their mother.

Apparently, the Fallen, for all their power and strength, had a very large empty spot in their memories when it came to the world they were born to. Which was not Risest, the fae world. A spot that was a little less empty now that their mother had decided to reveal her hand and make known the reasons for her sneaking around and stealing from her sons.

"Your mother clearly plans to invade, right?"

We'd been walking for hours in the trench of nightmare creatures. It was dark, with only the natural energy illumination of Zahak to light our way. It was very quiet in here too, and my worry that I was about to be torn apart by nightmare creatures had faded over time, replaced with fatigue and hunger. Zahak had found some naturally occurring water seeping from the rocks, but there was no food. I'd missed second breakfast, and that was not okay with me.

"Her actions suggest that has been her plan," he rumbled.

All of the Fallen had deep, hypnotic voices that wrapped around your essence and seeped into your being. But Drager and Zahak were the most devastating, and when I was unprepared, i.e. hadn't heard their voices in a long while, it always knocked me back a step.

"Why wouldn't she just come to you and let you know about the plan?" I asked. "You're her sons, and surely the entire point of sending you here in the first place was to prepare this world for a takeover."

The tunnel grew narrower, and I had to huddle in closer to Zahak, desperately trying to ignore the tingles of his energy caressing my skin. The longer I spent around the Fallen Five, the more adept I was at dealing with the waves of power they naturally exuded, but I doubted I'd ever be completely comfortable.

"I have a couple of theories, but until I get back up top and see what's happening, there's no way to know which is the correct one."

He didn't say anything else as the tunnel narrowed further. When he reached out and captured my shoulders, I barely managed not to gasp. His grip was firm as he steered me in front of him, and I tried not to panic at how close the walls were.

Or in truth, how close Zahak was.

This was not the place for heavy breathing. Gods no. It would be so obvious and then there'd be awkward questions, and I just needed to sort myself out immediately.

Astra, Zahak's sabre—a panther-like creature who was immensely adept at hunting—let out a purring rumble, and I was relieved to have her as both a distraction and a guard at our backs.

Despite Zahak's assurances that we were safe, and no

nightmare creatures made this section of tunnel home, I couldn't shake my unease. I hadn't felt this fear since Calendul, and I knew that whatever was out there would eventually make itself known.

Thankfully, the tunnel widened once more, and I found my rapid pulse calming. "So, what are your theories?" I pressed, desperately needing the distraction. Not to mention it was kind of important that we dealt with his mother and her plans, and for that, discussion was required. "It's so hard when you're without your memories."

The Fallen Five did not remember why they'd been sent to this world, and that in and of itself was suspicious. On top of that, his mother had been stealing books and tomes of information, learning about Risest and undoubtedly the best way to infiltrate it.

To my surprise, Zahak didn't hesitate to answer. He was less cryptic than Drager, that was for sure. "When we first fell to Risest, we knew our names and the name of the world we'd left, *Xalifer*, and that was the most of it. I mean, we knew we were brothers as well. We could feel the energy bond between us, but the rest was dark... empty. We assumed we had parents at some point, since most living creatures do, but there was a blank space when we tried to remember even a single detail. Over time, more memories emerged, and we started to believe our world had been destroyed. That we were the last of our kind."

I couldn't even imagine how that must have felt, being in a strange new place with no memories.

"I'm glad you had each other," I said gently.

He examined me for a long moment, the soft light he exuded highlighting the perfection of his face. He was tall, at least six-foot-eight, and exceptionally beautiful. The rugged planes of his face formed a being so masculine and strong that I found it hard to stare at him for too long.

Thankfully he released me from his focus and turned back to face the path we walked along.

"My brothers are more often than not a blessing and a curse," he said with a tinge of amusement. "Back to your previous questions, though, I think we're correct in stating that Mother was gathering information to invade us. The parts I don't understand are why we lost our memories when we fell and why she's waited so long to make her presence known. We've been here for a couple of centuries. We've held dominion over this land for almost as long, and yet she falls now."

"At the same time as me," I whispered.

It was a stupid thought, because I was one insignificant human in the grand scheme of everything, and yet I couldn't shake the feeling that my presence had something to do with the timing of this invasion.

"It's a worry that she didn't contact you first," I hurried to add, so he didn't consider my stupidly blurted thought for too long. "If you're all in this together, then she wouldn't have snuck around and stolen from you."

There was a deep-seated fury in Zahak's expression, clear, even in the dim light of his energy. "As I told my brothers, I've long thought that we didn't end up here by accident, and that the missing memories were also not a result of our fall. Whatever information we did retain was probably planted as well."

"Like the fact that your world was destroyed."

I'd spent a lot of time trying to work out the plot holes in this fantasy story. Mostly so my brain didn't implode at the fact that I'd *somehow fallen down the rabbit hole into a fantasy world.* A hole full of bitey rabbits.

"Exactly that. None were supposed to have survived," Zahak said, rubbing his hand across his face in a tired motion. "But considering how many fell with Mother, there's more of our world left than we originally believed."

His world: Xalifer. I tried to picture what it must have looked like, but honestly, all I could see was darkness. We needed more information.

"Have more memories returned to you now?" The appearance of his mother and other dragons had to have triggered locked away memories.

He paused, turning to see me better. "A few. And it sounds as if you already guessed as such."

I shrugged. "As an avid reader who lives life in fantasy worlds on paper, my brain is always trying to figure out the ending before I get to it."

For a second, it almost looked like he was reaching for me again. My body leaned in closer, anticipating the touch, but then he dropped his clenched fists at his side. "The truth is on the edge of my memory now," he admitted hoarsely. "My mother's voice unlocked her existence, and I am certain that we left Xalifer for a reason not related to its destruction, but I can't quite grasp the memories."

That was the most frustrating part of all: the Fallen Five no doubt held all the answers, if we could just figure out how to unlock their brains.

The tunnel widened further, the ceiling rising above our heads until I could breathe freely. It had been hard, for multiple reasons, to be in those tightly enclosed spaces. "Tell me about Xalifer," I said, needing imagery to fill in the darkness. "What was your homeworld like?"

His expression was hard to read as he tilted his head, keeping an eye on all our surroundings. "It was beautiful," he eventually said. "Lush and green, with lots of mountains.

Dragons love mountains, hence why Drager built his house in the sky. Risest, while holding similar landscapes, lacks mountains."

"Is it cold?"

I was building layers in my head, adding in elements to his home… to the world he grew up in.

"The south is," he said with a smile. "I remember flights through the snow as it surrounded my village." He paused. "No… not village. Castle. I grew up in a castle." He shook his head. "That was hidden from me until I searched for it."

Without thought, I grasped his hand, squeezing it tightly. "You might be royalty, or part of the guard."

As tingles and heat raced up my hand and into my arm, I went to release my hold on him but his grip tightened. My body responded in kind, as a tight ache deep in my center. A simple touch that in some ways felt beyond what I'd had with Drager, even when his energy filled me.

Zahak leaned in and I held my breath, anticipating what was about to happen. Was he going to kiss me? The heat and fire of his scent washed over me as he said, "We should rest here for the night. The area is somewhat deserted, and I can feel your exhaustion."

He released me and I almost fell flat on my face. The urge to fan my face was strong, and I had to suck in heated air as my lungs ached.

Astra growled, which turned out to be an excellent distraction. Zahak stroked her head softly, and I tried not to feel jealous of a cat. "Astra was an apex predator in these tunnels when I found her," he continued. "She'll be a great deterrent to any attacks."

Her growls turned to purrs as she butted her head against his hand. I'd learned with Astra that it didn't matter if you were an ancient black panther-like beast over six-feet long, as tall as me, with tentacle-weapon whiskers and lethal teeth, you were always a kitty at heart.

"I'm fine with resting here for the night," I said softly. He was correct. I was exhausted from the events of the day so far, including the many hours we'd been walking through the trench.

Zahak led us toward a small alcove which was protected by rock walls on two sides. I sat in a corner, my back against the wall and Astra crawled in next to me to snuggle against my right thigh. Zahak didn't join us though.

"Where are you going?" I asked. The thought of him leaving had panic racing through my body. Astra was amazing, but there was no substitute for the dragon shifter.

"To see if I can find food. You're hungry."

He leaned in and briefly ran his finger across my cheek. A fleeting movement, but I felt the burn of his touch even as he turned and strode off into the darkness. A darkness that surrounded me the moment my source of light was gone. Digging my fingers into Astra's fur, I tried not to freak out. *If you can't see them, they can't see you. If you can't see them, they can't see you.*

The fact that this was wholly inaccurate—my senses were weak and pathetic compared to most faerie creatures—didn't stop me from repeating it over and over in my head.

Astra purred and rumbled at my side as one of her huge paws landed in my lap. A second later, her fur started to twinkle, her energy able to project ambient light as well. "Thank you," I choked out, leaning down and pressing my face against hers. "You're a wonderful friend."

She purred even harder, and the warmth in my chest grew stronger. I loved this scary-ass cat like she was my own, and I'd throw myself in front of a nightmare creature to save her. Animals… they wrapped around your heart and never let go.

Buried against her warmth, I must have dozed off in my exhaustion. No doubt not the safest action when we were in danger like this, but hey, I was only human. Still, when I heard the scrape of rocks a few yards away, my senses came back online with force.

Astra was on her feet in a beat, prowling forward, her entire body rumbling as menacing growls erupted from her. Whatever comfort and relaxation I'd managed to achieve by napping with my kitty was dashed like a bucket of ice water had been dropped on my head. On my feet now too, I shuffled forward, hand on Astra's back as I squinted into the darkness.

Whatever was out there wasn't Zahak, because Astra wouldn't have shifted an inch from our comfortable cuddle. She was in protective mode, which meant a threat was moving toward us. Astra's rumbles increased, and I noticed in the twinkling lights of her skin that her tentacles were growing longer, extending from her face as the serrated edges sharpened.

She was readying the weapons at her disposal, and I could do nothing but peer with anxiety into the darkness. Was anxiety a weapon? If so, then I was armed to the fucking teeth.

The shuffling grew louder until eventually its maker was visible in the dim light Astra projected around us. Which was the exact moment I almost peed myself.

A creature stood before us, and I knew this was the end.

Oh my gods, we're about to die.

CHAPTER 3

MORGAN

The creature was unlike anything I expected to see in a faerie world—even in the nightmare portion of it. It looked like a bear, well over six-feet tall and up on two legs, with short black fur. It had a more elongated snout than a bear with rows of crocodile teeth, and glowing red eyes.

Screams were trapped in my throat as my fear increased tenfold. If I hadn't felt that fear inducing energy from Cal and the Fallen Five before, I'd have probably lost my mind at the sensations rushing through me.

The creature shuffled forward, and I wondered if it had been recently watching serial killer documentaries—nothing like the slow shuffle of a killer to really get the blood pumping. But as more of the giant creature grew visible in Astra's light, I noticed that it wasn't shuffling to induce fear. There was something wrong with it.

"Is that what the nightmare creatures look like down here?" I breathed.

Astra snarled, unable to communicate with me, which was once again super inconvenient. The bear-crocodile shuffled even closer, until it was mere feet from us, and I almost screamed when a chunk of its fur slid off and landed with a soft plop on the rocky floor. Chunks were missing all over it, to the point that I could see bone in some sections, along with a lot of red muscle and sinewy veins. A gurgle escaped as it took another step forward.

"We have to move, Astra," I said in a rush. "That cannot be a normal nightmare creature. It looks sick."

I'd seen a few nightmare creatures at the academy and not a single one looked like this. I mean, there was nothing more nightmarish than zombie-like decaying monsters, but I refused to believe this was normal.

Pressing against Astra's side, I attempted to shuffle her out of the alcove so we could make a run for it. We needed to find Zahak; he'd know what to do. Not to mention that if we stayed in this little alcove, the bear-crocodile zombie would have us trapped in seconds.

Of course, no one moved a sabre unless they wanted to be moved. Her body swelled up as she rumbled the most menacing growl I'd ever heard from her, and I felt her tense as if she was preparing to attack. Just as she moved, a small squeal escaped my pursed lips, and there was a whip of command. "Astra, no!"

The dragon shifter's words slammed into me, and even the nightmare creature ground to a halt, another chunk of fur falling from the side of its head, giving us a lovely view of its skull.

Nice, I'd be adding that image to my nightmare brain bank as well, thanks so fucking much.

Astra retreated without touching the beast, and now she was the one nudging me out of the alcove. Apparently, there were no communication issues between her and Zahak. The moment we were out of the line of fire, the light grew super bright in the tunnel and I had to close my eyes against the blast of heat as Zahak incinerated the bear zombie.

Holding on to Astra, I let out another embarrassing squeak at a soft touch across my cheek. Opening my eyes wide, I found Zahak close. "Are you okay?" he rumbled. Between my shock and finding him this close, I was at a complete loss for words. All I could do was stare. "Morgan," he pushed, "I'm going to need you to answer me, sweetheart. My dragon is on edge, and killing the beast hasn't appeased us one bit."

Zahak and his dragon. The pair who had removed heads and placed them on spikes for me like a lovely bouquet. He was always stepping in and saving me, protecting me, and it was so overwhelming that my emotions choked me again. My gaze darted beside him to the scorch mark, which was all that remained of the bear. "What was it?" I rasped before wetting my lips. "It looked like a decaying zombie-bear."

"Morgan…" His voice was deeper than ever. He wasn't budging until I answered his question.

"I'm totally fine. It didn't touch me."

He examined me for a beat longer, and as the tension released from his body the animalistic gleam faded from his eyes. He straightened to his giant height and looked around. "That was a *cranbil*, but it has been affected by an energy I've never felt before. I found other creatures decaying in the same manner. It's as if a disease is spreading amongst them."

Which explained why his command to Astra had been so strongly issued. "If Astra bit into them, she might have been infected," I said, a shiver chasing down my spine at the close call we'd just had. "And I'm guessing there's no chance of food if the creatures are diseased."

He looked grim. "I'm sorry. I can't risk you eating any of the normal prey down here. We're just going to have to pick up the pace."

Without thinking, I placed my hand on Zahak's arm, comforting him. He'd sounded frustrated and worried about not being able to provide me with food, but he'd literally just saved our lives, which was more than enough.

I jolted at the burst of heat and power under my palm. I'd felt a similar burst the first time I'd voluntarily touched Drager, but we'd been locked in the energy of a fertility ritual at the time.

There was no ritual with Zahak, and yet I still couldn't remove my hand.

This is our bond, la moyar. You will come to understand soon.

For the third time in ten minutes I squeaked, and if I did it again, I'd have to slap myself. But... *he was so clearly in my head!* What the actual fuck? His voice, deeper and more vibrational in my mind, echoed through every part of me, settling like fire into my gut.

Can you hear me? As weird as it felt, I had to try to project my voice back.

Deep laughter echoed through my mind. *You'll grow used to it with time. I won't ever push through your natural barriers, unless I need to for your safety.*

I narrowed my eyes on him. *I'm too human for this. At least pretend I can keep you out when we have an argument.*

The shimmery gold in his eyes darkened, and he didn't push me further. His energy withdrew from my body, and I refused to let the melancholy of the loss overcome me. Sure, for the first time in my life I hadn't felt alone, but I'd spent too many years scraping up independence to ever accept needing another person to make me whole again.

I couldn't do it.

Jerking my hand off Zahak, I tried to calm my breathing, and he let me have my moment as he looked around the cavern. "Now that we're aware of the situation under here…" he said. Zombie-talk was an excellent distraction. "…I'm not sure we should linger any longer. I know you haven't rested, but do you think you can keep going?"

My body was sore, legs aching, but I was way too hyped to sleep. Touching Zahak was akin to slamming down ten energy drinks. "I can keep going for a while."

He nodded, and his expression grew even grimmer. "I don't think it's a good idea for you to consume the water any longer. I couldn't detect anything in it, but this disease is like nothing I've ever experienced in my lands. It's a darkness, slimy and cloying, and as a human I worry how you'll be affected."

"I won't last long without water," I reminded him. I refused to panic about it though. If I was about to die of thirst, I'd risk the water. I'd already had some, and so far felt completely fine.

"I'm going to get you out of here fast," he promised me.

Before I could ask an important question like *How?* he reached out and looped his long arm around my waist, lifted me into his side, and then took off through the tunnels. "Zahak!" I shouted, but my voice was lost in his speed.

I'd traveled like this once before with Drager and had to close my eyes to keep the contents of my stomach inside my body. Zahak was no different, even with most of our surroundings in darkness.

Why bother to ask if I was too tired to walk? I shot snippily at him, using our mental connection before I even realized I was.

His response was more husky laughter, and no lie, I grew a little addicted every time I heard that sound. When he spoke, he was strong and stoic, along with very scary. But that laugh felt different... almost as if it was just for me.

Zahak moved us at warp speed for a long time, and I took the opportunity to nap. I was sure he'd let me walk again at some point, and when that happened I needed as much energy as possible. The lack of food and water would slow me soon enough, I didn't want to add lack of sleep in there as well.

After what felt like hours, the dragon shifter's steps slowed, and I was able to sleepily open my eyes. "Whoa," I murmured, as light filtered through the chasm, displaying just how deep we were under the mainland of Isle of Denille.

"This is where natural structural shifts have occurred," Zahak said quietly, looking around. "Greenery has crept back in here, thanks to the energy of the sun."

He set me on my feet, and no joke, it took a beat for me to find the strength to keep myself upright. Apparently, all it took was a few hours of a giant dragon carrying me around and my legs were ready to retire.

When I was able to stand without wobbling, I followed Zahak to explore. "Everything here looks normal," he rumbled. "When I first arrived in my land, there was a thriving ecosystem of greenery under here. Hence how Astra and the few remaining ocher sabres were able to survive."

"Why'd you close it, then? Shouldn't you have just left them alone?"

He took a minute to answer, and I wondered if I'd touched on a sensitive subject. My ignorance of certain customs and checkered histories here had gotten me into trouble more than once. "In hindsight," he finally said, voice huskier than ever, "I should have left them be. Our arrival awoke them from the instability that had been controlling their lives for far too long, and they all wanted a new start. They asked me to destroy the chasm so they could have a clean slate. But I don't think the world above was what they expected. They live separately now, outside of their nightmare clans, and while there are aspects that they find easier, I know they mourn their losses."

Astra purred deeply, and I found myself reaching out and rubbing her head gently—the echoing sadness in her purr was painful to hear.

"There's a chance you could reverse it one day," I suggested, no doubt unhelpfully. "We must learn from our pasts to create better futures. I get that you five are considered gods, but that doesn't mean you're infallible. It really just means your mistakes can be on a grander scale. But this might be... fixable." Right?

He watched me closely, giving no indication if he appreciated my unsolicited advice. Thankfully, before it got too awkward in here, Astra made a sound I hadn't heard before. A deeper rumble, and her eyes glowed red.

"Is she okay?" I said as unease trickled down my spine once more. We knew there were zombie-nightmares in here, and I doubted that bear was the last we'd see. Were we about to be attacked again?

"She senses a new energy," Zahak said as he leaned down toward her. "What is it, girl? What do you feel?"

It was clear that nightmare creatures were more in tune with this world than Zahak, and he trusted her instincts. Astra rumbled in that deeper, unusual way, and started to prowl forward. She was in hunting mode, even though her fangs weren't visible... yet.

We followed behind, Zahak reaching out to sweep me closer, and I tried to ignore the explosion of tingling energy between us. He wasn't speaking in my mind, but the connection lingered and strengthened as we spent time together.

Thankfully, I had a rather large distraction in the form of Astra, who continued to prowl deeper along the path. Small shrubberies that I couldn't identify grew in the rock floor here, and even larger branches emerged in cracks of the side wall, where water trickled along.

Her rumbling grew louder and louder, and when she paused and then stepped to the side, I finally noticed the beast that had drawn her attention. It was larger than Astra by a good few feet, sprawled out on its side, unmoving.

"Oh no," I cried, feeling my eyes heat. "What happened?"

It was an ocher sabre like Astra, with the same black coat and ancient beauty, but this one was clearly dead, its fur and flesh having fallen off in chunks, leaving just the decaying carcass. It didn't smell bad to my nose, but it had drawn Astra with her advanced senses.

For a long moment she simply stared down at the fallen beast while Zahak and I remained silently at her side, before she tilted back her head and let out a mournful cry. That sorrowful bellow filled my body until my chest ached, and I didn't even attempt to halt the tears trailing down my cheeks. Astra was mourning more than just the loss of one ocher sabre here; she was mourning the loss of the last of her kind.

"I'm sorry, old friend," Zahak said, placing his hand on her back in support, voice gruff. "I will find out who did this to my creatures, and then I'll take great pleasure in destroying them."

Astra's cry turned less mournful as her fangs emerged. She wanted to destroy them too, and I had to admit, as I stared down, my throat tight, I was on board with the plan.

These creatures did not deserve this. They'd been minding their business, living down here in their world, and they did not...

My angry thoughts were cut off by a tiny cry, so soft that Astra and Zahak, who were conversing with rumbles and angry words, didn't react. Wondering if I was losing my mind and imagining sounds, I shuffled forward.

"Morgan, what are you doing?" Zahak immediately noticed me edging along the side of the dead beast, and even though I was fairly certain this was all just my crazy imagination, I held up a hand, asking for an extra moment.

To my surprise, he let me continue with my task, and as I rounded toward the back of the sabre's corpse, another little cry emerged. This time the dragon shifter reacted, his body stiffening as he laser-focused on the dead creature.

Using my foot to shift the tail, I was almost certain this was where the sound had originated.

Oh my god. Oh my god.

Staring down, wondering if I was hallucinating, I examined the most perfect creature I'd ever seen. A baby ocher sabre, safely protected under its mother. Her last task had been to shield her cub from whatever had taken them all out.

How was this possible?

CHAPTER 4

ZAHAK

It *was not possible.*

My movements were slower than usual, as shock held me in its grasp. Not so slow though, that I didn't reach Morgan before she managed to pick the cub up. "No," I growled, then forced myself to temper that tone. "Don't touch it yet. It might be diseased as well."

"Z, it's a tiny baby and it needs us," she cried, her eyes watery as her fucking sadness destroyed me. The fact that there wasn't anyone here I could kill to make her happy was super inconvenient. This situation wasn't one I could fix with violence, and since I was rusty at almost every other emotion, it left me a touch lost.

"We can't be sure it's not infected like the mother," I repeated grimly. It wouldn't matter how much she cried and pleaded with me, endangering my mate was never going to happen.

Morgan blinked up at me, fire replacing her sadness. "I'm

willing to risk it," she snapped back, and it was clear that she didn't fear me… or she had very little sense of self-preservation. No one argued with my brothers or me, and yet Morgan had been fighting Drager from the start.

She was clearly ready to fight me as well, and I had long ago accepted she was strong enough to be my mate. Despite her fragile appearance, she would survive when I claimed what was mine.

"You're a ruthless bastard at times," she said softly, but with as much menace as her human body could muster.

Morgan had no idea how ruthless I could be. Especially when it came to her.

"Astra," I bit out, the tension of my beast rumbling in my chest. "Check the scent."

She prowled forward, her energy riddled with fury as she circled the carcass. As one of the last of her kind, she existed in a place of isolation and loneliness, and when we'd seen the dead sabre it had broken both of us. If this cub was unaffected, then there was a chance for her to retain a small piece of her heritage.

As Astra leaned down and sniffed slowly, Morgan stopped fighting my hold, watching the sabre closely. My fingers flexed against her soft skin, and I found myself focused on the woman in my arms. A woman still emotionally—and possibly more—tied to my brother. We had a lot to unravel before I could release the million-year-old instinct that was driving almost every part of me. A true test of my patience and discipline.

Astra's purring rumble grew louder as she sniffed closer. Part of me wanted to warn her away as well, but in her own way she was as ancient and powerful as me, and I'd learned over the years to trust her instincts. She wasn't much for our language, but she could communicate with me mentally when needed.

Safe.

"The cub isn't infected," I said, reluctantly releasing Morgan.

With a sad little cry, she landed on her knees beside the sabre, scooping it into her arms. The cub appeared to be asleep again, seemingly using all its energy to alert us to its presence. Morgan immediately tucked it in against her chest and started to rock like it was her own young.

"Panther cubs stay with their mommas for over a year," she told me, reciting facts in a hurry. "I know sabres aren't panthers, but they're the closest comparison to what I know in the human world. And this cub can't be more than a few hours old, right? What do you know about them?" She shot out questions, looking between Astra and me, as if one of us better answer her immediately.

My human was fucking adorable.

"We know very little about ocher sabre cubs," I said honestly. "Astra and I thought she was the last of her kind. This beast must have survived down near this section of light, feeding on the plants that grew here."

Morgan wrinkled her nose. "Well, they're no doubt similar to regular sabres," she said just as rapidly. "Tell me about them."

Another demand, and another rumble inside from my dragon, whose attachment grew deeper with each interaction.

"If you and your cub want to live long enough to learn about this species," I told her, "we need to move again. And the only way to move fast enough is if you let me carry you."

She was hungry and tired. "Can we rest for the night, please?" she whispered. "I need some sleep, and I can't sleep in your arms while carrying this cub. Just tonight, and then tomorrow you can rush at whatever speed you want."

I wanted to argue, but since I could sense no immediate danger, I decided that I could give her this. "Five hours," I said shortly. "You can have five hours and then we're moving again."

She shot me a smile that could only be described as joyful, and fuck if my chest didn't grow a little tighter as I stared at her. She was dangerous, this miraculous creature clutching a tiny cub in her hands.

Incredibly dangerous.

Astra scouted out a safe spot, her nose better than mine when I was in my bipedal form. We ended up in another alcove, which was walled in on three sides, so we only had to keep an eye on one attack point. Morgan's relief as she sat and leaned back against the wall had my dragon purring like a fucking sabre. He liked taking care of her, and the satisfaction was new for us both.

"You can sleep, sweetheart," I told her. "I will keep watch until it's time to leave again."

A huge yawn overtook her face. "The cub is going to be fine for a few hours, right?" she managed to ask around the yawn.

"Yes," I said with surety. Its energy was strong. "They're a formidable breed, and that little one has not succumbed to any weaknesses yet." Whatever energy had filtered through and infected the creatures down here had missed the cub. Maybe he hadn't quite been born yet, but either way it was another miracle.

"If there's only one ocher sabre down here," Morgan said around another yawn. "How is this cub even possible?"

Her mind was delightfully human at times. "I have no idea, but this breed is special. There's definitely a chance that they could create young on their own, if that was their choice." I felt Astra's interest in my theory, and I knew she'd spend a lot of time mulling over this new hope for the future.

Morgan's smile gentled as she glanced down, and I fought the urge to remove the beast from her. The possessiveness of my dragon knew no bounds, and we hadn't sealed the mate bond yet, so we were extra fucking testy when it came to others being near our mate.

She drifted off to sleep on her side with the cub tucked in close to her chest. Astra disappeared into the cavern, patrolling, as she was too furious to rest. Finding one of her kind dead had enraged her gentle soul.

I remained with Morgan, watching her silently, memorizing the way she breathed, deep and even. She was so exhausted that even on the hard ground she was soundly asleep. The longer I watched, the angrier I grew at her sprawled across loose stones that left red marks against her skin.

When I couldn't handle it any longer, I lifted her and the cub from the dirt and stretched out so they could rest on top of me. She stirred briefly, mumbling incoherently, then she was sound asleep again. The cub opened an eye and purred, before it too fell back to sleep. Bastard had already claimed my mate. "It's temporary," I warned it. "You don't get first hold. That's mine."

Another purr, and I found myself somewhat amused. I'd always have a soft spot for the ocher breed, thanks to Astra.

Heat and dragon energy rose and surrounded Morgan, and she slept deeper than ever. Leaned back against the wall, I kept both hands on her, securing her against me as I fought the urge to strip her naked.

The barrier of clothing between us bothered me—I wanted to touch her skin and taste her essence. I wanted to take everything her fragile body offered, but I wouldn't until she was ready.

I could keep my beast under control.

I had to keep it under control.

Getting my cock under control was a different story, as that ring of muscles near the base, my knot, throbbed once more. Fairly sure it hadn't stopped for weeks.

When Astra returned, her energy low and mournful, she took up vigil near the entrance, and I closed my eyes. I'd never allowed another to be near me during rest, except Astra.

And now Morgan.

With her against me, my energy relaxed in a way that I had no experience with. There was a level of comfort in her presence that I'd never felt before, a peace that drifted through the darkness of my core and allowed my body and thoughts to calm.

As she lay against me, and I rested with her, her energy increased, and the rumbling of her stomach eased. We were nourishing each other, giving whatever the other needed in that moment—a balance, which had been sorely lacking in my long life.

Very little could mar this moment as I began to understand what I'd been missing all these years. There was still the issue of Drager, though; his energy remained within her. Deciding that had to be finished, I spent time infusing my own energy into her, cleansing him from her system.

If he was here right now, I'd have ripped his head off. *Fucker*.

Of course, until we dealt with the issue of our mother and this invasion, there was no choice but for the five of us to work together. Our strength was in unity, which meant putting our differences aside.

Drager always found a way to skirt the consequences of his actions, but eventually he'd learn exactly what happened when one took what wasn't his to take.

Fractured memories of my life before the fall swirled in the back of my mind, brief images of the world we'd escaped from. I remembered mountains, painted red. My mother's voice was clear in my mind but her face was shadowed. Along with her beast... Did she have a beast? And if so, why couldn't I remember it? Did a female dragon differ to the males?

So many memories blocked by whatever energy had forced us from Xalifer all those years ago. We'd carved out a life for ourselves here in Risest, and it pissed me off that just as Morgan arrived, my family decided to invade.

Morgan had mentioned that earlier, but I'd been more focused on keeping her safe. Now I gave it real consideration. What if it wasn't a coincidence that this attack was coinciding with Morgan's arrival? Our lives had been consistent for the past couple of centuries, and she was the one factor that had changed it all.

What even were the odds of a human stumbling into a fae world and then finding out she's the true mate to one of us? Very low unless it was fate pushing us together. We'd found no mates amongst the fae, despite the very real efforts of my brothers.

Morgan was different. An anomaly. A human who had the strength to fight back against us, and who used her voice and knowledge to help us. Morgan was my true mate—if I had to kill Drager to prove it, I would, without hesitation—and maybe this new revelation meant more to Mother and Xalifer than we realized.

Morgan might have been the key that triggered it all.

CHAPTER 5

MORGAN

I had never been a person who enjoyed camping. Sure, the romantic aspects drew me in with campfires, no distractions, and living amongst nature. But then reality dragged me back and I decided that sleeping on the ground was my idea of a punishment, not enjoyment.

This day, though, in a cave of nightmares, on a world not my own, my exhaustion was so great that I barely felt the cold, rocky surface—helped along by the miraculous sabre cub snuggled against my chest, offering a small warmth.

I already held a sliver of possessiveness toward the tiny creature, like it was my young I had to save.

My biological clock wasn't ticking yet at near twenty-six, but I'd have died for this baby without thought. Of course, I did have some thoughts, and they went a little like *How the fuck am I supposed to save a baby of a near-extinct species? What is going on with Zahak and me, and why am I searching for his presence in my mind already? Is it weird that I feel less uneasy with him when I've been with Drager for much longer?—and much more intimately?—and there's always an element of mistrust between us?*

Thankfully, as I sank deeper into sleep, the chaos of my thoughts eased, until the cold started to seep into my skin, sending shivers through me, the cub's warmth not enough to keep me warm, especially as Drager's energy faded. Despite his assurances that we were building a permanent bond, no matter what he did, the energy he infused inside me never remained.

Another shiver overtook me, and I was almost roused from sleep until a delicious warmth surrounded me, as if someone had draped the coziest blanket over my body.

Sleep deepened once more, and it wasn't until I found myself waking naturally that I realized why I'd been so warm and comfortable in that final hour of rest.

"Fuck," I murmured, shaking my head to clear my vision.

"Good morning to you also," Zahak said huskily.

Oh, double fuck.

I'd slept on Zahak.

Right on top of his huge body. Cuddled into him like he was my safety blanket.

"Uh, sorry." I cleared my throat. "Did I crawl on you through the night?"

Please say no. I needed less shame in my life.

"You were cold," he said simply, like that explained everything, when I still had no freaking idea whether he'd carried me into his lap, or I'd searched for him in my sleep. A tiny purring against my chest was a perfect distraction, and I forced myself to focus on the fact that I'd kept the baby safe. That was the most important part.

Trying my best to get off the shifter in an unawkward way, I flailed for a beat before his firm hand landed on my ass, down low, cupping me as he effortlessly lifted me up to my feet. Knowing my face was beet red, I focused on the cub until I got myself under control, even as his warm laughter echoed through my mind.

He more often than not showed his amusement through our connection.

"Our mental connection feels stronger," I noted, when I'd managed to contain the swirl of desire and confusion inside me.

Zahak, also on his feet, scouted the area briefly before his focus returned to me. "My energy nourished you last night, and it was an unintentional building bridge in our bond."

Wait, what? "Nourished?" I queried.

His hand, huge and possessive, grazed across my stomach. A gentle stroke, before he released his hold. "Have you noticed that you're no longer hungry?"

Breathe, Morgan. Breathe.

Zahak touching me in this manner, branding his energy against mine, was destructive. Coherent thought faded along with any fear I'd been feeling to be in this trench. My one desire was to push this giant of a shifter to the ground once more and curl up against him. Only this time, we should do it naked. There was more laughter in my head, and it was a glass of ice water down my spine when I realized he'd heard my thoughts.

No, la moyar. But I can scent your arousal.

What. The. Fuck? Did he just say *scent*?

The urge to crouch and sniff myself overcame me, but I managed to refrain. I'd been embarrassed enough today.

Zahak leaned in so his voice was a rumbling balm across my senses. "There are two reasons you're not naked and in my bed for the next five years. One, you're not ready. And two, the world is combusting around us. But the moment I get those issues dealt with, you're mine."

Mine.

A word as equally destructive and desirable as his touch. As a modern woman, there was no way I should have a slow curling of heat in my stomach, dripping intimately to my center until my entire body ached. *Mine,* should have had me running and screaming about red flags, and yet... were they red? There was pink in there. It was looking very pink. I mean, red was practically a shade of pink if you thought about it. Like, really thought about it.

The facts couldn't be denied. Not even in our most intimate moments had Drager displayed one tenth of this possessiveness that Zahak did every time he was near me. Zahak had never fought our bond, claiming it without question or concern, and maybe, just maybe, that was why his flags looked pink.

He stepped away then to greet Astra, who had just returned from wherever she'd been, and I focused on holding the cub and breathing until I had myself under control. He was right about one thing: I was absolutely not hungry or exhausted any longer.

"We should get moving," Zahak said, and I was able to focus on him without any hot flashes. "Astra said the disease is worsening, and we'll have to deal with a lot more of the zombies if we stay here any longer."

"I'm good to move," I said, glancing down at the cub, who was finally opening its eyes. They were gold, looking up at me without confusion as it purred and rubbed its head against my chest.

Astra made a rumbling sound, moving closer to me, and I leaned down so she could sniff and lick the baby. "She said it's healthy and very content to be held by you," Zahak said, voice deeper than ever.

"How do we feed it?" I asked. It wasn't like we could head to a store and buy sabre formula. I wasn't even sure if they had shops here, or if most of the fae races grew and hunted their own food. I'd just always been in places where food was provided, and stupidly had never asked where it came from or how it got there.

"It'll be absorbing your energy at the moment," Zahak said. "It's young, so it'll only need minute amounts, and once we're topside we can search out the *hefle* bush, which is their first source of plant life. Or at least, it was Astra's, and I only have the knowledge she has."

"Good enough for me," I said, shifting the cub higher on my chest. "Let's get out of here."

I expected to be walking myself today, since I'd had a really nice—scarily nice—sleep on Zahak last night. As I took that first step, my feet were swept out from under me as he held me wedding style against his chest.

"You're a pain in the ass, you know that, right?" I sniped.

Zahak, who wasn't moving yet, shifted me higher so our gazes could meet. "If being a pain in the ass keeps you safe and alive, then I'll be a pain in the ass. I don't care, la moyar. I'll destroy the whole fucking world around us if it keeps you alive."

He'd shown that more than once already with my bouquet of heads. He'd been a definite pain in the ass for those fae, or *a definite murderer*, but who was counting?

Fourteen.

Smartass dropped that number right into my head, and I pressed my lips tightly because it felt wrong to laugh about the death of fourteen fae, even if they had been plotting to kill me.

"I knew you could hear my thoughts," I said out loud.

Zahak shook his head, and I settled back against his chest as he started to move. "Only the few you let slip. I haven't pushed past your natural blocks, and I won't."

The juxtaposition of his personality confused me. He was possessive and touchy, always with his hands on me, always checking I was okay, but then he gave me my mental privacy and didn't force the physical side of our relationship because he knew I wasn't ready.

It was confusing but it also made me feel safe in his presence.

As our speed picked up, I had to close my eyes again, focusing on breathing as I kept a firm hold on the cub.

We need to give her a name. I sent this thought to Zahak, unable to speak out loud when we were moving so quickly.

It's a male, he replied immediately. *And Astra has asked if you'd like the honor of naming him.*

A male. *I'll see if I can find a name to suit him. He's a little fighter, already overcoming the odds and surviving in the zombie caves.*

Zahak was quiet for a beat, and then I heard a scuffling sound nearby as he picked up more speed. Had the zombies found us?

His mother protected him, even in her frenzied, mutated state.

I would do the same. The thought slipped out, and I quickly added, *if I was his mother. I couldn't imagine not doing everything in my power to protect my babies.*

Zahak's hold on me briefly tightened, as if a reflex, before he gentled. *You'd be surprised how many mothers still protect themselves first.*

I wondered if he was thinking about that voice in the sky, the mother he held fractured memories of who was clearly not here for a happy family reunion. *My mother wasn't the nicest person*, I said, feeling the need to relate. *She grew up beautiful and spoiled. She was a beauty queen and the only child of parents who needlessly provided absolutely everything she wanted. No question asked.*

Zahak remained silent, but I could feel trickles of curiosity through our bond. He wanted to know more…

When she got married, my dad also made her the center of the world. Weirdly, I always thought that family dynamic worked well, you know. The dad makes the mom the center of the world, and she in turn makes the children, while they're young anyway, her priority.

A soft rumble in my mind and then he said, *Did she make you a priority?*

It was interesting how much easier this form of communication grew as we used it. I just had to think openly, and he could hear my thoughts. As my energy with Drager faded, Zahak's and mine grew together.

She did. She really did, but the part that ended up being destructive was that in the end, it wasn't for me. It was for her. Her obsessions. She was aging, starting to grow less important and less beautiful in this world designed to forget and ignore our older generations. So, she clung onto me, controlled me, tried to turn me into a version of herself. Everything was fine until I grew old enough to start wanting my own identity. To start making my own choices.

Narcissists cannot handle that, and that was when she'd lash out. Call me names. Tell me I was fat and useless, and that I owed her and Dad for their love and support over the years. It would go between guilt and shame and anger constantly, and I was losing parts of myself trying to keep her happy.

This time his silence felt heavy… angry, and I wondered if I should have kept this to myself lest I find my mother's heads on a spike next.

Lexie got me out, I hurried to say. *She taught me how to survive and take back my freedom. From then, I stopped allowing my parents to control my emotional wellbeing. I've been happier ever since.*

Happier, calmer, way more stable. Even stuck here in the chasm of nightmares, I'd still choose this day than being back home.

Without a single doubt.

MORGAN

Zahak's silence was heavy, and in his arms, I could feel the deep vibrations of his anger.

I find myself on the edge of losing control when I feel your pain, he said, and even in our minds his words were clipped. *I'm not a young shifter, with over two hundred cycles of life, and I've prided myself on making logical decisions for most of that time. You destroyed all that in days.*

Reaching out, I patted the hard muscles of his chest. *I will admit to not having any knowledge or experience with this type of bond. I hope I don't fuck it up, or destroy more of who you are, but you have to remember that I'm human, and until a month or so ago I thought we were the only sentient, humanoid beings in the worlds.*

Another chest rumble, deeper than before, but less intensely. *I welcome the destruction.*

That was all he said, and for some reason I was satisfied by those four words. Even if I was breaking his world apart, he wasn't unhappy about it.

Zahak's pace increased, and the cub started to squirm. I'd already wrapped one hand around him for stability, so with the other I stroked the soft fur on his back. Astra's fur was dense with a coarse protective layer on top, but the cub didn't have the same. He was still soft and fluffy. His rumble was delicate compared to Zahak's, and I found it comforting as he purred against my chest. At some point we dozed off, and when I woke once more we were still moving fast. Prying my eyes open a touch, I was surprised by how bright it was now. Enough illumination that I could see the plethora of zombie creatures as Zahak raced past them.

Within seconds I had to squeeze my lids shut or risk barfing all over the place, but it was clear that we were heading towards the largest opening we'd seen so far in the chasm.

Do you think we'll be able to escape soon? I needed to be free of this place. The time spent underground was starting to wear on me.

There's a small obstacle ahead, and then I believe the fissure will be large enough for me to safely fly. We won't need to make it all the way to the beam of light.

With relief, I relaxed against him once more. *Wait, small obstacle?*

He didn't reply, instead his pace slowed, and I opened my eyes to find a literal nightmare before me. Hundreds of nightmares.

Creatures jammed the path, leaving no room for the dragon shifter to race through. Zahak set me gently on my feet, and then shifted his stance to block me with his body. The cub stretched against my chest, and I noticed his eyes were open, but he seemed content to stay against me. "Small obstacle?" I repeated in a daze.

Zahak and I needed to discuss that term in more detail,

because I wasn't sure he knew what it meant.

"Morgan, I'm going to need you to back away from me," Zahak growled, and after mostly bond talking, his voice sounded deeper than ever.

"They're behind us too," I panic-whispered.

"I know," he bit out. "We have one chance, but I need to shift. If I call on the energy with you so close, you'll be destroyed in the process."

Oh, right. Right! We had a fire-breathing dragon on our team.

With the nightmare creatures closing in on us from the front and back, in varying states of decay—some looked almost whole, while others had lost most of their skin and were basically just animated muscle and bone—there was only one direction for me to move: to the side. Astra came with me, her comforting heat keeping me from freaking the fuck out.

Close your eyes.

Knowing how intense the light was when they shifted, I not only closed my eyes but also turned away. Heat built almost immediately, and inside I felt a similar burn from the energy I'd absorbed when I'd slept on him.

Zahak's energy felt different to Drager's, that much I knew for sure, but there was no real time to analyze the reasons for it. Not that I really needed to analyze it when Zahak had already explained quite bluntly that he was my true mate and Drager had been stealing our bond through the Fallen Five's connection to each other. A fact that was rapidly growing harder to deny.

Zahak's roar rocked the cavern, and as the light died off I opened my eyes and spent a solid few seconds gawking at the furious, black-scaled beast in the middle of the cavern. Despite us being in a vast section of the trench, it all felt smaller as Zahak lifted his head and once more roared to the world.

The zombie nightmare creatures didn't react at all, which was all the evidence anyone would ever need that they weren't in their right minds. Zahak was terrifying in his humanoid form, but like this... there weren't adjectives strong enough. You could only understand if you were here experiencing the intensity.

The cavern grew hotter, and I stumbled back until I was plastered against a side wall, the stone against my back burning through my clothes. Astra positioned herself in front of me protectively, and I wondered what the odds were of Zahak being able to take on this many creatures alone.

I got my answer mere seconds later, when his fire blasted through the trench, and I ducked low and turned away so the cub was protected. My bare skin felt like it was being sand-blasted, until Astra shifted again, blocking the worst of the fire and power.

With my head down, I tried not to freak out, but there was no way for me to know if Zahak was winning or losing.

Losing...? Not a chance, la moyar.

A little pee might have escaped at the rumble of his dragon in my head. It was deep and animalistic, burning through my mind as hot as the fire he sprayed around the cavern.

The way he'd rumbled *la moyar* sent shivers down my spine. I had all but lost my battle to remain impartial to this dragon, of wanting to wait until we were back with Drager and could hash everything out to get it all in the open. That one rasp told me there was no way I'd make it that long.

My bastard brother took advantage of our bond, the beast snarled, sounding extremely put out. *He knew it, and he needs no consideration because of it.*

If I hadn't already been crouched behind Astra, my weakened knees would have sent me down to the ground. I'd thought Zahak as a man was intense and destructive, but his dragon was like nothing else in the world. My poor human senses were overwhelmed, as my mind spun in an attempt to make sense of it all.

When the heat finally died down, I got back to my feet, steadier than expected. "Well, fuck." I gulped as I took in the scene.

The zombies were all gone. The decaying fleshballs of nightmare creatures were reduced to nothing more than ash and scorch marks on the stone. Zahak, still in his dragon form, watched me closely with those dark, fathomless eyes.

Come to me, mate.

I resisted at first, and this time I received the delight of a dragon laughing in my head. Streams of smoke trailed from his massive jaws at the same time. *You have no idea how long I've waited for you*, he said, softer than before. Never soft for a dragon, but there was a soothing quality to the rumble. *I could stand here for decades waiting for you to choose me.*

Choose me.

I'd also been waiting a lifetime for someone to choose me, and even if I hadn't had the tugging sensation of our bond in my chest, I'd have gone to Zahak.

Stumbling forward, I crossed to the beast, whose size was terrifying and overwhelming, but I never hesitated.

Climb on my back.

"Say what *the fuck* now?" I tilted my head like a confused puppy.

I was rewarded with another rumbly dragon laugh. *I don't know what the human translation for that is, but in this language, your usage of the word fuck is… amusing.*

It was my turn to laugh. "Yeah, I've always had a potty

mouth. Defiance against my mother who told me that ladies never cursed, but apparently she didn't care if they lied, manipulated, and gaslighted. You know, because a curse word is the only sign of depravity."

The dragon roared. It wasn't loud enough to deafen me, but it was close, and trickles of rocks rained from the ceiling. *Best not to speak of your mother any longer.*

Advice I was going to take. Zahak lowered himself until his massive body was nearly sprawled across the hard ground. His wings tucked in behind him, and I hesitantly stepped forward.

"How do I climb up?"

Even on the ground, there was no way for me to reach his back. Especially not with a sabre in my arms.

Give the cub to Astra. She'll get him up, and then you can use that bend in my front leg as a foothold.

"This is a lot like fight training and obstacle courses at the academy," I muttered. "Only without the help."

I almost killed that handsy little bastard, Zahak growled.

He was clearly talking about Mika, a helpful fae with the tendency to elevate my body through a firm hand on my ass. Probably best not to bring that up either.

Focusing on the task at hand, I lifted the cub from my chest, and he opened his eyes and rumbled louder than ever. *They sleep a lot at this age,* Zahak explained. *He's okay. Astra will get him up safely.*

She prowled forward, and I offered the baby to her, trusting she'd do exactly as Zahak had said. Astra nudged me, almost as a greeting, and then used her mouth to pick up the cub by the scruff of his neck.

As much as I wanted to freak out at seeing those lethal canines so close to the vulnerable cub, I knew this was how cats carried their young back home too. Astra turned away, and in about three leaps made her way up onto Zahak's broad dragon back.

"Showoff," I muttered, and I swore both sabres and the dragon laughed at me, as rumbles and purrs filled the cavern.

It wasn't easy being the weakest, smallest, and least powerful of the group. It meant I got to spend a lot of time treated like a toddler who was learning how to walk and had a tendency to fall and hit their head.

I hated the feeling. Then and there I decided that I was going back to fight classes the moment I could. I might never be one of the gods, but I could sure as fuck be less weak.

Zahak didn't move as I touched the groove in his leg. With a sigh, I attempted to lift my foot high enough to reach the crevice but I only made it halfway. Eventually, I had to wedge my foot into another small spot for leverage. Once I was up past the joint of his leg, he extended one of his wings, and I was able to use that as a handhold to get onto his back.

The scales were slippery in one direction, and somewhat rougher and jagged in the other, and once I figured that out I could use them to anchor my boots. If I slipped and fell down those scales the wrong way, it'd be like going down a cheese grater, and that was all the incentive I needed to stay on my feet.

Finally, after what felt like a hundred years, I was on his back with Astra. She nudged me to sit near the joint of his neck and body, and I was almost able to stretch my legs on either side. "I really hope I'm better at this than the one time I rode a bike," I muttered, my stomach tied up in knots.

The bike ride had ended with an ER trip and ten stitches.

I was going to guess that falling off a dragon would be much, much worse.

CHAPTER 7

ZAHAK

Astra was the only one who had ever ridden on my dragon form, and only when the distance we had to travel was too vast for her to keep up. It was not offered lightly in our race, but as Morgan settled on my back, her weight barely even discernable, there was no urge to hurry through the process. My wings spread as wide as they could go in this cave, lifting us from the rocky ground. Morgan let out a small gasp when my wings scraped the side of the walls.

Are you okay? Her timid voice sounded less human in our dragon mind.

Fine, sweetheart. Rocks are no match for dragonhide.

In her mind, trickles of pleasure emerged when I called her *claim of my heart*, and I wondered what the translation was in her language. Whatever it was, she'd hear it all the time from me, along with *la moyar*. The fear of scaring her with our intensity did hold me back. For now. But she'd understand soon enough.

Drager would understand soon enough.

Morgan was my true mate. All he'd felt were echoes of it through our pod bond.

As we rose higher, Morgan's legs tightened, and when I turned my head it was to find her clinging like a bear on the side of a tree. There was no panic in her mind; she had that locked down tightly, but it was visible in the tense lines of her body.

This was a new experience for her, but eventually she'd grow more comfortable traveling like this. The strongest roots did not grow overnight. They took time, of which I had plenty.

Z, the light is brighter.

Excitement filled her voice as the tension in her hold eased. Twisting my body, I fit the best I could through the broken crevice high in the cavern. The lights of Risest surrounded us, and as the pinkish glow grew brighter I noticed subtle differences in the color.

In my dragon form, I could see a far greater spectrum of light, and this was not the dusty pink of Risest's normal illumination. Morgan didn't notice until I finally burst free above the Isle of Denille, not far from the academy.

"Z," she gasped, stretching up on my back as she peered around. "What happened to the sky?"

I lifted us higher, swiveling my head to take it all in. The shimmering, dusty pink had been replaced by a deep crimson, streaked in darkness across the far reaches of the lands.

"Why is the sky red?" Morgan whispered.

The invasion, I replied using our connection. There was no ability to converse out loud in my dragon form, my vocal abilities limited to rumbles, growls, and long spurts of fire when we were pissed off. *This is also why disease runs through my trench. They're a plague, and they're going to destroy this world if we don't stop them.* Knowledge borne of instinct in my ancient soul.

Morgan craned her neck so hard she almost overbalanced. Thankfully Astra saw it coming and shifted her position to brace against our human.

Careful, I warned, the aforementioned rumbles starting in my chest.

Shit, sorry, she gasped, and I enjoyed her using the mental connection instinctively. *It's just... what is happening? Those dragons we saw falling changed the color of the sky? How?*

How they were doing this, I didn't have an answer for yet, but I intended to figure it out.

We must find my brothers.

Morgan leaned down and clung on tighter. "Yes, let's find them. I need to know if Lexie is okay and..." She trailed off, but we both knew who the other name on her list was.

Drager.

Despite my anger toward my pod-mate, I also wanted to ensure he was safe, and with that I decided to tap into our pod bond. A bond we'd both steadfastly ignored for decades. The barriers were old and strong, but they crumbled in seconds, as if they'd been waiting for one of us to make the first move.

Brother, I rumbled.

His reply was unclear, almost drowned out by static between us.

Drager? I tried again.

He shot back more words, and I managed to catch *...come to Lancourt. We're hiding up here...* before his mind closed off from mine.

Unease settled deep in my gut. It had been Drager, his

energy signature unmistakable, but we'd never had interference like that between us.

Morgan's softer energy filled my mind, easing away the anger and confusion. *Did you get in touch with him?*

Yes. I wasn't hiding anything from my mate, so I let the concern filter into my words. *But it was a broken connection. He said they're hiding at Lancourt.*

Morgan remained silent for a beat, and then she surprised me by leaning forward to rest her cheek against my scales. Maybe she was exhausted, but it almost felt like a hug. *It's going to be okay, Z. Drager wouldn't call you to Lancourt if it was dangerous. He's an asshole, but that's next level. It must be this new imbalance impacting your mental connection.*

I wanted to believe that was the case, but Drager had not proven himself trustworthy over the past few decades. His obsession with power, land, and control had filtered into his relationship with his brothers.

We should approach with caution, I warned her. *Astra can scout first for us.*

I waited for her to argue, to defend Drager once more, but to my surprise she remained silent. "That might be a good idea," she finally said out loud. "Just in case."

It appeared my little mate had some doubts of her own, which settled as satisfaction deep in my chest. She didn't trust Drager either.

Banking to the left, I rose above the isle, relieved to see that the general landscape appeared untouched. My land was harsh in its beauty, rocky and barren in sections, tempered by edges of lush forests. The contradiction fit perfectly with my dragon soul, which was beauty and destruction intermingling to form a perfect balance.

Through our bond, I felt Morgan's curiosity, as she leaned forward and took in the Isle of Denille.

"It's not how I expected," she said conversationally, and I had no idea if she was talking to me or herself. Or even Astra. She chatted to my sabre as if the beast could reply. I wondered if it was possible for a human to develop the mental bond required to converse with a sabre.

One of many questions I had regarding Morgan and humans in general. Drager had always held a fascination with Earth and its inhabitants. Despite citing that his library was simply there to gather energy, I'd always known it was so much more. But I'd never really cared until the night of the fertility ritual. The night my entire fucking world imploded, and I awoke as a different beast.

"Z, your land is beautiful," Morgan said in a whisper. "Look at that river!"

The isle was filled with crystal-clear waterways meandering through the lands. We also had oceans along the east and south, treacherous but stunning. *I never expected to love anywhere outside of the world I was born into*, I told her, *but my dragon heart is at home here*.

And those bastards who thought to invade and steal away what we'd built were destroying it with their mere presence.

Morgan picked up on my fury, and I felt her hand stroke my scales. The surge of energy that followed her touch had the dragon raging to claim her once more, and he was much harder to control in this form.

She distracted us as she said, "We never got a chance to work on unlocking your memories. Do you remember anything else?"

The arrival of decaying nightmare creatures had disrupted most of our plans in the trench. I was just thankful to get us out alive and unharmed. Above, from what I could see, the fae and creatures of the isle were acting as per normal, so the disease had not escaped the trench yet.

We had to put an end to it before that happened.

My memories are jagged. A series of bright lights, with barely visible images buried deep inside. We were just coming of age when we fell, I remember that much. I remember her voice. Our mother's, but her last words are shrouded in more of the light.

Light and static, similar to my mental conversation with Drager.

Ty, Emmen, and Kellan were still blocked in our bond, and whenever I reached for them, there was echoing silence, not even the static. On all fronts, my bond to my brothers was being interfered with, and that spurred me on.

If she'd hurt them, I would ignite her world until it was ash, and dance in the fucking darkness.

They're going to be okay, Morgan said, in her soft, reassuring way. *You're strong and powerful, with the lands of Risest supporting you. Your mother will have underestimated you. I don't care how much information she was gathering behind the scenes, she doesn't truly understand what you've all built here.*

I wanted her to be right. I wanted to believe every reassuring word she sent my way, but deep in my chest, where instinct guided me, unease stirred. For the first time in my long life, I had so much to lose.

If mother had invaded two months ago, she'd have found a different dragon in me. If she was planning on bringing us back into the fold, I'd have considered her proposal, depending on how she intended to use Risest. But now... Now I was fucking furious and there was no mercy in my soul.

Not for those who threatened my world, my fae, and my brothers.

Especially not for those who threatened Morgan.

If I had to kill every single being from our birth world to keep them safe, I'd do it.

No hesitation and no regrets.

CHAPTER 8

MORGAN

Zahak grew quieter as we crossed his land, and with no immediate threat on the horizon I found myself relaxing against his back. He flew about a hundred feet over the Isle of Denille. It was a beautiful landscape, with pockets of forest and greenery—different species of trees to those in Ocheran—and less grass. Sections were rocky and barren, but then there were other sections with flowering meadows and gorgeous meandering streams.

When Zahak changed directions, I caught a glimpse of the trench once more, a visible crack in the land. Through the gaps, nightmare creatures were visible, decaying and stumbling around. *Do you think they'll get out and spread this disease?*

Zahak angled his neck to look below us. *There are those with the ability to fly, but it appears they're too decomposed to try and escape. I hope that remains the case.*

We all hoped that was the case, because I had the very real

sense that one escapee could spread this illness far and wide, wiping out the rest of the fae world.

Zahak continued in his dragon rumble: *Until we know how the invaders are doing this, we can't be sure that it's not already spreading to the rest of Risest. So far, though, I don't feel that darker energy above the land.*

I'd also noticed that the creatures we'd seen above the trench had all appeared normal, but that was hardly enough evidence to assume that only the trench was affected.

Since we're not sick, yet anyway, we have to assume that the energy which called forth the illness, happened when those shifters invaded. It made sense with the timeline, and Zahak didn't appear to disagree. *Drager and the others will have more information*, I decided. *We just need to find them.*

Zahak's mind was full of energy and a real sense of unease, even as he remained silent. He continued at a steady pace, and I never felt nervous about sliding off. After about an hour, Astra scooted forward and dropped the cub in my lap. "He's okay?" I asked out loud.

The sabre nodded.

He gathered energy from her while they slept.

Zahak's voice in my head sent shivers down my spine, but I managed not to physically react. It surprised me how comfortable the mental communication felt already.

His theory about being a true mate grew more likely with every second we spent together, and I knew my hesitation at embracing this bond was a protective measure. If I allowed myself to fall into Zahak and he hurt me, I'd never recover. So far, though, this Fallen had given me no reason to mistrust his motivations or believe him to be like Drager. Drager, I hadn't trusted for a second, which had been pure instinct guiding me. It was completely different with Zahak, which had to mean... well, it had to mean a lot.

The cub cuddled against me, eyes open as he pawed at my shirt. His claws were sharp, but he stopped short of making me bleed. It appeared to comfort him, so I let him go, only wincing when he scraped exposed skin.

When one claw left a deeper welt, Zahak growled and the cub ceased his movements, snuggling deeper against me, eyes closing once more. He was still such a baby, barely able to stay awake for long.

"He wasn't hurting me," I told Zahak. "I just have sensitive skin."

Another rumble, but he didn't say anything through our bond. Secretly, I liked his protectiveness. Zahak had this way of protecting without infringing on my independence. He let the situation go until either I needed assistance in stopping it or I was in pain, and that was when he stepped in. Drager stepped in before the situation even started, needing to be the one controlling everything. *Fuck*. It was odd and disconcerting to have feelings for them both.

Different and confusing feelings.

I needed to talk to Drager, to find out if he felt the mate bond too and had just been hiding it from me all this time or if he simply—

He felt the bond because of me.

As a dragon, Zahak's mind was closer merged to mine, and he'd heard those thoughts. Maybe I'd been projecting them louder than usual too. I felt a swell of heat beneath me as his body expanded along with his anger. I was about to comment, hopefully with a soothing type of statement, but I paused when I caught sight of familiar territory. We were closing in on the academy.

The white of the building appeared brighter against the darker crimson sky. I'd been doing my best not to focus on the fact that my beautiful dusty pink was gone. The crimson wasn't the worst part either, nope, there was also darkness hovering out in the distance. Heavy clouds, even though I'd never seen a storm here in my time.

Until this day, I'd never even seen a cloud marring their sky.

The Fallen Five had lifted the darkness when they fell, and now it was closing in once again.

They've taken over the academy.

Zahak's anger continued to swell with each of those mentally bit out words. The rumble of his tone sent shivers down my spine. Not the usual shivers I felt around him, but ones of pure fear and dread.

My human eyes did not see what had him all riled up, but I trusted his instincts.

Zahak changed directions, flying lower across his land, and I found myself ducking lower as well, like I'd make any difference in keeping us undetected.

We need to get closer, but there's going to be scouts and guards in the area.

And it wasn't as if hiding a dragon was easy. *We should land and go on foot until we reach those trees on the other side of the lake,* I suggested.

Yes, we will use our knowledge of this land to take it back. Those bastards forgot one very important detail when they decided to invade. This is our world, and we know every part of it. They might have stolen information, and they might have pitted my brothers and I against each other, but in the end we're a team and we're strong.

It had been mentioned multiple times that when the Fallen Five worked together, they'd been near unstoppable, literal gods in comparison to the fae of this world. But I was worried about this new batch of shifters. Did they have the same strength as the Fallen Five?

We wouldn't know until they faced these interlopers. A thought that filled me with dread and terror. I'd only just discovered this world and the dragons. I couldn't lose them. I wouldn't survive it.

Zahak banked to the left and I had to focus on remaining in place while keeping a firm hold on my sleeping cub. He turned away from the academy, his body lowering, wings expanding into a glide as he smoothly descended. When he landed, he dropped on his belly and I was able to maneuver myself off with the baby clutched close to my chest.

My legs were shaky, but I caught myself with the help of Zahak's wing, which he shifted into position to stabilize me. Astra leapt free, and then we backed away so he could shift.

I turned and closed my eyes, only opening them again when I felt a graze against my cheek. Zahak stood right before me, his eyes filled with darkness. He was so tall and broad that I felt tiny as I stared up at him, helplessly trapped in his gaze. His dragon form was intense, but it was different to how I found him when he was in his bipedal form.

Zahak's smile was slow, and I realized that once again I'd let my inside thoughts blast so loudly that he'd heard through our bond. "We're true mates," he repeated, and the poor guy was probably hoping he'd eventually get through to my slow human brain. He cupped my face in his hands. "As I've already told you, the only reason you're not naked in my cave is because our world is under attack. But don't mistake that for anything other than me exerting a painful degree of patience. You belong to me, and I intend to claim what is mine."

I remained trapped under both his gaze and his hold. I felt no fear as heat unfurled all on its own inside me. Natural this time, without having to be infused by Drager....

Zahak rumbled. "Remind me to kill that bastard when this is all over."

He released me, and his intensity faded enough that I was able to breathe freely. "Come on, sweetheart," Zahak said, focusing on the landscape. "We need some intel, and to figure out if my brothers are being held there."

Whenever he called me *sweetheart*, my body went all warm. *Little human* had done the same when Drager started to use it as a term of endearment, until I realized it was a free-for-all pet name. Zahak had never called me *little human* though, and that meant a lot.

Shifting the cub higher against my chest, I followed Zahak as he prowled into the closest forest. We were still on his land, a beautiful stony landscape, but as we entered the coniferous style forest of the isle, it didn't take long before the trees morphed into Ocheran's more deciduous species.

After walking for about ten minutes, I had to ask, "Where are all the animals?"

Last time I'd been in an Ocheran forest, there had been many curious creatures wandering around. This time, though, not a single one was to be seen.

"They're there," Zahak murmured, glancing around as we strode deeper into the forest. "But everything is hiding. The energy and balance of Risest is out of alignment, and they all feel it."

"At least the invaders aren't killing everything in sight." I searched for a positive, even if it felt like there was none around.

Zahak rumble. "I don't think that's their plan. Not yet anyway."

We were edging closer to the lake, and he only spoke again when he pointed out the hefle bush and explained how to take the long, bell-shaped white flowers and milk them for sap. The cub lapped it up, delighted by his new treat.

We stashed extra flowers in our pockets for later, before entering the danger zone on the edge of the lake. Zahak, Astra, and I got low, keeping trees and shrubbery in front of us to ensure we remained out of sight. When we found a good place to settle, we gave our full attention to the academy.

When I'd been in the air on Zahak's back, I hadn't been able to see what had him riled up, but we were close enough for me to notice the dragons on the front lawn, standing between the lake and the building. Seven of them, all in their beast forms. Their dragon hides were mostly brown, duller than the bright hues of the Fallen Five. They also didn't have gilded wings, and I had to assume that in their world there were different races and family groups as well.

"They have guards all around the building," Zahak said softly, and I didn't doubt that his vision was picking up a hell of a lot more than mine. "Nine at least, and there's energy from more inside."

"We're so outnumbered," I whispered back, prickles of fear entering my words.

Zahak didn't argue with me, and I really wished he would.

Cuddling the cub closer, I drew in the comfort of the tiny sabre, and wondered what the future held now. "Can you sense your brothers?"

Zahak closed his eyes briefly, and I wondered if he was trying to reach out to them through their unique connection. He'd managed to chat to Drager with interference, but he hadn't been able to get hold of the others at all.

"One of them might be being held in the basement prison

cells," he finally replied. "I'm getting flickers, but our connections are all but severed."

"We should head for Lancourt and find out what Drager knows," I reminded him.

He didn't look my way, but I felt a sense of resigned acceptance as he nodded. "Yeah, we don't have much choice. I'm strong, but I'm not sure I can take on a dozen shifters on my own."

As he said that, a fae exited the front doors of the academy, head bowed as she headed for one of the guards. I couldn't hear what was said, but when she lifted her head, a small gasp escaped. It was Rolta. Even from this distance, there was no hiding her stature. The infiltrators had the headmistress of the academy under their control and doing their bidding.

They had the entire academy under their control.

CHAPTER 9

MORGAN

From our position in the trees, we watched the dragons for a long time. Zahak remained so still that I would have thought him asleep, except I could see his unwavering gaze. After some time, I alternated between dozing and cuddling the cub.

I still didn't have a name for the baby sabre, but as we sat there, I had time to give it some serious consideration. Astra's name, which I loved, reminded me of astrology, so I decided to stick with that theme.

After running a few options through my mind and discarding them immediately, I finally settled on a name that felt right. Strong, fierce, and linked to Astra: Leo.

Which, oddly enough, was also my star sign.

Zahak shot an amused glance my way, his first break from steadfast observation of the academy. It only lasted a second, before he was back watching the dragon guards like his life depended on it, but it was enough time for heat to fill my chest.

"Learn anything new?" I asked.

There was a stirring of energy in my mind, but he spoke out loud: "There are twelve soldiers on the grounds. If there are more, they're beyond my current energy span. The power of Mother is not here though."

"Is that what you've been searching for? Your mother?"

His expression was as dark as the pigments in his eyes. "She's the one we should concern ourselves with. My memories remain clouded, but the emotions are stronger. When I focus on her voice, all I remember is feeling anger and fear. I imagine that at one point I was a child, and she hurt and controlled us. Which doesn't bode well for her plans now."

Fire unfurled in my stomach until my limbs were shaking. I wasn't surprised at the level of rage coursing through me. Parents hurting children was a trigger for me. If I could cleanse the world of one type of human, it would be those who abused the innocent and unwavering trust of children.

Leo reacted to the elevation of anger inside me, making small rumbles as he clawed my shirt. He wasn't the only one as heat rose in the forest around us and scales streaked across Zahak's skin before vanishing. His dragon was on edge; we were all on edge. "We should make our way to Lancourt now," he growled. "But I don't want to fly in and make us easy and obvious targets. There's no way to hide a dragon, so we need another plan, one that Drager wouldn't have thought of to alert our mother."

I considered our options, wishing I wasn't a human with very little knowledge of this world. "Lexie said they had transports, but I never saw what they were," I told him. "Do you have any idea?"

Zahak nodded. "Yes, they use *crion*. They're a subservient

bird race," he continued. "Think the opposite of a yonter. They live to please, especially Drager, who takes advantage of their nature."

Lexie had mentioned crions when we were walking through the forest as a means to get to the academy faster. Drager had declined and carried me, so I'd never seen one. "If they live to please him, it might not be in our best interest to use them then," I said, my suspicions toward Drager unwavering.

Zahak nodded once. "My thoughts exactly."

"There must be another option," I mused. "We just need a creature strong enough to fly us, but smaller than a dragon." I shook my head at my stupidity in overlooking the yonters. Zahak had even mentioned them. "Calendul. We need her."

"Calendul?" he queried.

I nodded. "Yes! She's the yonter who carried me down from Lancourt, and she's loyal to Lexie. I'm sure she'll help. She might even know where my best friend is, because I'm freaking the heck out that she's hurt."

Or worse.

I'd never say the *or worse* out loud because the universe needed no encouragement to fuck things up for us.

"Okay, let's find her."

Zahak didn't question my suggestion, trusting me enough to follow my lead. Even though he was superior to me in many ways, he never acted as if he was. His attitude, after Drager, was just so unexpected that I didn't know what to do with all the feelings swirling inside me.

"Do you know where the yonter territories are in Drager's land?" I asked him. "I assume that's where we'll find Calendul."

"They sit between the Green Hollow and the land of the Lightsbringers."

I blinked at him. "Lexie's home?" The thought that she might be there with her family had a surge of adrenaline pumping through my veins.

"Yes, Lexie hails from the Lightsbringers, and Green Hollow is another of the clans in Ocheran."

Green Hollow was familiar as well, and with it, an auburn-haired fae crossed my mind. I'd seen Florentine of the House of Green Hollow twice. The first was at Dragerfield Library, when she paid tribute to her *god*, and the second when I was assigned the glamorous job of interviewing Drager's fae to discover if any of them were traitors. Both times she'd regarded me with confusion and suspicion. I'd liked her, though, for some ridiculous reason, as I didn't know her. But our brief interactions had shown her to be smart and protective of her clan. Two qualities I admired.

"We should get moving," Zahak said, sparing one last glance at the academy. "It's not a short journey, and I can't shift into my dragon form without alerting them to my presence. We're going to have to walk."

I didn't bother to mention my human frailties again. I hadn't eaten in what felt like days, but I wasn't hungry or fatigued after my night spent sleeping on a shifter god. I also wasn't thirsty. My body was freaking out about not eating or drinking, but at the same time we didn't appear to need it.

Whatever Zahak's energy had done when I'd slept on him was nothing short of a miracle, but I'd long given up questioning the weird and wonderful in this world.

We started off at a reasonably fast pace, or so I thought, until I realized everyone was slowing themselves down for me. Not that they said a word or made me feel bad about it, but I was observant enough to notice. I also wasn't the fittest human, despite my few classes in the academy, and as soon as I felt small pains in my calf muscles Zahak reached out and swept me into his arms.

"Nice of you to ask permission," I said with a snort, settling in because fighting this giant male was useless. Leo curled up against my chest and took a nap while I closed my eyes and hoped to do the same.

"You were in pain," he said simply.

I didn't bother to explain that a little discomfort wasn't pain, and humans were used to feeling their muscles strain. He didn't understand our bodies, and I liked that he cared about my pain.

Zahak's pace picked up. I had to close my eyes once more. His voice filtered through my head a moment later: *You're my mate, and you're testing my dragon.* He growled. *I'm not a saint, even if you think of my actions as such. If you keep pushing, I will take what is mine.*

His voice was gruffer than it had been, and even with my duller senses, I started to pick up that Zahak's energy was out of sorts. Even still, my insides tightened at that sexually charged threat. His tone was laced in a barely contained violence, animalistic, and yet I wanted to push just a little. Lexie would be smacking me upside the head if she were here, and I got it, I really did. If my best friend was obsessed with a creature who might get her killed, I'd be upset too.

But I just couldn't bring myself to stop.

How would you take me?

Fucking hell. My mind had always needed a keeper, which hadn't been a huge issue until my thoughts could be projected.

You're pushing it, mate.

I was, and I couldn't make myself stop.

Zahak picked up even more speed, and I was forced to focus on keeping the nausea at bay. I knew why he was rushing, as that sense of agitation I'd noticed a moment ago continued to grow. Maybe the reality of seeing those shifters at the academy and the evidence of this invasion had him extra fired up.

Wanting to distract the both of us, I asked, *What does a female dragon look like? Are they the same as males?*

Zahak's chest rumbled. *I don't remember…*

It bothered him to have these massive gaps in his memory, and now I wished I hadn't brought it up. His next rumble was harder and stronger, waking Leo, who pawed at my shirt.

Z?

"Something is wrong," he raged out loud. "The energy here is—" Another snarl and growl took over him. "Ever since we left the trench, I've been fighting my darker nature, and whatever energy is around the academy is hammering at my control."

He slowed and with a jerk I was dropped to my feet. Staring up at him, I swallowed hard. Whatever energy he was feeling had his body larger than usual, scales trailing over almost all his visible skin.

"Morgan," he bit out, heat pouring from him as he leaned forward and braced his hands on his knees. "You need to get away from me."

His words were difficult to understand as the intensity of what was driving him out of his mind increased to the point that even I could feel it. Like a swarm of bugs had descended over my skin, and I was fighting the urge to itch at it.

Astra moved to my side, nudging me away from Zahak. I backed up, taking their warnings seriously. As the heat increased, light did as well, and it appeared that his hope to not shift and keep his presence low-key was about to be dashed.

Veins popped in his neck, more scales covered him, and his limbs lengthened, along with his body. He kept growing larger, but so far hadn't turned into a full dragon. He was in a hybrid human-beast form, and even as the scales covered him he retained his normal face and body structure. Just bigger. Everything about him was bigger.

His head jerked up, and I met eyes as black as death. He locked me in his stare, and true fear raced down my spine. "Run," he rumbled, taking a step toward me before he managed to stop himself. "Get to Calendul!"

Without another thought, I did as I was told, taking off between the trees with Leo in my arms and Astra at my side.

Behind us fire burst to life, and I wondered if this was finally the moment I'd been anticipating.

Death by dragon.

CHAPTER 10

ZAHAK

The energy had taken a while to infiltrate through my barriers. When we'd left the trench, I'd felt uneasy but expected it was because my world was under attack. Eventually, though, as I'd sat by the academy observing our enemies, I'd succumbed to the darkness until it had all but pushed my dragon beyond control.

"Run," I rumbled at Morgan, having no idea if she could understand me. My vocal cords were thickening, my skin hardening as scales covered me. Their protection was usually welcome, but today, when logic was lost to the animalistic nature of the beast, I worried about what it all meant for Morgan.

We wanted to hunt. We wanted to feed. We wanted to take and consume.

And none of that had a single fucking thing to do with food.

It was our mate that we needed.

A strangled squeak escaped Morgan, her eyes wide as she stared at me, and with what remained of my sanity I cursed her lack of survival instincts. She tempted death with her mere presence, and barely appeared to notice or care.

Humans were frail; she'd never survive me in this form. I needed her to leave so I could focus on getting myself under control. The invaders, including my mother, had done this to me, and until I figured out how to strengthen my barriers against it, Morgan was in danger.

"Get to Calendul," I raged, gripping a nearby tree, digging in claws. Morgan's scent was richer and muskier than it had been a few seconds ago, and it drove me insane. Being close to my mate and not being able to claim her had me raging in both beast and man.

The relief I should have felt when she finally *fucking finally* took off into the trees, Astra by her side, and Leo in her arms, was diminished by pure rage.

Mine. My mate. She was running from me, and my dragon wouldn't stand for that.

Not now, when she was unclaimed.

As the darkness pulsed through my veins, I dug my claws deeper, the slightest sliver of sanity reminding me that we would catch Morgan in a split second if we didn't give her a decent start.

No amount of head start would be enough though.

But I had to fucking try.

In this hybrid dragon form I was too strong to be restrained by flora, and as I ripped the trees free I charged into the forest, following her scent. Now that we were in pursuit, I found that I could slow my steps. The beast was in charge, but we were one and the same, so my sliver of reasoning kept us under control.

If we reached Morgan before she made it to Calendul, that

sliver would snap and we'd take our mate. Take and claim, just as our kind was designed to do. Patchy memories or not, that part was pure instinct. We had one mate, and Morgan was it.

Find. Hunt. Claim.

Find our mate and never let her go.

Find. Hunt. Claim.

The chant in my head pushed me faster. Her scent grew stronger… muskier… and it was from arousal not fear. Did she not understand a dragon was hunting her down? Or did she just not care…?

When I reached a fork in the road, her scent turned down a path too small for me to follow. Astra was guiding her, giving them the best chance of staying ahead of me, and I was both furious and thankful.

At this stage, I wanted to destroy everything standing between me and Morgan, but I also wanted her safe.

Find. Hunt. Claim.

Taking a route around the small path, I crashed through trees, creating my own openings as I slashed. A low shriek in the distance told me I was getting closer, and with that the beast surged beyond my remaining sanity.

My mate was close, and it was time that we sealed this bond, once and for all.

Mine.

CHAPTER 11

MORGAN

Astra kept nudging me into a pace that was uncomfortable for both my legs and fitness levels, but as the heat of Zahak's dragon filled the forest around us, adrenaline gave me the boost needed to keep going.

"Is he going to kill us if he catches us?" I breathed, too freaked out to be embarrassed by the way I was puffing along.

Of course Astra couldn't answer, but she did keep head-butting me.

Part of me wondered why we were even bothering. I'd never be able to outrun a dragon shifter. I couldn't even outrun humans, and my current pace was about to end in five minutes when my lungs exploded.

Fear did drive me, but there was a part that couldn't stop thinking about Zahak in that dragon form. It called to me, and I was past the point of denying that we had a true mate bond. That would require me to deny both my instincts and feelings—along with the fact that he could speak in my mind.

It pissed me off to no end when the female protagonist in my books were *I'm unnaturally attracted, and I can hear his voice in my head. But nope, we're not mates. Can't be. It must be drugs.* Okay, I would admit to having a few of those thoughts initially, because my human brain was slow and freaked out. But I'd been in this world long enough now to know that fantastical happenings were the norm. It was stupid to deny it any longer.

Running from it was even stupider.

As I started to slow, there was a crash to my right and a shriek escaped before I slammed my mouth shut. Zahak was closer than I expected. Astra tapped her head against me once more, with enough force that I almost fell into a nearby tree. "Stop," I cried. "I can't outrun him. You take Leo and get to safety. Zahak won't hurt me, we're mates. He might be out of his mind, but there's nothing that can completely fracture our bond."

Was I certain of this random drivel I was spilling? Nope. I didn't know anything for certain, but I was trusting my gut here.

Through our bond, I reached for Zahak, only to find darkness. "He won't hurt me," I repeated, hoping to convince us both.

I held Leo out to Astra, but she raged at me, growling and stalking forward until I had no choice but to step back, all the while the crashing through the trees grew louder. Soon, there'd be no other choice but to face Zahak.

Of course, Astra didn't give me that chance, as she knocked into me once more, and this time I lost my balance and would have hit the ground if she hadn't ducked low to catch me on her back. Draped over her huge form, all I could do was hold on with one hand while desperately clutching Leo so he didn't go flying off into the forest.

Astra moved fast, trees a blur on either side. She howled and picked up the pace when Zahak's massive form appeared in the trees a dozen yards away, and as I clung to the back of the sabre, all I could do was stare at him.

The Fallen were all near seven feet as it was, but in this hybrid dragon form, he was even taller. And broader. His clothes were shredded across his body, scaled muscles pumping as he stalked behind us. Bastard didn't even look like he was running, and yet the distance continued to shrink between us.

Black and gold scales covered most of what I could see of his impressive physique, and I couldn't deny that a large part of me was into this prey-predator chase. There was fear as well, of course—I hadn't completely lost my mind. There was no being more dangerous than the predator stalking us, but I sensed I could handle Zahak in this form.

I just had to get Astra and Leo to safety first.

Making a split-second decision, I shifted Leo up to Astra's back. "Hold on, little one," I whispered, relieved when he dug his claws into the fur on her neck.

Then I released my hold and rolled off Astra.

All the air escaped my lungs as I slammed into the ground. Fuck, that had been harder than I'd expected. Zahak roared and the ground beneath me shook. Astra, who had stopped when I fell, looked like she was about to come back my way, but I waved her on. "Go," I gasped, lungs still screaming for air. "Get Calendul."

She bellowed, tentacles flying around her head as she stared into my eyes. I was about to yell again, when she shook her head and took off. Relief flooded through me along with prickles of fear. Despite this being my plan, now that I was alone with a mindless dragon-man, who was hunting me down like prey, I worried I might be too human to survive.

Pushing myself up, I was finally able to breathe freely, and thankfully none of my limbs or ribs felt broken. Just bruised. Turning to track Zahak as I got to my feet, I choked back another scream.

The path was empty.

Looking left and right, I tried to find his huge form in the trees, but there was no sign of the beast, even as his presence surrounded me.

He was out there.

Hunting me.

"Z?" I called softly. "I'm not fighting you, big man. I'm here and I'm ready."

A low rumble vibrated through the air, and my body reacted involuntarily. Heat filled my core, and I found myself pressing my thighs tightly together to ease the ache. Another rumble, and I flattened both hands on my stomach, leaning forward as I groaned.

What was he doing to me? What was happening?

The rumbles increased until they all but surrounded me. I spun to look behind. Anticipation of when he would appear had me near jumping out of my skin. The path behind me was clear, but as I turned back again, my scream couldn't be suppressed any longer. Zahak stood before me, towering like the beast he was, blocking out the crimson light filtering in through the canopy.

"Hi," I squeaked, swallowing roughly to try and get myself under control. "Hey, hi, hello. Fancy meeting you here."

He didn't respond to my nervous babble, remaining silent as he stared with eyes that were double pools of darkness. Zahak's power sank into my essence until my limbs trembled.

The fire inside grew, and I barely stopped myself from touching him. Through our mental connection, there was just that same rumble that had filled the forest before.

"Z?" I tried again.

Scales trailed up his cheeks, leaving only patches of his bronzed skin visible. The stare didn't break, but his lips tilted up a beat. "Run, little one," he rasped.

This wasn't like last time when he'd told me to run and all I'd felt was fear. This was telling me to run so that he could claim me, and there was no denying that I wanted this claiming. Drager was a distant memory in my head, and no matter what small connection I'd felt to him, it was nothing to how I felt with Zahak. This was deeper, *deep* in my soul.

"I don't want to run from you," I whispered.

The smirk grew, and it was a scary smile, but I wasn't scared. Had I ever truly feared him? Even the first time in Lancourt, when his black beast appeared, I thought I felt fear… but it was more confusion. Confusion and intrigue.

Instead of turning away, I took a step closer. Zahak remained exactly where he was, even as I tilted my head back and watched him. "Do you need me to run so you can hunt me?" I asked.

His chest rumbled, and I saw his fists clench and unclench at his sides. He was still fighting his instinct, trying to keep me safe, and I didn't like that.

"Okay, Z," I said with a chuckle. "Game on."

I slapped my hand against his chest, as if we were kids playing tag on the playground, and then I took off into the forest once more. My steps were light, and when I heard his pounding footfalls behind, the fire in my gut grew stronger until I was blazing. Heat traced along my spine, through my muscles and cells, and my eyes burned. There was no visible fire, of course, but I felt it inside.

Zahak's steps grew louder, and I welcomed the natural burst of adrenaline in this primal chase. As I ran, my clothes scratched at my sensitive skin, and I wished that they would just disappear. The instinct that we should be doing this naked was screaming inside me.

Swift winds behind indicated my dragon was close, and I resisted the urge to look over my shoulder. Our chase would be finished all too soon, and I wanted to drag it out.

When it came to Zahak and the way he made me feel alive… I never wanted it to end.

The moment he was close enough to capture me, he did, strong arms enclosing around me from either side, and I was lifted off my feet and hauled back against his hard chest. His body was burning; even through clothes it scorched my skin.

As his hold tightened, I was dragged higher. "You ran from me, mate," he rumbled, words barely understandable.

"You—" I coughed. "—told me to. You told me to run, Z."

A low rumbling laugh that did unspeakable things to me. "Since when do you listen to me, la moyar?"

Arching against him, desperately in need of relief from this power destroying me, I was not above begging for what I needed. The chase had opened a part of me that was into primal play, and I wanted more.

"Zahak," I finally growled. "Are you going to fuck me? Because I'm just here, all unclaimed."

I had no freaking idea where this bold side of me came from, but I was done waiting.

To my surprise, he lowered me back to the ground, and for a second my heart sank. Was he rejecting me? When I'd just opened myself up and offered every part of myself to a beast who could destroy me with one strike.

Sucking in a deep breath, I turned to face him, needing to see his expression. Before I had a chance to examine him closely, he reached out and clutched my shirt. In one yank, he tore it from my body, the material all but dissolving under his touch.

"What?" I gasped, and I would have stumbled back but he had moved on to grasping my pants, which vanished in the same manner. My chest heaved as I sucked in the hot air, and with that, Zahak's smile grew. "I'm going to claim you now, mate," he growled. "Will you fight me?"

His smirk remained firmly in place, and I got the sense that he was hoping I would.

Joke was on him, because I was into this, and I would not be fighting any longer.

CHAPTER 12

MORGAN

Zahak's hands slid up my sides, the scales smooth and rough at the same time just like on his full dragon form. Tingles detonated into my body under his touch as a low groan slipped out.

"Morgan," he rasped, and I realized my eyes were closed.

"Run for me one more time, la moyar."

Moistening my lips, I nodded breathlessly.

As I turned to leave, he clawed at my underwear, and then I was naked. Well, except for my boots, which was fucking weird, but what the hell, they'd help me run.

Run and be claimed by Zahak.

I shot one last look at my beast-man, uncaring that I was butt freaking naked in the middle of a forest, in a world under attack. As I'd thought before, this was how we were supposed to do this first claiming.

"Catch me if you can, big man," I whispered, breathless,

leaning in and slapping my hand against his chest once more. "Tag, you're it."

Racing off, there were no restrictions on my body now, no annoying material chafing my skin. Yeah, my tits were flapping in the breeze like they'd been hung out on the line to dry, but that was all good, because I was free.

Free in a way I'd never felt, with no pressure or restrictions crushing me.

Life on Earth had a way of suppressing our freedoms, and this was invigorating.

The roar that followed reminded me that there was more going on here than a casual sprint.

This was a primal chase.

Giving myself one chance to look back, I spluttered out a gasp and curse, before picking up my pace. Zahak's wings had appeared behind him as he raced after me, and I had no way of knowing how much danger I was in until he caught up to me. An eventuality that had me both excited and on edge.

Thinking myself clever, I changed course down a smaller path, and despite myself I had to look back once more.

The path behind was clear.

Where the hell had that dra—?

Before I could finish that thought, I slammed into what felt like a wall. Strong arms captured me and squeezed me tightly. At first there were flutters of excitement, until his scent washed over me. A scent I knew well, but it wasn't Zahak's.

"Hello, little human," Drager murmured as screams ripped from me, and I fought against his hold. He slammed his mouth against mine to cut off my shrieks, and I clawed and punched harder, but my strength was nothing on his.

"Let me go!' I snapped, when I finally managed to pry my mouth away.

Drager's expression darkened. "Not a fucking chance. You're mine. I had you first, and I claim you now."

My insides swirled, but it wasn't from arousal this time. It was disgust. The fact that I was naked with this shifter felt very dangerous.

"You're wrong," I choked out, my current fear very real. "You never truly wanted me. You just don't want Z to have me. You're the competitive one."

Drager's expression was more feral than I'd seen from him in a long time. His energy felt frenzied and out of control. "He doesn't get to claim what's mine. I'm taking you and he'll never see you again."

Without thinking through the consequences of my actions, I leaned forward and bit his chin. Hard enough that he dropped me, and I managed to land on my feet and scramble away from him.

He stared at me in shock, and again I really wished I wasn't naked. Risking a glance away, I looked for Zahak, but he was nowhere in sight.

"He's not coming, human," Drager snarled. "Mother said that he's the key to her plan, and I decided to make a deal."

If I'd had the ability to destroy Drager in that second, I'd have done so without hesitation. This was why Zahak had felt uneasy about heading to Lancourt; he'd known his brother was a betraying bastard. Drager always took the easy way out, and for his weakness we were all going to pay.

"How could you?" I whispered as tears sprang to my eyes. "You don't even care what they'll do to him? I defended you, saying you'd never sacrifice your brothers. Yet here we are, all so you could win this fucking game. You're a monster."

The skin around his eyes crinkled, a slight twitch before his expression smoothed once more. "Mother assured me that no harm will come to me or my brothers. She's not here for that. She's here to claim Risest. We were just holding it for her."

I almost felt sorry for this moron. "There's no fucking way that's the truth," I spat out in the hope he could grow a brain cell. "She stole your memories. You haven't seen or heard from her in a few hundred years, and you've held claim all that time. She's here for another reason, and you're too stupid and selfish to care about more than getting what you want this minute."

Crossing my arms over my breasts, I felt so uncomfortable that it was almost as if we'd never seen each other naked. My time away from Drager and his influence had woken me up to all the toxic behavior he'd displayed when we'd been together.

His flags weren't even remotely pink, they were as fucking crimson as the sky above.

Of course, he was still twice as tall and seventy times stronger, so when he reached out and grabbed me once more, I could do nothing except claw, bite, and swear at him. He just wrapped one long arm around my chest, pinning my arms to my side. Wings appeared behind him, black and gold, as he shot up into the sky, taking us out of the forest.

As we got higher, I frantically looked for Zahak, fear that he was hurt or worse a driving force inside me. Frantic cries ripped free when I caught sight of him a few yards from where Drager had captured me, fighting off four dragon shifters. His mother wasn't there, thankfully, since I knew she was the big bad, but he was still horribly outnumbered.

I choked on sobs as Drager flapped harder, taking us away

until I could no longer see Zahak. The roars of a pissed-off dragon followed, and I slumped against the bastard stealing me from my mate.

No matter what happened, I'd make Drager pay for this. Even if it was the last thing I ever did.

—————

Drager eventually landed and forced me to pee *so I wouldn't have an accident on him.* Like I was a fucking child. Then he dressed me in one of those horrific white pantsuits that chafed at my skin, and flew until the red of the sky faded into a dark night. There was no more bronze and gold lighting up the sky. Instead, we had eternal darkness, without a single star to break it up.

The same darkness seeped inside me as I hung in his arms, having used every ounce of energy to fight. It was freezing up this high, but Drager radiated enough heat to keep us both warm—a fact that bothered me a lot. I didn't want to be kept safe or alive by someone who could betray us like this. Betray Zah—

I cut off all thoughts of him. It was too painful to wonder what had happened. I'd been reaching through our bond, but there was only silence on the other end. Either the infiltrating shifters knew how to block bonds, or Zahak wasn't conscious, and both scenarios were terrifying.

To mentally escape, I spent my time plotting Drager's death, and figuring out what I'd wear to his funeral. An event I'd only attend to show respect for his brothers, who I actually liked.

I definitely wasn't wearing black or white, his favorite colors. I'd wear pink. Bastard would hate that joyful color.

As if he heard my mental hatred, his deep voice broke through the hours of silence. "You can't ignore me forever, human. I promise, this is for the best. Zahak is an evil bastard. He'd eventually grow tired of you and throw you away."

That asshole did not just go there! He fucking did not.

He was about to learn of my history, so he could understand why someone making decisions about what was best for me triggered me back to my damn childhood.

"My mother was a controlling narcissist," I said without inflection. My voice wasn't loud either, but he had supernatural hearing, so I pushed on. "It started small, with her insisting on choosing my clothes, even past the age where I should be picking my own outfits. She'd always push and prod me into what she wanted me to wear. Then it got a little worse, limiting my access to friends outside of school and canceling extracurricular sports. Eventually she decided to homeschool me. Did I tell you that before? She kept me locked in the house all week, under the pretense of protecting me from the outside world. I almost drowned in that fucking lake at the academy because she wouldn't allow me to learn to swim. For my own good, of course."

My breaths huffed in and out, and Drager's hold on me tightened uncomfortably before he loosened his grip.

"Her use of guilt was next level. I've seen my mother cry so many times now that I thought it was normal to cry daily. I used to force myself to shed tears as well, which led to a case of feeling sorry for myself regularly. That was one of the first habits Lexie nipped in the bud. Followed by many others, including my constant need to check any decision I made with my mother first, because if I made the wrong one she'd destroy me from the soul up."

Just saying Lexie's name out loud had my eyes burning,

as if I was about to practice daily crying again. Maybe that would have her appearing out of nowhere to kick me in the ass once more.

"I fought for college, and it was the only time my dad ever backed me. And it changed everything. I met Lexie and she showed me that the life my mother trapped me in was toxic. I might enjoy the quiet life of a librarian, and some might say it's no different to what I had before, but to me it's *all* different. I make my own decisions now. No one gets to tell me what is right or wrong for me. Or *best* for me."

Drager let out a rumbling huff, as if he finally got the point of my extensive backstory and ramble. "You said my call changed your life," he said after about thirty seconds of silence.

I just blinked, tilting my head back so I could see his expression. I'd been resolutely refusing to look his way, but I had to see if he was for real. "From everything I just said there, your response was to bring it back to you, and make it seem like you swooped in and made my life better?"

Drager shrugged. "You'll come to see in time. Unlike your mother, who is cursed with the stupidity and shortsightedness of humans, I do truly know what's best for you."

With that last frustrating and frankly insane statement, he changed directions and dove to the right. The landscape below us had changed while I'd been trying to appeal to the better nature Drager apparently did not have. It was now lush and green, all rolling hills and the prettiest village I'd ever seen.

For a brief moment I was distracted from my anger and fear as Drager descended between thatched roofed houses. They were dotted around a winding river, sticks with lights on the end scattered in the yards of each house, displaying gardens and crops instead of grass. Even in the dark I could tell it was gorgeous and picturesque, but if Drager had brought me here, then all this beauty hid evil inside.

Lexie had warned me, and I'd learned the hard way, to never trust a pretty face in faerie land.

MORGAN

By the time Drager landed, fae had emerged from their homes and were waiting for their *god*. He'd dropped us onto a cobblestone street which looked as if it was used for markets and other village activities. There were small stalls off to the sides, the red and gold banners closed to contain the goods inside, but I could already picture how bright and inviting they would look when they were all open and trading.

More of those wooden lanterns were sending soft light around the perimeter, revealing the various races that had come to greet us. A lot of the fae who could pass for humans were in the vicinity, along with some trolls, sirens, and a few nightmare fae. I found myself unable to stare directly at them, because it brought me right back to the trench.

I'd have given anything to be back there with Zahak.

Zombie creatures were nothing compared to being stuck with the fuckhead who had kidnapped me.

Drager's physical hold on me didn't cease; his huge hand remained wrapped around my forearm. He'd anticipated my need to escape but I wasn't stupid enough to race out into these lands without a clue of where I was or what dangers awaited me. I had to be smart about this and plan before I escaped.

Clearly, though, Drager believed me to be beyond such reasoning.

He'd always underestimated me because I was human, and for once I was glad of it. He'd continue to underestimate my ability and desire to get free from here, and he'd eventually let down his guard.

The first to approach us was a very familiar face: Florentine, and I now knew exactly where we were. This pretty village had an equally pretty name of Green Hollow. Florentine looked exactly as she had the last time I saw her, with suspicious eyes and full pink lips. Her auburn hair was so long that if she didn't have it braided back it would have brushed the ground.

Her green eyes were hard as she examined us. "Lord Drager, we had no word you were coming to visit."

It wasn't a question, but Drager didn't appear to notice or care about the bite in her tone. "I need a place to lay low for a few days, until I can figure out how to deal with the situation at hand."

Florentine's unwelcoming stance didn't shift. "We heard the war sirens. Our lands are under attack... Shouldn't you be out with your brothers taking down our enemies? After all, that's why we've lorded you to gods, correct?"

Yas, girl! Silently I was cheering her on. This arrogant asshole needed more than a few home truths. Drager's scowl left deep-seated lines across his forehead. "They've captured my brothers, and I am but one dragon shifter. I cannot take them on by myself, at least not without a lot of planning. Your village is well shrouded and protected by ancient energies. It's the only place to hide my energy."

The low-lying panic I'd been pushing down for hours reared up once more. If Green Hollow was *magically* protected, then that meant Zahak wouldn't be able to find me. Among my many fantasies as we flew, was one where Zahak escaped from the infiltrators, tracked our path, and then stormed in here and killed Drager. After, we'd wear pink to the funeral, because the ending was always the same.

Like a Choose Your Own Adventure book, one path led to me killing Drager, and the other had Zahak as the dragon slayer. But the happy ending remained consistent through all the options.

Drager had crushed one adventure path without even knowing it, the bastard.

Florentine didn't appear to be willing to bend, but unfortunately for her the rest of her village was not as astute. They all wore dragon bullshit on their faces and appeared grateful for it.

"Please, you're more than welcome, Lord Drager," said a tall male from behind Florentine. He had the same red hair as her. "I'm Joseph, and I apologise for my sister; she's a little overprotective. But we are honored that you would choose our village to regroup and plan."

Florentine attempted to maim him with a glare, but he was unbothered. "I'm the matriarch of the strongest family," she bit out. "It's my job to be protective."

"I'm the strongest family," Drager boomed. "You have no need to protect them from me. I'm the one who has kept you all safe for decades. It's going to be fine. I promise."

Nothing like making promises you couldn't keep. I opened my mouth to insert my own opinion, but Drager's hold on me tightened painfully, so I decided to leave it for another day. Clearly, we were here for the foreseeable future, and I had to survive it, even if it felt like my soul was bleeding. A cut that wouldn't heal, and as dramatic as it sounded, with the pain in my chest I was surprised not to see a pool of blood at my feet.

Drager might have faked our bond through his infusions of energy, but now that I knew what a true bond felt like, there was no mistaking the two. It was akin to having the best designer bag and then getting a knock-off. On the surface, they appeared similar, but you didn't even have to look that closely to discover the knock-off quality was low.

Drager was totally a knock-off.

"We will lend you our house, for it's the grandest in the village," Florentine's brother continued, and if he didn't shut up soon he'd be on his way to his own village funeral.

Florentine and I could both wear pink. It'd be nice.

"That will have to do," Drager said, with all the grace of an arrogant sociopath.

I'd been attracted to Drager from the first second I saw him, even as he terrified me, but now all I felt was hatred and anger. No, not anger: absolute fury. His controlling and manipulative behavior had been there from the start, and I'd had no choice but to accept it because he was a god. I'd assumed that due to his station in life he had never been taught how to treat people with respect.

But then I'd met his brothers, and outside of Emmen's attitude problem, none of the others showed the same arrogance. It was clear that I'd just been making excuses for Drager because of my attraction to him. I should have slapped myself long ago.

Shaking my head in disgust, I turned away and found my gaze meeting Florentine's. She was watching me closely, her focus moving between my face and my arm, where Drager held me prisoner style. I couldn't tell exactly what she thought about the situation, but it was clear that she did have thoughts. Many of them.

Joseph waved for us to follow him. Drager pulled me along, and once we left the town square we entered the small streets of the village built along the river. Even in the darkness, the body of water appeared huge, with the village co-existing around it.

"Here we are!" Joseph exclaimed, sounding very pleased with himself. He'd brought us to a house that wasn't all that large or grand—it looked very much like the others in the village, which made me like Florentine even more. She was the leader here, and yet hadn't set herself above her people.

It appeared her intentions were pure and genuine, holding Green Hollow's best interests at heart. Drager could learn a lot from her actions.

The lanterns around the property flickered, lighting up a white house with a yellow thatched roof. It had a yellow door and window trims too, but the color looked faded, as if it had been painted a long time ago. A short path led to the door, and there were no fences or gates to separate any of the houses.

As we made our way into their property, I squirmed against Drager because his hold was cutting off blood flow. My fingers were starting to tingle. "Stop fighting me," he muttered.

"Never," I shot back. "I don't know what you did to make me think there was a true bond between us, but all I feel now is hatred and disgust."

His grip tightened, and my next words died under my whimper. He eased up almost immediately, and I felt some relief as he stroked his thumb over my skin. "You drive me insane," he rumbled, loud enough for Joseph to hear, though the fae showed no sign of it.

"The bedrooms are on the top level," Joseph said, turning to wave his hand again. "This is the living and eating space, with cooking facilities through there." He pointed to a small door on our right.

It was a simple, sparsely furnished living area with only large cushions on the ground, and a fluffy white rug. They had no televisions in this world, but there were shelves filled with books. The urge to explore new stories hit me, as it always did when I found myself in a library, but now was not the time nor the place.

A dining nook was situated to the right of us, with a round wooden table and six chairs, all carved in a light gray wood. "My great, great grandfather made this for us." Florentine said as she entered the house and noticed my observations. "It's from the last old variety of *wickery bramble* and it's where we ate every morning and evening growing up."

Drager spared her a brief glance, before he dismissed her to speak with Joseph again. "I need a means of spreading information through the villages without it getting back to the infiltrators. We must band together, and if we can gather enough warrior fae to distract their guard, I can take on the main instigator."

"Your mother," I sniped.

Joseph looked taken aback by my statement. "Mother?" he breathed.

Drager's chest shook beneath me, but I honestly couldn't care less about his anger. It barely matched my own. In my head, Lexie was screaming at me to lay low and stop prodding the beast, but I didn't even know if my best friend was alive, so I couldn't find it in myself to shrink.

"We don't know who is really in charge," Drager lied,

"but I intend to get to the bottom of it. We must be informed to win in this war."

Joseph nodded, his confusion fading as he extended complete trust to his leader.

Florentine, who wore a look of distrust, didn't extend the same faith.

She was the one I needed help from to escape this place. I just had to wait until Drager felt confident in my compliance, and then I'd decide what to do.

To claim my freedom.

CHAPTER 14

MORGAN

The next day I remained in the tiny bedroom I'd been assigned. It had a twin bed, a shelf holding small carved statues depicting fae animals—mostly *dunedins*, sabres, and a yonter—and very little else. With nothing to distract me, I spent my time planning, fuming, and mourning.

My melancholy was more than knowing Zahak was out there in danger. It was also the irrevocable destruction of my relationship with Drager. Yeah, sure, my emotions toward him had clearly been borne from a Stockholm Syndrome of sorts, but they had still felt real to me.

So, I mourned.

It was the next morning when Drager finally made an appearance. "You will leave this room today or I will drag you from it."

He didn't deserve an acknowledgement or a response.

"Morgan," he growled, warning in that one word. He wasn't kidding, and as he went to grab me, I pulled myself up quickly and scooted back on the bed.

"What do you want, Drager?" I snapped. "Can't you just go out and steal the world without any help from me?"

He was dressed in armor again today, darker and less ornate than the last style I'd seen him wear. Everything about him appeared darker, despite his blond hair and glowing sun god persona.

"Do you need my energy?" he segued, and as my brow furrowed into a heavy scowl, I decided to make it very clear how I felt about that.

"If you touch me, I will cut your dick off and feed it to a yonter. I swear to fuck. Don't tempt me."

Drager didn't look put out. If anything, he was amused. His grin grew, and the darkness in his eyes eased until he was all but laughing. "You have such a way with words, little human. I missed that when you were stolen from me."

Of course he thought Zahak stole me. There was no part of him that could fathom the simple truth—when that blast of energy shot us away from the academy, my body had gone with Zahak. My soul went to its home, and I would have given anything to be back with him.

"I still can't believe you left him to be captured." I cleared my throat. "He's your brother, and despite everything, he would never have done that to you."

Drager's laughter faded in a heartbeat. "For you he'd have fed me to the dragons and never looked back. Why am I vilified for doing the same?"

Furious, I was up on the bed so I could match his height. "The difference is, there was no need to sacrifice Zahak to save me. You did that for your own selfish gain. He murders for me, and you murder for you. That's how it has always been with you, Drager. You are first, and the rest of us second."

The heat increased in the room; he was so furious that I wouldn't have been surprised to see his dragon appear. Already he was half covered in scales, eyes black once more.

Forcing my voice lower, because I wouldn't survive his shift this close, I delivered my final thoughts on it all: "Until you learn how to love another as much or even more than you love yourself, you'll never truly understand. I know there's a decent dragon deep down inside you, but you're going to need one hell of a character growth to get there."

He exhaled with force. "You're not my equal, and for that I don't have to pay attention to what you say. *You are a human.*"

A human that he wanted to possess, and therefore, I had all the goddamn power.

Crossing my arms, I glared and didn't back down. Drager finally threw his hands in the air and turned to leave the room. "I'll get Florentine to shower and dress you, since you're acting like a fucking baby."

Then he was gone, taking his massive energy and presence with him. For the first time since he stormed in here, I could breathe freely, and I was ashamed to feel tears in my eyes. Traitorous tear ducts.

I refused to mourn my relationship with Drager for one more second.

We never even had a relationship to break.

Hopping off the bed, I attempted some deep breathing exercises, even strolling over to the window to see the outside world. This land had calmed me before, but of course now I got to witness stunningly eerie crimson skies instead of my favorite dusty pink color.

I was about to turn away from the view, when movement caught my eye near a patch of trees filled with giant yellow and orange flowers. Every part of Green Hollow was natural and meticulously cared for, and that section was no exception. And in those flowers and pruned shrubs, I'd definitely seen a creature move.

My heart stuttered as a sleek dark coat came into view, before it disappeared again into the shadows. *Astra!* I was almost certain that had been Astra hiding in the bushes, appearing only briefly so I knew she was waiting.

I had to get to her.

Scrambling off the bed, my bladder protested because I hadn't peed in far too long. In fact, I could have used a few hours in a bathroom to get myself all sorted, but it would have to wait.

The landing was empty, and so were the stairs down to the ground floor. Taking them three at a time, I managed not to trip and die before reaching the living area. Holding my breath and hoping Drager was still outside searching for Florentine, I raced as silently as I could into the stone-lined kitchen, which held two sinks and a large fireplace with cooking pots hanging over it. More importantly, there was a back door, which opened silently.

According to Joseph, nothing in this village was ever locked, and that was going to come in very handy today. Drager had already warned me he'd feel it if I crossed the invisible magical barrier around Green Hollow, but Astra was inside. Somehow, she'd done so without any detection.

The sun's warmth surrounded me, along with a mild breeze holding a hint of a sweetness. The scent reminded me of honeysuckle, though clearly the Risest version. With the sheer quantity of flowers filling this village, it could be any number of them that smelled sweet. There was no time for a horticulture lesson though; I had a sabre to tackle-hug.

No one stopped me as I raced across the open land, and I felt less panicked when I entered the tree line, shade engulfing and hiding me from the outside world. Slowing, I caught my breath and looked around. "Astra?" I whispered. "Are you here, girl?"

There was a rumble from my left, and I turned to see her gorgeous form spring into view. Clinging to her back was our cub. "Leo!" I exclaimed, tears once again rolling down my cheeks.

My emotions were on the edge, needing only the slightest upheaval to tip them over.

"Thank fuck you're both okay," I sobbed as I threw myself forward and wrapped my arms around them. The sabres let me cry out my love for them for many minutes. I eventually pulled myself together, backing up and taking a few deep breaths. "How did you find me?" I asked, staring into Astra's eyes, which were filled with ancient energy.

Of course, the one issue with our relationship was that there was no actual way for humans and sabres to communicate. Zahak had shown signs of mental speak with her, but I had no such ability. She understood me, though, that much I knew for sure.

"Did you follow me yesterday when Drager kidnapped me?"

She nodded her huge head, and I wondered how long she'd had to run below the flying beast to keep us in her line of sight.

"Is Zahak okay?"

Simple yes or no questions were the key, but of course there were many nuances to "okay," and I could immediately tell that tripped her up.

"Is he alive?"

Another nod.

"Is he free to come look for us?"

This time it was a definite shake, and low rumbling growl.

Squeezing my eyes closed briefly, I fought to stay calm. A losing battle.

"You should have stayed with him," I whispered. "I'm not in any actual danger here, outside of Drager being a demanding fuck."

Another growl echoed in the forest, but this time it wasn't from Astra. Spinning, I placed my body between my sabres and my kidnapper. "Leave her alone," I snapped, before he even said a word. "She's done nothing wrong and she's not Zahak, here to steal me away."

Drager's eyes were narrowed slits, fury seeping out. "I'm not worried about the creature. Zahak might have forced her to follow, but he can't communicate or sense either of you here. Not even a bonded pet is an exception."

Astra growled and I joined her. "She's not a pet," I told the ignorant bastard. "She's family."

He dismissed us both with a wave of his hand. "Then if you want your family to remain alive, you'll get your ass back to the village and get cleaned up. We have plans to make."

I hesitated, wanting desperately to fight his demands, but there was more at stake here than me. For all of Astra's strengths against most of the inhabitants of Risest, she was still less powerful than their gods. I couldn't risk her.

"As long as Astra and Leo can stay, then I'll comply." For now.

Drager spared a glance at the cub, and it was clear he wanted to ask a lot of questions, but in the end he got what he wanted so didn't really care.

"Deal."

Great. Now I had to play more of his stupid little games.

Having Astra here did feel like I was one step closer to Zahak, and that filled me with renewed hope. He wasn't dead, and I was determined that very soon we'd be reunited.

CHAPTER 15

MORGAN

Back in the village, in front of their home, Florentine and Joseph waited for us. "We thought you had escaped," Joseph said with a forced laugh. "Not that there'd be any reason to run away, would there? We're safest he—"

His word was lost in a strangled gasp as Astra came into view, quiet and stealthy, settling in at my side. Her presence, as I'd discovered in my short time at the academy, often left those who had never experienced this ancient breed of sabre speechless, and today was no exception.

Florentine hid her reaction a fraction better, but I could see the awe and fear in her deep green eyes. "This is Astra," I replied, ignoring Joseph's statement about escaping. He wasn't the smartest fae on the shelf, unfortunately. "She'll be at my side while I'm here, and for everyone playing at home, she's the literal definition of fuck around and find out."

The fae siblings wrinkled their brows in a very similar manner, while Drager just shook his head.

"So don't find out," I continued, feeling pleased that I got to use one of my favorite lines.

The silence was heavy as my unsubtle threat registered. The siblings didn't look impressed, but they also didn't return any threats of their own. I chose to believe that was *not* because of Drager's presence.

"Lord Drager said you require new clothes and the chance to clean up," Florentine said stiffly. "I'm here to assist."

"Thank you," I replied, and placed my hand on Astra's head to stroke her fur.

Florentine indicated I should follow, and I did without hesitation, still desperate to pee. Astra and Leo remained by my side, and since it had been too long since I'd held my cub, I reached out and picked him up. Leo purred loudly as he settled against my chest.

His weight was more substantial than the last time I'd held him, which was hard to believe when it had only been a day or so since we were all separated.

"I didn't know there were two of these creatures left in Eastern Risest," Florentine said, staring at the tiny bundle in my hands. "Here I find you've claimed both. You're clearly a collector of rare and powerful beings."

Her digs were as subtle as my threats. "Honestly, they just keep falling in my lap, and I don't really know what to do with them all." I'd sensed a kindred spirit in her from the first moment I'd seen her in the library, and if I wanted her to help me now, I had to lay everything on the table. "I'm not the woman you believe me to be," I continued, sadness unintentionally seeping into my words. "I've been in the wrong place at the wrong time for so long now that I'm starting to think it's actually not wrong at all."

Florentine was clearly confused as she narrowed her eyes at me, while expertly navigating the edge of the raging river.

I tried again: "What I mean is that I thought I ended up in this world and sleeping with Drager through a series of coincidences and random bad luck." I shrugged. "Or good luck, depending on how you looked at it. But my relationship with him has always been one-sided. He tolerated me and gave me energy so I wouldn't fade from existence, and I gave him… me. I tried to be part of his world, I cared about that selfish bastard, and I thought there was a bond forming between us…"

"There's not?" she asked lightly. "Because from the outside he appears possessive of you. We've all been warned that if one hair on your head is harmed, he will destroy this village and everyone in it."

While his threat was unexpected, it also wasn't completely surprising. Not now that I knew his game. "Drager cares about Drager," I said, and there was no bitterness in my tone, just truth. "The bond between us is manufactured, and the only reason I drew his attention at all is I'm Zahak's true mate."

She ground to a halt, and I had to reach out and catch her arm or she'd have tumbled into the river. As it was, I barely managed to keep hold of her, Leo, and my balance. "Lord Zahak," she choked out. "Impossible. He would never tolerate being mated to a human."

Humans weren't exactly thought of as equals here, so I chose not to take offense. "Actually, he tolerated it much better than Drager."

"Lord Drager thinks you're mates too?"

The shocks kept hitting her, and if her eyes widened any further, she'd lose her eyeballs.

"As I said, Drager thinks we're mates because he felt a

connection to me through his bond to Zahak." It sounded a touch ridiculous when said out loud, but I was sure of my truth now. "Drager also can't help but compete with his brothers. I'm a prize he must win, even though the only bond between us was forced through energy sharing."

I was simplifying a complicated situation, but it seemed that finally Florentine understood. "You don't want to be here with him, do you?"

My snort of laughter held exactly zero humor. "If I could rip out Drager's heart with my bare hands, I'd have done so when we arrived."

That got a smile out of her. "Come on," she said, shaking her head with a chuckle. "We should keep moving."

Our pace was faster now, and Florentine's entire attitude had changed toward me. No longer was I getting the side-eyes and grimaces whenever she looked my way. Now she was relaxed and open as she chatted about Green Hollows. "My family founded this valley a few thousand years ago, and even during the darker days of these lands we were immune from much of the turmoil. There's a natural magical energy that surrounds our hollow. Hence why I protect what we have so fiercely."

"I've admired that about you from the first moment I saw you approach Drager," I said with a nod. "And I completely understand why you don't particularly welcome or trust the Fallen."

This got me another warm smile. "They might have been a positive change for much of the land, but I never trusted their motivations. Maybe because we never really needed them. For that, I'd rather remain as independent of their influence as possible."

The urge to reach out and squeeze her hand as I would have with Lexie was strong, but I refrained. We were building a fragile rapport here, and I wouldn't risk that by acting impulsively.

"I have my own feelings about the Fallen," I admitted. "Some positive, thanks to this bond with Zahak, but there's also a part of me that disagreed with their unilateral control over you all. They are judge, jury, and executioner, with no process to check their actions."

We'd reached a narrower section of river now, and Florentine gestured for us to leap over to the other side, which we all did with ease. She led us along this bank until we reached the mouth of a cave, the river disappearing inside.

She led us into the cave as she said, "The Fallen did not destroy as I expected." Her tone was one of resigned acceptance. "And they did not abuse their power. If they had, we would have fought back. In the end, most fae would agree that it has been to our benefit to have them here."

Also the conclusion I'd eventually reached, which had allowed me to stop questioning their dictatorship style of leadership. "But you'd still rather they remained out of your lives?" I added.

Her smile was brief. "Yes."

Our conversation faded as we took a left fork in the cavern, and ended up in a large space that was filled with pools of water. It was warmer in here, and I relaxed as steam surrounded me.

"These are natural thermal springs," Florentine said, pushing back some wayward strands of her hair that sprung to life in the humidity. "They'll cleanse and heal your body and spirit. There's also a section over there that we use as a bathroom, because not everyone has a toilet in their house." Florentine's house did, but theirs was the *finest house in the hollow*. She went on to explain how it all worked in more detail, and I promised my aching bladder that we'd be out of pain soon enough.

While we were chatting, Astra padded to the side of one of the thermal pools, sniffed at the waters, and then appeared satisfied as she dropped down onto her belly. "Looks like my spot has been chosen," I said with a laugh.

Florentine returned my smile with a genuine one of her own. "I'll be back soon with a drying sheet and some clothing. Please, take your time and relax. The waters have all you need to be cleansed."

She nodded her head once, a half-bow, and then turned and left the cave. I padded over to Astra and placed Leo on her back, where he clutched at the fur and snuggled in once more. Then I stripped off the clothes Drager had put me in, so relieved to be rid of them. After using the toilet section of this underground cavern, I made my way back to where the pools were, ready for this cleansing that Florentine spoke of.

Cleansing of more than just my skin and body, but also my essence.

As I sank into the warm water, an involuntary exhale left me, and with it worries and pain were released. Not all my pain, of course—the ache in my soul for Zahak was consistent and increasing—but the physical pains from kidnapping drifted away in the steam. Closing my eyes, I settled against the side of the warm stones, finding them smooth as they cradled my body.

Astra's purring was contented as she lazily dipped a paw into the water, swishing it around, before bringing it up to swipe at her eyes and ears. She then set to work cleaning Leo, and I imagined she would be a wonderful mother. Along with a scarily protective one. Having no idea if that was a future possibility for her or not, it was nice that she had Leo to care for now.

Time was lost as I drifted in thought, half asleep, even as I found myself reaching through the bond to try and find Zahak.

Z… where are you?

It was a fruitless task of course, being here in Green Hollow's protected lands, but I couldn't help myself. I'd have given anything to hear his rumbles in my head. I held on to Astra's assurance that he was alive, and just wished we had more time together to truly develop our bond. If we'd have cemented it in the forest, nothing would have kept me from his mind.

I believed that with every part of my being.

"She's still alive, you know?"

My eyes sprang open, and I instinctively covered my breasts, knowing that even in the dimly lit cave, Drager's eyesight was strong enough to see everything.

"What the hell are you doing?" I snapped. "Why are you suddenly so creepy? Were you always watching me like this?"

He shrugged, and I was shocked to find no denial forthcoming. "Lexie," he continued, as if I hadn't said a word. "She's alive and in the same prison as my brothers. So, you don't have to worry."

I just stared at him.

He'd given me an unexpected gift. I'd asked him about my best friend when he'd first kidnapped me, and he'd refused to answer. At the same time, though, the nonchalant way he spoke of them all being held prisoner was horrific.

I shook my head and let my disappointment spill out "How can you know that they're all in trouble and do nothing to save them? You ran like a coward to hole up here in your little protected hollow."

He rose from the wall he'd been perched against and

headed in my direction. I scooted back in the springs until I was as far from him as I could get. Astra was on her feet now too, but I gestured for her to back away. "Don't fight him," I told her quickly. "You getting hurt won't save me."

Astra snarled and growled, her impressive teeth on display. Thankfully, Drager stopped a few feet away, giving us our illusion of safety and space. "I can't save them without risking everything," he snapped, his face no longer impassive. "I didn't run like a coward. I used my fucking brain and knew I couldn't beat her on my own. I need time and numbers, and that's why I've come here. This is our chance to plan our attack without any outside interference."

"So, you do plan on trying to save them. All of them, even Zahak?"

His hesitation was minute, but I saw it. "Yes," he said, and I wondered if he was lying to me as easily as he'd lied to the others outside.

"What if I choose him?" Rhetorical question, because I'd all but made my decision the moment we were blasted into the trench together.

The darkness shading his face deepened. "As long as we stand side by side, and you can see which one of us is truly the stronger option, then I will accept your decision."

None of what he said made any fucking sense to me. "Why did you kidnap me, then? If you had a plan to not only save them but also give me a choice of mates?"

Drager shrugged. "It was the only way to ensure Mother believed I was happy to take off to Earth and leave her to her evil fucking schemes. Apparently, your delicious ass convinced her that I'd be shallow and cowardly enough to just run off and let them take this world."

His mother hadn't been the only one convinced.

I wasn't usually confused by the twist in a story, because I often saw them coming, but I'd truly believed Drager was as selfish and weak as he'd acted.

It seemed, though, that he had a touch more character than I'd given him credit for. I felt better knowing he wasn't the complete monster I'd assumed him to be, but it also didn't change my feelings for him. Whatever had happened between Zahak and me in that trench was already stronger than all my time with Drager.

Not that I was breaking it to him any time soon.

I needed him to stay on this course of taking down the interlopers and saving his brothers.

All of our lives depended on it.

CHAPTER 16

MORGAN

Drager left me to bathe alone, and by the time Florentine arrived, a stack of clothing in her arms, I was more than ready to get out. Drager's confession had my mind in a swirl, and I couldn't return to a place of rest and relaxation.

"Lord Zahak killed five of the Fallen," she said as a way of greeting.

I all but launched myself out of the water. "He's here?" I gasped, automatically reaching for the bath sheet she held out.

Florentine shook her head. "Oh no, I'm sorry! I should have realized," she grimaced, "no, he's not here, but one of our members was scouting around, and he's just arrived back with news of what happened after Lord Drager captured you."

My heart was pounding so hard that I was sure everyone could hear it. "Z killed five of them, and then what happened?" A whispered question, and an answer I wasn't sure I could handle.

"More arrived, and they managed to blast him with what was described as an energy ball. He was knocked out, and they dragged him off."

Astra's rumbling purr was low, and I felt her sadness in that one sound. Or maybe I was projecting, because the intensity of my own pain almost sent me to my knees.

"But… he was alive still, right?"

Florentine nodded rapidly. "Yes, very much alive."

Thank the gods. Not that I was happy about him being taken down…

"How many did they send the second time to contain him?"

Florentine's smile grew. "More than a dozen, according to Philip."

That was my Zahak. Yeah, at some point I'd claimed him. And despite my panic for his wellbeing, I was also weirdly proud. All of the Fallen Five were formidable males, but for me, Zahak was just a touch more than his brothers.

The fact that they'd needed a near army of shifters to take him down was proof of that. Not that I'd ever needed the proof.

Drying myself quickly, I said in a rush, "Drager told me that their mother doesn't plan on killing them, at least not yet, so we have time to figure out how to rescue them."

Florentine's open expression soured. "Does our Lord actually plan on rescuing his family? I was under the impression he was just hiding out here in the one place he couldn't be detected."

I'd been under the same impression, but now there was a tiny dot of hope that he wasn't as selfish as we'd all initially imagined. "I think he has a plan," I admitted, as I took the clothing she patiently held for me.

Florentine's expression indicated that she'd believe it when she saw it, and a part of me felt the exact same way.

I dressed in soft white underwear, before pulling on the dark gray linen pants and matching linen shirt she'd provided. She had also included sandals which appeared to be woven from vines and were far more comfortable than I expected. I didn't throw my boots away; I'd need them later, but it was nice to wear casual clothing.

When we emerged from the cave, with Astra padding at my side and Leo asleep again in her fur, it was to find dozens of fae gathered in a grassy knoll near the bathing cavern. Drager stood at the helm, a head taller than everyone else there. We couldn't hear what was being said from where we stood, but it was clear that the shifter god was moving his plan into action.

"He's wasting no time," Florentine muttered.

I refrained from giving any further opinions on the situation. Drager had extended his olive branch and I was taking it. Not that I'd ever forget what he did. If he wanted to rebuild a friendship between us, he had a lot to make up for, but in the interest of saving everyone, I was willing to embrace a temporary ceasefire. For the short term.

Since my time in the trench with Zahak, my urges to jump Drager's bones were gone. It had been fading from the moment Zahak appeared in my life, and now that I was awake and aware of their little rivalry, I felt almost no pull toward the enigmatic leader of Ocheran. I was onboard with Zahak's theory that all along my connection with Drager had been because of him.

It was always him.

We stopped near the back of the crowd listening to Drager.

"...figured out some of their weaknesses," he was saying, "because they're my own. Those assholes who have taken over our lands are from my homeworld. The army she's brought can be destroyed, because they're not as strong as me and my brothers."

Evidenced by Zahak taking out five of them.

"But we need to be smarter and more strategic about it. Destroy them one by one until our armies are equal in numbers. We also need to free my brothers. The five of us together are stronger than even our mother realizes."

There were murmurs and cheers from the fae, and I heard some intense discussions spring up. All of which was interrupted when a breathless fae appeared on the side of the crowd, looking as if he'd just run a marathon. His short blond hair was perfect, of course, but there was a tinge of pink in his brown cheeks. "Warriors approach," he got out in short bursts of panting. "Lightsbringers."

Lightsbringers! Lexie's family.

I turned to Florentine, and she confirmed my theory. "They're our strongest warriors in Ocheran. Drager called for them when he first arrived."

Well, well, it appeared that he did have a plan, it wasn't just spewing empty promises to get me to calm down and stop planning his funeral.

"Allow them entry," Drager said pompously.

"Like we could stop them," I heard Florentine mutter. "They control more of the natural energy than we'd ever hope to."

The barriers around Greens Hollow protected this gorgeous little village and its inhabitants from detection, but they didn't increase their power. Another reason Florentine was so protective of her village. They had much to lose and very little means to defend their treasure here.

The Lightsbringers warriors, from North Sandingshire province, were impressive as they marched into the clearing. Impressive and heartbreaking. They reminded me so much of my best friend, and it hurt to see them in formation as they waited before Drager.

They had the same tall, lithe frame as Lexie, and bore similar bone structure. Not so much that you'd think they were related, but enough that it was clear they were all from a similar province.

"Lord Drager…" A female stepped forward. Her hair was slicked back and so black it had blue flecks in it. "We are here at your command."

Drager nodded, in an almost respectful way. "You made good time, Commander Lightsbringer."

Her expression did not change, but her eyes grew harder. "They hold my daughter, Lord Drager. I was already on my way when we intercepted your call."

Daughter. Not that I hadn't been paying attention before, but now I was laser-focused.

My best friend had never spoken much about her family, no doubt to keep this side of her life secret from the unsuspecting human, but she had mentioned that they were greatly ambitious and traveled a lot. I'd always been under the impression that Lexie wasn't particularly close to her parents, but that she did love and respect them.

The distance between them didn't originate from her, and I still wondered to this day if fate had thrown us both together for a reason. We'd needed to find family after the ones we'd been born into let us down time and time again.

"We should not linger any longer than necessary," Drager said, addressing both the Lightsbringers and the fae from Green Hollow. "More of their troops arrive daily, so we have to end this now, before they plant roots too deep for us to sever."

Florentine leaned in closer to me. "How does he know so much about their plan? Are we sure he's on our side and not just leading us to slaughter."

I kept my voice low as I replied: "He told me that he pretended to be on his mother's side to get her to let him go free, and he used me as the bargaining chip to make it appear more legit. That being said, I don't fully trust Drager. From my experience, he puts himself first always, and will not risk himself to save others." Her frown deepened and I sighed. "Unfortunately, I don't believe we have much choice but to follow along with his plan for now. Just be on guard for any betrayal."

I'd already felt the sting of Drager's betrayal once, and I was not letting that take me by surprise again.

Drager finished up his speech: "We will leave before first light. So, tonight, we feast and plan, for tomorrow we are at war."

Florentine was silent beside me, but if her expression was any indication, this was her worst nightmare come to life. I couldn't blame her. There were no winners in war, but in this case I was hoping that at minimum we got to free my friends.

Free Zahak and Lexie, and the other Fallen. Then I'd be able to function without this low-level thrumming of panic in my soul.

The crowd dispersed, and I stood there for a long time watching the Lightsbringers set up a camp in one of the largest clearings beside the river. There had to be a hundred or more of the warrior clan here, and even knowing how strong these infiltrating shifters were, I was optimistic that if the fae all worked together, they could hold them at bay.

An optimism that would only grow stronger if we

managed to free Zahak and the others. Drager couldn't take them all on alone, and I knew he'd turn dragon-tail and run if it appeared his life was in danger.

His motto was *Drager first*, and the rest of the world a distant second. God or not, he had a lot to learn from the fae who showed up and stayed through the danger and hardship. The ones who never gave up on each other or their families.

Drager might have acted the way he did with a plan in mind, but it wouldn't matter what my plan was. I'd never have stood there and let my family be captured and taken away. He had no freaking idea what was happening to them under the control of crazy-momma-dragon, and I'd have rather been in the cage with them, then out here safe.

Maybe that meant I'd never win a war, but even so, I'd still make the same decision.

Always.

CHAPTER 17

MORGAN

The next few hours passed in training and preparation. A multitude of races joined in from other provinces around Ocheran, including trolls, harpies, sirens, centaurs, nightmare creatures, and even a race of fae I'd never seen or met, who were referred to as warrior fae. I got the impression they were originally from the trench. They stood about seven feet tall and looked like orcs, with leathery green skin and tusks. They could also blend into shadow like Professor Malin, the ghost walker who taught at the academy.

Nerves built slowly as we whiled away the time until we were to set off. Being human, I eventually had to sleep, but it was restless and fitful. The only reason I felt comfortable enough to sleep at all was Astra's presence at my side. She stretched out along the floor, and I cuddled Leo in my arms.

In the early hours of the morning, when the sky was still a crimson so dark it was almost black, Florentine shook me awake. "Prepare yourself to leave," she murmured, jumping back when Astra growled. Growled but didn't attack. If Florentine had been a threat, she'd never have gotten close enough to touch me. "There are clean clothes and *plumth* leaves for you to clean your teeth on the side table," she added quickly. "I'll meet you outside."

I nodded, shaking off my disorientation. We were marching on the invading shifters today, and I needed to be focused. Sliding from the bed, I pulled the covers up neatly, wondering if I'd ever be back here again. A yawn overtook my face, and I shook my head again, and did a few quick jumping jacks on the spot. "Come on, Morgan, wake the heck up."

Placing Leo on Astra's back, I focused on the pile of clothes Florentine had left on the table. She'd lit candles as she exited the room, and in that low light, I examined my own set of armored clothes. Made from material much thicker than I was used to wearing, the dark blue pants and shirt had stitched plates of gilded metal to protect my thighs, stomach, and chest.

Surprisingly it was light and easy to move in, my movements unrestricted when I leaned down to lace up my boots. I didn't have a hairbrush, so while I was chewing up the minty leaves, I finger-combed through the tangles and managed to pull it back into a rough ponytail.

Being morning, I desperately needed to pee, so I used the small bathroom in the house. It didn't have a shower or bath, but there was a drop style toilet, and running water to clean myself up after.

Once I was done, we hurried down the stairs and out the front door, and then made our way to where Florentine waited for us. Judging by the abundance of lights in the distance, the army was gathered and ready to depart. The nervous swirls in my stomach kicked into gear hard, and I had to swallow roughly against my dry throat. "Everyone is marching out now?" I asked as she waved me to follow her.

"Yes. We'll all travel together until we reach the *Harlont Forest*, and from there we'll be splitting into teams to handle different aspects of this attack. They've been coordinating all night. Drager has requested that one of us stay with you in the forest, so you don't get lost or hurt during the scuffle."

He loved to treat me like an errant toddler, but I didn't argue. I understood and accepted my position here in a world of fae. I was a human, and my only role was to *somehow be a mate to their gods*. Or god, singular. I had no doubt where my soul truly belonged now.

When we reached the back of the massive group, most of whom were dressed as I was in dark armored clothing, Florentine handed me two small bars of food, tinged red and slightly sticky. I'd had them before, and knew they'd be sweet from the dried fruits they contained.

"It'll give you energy," she said. "We'll be traveling as quickly as possible, via fae portal, which is only used in extenuating circumstances because it requires a lot of power to create. Luckily, we have the Lightsbringers here to help." Her words were matter-of-fact, without any jealousy or annoyance.

"Thank you," I told her, chewing the bars quickly. Looking around, I was surprised that I hadn't seen Drager this morning. *Wait, no*, I actually wasn't surprised. No matter what he said about us having a bond, he'd always been ambivalent about spending time with me, managing to go days without us crossing paths. I existed for him when I was right in front of him.

He's kind of leading an army rebellion against his family. As the annoying voice in my head reminded me that I wasn't the center of the universe, I had the sense that it wouldn't matter with Zahak. For him, I'd be the center, and he'd fit the rest in around me. Did I have empirical evidence of this... well, no. But I'd felt it from the first moment he saved me in Lancourt.

Florentine distracted me from my obsessing over a couple of gods. "Are you nervous?" she asked as we started to move, the regimented Lightsbringers leading the way.

"Terrified," I admitted. "I've never been involved in a battle. All I can think about is all the ways this could go wrong. Death and loss. Pain and suffering. I don't want to witness it, even knowing it's my duty to not look away. To be here as we take back our world."

She didn't react to my usage of *our* and I couldn't believe that slipped out. But it was how I truly felt inside.

"You're favored by the gods," she said, and there was no note of bitterness in her voice. It almost sounded as if she felt a touch sorry for me.

"The gods of this world can only do so much," I replied with a sad smile. "And considering they will battle against foes almost as strong as they are, no one is safe."

Florentine didn't argue, because there were no words of truth that would be reassuring. Astra nudged me a few times, comforting in her way, and I let my hand rest against her fur. Leo purred and moved closer to nuzzle my hand, and I marveled at how much bigger he looked already. The cub was double the size from when we'd found him in the trench, and since I'd only ever seen him drink from the milk of the hefle bush, I had to assume most of his growth was from Astra's energy.

That thought reminded me of the night I'd slept on Zahak and how his energy had sustained me. That was the first and only night we'd spent together, and yet I felt as if I'd known him for a hundred years longer than that. Time had moved oddly from the moment I entered this world, and apparently it wasn't going to start acting normal anytime soon.

When we'd been marching for about twenty minutes, deeper into the forests of Ocheran, Drager's voice lifted above the crowd and everyone drew to a halt. "We'll be taking the portal from this point," he called. "Grab your travel connection so you're not lost in the energy."

Florentine stood straighter. "Okay, looks like Drager himself will be tapping into the energy. Interesting." What exactly was interesting I never got to find out, as she patted my shoulder and added, "I'll head over to my brother and see if he has a connection. I expect Drager will ensure your safety during this journey."

I expected the same, since I was a human navigating a world filled with fae and would be the most vulnerable. "Thanks, see you on the other side." We exchanged smiles as she turned and walked off.

The rest of the crowd were pairing up, and I watched as they linked themselves, gripping forearms for the strongest hold. The crowd thinned as the pairs stepped farther into the forest.

"What the heck is going on?" I murmured, pressing my hand against Astra as I craned my neck to see better. The tail end of the crowd still blocked my view of the portal.

Drager hadn't found me yet, but I expected he was at the portal, ensuring everyone crossed safely. By the time there were only fifty or so fae left, I was finally able to see the whirls of light. The pairs would approach together, with their hands locked around forearms, step inside, and then zip, they'd be gone from view. "Holy crap. It's a portal." I mean, I knew it was a portal, but still seeing it was an entirely different experience.

One of the villagers from Green Hollow turned, as if I'd

been talking to him. He was a satyr, with a tawny-colored hide, and black skin. His eyes were tawny as well, and he was striking in all ways. "The energy will attach to your body, and once you pay with a taste of blood, you're shot through to the other side."

Right. Okay. *I have some questions...*

"You have to pay with blood? How much blood is a taste? Specifically."

This felt like one of those *read the fine print before signing* deals. "You'll barely feel it," he said with a faint smile. "All energy transference comes with a price, and this one is blood."

Was that why Drager had tapped into the portal, as Florentine said? He was taking blood, which to my understanding, was akin to taking power. Lifeforce and all of that.

"Why do you have to team up?"

The satyr didn't answer until we stopped moving forward once more. "For balance," he said. "The energy from both sides compete, and you can get pulled off course. With two, you work together to keep yourselves balanced." Here was hoping I'd be able to balance out the giant that was Drager.

"Thanks for the information," I told the satyr. "My name is Morgan. It's nice to meet you."

This time his smile was brighter. "Tomi, and I have to say, you're nothing like I expected."

Astra rumbled loudly, and he jumped a few feet back. Not that we'd been particularly close to start with.

"Seems that humans didn't have the most accurate representation here before I arrived," I said with a laugh, stroking my hand across Astra's head to ease her annoyance. I hadn't met another human in Risest, but I'd heard that the rare times they crossed into this world they existed mostly as pets and concubines to fae. "Glad that I've been able to fix the preconception of my race a little."

Tomi gave me a brief nod, before turning away and focusing on the portal. It was only when it was finally his turn, joining hands with another satyr, that I realized a very important fact: Drager was not here.

There was literally no sign of his huge form anywhere, which told me one thing…

He'd already gone through and left me here alone.

Fuck.

CHAPTER 18

MORGAN

He left me.

That bastard knew I was a human out here trying to navigate a fae world, and he never even checked to see if I had anyone to travel through the portal with. I'd been so sure he'd be waiting for me at the end, I'd never even bothered to worry about it. Even Florentine, for all her frustrations and suspicions of Drager, had assumed the same.

"What do we do, Astra?" I asked, looking around at the completely empty clearing.

Another nail in the coffin of Drager ever being my mate. The evidence had always been there, I'd just buried it deep. Like a dumbass human.

Astra's purring grew louder, and she started to nudge into my side, pushing me toward the portal.

"You can balance me?" I asked, nerves kicking in again.

Her rumbles increased and she nudged me harder, which I took for an affirmative.

Reaching out, I gathered up Leo, tucking him in against my armored chest. I'd hold him with one hand, and Astra with the other, and hope it was enough to keep us on the path.

The swirling grew brighter as we stepped closer, and it reminded me of the lights that erupted from the dragons when they shifted. Was this glow due to Drager's influence on this portal? Or was a similar energy used for both transformations?

Astra purred loudly as we stopped right before the brightest section. I couldn't see what waited on the other side, and knowing this was one huge leap of faith, I exhaled rapidly, and lifted my foot to step inside, right as a strong puff of air knocked me backwards.

It was only my grip on Astra's fur that kept me from stumbling, and before I could freak the fuck out, Drager stepped from the portal.

All my fears vanished in the heartbeat of time it took for rage to rise up. "Human, what the hell are you doing?" he said, sounding like he was the one put out. "Why haven't you crossed the portal yet."

I was speechless, which, honestly, rarely ever happened. But. The. Fucking. Audacity. It left me unable to comprehend how his brain even worked. How he could walk around in a real world, acting like such a—

"You're a fucking idiot," I snapped. "You left me here. Left me here to figure out a magical doorway on my own. Luckily, Astra is still at my side, or no doubt I'd have been eaten by a dunedin or fantine."

Drager tilted his head to the side, as if confused by my outburst. "I assumed you would be with Florentine. It wasn't until I saw her in the forest with her brother that I wondered where you'd gotten to."

A derisive laugh escaped me as I shook my head. "I'm not really on your mind that much, am I? You never thought to even check if I needed help crossing the path? And you think to call me mate…" Not a chance, bro.

Drager tilted his head back the other way. It reminded me of a puppy trying to understand weird human language. "Being a compatible mate doesn't mean you're always at my side. It means we could breed and bring more of my kind into the world. I expect any mate of mine to act independently though, and I thought you were a woman who wanted the same freedoms. You've never told me otherwise."

I'd never really told him much of anything, if we were being honest. Mostly because Drager had never bothered to ask, and the one time I'd opened up to him after my kidnapping, he'd still made it about himself.

"There's no way the world needs more of you," I said coldly, before stepping forward. "And Astra will guide me through the portal. This *independent* woman doesn't need your help."

Bye, bitch.

He reached out as if to grab me, but I'd anticipated the move, and dodged him successfully. With a little help from Astra, we entered the portal a beat later. On the inside, the light swirled brighter; I felt tiny pricks across my skin. The portal's desired taste of blood wasn't painful, more of a sensation that I'd just walked through a bush with irritating sap on its leaves. Astra nudged me as the light grew brighter, and I closed my eyes and gripped her fur tighter while keeping a hold on Leo. A tugging sensation started low behind my navel right before I was jerked along the path fast enough to induce nausea.

Barely managing to hold on to the contents of the fruit bars I'd eaten, I focused on Astra, completely understanding now why pairs were needed. I'd have never been able to stay on course without the yin to my yang.

The exit was somehow rough and smooth at the same time, and it was a huge relief when that prickly sensation ceased. As I stumbled to a halt on the other side, strong arms caught me, and I jerked my head up to see…

"Mika!" I exclaimed, before quickly lowering my voice. "What the hell are you doing here?"

He grinned, those perfect teeth standing out against his darker skin. His mop of curls was less perfect though, and despite that smile it was clear he was exhausted. I'd trained with him multiple times and never saw an ounce of fatigue, but today he was weary. "We're at war, Morgs, didn't you know?"

Morgs. He'd adopted Lexie's nickname for me, and it hurt to hear it again. "Have you not been trapped in the academy the entire time?" I asked him.

He didn't answer, wrapping his hands around my shoulders and jerking me away from the portal as a giant stepped out. He must have felt the energy of Drager returning, saving us both from being pummeled by a god.

"Thanks," I choked out, rubbing my arm when he released me. He'd used more strength than needed, but then again, he was naturally so much stronger that he probably didn't even realize.

The sound of battle rang out in the background, but I couldn't see anyone close by. "How long have you been fighting the shifters?" I asked him.

Mika glanced up at Drager, as if afraid to say anything in his presence. "A small fraction of us managed to escape the academy when it was infiltrated." His answer was rushed as he continued to side-eye Drager. "We've been in these pockets of forest ever since, spying and learning, all while we waited for the gods to arrive. When we saw some of them dragged inside, we knew that we were on our own."

"We're here now," Drager rumbled. "I'm sure you weren't too effective without us."

Mika managed not to punch him in the face; his control was stronger than mine. "We've been irritating them at least," he said with ease. "Confusing them and splitting their guard so that there are distinct weak spots in the academy boundary now."

That's what I wanted to hear. "Can you get me inside?" I asked him. Astra growled at my side, and I patted her quickly. "Astra and me."

"And this little guy?" Mika said with some amusement, referring to Leo, who was still curled up against my chest.

I'd almost forgotten he was there. He just clung on like a tiny, purring hot water bottle of love. "Yep, and Leo."

"This is too dangerous," Drager interjected before Mika could say another word. "Wait until we retake control."

Spinning on the spot to remind him that he wasn't my fucking keeper, I didn't manage to get a word out before Mika politely said, "In all due respect, right now is the best time of all. You all appearing out of nowhere has really thrown them off. The layers of security are almost nonexistent today, and if we move now I'll be able to get Morgan in safely.

Facing Drager as I was, I got a front row view to his annoyance. He wanted to argue, but then again, we knew how much he actually cared for my safety. "Fine, take her, but if she gets hurt at all, I'm going to rip your spine out. Understand?"

Mika swallowed roughly. "Understood, Lord Drager. Morgan is a friend of mine, and I'd be sad if she died."

A snort escaped me, before I swallowed it down. Fae certainly had a way with words and emotions. "Come on, hero," I said to him, turning my back on *Lord Drager*. "Let's do this."

Drager's hand on my arm stopped me, but I didn't turn to him again. I was done with giving parts of myself to this shifter when he'd never shown once to be worthy of them. "Be careful, little human," he said softly. "I'll be displeased if you're hurt."

"I'm no longer your worry," I said just as softly. "See you later, dragon man."

It felt like a goodbye, in more ways than one, and I let that settle deep into my heart. There was no pain this time, and I wondered if I'd ever had deeper feelings for Drager, or if I'd been caught up in the magic of the world *and the sex*, giving my time with him more meaning than it had truly had.

The magical blinders were gone now, and I think both of us knew it as I walked away with Mika. Astra, in particular, had an extra pep in her step as she prowled along.

"Phew," Mika muttered when we were alone once more. I never looked back, but I was sure Drager no longer stood there anyway. "The tension, girl. The freaking tension."

My laugh was all sadness. "It's complicated, but also… not. If that makes sense. I think maybe that chapter of my life was a stepping stone to the actual story I'm supposed to live."

Mika released a slow breath. "That's very profound. I hope I'm around to hear this story of yours."

The sound of fighting grew stronger as we pushed farther into the forest. Astra remained glued to my side, but Mika glanced down at her. "I think it might be best if she remained here as well. It's not that I think she's a liability and will get us caught… I know she can turn herself invisible if needed. It's just that her energy is so much stronger than ours and that might draw their attention. You have almost none, and I've learned how to temper mine into nothing. Can she do the same?"

Astra turned her head to the side and examined him, and I had to guess by her lack of a *nod*, which was our only form of communication, that she couldn't dim down her energy that much.

Reaching out, I placed my hand on her shoulder, and rubbed gently. "Stay here and keep Leo safe. I'll get our Z back, okay?"

Her entire body rumbled, and it was scary, but I knew it wasn't directed at me, so I didn't react. "I love you, Astra," I whispered, leaning in to kiss her nose. "I'll return soon. I promise."

With one last rumble and head tilt, she turned and headed toward the sounds of battle, and I hoped with all I had that they would be safe until we returned.

With a sigh, I focused on Mika. "Okay, friend. It's time to make good on your promise and keep me alive. Do you have a plan of how we're getting into the academy undetected?"

Because I sure as fuck wasn't going to be able to pretend to be a seven-foot-tall dragon shifter god to trick their guards into thinking we were one of them.

Mika's grin did fill me with confidence. "I've got you, Morgs. Don't worry yourself."

He started off with determination and I hurried to catch up. "Do you know if all the prisoners are okay?" I asked. Now that we were close, my heart was racing at the thought of what I might find inside; I needed to prepare myself.

His expression dimmed. "They were all okay, the last time I saw them. Alive and fighting, if not a little banged up."

"Lexie too?" I pressed.

He nodded. "Yes. Lexie too. As far as I know, they're all being held in the cells under the academy. The students and staff are mostly contained in their rooms."

Sounded like they turned the academy into a large prison, but at least they weren't killing indiscriminately. Not yet anyway. This war we brought to their door would no doubt change everything, but I wasn't part of that fight.

My fight was in those cells below the academy, where I'd have to figure out how to free my friends and family.

CHAPTER 19

MORGAN

Mika was relaxed right up until we reached the edge of the tree line.

"Okay, Morgs," he murmured, peering out through the bushes we were crouched behind. "This is the part where it gets real."

"I'm ready." There was nothing more real to me than this moment. From the instant Drager had snatched me out of Zahak's arms, stolen me away and left his brother to the mercy of the shifters who fell from the sky, I'd had a hole in my chest.

It wasn't an obvious hole to anyone from the outside, but to me it felt as if vital organs had been ripped from my body, leaving behind carnage and destruction.

The fact that I was finally back on academy grounds, with Mika, about to infiltrate the building to find Zahak, had a new pulse beating against the pit of despair. Finding Lexie was of equal importance, and then the other Fallen Five just a touch below that.

For a stupid, inexplicable reason, I felt they were all family.

My found and chosen family, and damn if that wasn't the best kind.

"We just need to wait for this last guard shift to change," Mika continued, his focus on the east perimeter of the building. We were in a small pocket of forest, crouched low. His body was tense, the striations of his muscles more defined than ever. Despite the dust and debris on his clothing, his skin was clean and vibrant—fae were rarely dirty, except for those of the nightmare variety, who naturally rocked the whole grunge vibe.

"What race of fae are you?"

Was that a rude question? Probably. But these fae who looked like genetically blessed humans, and were referred to as highborn fae, were a great mystery to me. They had to have their own race, right? Highborn wasn't a race. Whatever the translation from their language to mine was, that couldn't be a race.

Mika's grin was wide as amusement danced in his eyes. "You've been learning about the fae races, right?"

I nodded. "Yep, and I'm aware of harpies and trolls, and many of the races who couldn't pass for extra-hot humans, but what is your actual race?"

He didn't even screw up his face at my mention of fae passing for humans, and I was once again reminded of why I liked him. He'd never treated me like a disease festering in his world.

"We're part of the elfin community," he said simply, as if I should understand what that meant.

"Elfin community," I repeated softly, before it all fucking

clicked into place. Like a lightbulb bursting to life above my head. "Elves. You're elves!"

Mika was full-on laughing at me now. "Look, we don't really refer to ourselves as such, and over the years highborn has been the unofficial designation, but yes, we're elves. That's our race."

Of course. It fit them perfectly, and I couldn't believe I'd waited so long to ask. "I don't really like the term *highborn*," I admitted, shaking my head. "It gives the impression that everyone else falls under lowborn, which is far from the truth."

Mika nodded, sobering as he turned back to observe the academy once more. "Yeah, I've always felt the same. There is a hierarchy here in the races, and the *highborn* do fall near the top, but it's not so simple to refer to the other races as lower. Just different, I guess. The nickname should probably be retired at this point." I agreed, but it seemed our time for conversation was finally over as he straightened and said, "Okay, stay right behind me."

I did exactly that, following in his footsteps as we left the safety of the forest. As our position grew more exposed, trickling fear down my spine increased. Like icy water, dripping across my skin. It felt wrong, being out here, knowing dragons could come from any direction, even above.

At least they couldn't really sneak up on us. Not with the size of them.

I had no idea what we'd do if a dragon suddenly appeared. I mean, neither of us stood a chance of fighting them. Mika didn't even have a weapon visible on him. Not that I expected any fae weapon would work against a dragon.

Keeping my head low, I focused on stepping exactly where he was, as if we were navigating a field of landmines. "Brace yourself, Morgs," he said softly, and before he gave me a chance to panic—*brace yourself was not what you wanted to hear in a war*—the ground fell away beneath us, and I tumbled down with him.

Landing hard, I ended up *bracing myself* on the freaking dirt, all the air knocked from my lungs. Mika stood above me as I flailed around like a puffer fish out of water, his brow furrowed as he stared down. "Humans don't land on their feet?"

If I wasn't trying so hard to breathe, I'd have kicked him in the balls. Elves had to have balls too, right? Who the fuck knew.

Eventually my lungs recovered and I pushed myself up, still glaring. "Humans aren't cats," I huffed. "We don't just land on our feet. Especially when those feet are running on the ground, and then suddenly that ground turns into a hole." I wanted to shout, but I had enough awareness of our situation to keep my reprimand to an angry whisper.

"At least we didn't get eaten by a dragon," Mika said with a shrug. "This is a dunedin burrow, which I've been using to sneak in and out of the academy for the last few days."

Great, we might not have to worry about dragons, but now we had carnivorous little bunnies to keep an eye out for. As if he'd read my thought, Mika patted me on the shoulder. "Trust me, I can handle a dunedin. You're perfectly safe down here."

I glanced over my shoulder, not feeling quite as confident as he was. We'd tumbled into a hole that was about three feet wide and at least ten feet deep. Connected to this hole were tunnels, running both behind and in front of us. "Large enough to drag a highborn fae down when they ambush us," Mika whispered near my ear as I jumped and stifled a scream.

Laughter shook his body. "I'm kidding. They've never

taken one of us, and they're not about to start today." He grew serious after. "Once again, stay right behind me, and don't look back."

What the fu—? I never even got to finish my horrified thought before he took off, and I was forced, once again, to run like I wasn't an unfit human trying to keep up with an elf. Weren't elves known for their speed and light feet? I was known for my ability to eat a cheese wheel and read four novels in a weekend.

We were not the same!

Adrenaline kicked into gear and saved me once more, as I pushed hard to keep up with Mika. When we moved away from the entrance, the tunnel grew darker, but there were small dots of illumination up high that kept us from crashing into anything. As we ran, I swore I could feel the eyes of the murderous bunnies on me, but I did my best to pretend they weren't there.

This was about getting to my family, and I'd have done scarier tasks than race through these tunnels for them.

Mika started to pull ahead, but I was maxed out and couldn't keep up. Thankfully he must have noticed, because in the next few yards I was right behind him again. My lungs and thighs were screaming at me, and I resolutely ignored them, all the while knowing I was running out of time for that plan to work.

"Almost there, Morgs," Mika said reassuringly. "The path isn't direct, but we'll come out very close to a side entrance near the basement cells."

I'd have replied, but my entire existence was currently focused on breathing and not passing out. When I was almost out of life, Mika slowed his pace, and the tunnels grew a little tighter. We had to duck down, slowing us to a fast walk.

It was still too fast.

I huffed embarrassingly and tried to catch my breath, but it wasn't like he hadn't seen me the same way during fight training classes. He was well aware of my human shortcomings.

Yeah, okay, there were plenty of fit humans.

He was aware of my *Morgan shortcomings*, including my many years spent training as a bookworm.

Eventually we stopped, and I leaned on a hard stone wall, small fragments of dirt dislodging as I got my breath back. "We have to climb out now," he told me. In the low light his expression was serious. "This is the most dangerous part of this journey as we'll be exposed right near the academy. Wait here until I check it's clear above."

I nodded, still beyond words, and his smile was gentle this time as he brushed a hand over my heated cheek. "You did great, Morgs. That was a pace I've never pushed you to before, and you found the strength to keep going. I'm proud of you."

Shock almost knocked me over, as heat bloomed in my chest. Heat that didn't come from running like an Olympic sprinter, but of someone acknowledging my worth and strength. Thanks to my mother, there'd always be a part of me searching for acceptance and acknowledgement. It was a daily battle to practice contentment within myself.

"Thanks," I managed to get out, and Mika nodded once before he took a few more steps along the passageway. He glanced up just as he launched from the tunnels.

Moving to where he'd disappeared, I found myself under another hole to the land above. Another spot for the dunedin to emerge and ambush their prey. The sky was crimson, and it occurred to me that I wasn't going to be able to jump up and scramble to the exit—it was at least twelve freaking feet above. What if Mika didn't come back?

Holy shit. That was when the panic really kicked in. I was trapped in this hole, with no means to get myself out, and if he had been taken the moment his head popped up out there, no one would even know I was down here. I mean, outside of the dunedins, which were probably sniffing me out right now as they perused their cookbooks for the best way to tenderize a human.

"We taste like chemicals," I shouted randomly, feeling eyes on me everywhere. "It's all the processed food. Trust me, you'll hate the taste."

Acting crazed came easily when I was in a panic, and when Mika's face appeared above in the hole, glancing quizzically down at me, I almost passed out once more. "Get me the fuck out of here," I whisper-yelled. "I'm freaking out."

He snort-laughed. "I can see that. But no need to panic. The coast is clear. I'm about to throw a rope down for you to climb out with."

He disappeared again briefly, and I wondered if I'd just heard him correctly. Did he say rope? Had he already forgotten my attempts to scale the ropes in the obstacle course?

Sure enough, not ten seconds later, a brown, thickly woven rope dropped into the hole. Grasping it in one hand, it was rough against my skin.

"Ready, Morgs?" Mika whispered.

No. Not remotely ready, but I had to get to my family, so I'd find strength. *Somehow.*

"Here I come," I said with confidence. Lifting my hands above my head, I held on tighter and pulled myself high enough to get my boots lodged together under me. I pushed up again, and managed to make it another foot, before I was just dangling there, unable to move an inch.

Mika's laughter washed over me, and if I wasn't literally

clinging on for dear life, I'd have flipped him off. "Hold on, friend," he called down, and I let out a strangled shriek when the rope was suddenly jerked up. In mere seconds, he hauled me out of that hole and helped me scramble over the edge.

"Why…" I huffed, "if you planned on pulling me out anyway … did you tell me to climb?"

He was still laughing, his chest shaking in silent chuckles. "Mostly to see if you'd cuss me out. But instead you showed your inner strength once more." He rolled up the rope until it was a small bundle, which he stowed inside his armored vest. "And now it's finally time to find your friends. We're at the academy."

I'd been so busy worrying about getting out of the hole that I'd missed the fact that there was a huge white wall behind us. The Fae Academy.

A thrill of anticipation pushed down my pains and exhaustion. I was going to find my family, and we were getting them back.

Finally.

CHAPTER 20

ZAHAK

Their knowledge of what debilitated us was how they kept us contained. That day in the forest, the shifters who ambushed me used energy to turn me into a mindless beast. I'd been on edge already, having not claimed my mate yet, and they pushed me right over.

A similar energy, blasting from a crystal in front of my cell, was used now to keep me disoriented and unable to escape.

"Zahak!" Emmen raged against his cage. We were all trapped in barred cells, open so we could see each other, but too reinforced for any of us to break free. All of us were affected by the energy of the crystal, but I was the only one with a direct hit. "Why do they keep it firmly on him all the time?"

The crystal had turned me into a hybrid beast-bipedal form, holding me in a partial shift. It blocked me from my mate, and my mind was fracturing under it. My ability to converse was all but gone, along with most rational thinking, but there was one thought that hadn't been stolen: *Morgan.*

The sole reason I still held any sanity. If we'd have made it through the bonding ritual, nothing could have stopped our mental connection, but we never got that far. Which they were using to their advantage.

They being our mother, who needed to die.

"He's the strongest," Kellan said softly.

"They're going to kill him if this keeps up," Tylan added with a rumble.

My brothers were here, along with Lexie, who had fallen quiet earlier today. She wasn't dead, but she was hurting from her time trapped in this room. The weapon was strong against us, but destructive for her.

The door above clanked, the signal that one of our guards was about to appear.

It was always the same robotic shifter, with food and liquids.

They weren't starving us, at least not yet, but we also weren't receiving the amount of food we needed. Shifters needed a lot of sustenance for our high metabolisms, and they kept us weak on purpose.

Not that I'd ever be too weak to rip their fucking throats out. I'd already tasted shifter blood and I was raging for more. Their weaknesses were the same as ours, and I was ready to tap into every piece of knowledge I held to destroy them all.

Their current advantage were these crystals, which I knew nothing about, but I was going to figure it out. As soon as I got free from this cage.

"Breakfast time, assholes." The shifter walked into the room full of confidence, unaware that death awaited him. It might not be this morning, but it would be soon. Already I was learning how to filter through the waves of crystal energy. Eventually, I'd be stronger than its blast.

Gripping the bars, they flexed under my hold as I pulled myself to my feet. I never faced these bastards lying down. I'd heard them comment on how I shouldn't be able to stand with the constant blast of sonar power, and it was good to see concern in their expressions. They should be concerned.

My mate was out there with my traitorous brother, and I had to get free and save her. Save her, and then kill Drager, in that order. This plan pulsed through my veins, and into the fragments of my mind, and for that, I held on to sanity.

The shifter guards never got close to our cells, placing the plates on the floor and using a long-handled stick to push them until they rested against our bars. He gave the plate a solid jab at the end, so the stick didn't come close enough for us to grab it. They'd learned that the hard way when I killed the first guard sent down. Emmen got the second.

These fuckers adapted quickly, unfortunately, which is how they knew to keep me debilitated at all times.

I'd thinned out their numbers on the way to the academy, and I'd learned a lot about them in the process. I would be faster next time; they'd barely see death coming.

My senses were too addled to check my food for poisons, but when Emmen announced his was clear, I placed the first bite into my mouth, and chewed resolutely. This was about keeping my strength up, even as my energy was shattered into fragmented pieces.

"You're a mindless beast," the shifter guard snarled, and it bothered me that they all spoke the fae language. How fucking long had they been watching us. "I can't believe you're the fabled princes of Xalifer. Our world would have crumbled under your rule. All we see is violence in this land, and that's due to you."

The irony of this asshole acting like we were the violent savage ones when they'd launch all-out war wasn't lost on me.

Or my brothers.

"I'm going to really enjoy using *my violence* to rip your head from your shoulders," Emmen said with a laugh. That particular laugh, when he used it, was always our signal to get the fuck away from him. When Emmen was at this level of pissed, he acted as mindless as I felt from the crystal's blast.

The guard must have understood the depth of Emmen's threat, as he raced from the room without another word. The clanging of the door above was loud, and no matter what he'd said, it was clear that as the royal sons we were stronger than them.

"Lexie," I heard Tylan snap, and I wondered if he'd been calling her name for a few seconds. In this state, I missed more than I liked. "You need to eat, little elf. You need to eat or you'll die, and then Morgan will kill us all with her bare hands."

She would.

Lexie was my mate's family, and the loss would destroy her. I couldn't let that happen.

A rumble spilled from the beast-shaped structure of my face. "Lexie," I rasped. "Open your fucking eyes."

The dragon voice was unlike any other, and the depths of that rumble appeared to rouse her. "I'm awake," she groaned, sounding weak.

"Eat," Tylan said, his voice softer. "You need to look after yourself."

Those two had been blasted away together when the

shifters had invaded, and I'd heard parts of their story, which involved ending up near the yonters, and getting captured on their way back to the academy. Whatever happened appeared to have formed a bond between them, because Tylan had been pacing like a worried mother when she didn't respond.

Lexie released a low groan, and I heard the scrape of her plate as she reached through the bars. When we were satisfied that she was eating, my brothers continued with a conversation from earlier, rehashing returned memories, and analyzing what we'd learned from our mother when she visited yesterday.

She'd arrived in our cells, a tiny female with icy blond hair and equally icy blue eyes. Her skin was so pale that it was hard to believe any of us were born from her. "You five were supposed to rule our kingdom," she'd said, conversationally. "But without mates you're too weak. So we sent you away to find them."

I missed a lot of her other information, but it was clear that she hadn't told us everything. If I'd been in my right mind, I would have demanded answers, but all I'd been able to do was grip the bars and rage at her betrayal.

"Why did you invade our world here?" Emmen had asked, pressed against the bars. "Why have you imprisoned us if we're not enemies?"

Her smile was as cold as every other part of her. "Who said we're not enemies?"

With that, she'd swept out of the basement cells, and we hadn't seen her since. Just the guard, three times a day with food and water.

"Let's refresh what we know," Kellan said, uncharacteristically serious. "It appears more memories return as we push harder at the cracks."

All I had were cracks, and memories seeping out in all

directions. But I couldn't put them together coherently. If I could just get that fucking crystal away from my cell, I might have a chance. As it was, all I could do was sprawl out and listen to their conversations, keeping Morgan's face firmly in my mind.

I refused to fall into the darkness hovering on the edge of my being. Not until my mate was safe.

"We're the five royal sons of Xalifer," Tylan started. "There are no female shifters, only the mates of the dragon males. Which must come from offworld, since only male shifters are born in Xalifer, right?"

This was all information that we'd either overheard or remembered. Our mother wasn't a shifter, she was a human. Just like my mate.

"It stands to reason, based on the evidence that we have so far, that humans are our mates," Kellan said. "But we were sent to Risest instead of Earth. Was it an accident?"

There were too many unknowns still. Like Xalifer itself. We couldn't really remember it, outside of those mountains we flew around. Along with the memories of its destruction, which were clearly manufactured, since it was currently orbiting somewhere near Risest.

As their conversation continued, another blast of the crystal knocked me out of commission for a time, and all I could do was hold on tightly to Morgan's image in my mind. With a groan, I dragged myself up the bars once more. "I need to get out of here," I forced the words out slowly, one by one. "I can't do this for much longer."

Lexie, to my surprise, answered first. "Zahak," she said softly, "can you feel that? The energy?"

I was about to growl out my fucking annoyance, because I couldn't feel anything except the destruction of my being. But then, without any warning, the shattered memories in my mind solidified. The crystal blasted me just as hard, but it was no longer infiltrating my barriers as thoroughly.

Instead, there was a clarifying moment when I figured out what Lexie had sensed.

Morgan. She was here.

CHAPTER 21

MORGAN

After my anxiety in the dunedin tunnels, skulking down the side of the academy in the shadows felt relatively easy. There were no signs of shifters on this side of the building, and I found myself relaxing. Which was ridiculous considering the circumstances, but I guess there was only so much adrenaline available in a certain period, and you had to crash eventually.

"The entrance is here," Mika whispered, pointing toward two nondescript wood doors on the side of the wall, reminding me of an outside basement entrance. "This leads right into the cells, and it's also the point where we'll find the most danger. There are guards inside. They move between the levels frequently. I'm hoping with the battle in the forest that most of them will be out there, but don't let your guard down."

Like my guard was going to do much, but I could scream and warn at least.

"Could you take on one of them?" I asked, needing this knowledge before we entered the basement.

Mika didn't hesitate, trademark cheeky grin on display. "I could distract them for a few minutes so you can run." His grin faded. "And I expect you to run, Morgan. Don't be a hero, just get out of there and hide until it's safe to leave. We don't both need to die today."

My head was shaking before his words even fully registered. "I won't do that. Don't even suggest such a thing."

It wasn't that I was brave, but the whole theory of *you've just got to be faster than the slowest person to survive a dangerous situation* was only funny as a joke. If Mika sacrificed himself to save me, it'd destroy a part of my soul.

Mika squeezed his eyes tightly for a beat, letting out a long breath. "Let's just hope it's not a decision anyone has to make. Come on."

He was done waiting, and I felt the same way. No need to stress about dying when we might walk into the basement and find it was completely unguarded—that was the hope anyway.

As he opened the doors, I swore I could feel Zahak's energy mingling with my own, beating against my skin, wanting to burst free. *Zahak.* I tried to reach him through our bond, and while I could feel him now, the connection felt like it was shattered glass, fragments everywhere.

What were they using to disrupt our mental connection like this? I wondered if they would have been able to do the same if we'd cemented our bond. A process that I assumed involved sex and knotting—because what fun would it be if it didn't?

If I was writing this story, true mates would seal their bond with at least a dozen orgasms. It was only fair. Then we'd be tied together. Forever.

A truth that should have me panicked and riddled with anxiety, but at this point in time we probably wouldn't make it through this week, let alone eternity, so I'd leave that as a next week's problem. If we lived that long.

Climbing through the doors, we landed on stairs that descended into the dark room. I worked hard to remain as silent as Mika, who moved like he was part of the shadows themselves. Half the time I couldn't even see him in the dim light.

This entrance wasn't one that appeared to be used much, as evidenced by our tracks visible in the dust. I hoped that with the light so dim, no one else would notice them.

When the stairs finally ended, we stepped into an equally dark area, flickering lights down a long hallway the only illumination. Mika didn't speak, but he did raise a hand. I stopped and all but held my breath as he checked for any dangers, and when he found none he signaled that we should move again.

We crossed through what I figured out was a storage room, full of shelves stacked with boxes and drums of liquid stashed haphazardly. There was a stale, damp scent in this area, and I was thankful that it dissipated as soon as we left that area.

When we reached the next thoroughfare, the pulse of Zahak's energy picked up, and it was all I could do not to push poor Mika into a wall and start sprinting. Reaching Zahak was my sole focus, but I had to stay alive to do that, so running into the unknown would have to wait.

It took every ounce of my control.

Mika stopped us again just before we entered the room with the lights, and I watched him closely as he tilted his head to the side, eyes squinting, then back the other way, and not for the first time did I wish to have stronger senses to hear and scent what he was.

Eventually he appeared satisfied that it was safe to move forward, and rounding the corner we were finally in the cells. From where we stood, I noticed at least a dozen rooms, all barred with a shimmery silver metal. The first few were empty and sparse on the inside: stone floor and walls, a single bed, and what looked like a sink in the corner.

I felt Zahak with each step, like a pulse in my veins… in my blood… in my chest. My heart hammered so hard that I wondered if I was about to give us away, and I tried to breathe slow and deep to calm myself.

It was hard to remain quiet in these circumstances.

Before we reached the occupied cells, a low-level thrum infiltrated my hearing, and then my brain. Soon it was rattling around in there, giving me an instant headache. Mika must have felt the same, as he held up his hand once more to stop me, only this time I couldn't stop.

I'd just caught sight of a familiar face: Tylan, the dragon shifter from Lastoa, with his woodsman vibe and thick beard.

He didn't look disheveled as he stood at the bars, gripping them tightly, but there was a manic look in his dark eyes. Manic and shocked as he stared at me like I was a mirage. Stepping around Mika, I did my best to ignore the pounding headache, even as the thrumming grew impossible to block out.

Mika didn't prevent me from moving toward Ty, and I all but slammed against the bars of his cell. His arms slipped out around me as he clutched me tightly. "Where the fuck did you come from?" he growled, voice hoarse.

I had no chance to answer, as a roar ripped through the room, so loud that I found myself crouching and pressing my hands over my ears, worried my eardrums were about to explode. When I was finally able to look up, I knew exactly what cell I'd find Zahak in, and I couldn't stop from crying out.

He was slamming against it, more beast than man. Actually… I looked closer. He was literally part beast and part man. It appeared that one of his legs was a dragon limb, while the other was humanoid. Half of his torso was elongated like a dragon, and his face had a snout and a lot more teeth than he usually had in his bipedal form.

It was as if he'd gotten halfway through a shift and was stuck.

He raged and threw himself against the bars until the entire room shook. If he kept this up, he was going to bring the damn academy down on top of us.

"Zahak!" Tylan's shouts could be heard between the roars. "You're hurting her."

That appeared to get through to the beast as he instantly stopped, and the silence that followed was almost as echoingly loud as the roars had been. Pushing myself up, Mika stepped in behind as if to help me, until Tylan shot out an arm, barring him. "Don't get too close to her. He's barely holding on."

I heard him, but I was so focused on Zahak that I didn't turn to see where Mika ended up. My feet moved without thought, and it was only as I got closer to Zahak that I winced when the thrumming grew worse.

It was so bad that about six feet from him the pain in my head had me near passing out. "Back," Zahak growled, and I was so relieved to hear a coherent word from him. "Back away, mate."

"Do as he says," Emmen muttered from nearby. The shifter from the wilds of Santoia was always grumpy, but he looked even more so as he stood at the bars, arms crossed.

"They have a sonar-waves crystal aimed right at Zahak. It's breaking his cells apart with each blast. It's only his strength that has kept him alive."

I tasted blood, and realized my nose was bleeding as I reached up and wiped it away. I couldn't get closer to Zahak, that much was clear, but seeing him like this was almost as destructive as the crystal itself. "Is this how they took him down in the first place?" I bit out.

"Yes," Emmen said shortly. "It's how they took all of us down. We didn't know about this weaponry, and even now I have no idea how to counter it."

It made sense that these bastards, with all their knowledge of the Fallen Five, would have the advantage in battle. "Does Drager know they have these weapons?" I asked quickly. As pissed as I was over what he'd done, I also didn't want the fae warriors he'd gathered to walk into a terrible ambush.

"Since that fucker betrayed us, I'm sure he's aware," Kellan added, sounding far less relaxed than he usually did. The gorgeous water-loving dragon stepped forward in his cell as well, and I marveled at how they all looked as perfect as always.

There was just one member of my family unaccounted for. "Where's Lexie?"

Zahak, who hadn't moved or taken his eyes from me, pointed to the cell beside his. A cell I'd thought was empty. But there was a shadow on the ground near the back. I was pushing forward again, until a blast of energy had me falling to my knees.

Fuck it, I'd crawl.

"It'll kill you," Emmen warned. "You're human, and this is taking down fucking shifters. Just back up. Lexie is weak but alive. She's getting side blasts of the weapon trained on Zahak."

"Why—" I gritted my teeth, wiping more blood from my face. "Why is it only on Z?"

Strong hands gripped my sides and yanked me backwards, and the relief was almost immediate. Zahak rattled the entire room again, calming only when Mika released me. "Let me try and disrupt the weapon," he murmured to me. "I need to hurry though, because Zahak's going to bring the entire guard down here."

I met the black eyes of my mate and held out my hand. "Calm, Z," I whispered, knowing full well he'd hear me. "I'm here. I'm safe. And we're going to get you out."

Like fucking magic, he stopped rattling the academy, and stilled in his cell.

"Unbelievable," I heard Emmen mumble behind me.

"She's the fucking dragon whisperer," Kellan added with a snort.

"Could have used her for the last few days to keep his ass calm," Tylan said with a harsh laugh. "Some of us need our beauty sleep, and with that big bastard raging all night…"

Kellan laughed as well. "Speak for yourself. If I get any more beautiful, the world will unravel."

He might have been joking, but he also wasn't wrong. All the Fallen were beautiful, especially Z. Fuck, even in a half-shifted form he still drew my gaze. Drew and held.

Z?

Mate.

A single growled word burst through the fractured patterns in our bond. Fractures that I now knew had to be from the energy of this crystal tearing my mate apart, even as his dragon did everything in his strength to hold them together.

"How do we destroy the crystal?" I was finally able to

focus, looking down to notice the shiny box on the floor before Zahak's cell.

"We have no idea," Tylan said with a low huff. He sounded exhausted. They all did. "That box holds the crystal, and there's a direct pulse of sonar energy every few minutes. They seem to be able to send it in all directions, or to a very specific location, like they're doing with Z. It's stronger that way too."

Mika met my gaze, and I knew we were both thinking the same thing. This crystal had taken down the Fallen Five, and I couldn't get close without my brain exploding, so how were we supposed to free them?

Whatever we decided, we needed to do it quickly, because a door clanking above alerted us to the fact that we were about to have company.

MORGAN

"Y ou try and free Tylan and the others," Mika told me as he took a step toward the crystal. "I'll see if I can knock the box over and redirect that blast." It was just a small bronze box on the floor, and I couldn't see the stone inside, since it was facing Zahak.

Racking my brain to figure out what disrupted sonar waves, I prayed that Mika would be able to reach the weapon. We needed to stop its power now, before the guards arrived.

"Does it affect you even in dragon form?" I asked, moving back to Tylan's cell and running my hands over the bars. There was no door, and I had no idea how they'd gotten them all inside.

"Yes," Kellan said ruefully. "I fell from twenty feet when I was blasted, because it yanked me back into my bipedal form."

Which explained why none of them had shifted into their

beasts to get out of here. Despite not being in its direct blast, the general waves were enough to keep them weak and unable to shift.

"We need our own soundwave to counter theirs." The thought came to me as I grappled with an impenetrable cell. "I'm sure I've read that somewhere. Two sonar blasts can disrupt each other."

I had all their attention now, except Mika, who was slowly moving forward against the pulse of the weapon. "Explain, human!" Emmen, who was just the sweetest dragon, snapped at me.

"Can you five create any sort of soundwave pulse with your beast forms?"

Footsteps could be heard on the stairs, as the guards got closer. "Hide," Zahak growled, and I knew that we had run out of time. We had to get out of sight until the guards left again.

"Mika," I whispered. "Get over here. We need to hide."

"I'm close," he shot back, and I took a step forward, wincing against the pain, but determined to stop him before he got himself killed.

Through pure determination and inner strength, he made it to the crystal box, reaching out for it. A shifter guard appeared in the entrance of the cells, near where Lexie was, wearing a look that promised murder. Mika, hand hovering above the box, met my gaze. We exchanged a glance that lasted no more than a second, even though it felt like a lifetime.

A resigned look fell over his face, and I cried out at the same time. "No! Don't do this!"

He shot me one last sad smile, before he reached out and grabbed the crystal with both hands.

This time, the pulse was so intense, it exploded through

the room, and I was thrown backwards into a stone wall, which hurt like a bitch.

"Give them hell…" Those were the last words I heard from Mika before another explosion rocked through us all, and I found myself fighting to remain conscious. Pushing myself up, I choked on the blood filling my mouth, knowing I was in a bad way.

There was a rough clang as Zahak burst from his cell, tearing out half the wall, before he lifted the guard with both hands and *tore him right down the damn middle*. Like ripping a piece of paper in half, only this paper had organs and blood, which splattered all over the cell.

Despite my yearning to remain conscious, I lost that battle as my head tilted forward, my arms too weak to keep myself upright.

I heard *"La moyar"* briefly, and then Zahak's strength and energy washed over and through me, and I let the darkness take me, trusting I'd be safe.

———

Pain. It was everywhere.

My brain attempted to protect me by remaining unconscious, but the stabbing in my head brought me back. I wanted to scream, but I couldn't find the strength to open my mouth.

Mate. His voice was soothing. *Let me heal you.*

Zahak slipped into my mind, and then further into my soul, seeping his energy into me. It was a cooling wave, a balm over my injuries, and it worked. His power repaired the damage from the sonar weapon.

A gasp escaped as I shot up in his arms, staring at his face, which was once again my Zahak. The dragon had sunk back below the surface, and all I saw were his gorgeous eyes. Zahak, despite everything he'd just gone through, was once again a being of elemental beauty, carved by the gods themselves.

Ironically, since he was revered as a fae god.

"Z?" I whispered.

He closed his eyes briefly, as if saying a short prayer, and when he opened them again, a sliver of gold appeared around his pupils. "I'm here," he murmured. "I have you, and I won't let anything tear us apart again."

I'd never believed anyone the way I believed him in that moment. Memories of what had happened took longer to filter in, but eventually it all came back to me. Pushing gently against his chest, I attempted to see the other cells.

"What happened? Where is everyone else?" He didn't respond or move out of my way, and that was when the dread set in. "Zahak," I choked, imploring him with my gaze to tell me. "What happened? Lexie? Mika? Are they okay?"

When his face fell, my heart skipped a beat in my chest.

"No!" I pushed at him again, in a full-blown panic. My physical injuries were healed thanks to Zahak's energy, but not even he could help with emotional pain. "No! Please no." I was sobbing. "They have to be okay."

"Morgs…" Lexie's rasp had me full on snot-crying, and that was when Zahak finally allowed me to move out from under him to see her battered face. She was standing near the closest cell, held up by Tylan. The shifter didn't have a scratch, but she looked like she'd gone through a wood-chipper.

Zahak helped me up and I lurched toward Lexie and we fell into each other's arms. It took real effort not to squeeze her too hard, even though she was holding on to me like her life depended on it.

And we were both crying.

Bawling our fucking eyes out, and trying to converse at the same time, so it just sounded like snotty blubbering. All the while four gods stood awkwardly around us, even as we paid them no attention.

"I hate when they cry," Tylan said, voice strained.

Zahak just let out a rumble, and through our bond I felt that his emotions were still too raw to reply. *We need to leave.*

The fact that he was once again in my mind filled me with so much joy—many of the tears I shed were in happiness.

But there were a few for Mika. He wasn't standing here, and Zahak had given me the vibe that someone wasn't okay. I needed to know what happened to him, even if the truth would destroy me.

Lexie wouldn't lie to me, so I asked her outright. "Is Mika dead?"

She pulled back to meet my gaze, expression grim. "Yes. He absorbed the sonar weapon's energy long enough for Zahak to get free, but his injuries were too great to be healed."

It was a stab in the chest, hard and fast, and I caved in on myself for a beat. "He saved us all," I whispered, too broken to do more than breathe, tears slowly slipping down my cheeks.

"He will be honored," Zahak finally said out loud. "He died a warrior's death."

Fuck that. Fucking fuck.

I didn't care about warriors' deaths and honor. I just wanted my friend back.

"His energy did blast the crystal to pieces," Emmen added, and if I had any strength I'd have punched that bastard.

It was too soon to move on from his death and discuss all

the helpful ways his sacrifice saved us. Mika was my friend, and he'd risked everything to give us a shot in this war.

Emmen continued: "But I think I know how we can disrupt the sonar waves without sacrifice from now on." He glanced my way, but I didn't return his smile. "Morgan gave me the initial idea."

"Enough," Zahak said shortly. "This is not the time. Gather his body so we can honor him. We need to leave and regroup. Next time we step foot in this place, it'll be to destroy the Fallen."

A part of me knew I was in shock, unprepared to deal with Mika's death. He'd been here not two minutes ago, alive and fighting, and now he was gone. Just... gone from this world.

How did one accept and understand that? It made no sense. You should have weeks and months on a path to death, and then you'd still mourn at the end—I sensed there'd never be enough time—but it wouldn't be *so fucking sudden.*

Lexie's hold on me tightened, and I had the sense that while she grieved Mika, it wasn't the same for her. She didn't know him very well, and in all honesty neither did I, but he'd been one of the few fae to take me under his wing and accept me for who I was. He'd never mocked my humanness, and he'd made my time in fight classes bearable.

He'd been a friend, and as a person who never had a lot of those, I held tightly to the ones I allowed into my heart.

Fuck.

Zahak was a silent comfort in my head, absorbing my painful thoughts. There was no jealousy or possessiveness in his emotions, as he allowed me to mourn my friend.

You care with your entire heart and soul, he said, in a deep rumble. *Fate chose well for me, la moyar.*

My tears continued to fall, and I couldn't get them to stop.

Eventually, Zahak was unable to hold himself back, wrapping his arms around both Lexie and me, since we were still clinging together.

"Tylan," he grumbled.

That was the only word he uttered, but his brother knew exactly what he wanted. He stepped in and lifted Lexie away from us, cradling her bruised and battered form in his arms. It spoke to how injured she was that my strong warrior sister sank against his broad chest and closed her eyes. I loved that there was enough trust between all of us that she would allow his assistance.

Zahak had me in his arms in the next heartbeat, and even though I was no longer injured and could walk, I didn't put up a fight. We both needed this. We needed the bonding, healing and comfort.

Off to the side, Emmen approached Mika's body, and I forced myself to watch as my friend was lifted and draped over his shoulder. Emmen was gentle, and I wished that all of us were walking out of here alive and well.

Today, wishes were broken dreams, and I was without a star to guide me home.

You are home, Morgan.

Zahak's voice in my head reminded me that all hadn't been lost today. And Mika would want me to count my blessings and enjoy every second we still had together. I'd told him I couldn't live with his sacrificing himself for me, but in the end, it had been for all of us.

And for Risest.

He gave us a chance in the battle we still had to fight, which was thankfully tomorrow's problem.

For now, I was content to snuggle into Zahak and let my dragon carry me to safety.

Today, my fight was done.

CHAPTER 23

As we walked, I explained how we'd used the dunedin murder tunnels to make it across the open plains around the academy, but it was clear as soon as I mentioned it that the Fallen Five were way too pissed to sneak out of here.

They wanted everyone to know they were free. Especially those bastards who were trying to steal their world.

We exited through the academy halls, opening every barred door to release the students and teachers. "Stay with us," Kellan growled to the rapidly increasing crowd, his eyes blazing green, scales covering most of his skin.

As more of the doors were opened, I asked about Rolta, remembering what Mi—

It was too painful to think of him, so I laser focused on the headmistress of Fae Academy. "They took her away a few hours ago," Zahak said gruffly. "She controls this school and knows all the secrets. They'll be using that knowledge to their advantage."

It made sense. She was one formidable fae.

"I wouldn't be surprised if she's dead," Emmen said without inflection. "I'd be killing off any powerful fae."

With that depressing thought, we made it to the exit. Stepping outside with a few hundred fae behind us, we found pure carnage. Half of the forests surrounding the academy grounds were on fire, black smoke billowing into the air, flames an eerie red against the crimson sky. I had no idea what time it was, but I would guess afternoon.

"Lots of fire when dragons are involved," I heard a student murmur from behind us. They were pushed up as close as they could get to the Fallen without being in their actual arms like Lexie and me.

Lexie, me... and Mika. Only he wasn't alive to know about it.

My chest clenched hard, and I fought tears as the pain overwhelmed me. It was consistently there, but at times, the waves of grief knocked me harder.

Zahak's energy remained a cooling balm in my mind, and with each wave, his comforting grew. This was what a mate bond meant to me—he was my strength when I was weak and vice versa.

He'd healed my physical injuries, so my weariness could only be blamed on emotional turmoil, a fraction of which eased as a familiar black sabre bounded into view. Through our bond, I felt an increase in Zahak's energy when he saw Astra, and it was odd to sense his emotions.

"Astra!" I exclaimed when she stopped before us. "I can walk now, Z," I said, glancing up at him.

Indecision split his face for a beat, before he reluctantly set me on my feet. I patted his chest in a comforting manner, and wasn't surprised when he remained close. We'd been forcibly parted, hurt, and scared, and we were in no condition to separate again.

Leo, still clinging to Astra, purred at me, and I lifted him up to cuddle close. "Hey, baby Leo," I cooed, stroking my fingers across his soft fur. My pain dulled, the waves easing as he offered comfort in the way only animals can do. There was no explanation for it, but I swore having animals around decreased stress and pain.

"Astra said that Drager is calling everyone back to Green Hollow to regroup," Zahak suddenly announced to the crowd. "The crystal weapons need to be dealt with, and apparently they have an idea for shielding."

"Fucking excellent," Kellan snorted. "About time Drager did more than just whine and brush his hair."

I hid my smile; the love-hate relationship between these five amused me to no end.

Astra rumbled louder, and Zahak added, "She also said she'll lead us to the portal location."

The students behind us remained in a tight group as we followed a sabre into the burning forest. Within the trees, we were inundated with evidence of the battle. Bodies littered the grounds, and I found myself searching the faces of the dead, feeling sorrow and fear that I'd find another of my friends in the carnage. Not that I had a lot of friends in Risest, and I doubted Florentine would even consider us friends, but I'd mourn her death. Just as I did Mika's.

There were cries behind us, and I wondered if a few of the students recognized the murdered fae. "We will retrieve their bodies and send them off in a warrior ceremony," I heard Emmen rumble. His words infiltrated through the forest, followed by a shocked silence. "But for now, the battle carries on. Remain vigilant."

I could practically feel the focus of the crowd, and maybe it was the intimidation of our numbers, or maybe the infiltrators had taken off to regroup as well, but we saw no other shifters as we followed Astra. Larger fires sprang up as we pressed deeper into the forest, and Kellan used his water affinity—which allowed him to pull moisture from the air around us—to cool the heat and flames.

When we reached the portal, the Fallen Five ushered the students and professors through first, and then it was our turn to cross. Crossing back with Zahak was a very different journey—smooth, seamless, and with no sensation of my skin being pricked. "How'd you stop them from taking my blood?" I asked him.

"Your blood and essence are mine," he said, waving his pink flags again, "and no one takes what's mine." Pink really was my favorite color.

Whether it was safe or smart, there was no denying my heart any longer. His rumble and violence did it for me, and as long as it was never directed at me, then I'd cheer him on with every iota of who I was.

I'd die before I hurt you, la moyar. You know that deep down, which is how you're okay with the violence in my soul.

An undeniable truth.

Green Hollow, calm and cool compared to the forest we'd just left, was filled with fae. They were everywhere, in various states of dress and disarray as they lined up for healing. Drager's huge form was visible in the distance, but he soon crossed to us, weaving around the groups of soldiers.

Zahak's body tensed beside me, and I wasn't sure how this was all going to go down. The last time he'd seen Drager, it had been in a situation of betrayal, which would undoubtedly be dealt with at some point. I just wasn't sure today was the day.

It's not, Zahak rumbled, *but I won't forget. My brother will get the beatdown that's coming to him.*

You're not planning on killing him?

Zahak paused briefly, his energy hot as it pulsed. *I haven't decided.*

I let the memory of Drager in the bathing caves rise so Zahak could hear the explanation, and allow that to filter into his decision-making process. Zahak didn't comment, but the fires eased up a touch.

"Brothers," Drager said roughly.

Zahak stepped forward and slammed his fist straight into Drager's face.

Okay, then. Maybe the fires were hotter than I thought.

Drager flew backwards, completely unprepared for the strike, and I wasn't surprised to hear him groan as he sprawled on the ground.

"Nice hit," Kellan snorted. "That big bastard deserved that. Wish I'd punched him first."

"Same," Tylan and Lexie added.

Emmen remained silent, but I could feel his focus on his brothers as he shifted forward.

Drager, back on his feet, strode toward us, and I tensed, expecting more violence. But he never showed an ounce of unease. If anything, his face was impassive and a little sad.

"I deserved that," he said softly, wiping away streaks of blue-tinged blood from his lip. Wounds inflicted by one of their kind took longer to heal, but it would be gone soon.

There was an awkward silence after, and I took my time examining Drager, weirded out by how dirty and disheveled the usually immaculate shifter looked. His armor was blood-stained, his face streaked with his blood along with soot and mud. "Are you okay, little human?" he asked, noticing my observation.

"Fine," I shot back.

He nodded once. "Thank you for rescuing my brothers. Now we have a real chance at ending this invasion once and for all."

Zahak's response was a rumble, one of those deep, guttural sounds that shook his entire chest. I didn't even need to look at him to know he was covered in scales.

"We need to discuss our time trapped in the cells," Tylan said quickly. "And you need to tell us what happened during the battle and our current standing in this war. But first, all of us need to clean up and eat."

Zahak didn't even wait for anyone's response, reaching out to sweep me into his arms once again as he turned and marched away. His mind was a riot of red fury as he fought the urge to destroy his brother. He knew that we still needed Drager, so he had no choice but to walk away.

"Don't trust him, mate," he managed to growl.

"Not a fucking chance," I said, settling into his arms.

He'd either been in Green Hollow before, or he followed my memories as he took us to the bathing caves. We left Astra and Leo guarding the door, entering the main bathing area a few seconds later. As expected, others were in there cleaning up, but it only took one long rumble from the dragon for everyone to hurry up and get the fuck out.

When we were alone, Zahak set me on my feet once more, only so he could strip me naked, my armored clothing disappearing as if by magic… *er, energy manipulation.*

"Stay with me, we both need the healing," he said as he removed his tattered clothes—he hadn't bothered to fix them after reverting from that hybrid dragon form.

I was about to respond when thick chest muscles came into view and I immediately forgot words. *Holy shit.* I didn't have intimate knowledge of Zahak yet, so this was the first time I got to really see him. Zahak was bigger than Drager somehow, with visibly thicker and stronger muscles. Not quite as bodybuilder-defined as Drager, but I found I preferred Z's form much more.

He was so deadly masculine that my mouth was dry as I fought to swallow.

He had more scars than Drager too, and I desperately wanted to touch them, to learn their texture against his bronze skin. *You don't have to ask permission to touch me, Morgan.*

Dead. I was basically dead. Dehydrated to a husk because all the fluids in my body were seeping into my lower regions.

Zahak's laugh was low and sensual in my head, even as his face remained stoic. "What scars a god?" I asked.

He kicked off his boots, hands moving to the band of his pants. Morgan from a few months ago would have looked away, but there was not a fucking chance I was doing that today. I doubted I could, even if I wanted to.

"I have no idea. I was scarred up when we arrived here, so it was probably thanks to that crazy-ass mother we have."

I'd have raged about that, if I wasn't completely focused on the dark hair trailing down his stomach. He flicked the button on his pants, sliding them down an inch so the thick head of his cock appeared. At some point I leaned closer, drawn in by the sight, and almost bumped my head on his shoulder.

As more of his impressive length was revealed, I barely managed not to groan. He was a god-dragon alright, the evidence was clear. The dark ridging along the sides of his cock was more defined than Drage—nope, I was not comparing them.

There was no comparison.

When he was naked, standing there as if carved from

stone and beyond any human perception of beauty, I had to close my eyes to get myself under control. The breadth of his shoulders, tapering down to narrower hips, and those thick strong thighs… I was so screwed.

A feather-light brush against my cheek had my eyes shooting open to find him right before me. He leaned down so our faces were closer together. "Stay with me, mate," he murmured. "We'll complete the bond soon, but it won't be here where others could walk in and see you. I wouldn't be able to stop myself from killing them, so it's best we wait."

Equal amounts of disappointment and understanding hit me. Waiting was hard, but it'd be worth it. I already knew that.

Zahak lifted me and walked us into the closest bath, settling on the side wall, me firmly against his body. "Relax," he rumbled.

Right, easy for him to say, because all I could think about was that long, hard length resting between my ass cheeks. Eventually, the soothing waters worked their magic, and feeling safe in my mate's arms I fell asleep against him. For the first time in days, the hole in my chest was smaller, and there was no danger or fear, so I slept soundly.

CHAPTER 24

ZAHAK

Morgan had no idea how close I'd come to destroying my brother. It was only her presence that kept me sane. The fracturing power of the crystal weapon had ceased, but its aftereffects weren't completely diminished.

I'd never felt my dragon so restless, but as Morgan fell asleep in our arms, parts of my ragged soul settled with her. I'd never have believed it if I hadn't experienced this moment, but there was real power in a true mate bond.

Drager's energy reached me long before he entered the room, and I could tell that he'd come at this time because he knew I wouldn't risk Morgan with a fight.

He was right, but the fact that she was naked and so close to my traitorous brother was another tick in the *murder him when this is all over* column.

Gently shifting my mate behind me, I used energy to manipulate the water structure and keep her buoyant.

"Nothing I haven't seen before, brother," Drager said, pausing near the edge of the bath, staring down at me.

"If you want me to kill you tonight, you're going the right way about it," I said, barely an inflection in my tone. I was beyond rage, everything iced over in my vision as I stared at him. "Why the fuck are you in here, Drager? We have nothing to say to each other."

He held both hands up, and for once the arrogant dragon appeared contrite. "I wanted to try and explain my actions."

Before I could tell him to fuck off, he launched into the same explanation he'd given Morgan.

"When we were blasted apart, I landed basically at Mother's feet..." He went on to say that he'd had to do some quick thinking and faked an alliance to keep himself alive. "I figured I could play a double agent of sorts, gather up information, and then use that to save everyone. I also knew you'd want me to get Morgan to safety first, so I added her in to the deal."

My laughter held zero fucking amusement. "Don't pretend you did any of this for her or me, Drager. We all know the real reason. Morgan knows as well."

I'd seen her thoughts. She'd been ready to kill him when he took her. The only reason she stopped fighting him was the hope he would get her to me. Since he had, I'd show some mercy when I murdered him, and exclude the torture first.

"Look, I told Morgan that she could choose when we were both back together," Drager said, continuing to dig his grave, "but it was clear from the first second I saw her in your arms that there was never a choice. If you fuck her and don't knot, though, just remember that she's mine."

Rising from the water as stealthily as I could as to not disturb my exhausted mate, I enjoyed the flicker of unease that crossed Drager's face. Water poured from me as I used my energy to leap seamlessly up to land right before him. Drager still had both hands up, lifting them a touch higher. "Point taken."

He had no fucking idea. I hadn't even begun to make my point. Until he was broken at my feet there'd always be this tension between us. Drager backed away, his focus locked on my face, watching for any indication of my next action. Our mental connection was solidly blocked, so he was forced to use his instincts. "We're meeting in the next ten minutes to discuss everything we've learned," he added as he disappeared into the darkness. "You need to be there."

As much as I wanted to tell him to fuck off once more, he was right, and I reluctantly dried myself and formed new armored clothing to wear. Lifting Morgan's slight weight from the water, I did the same for her, forcing myself not to linger on her soft curves as I dressed her in pajamas— just plain shorts and a shirt, the style she appeared to prefer.

As I carried her, I infused a touch of my energy into her center, soothing away the wounds in her soul. When we emerged from the cave, it was to find Astra and Leo curled up together at the mouth of the cave. They joined me a beat later as I launched over the river. "Where did she sleep last time she was here?" I asked Astra.

She led me to a small house with yellow trim, where inside I followed Morgan's scent up the stairs to another small room. "She needs to rest," I told the sabres, "and I need to meet with my brothers. Can you keep watch over her?"

Astra rumbled and purred, rubbing against me briefly, before she settled on the floor. Leo was already jumping up into the bed to be with Morgan, and I shot him one last look, reminding him to be gentle.

"I'll be back shortly," I bit out, annoyed at having to leave my mate. When we were apart the world went to shit, and I was done letting her out of my sight. But for now she needed to rest and heal, and I had to deal with the war on our doorstep.

Keeping my connection with Astra open, along with my link to Morgan, I was able to force myself to walk out of the room. We needed privacy and time to seal the bond, but my dragon and I had reached our limit. No matter what happened next, that part of our story was about to unfold. Our mate bond had to be sealed before we went into battle again.

It was easy to find my brothers, in the forests on the edge of the main village. They were sprawled in a clearing, surrounded by logs, set up in the same square pattern of our previous meeting area—the spot we'd landed when we first fell to this world.

"Z," Tylan said, hurrying forward to greet me. "Is she okay?"

I nodded. His concern for Morgan didn't bother me, because it came from the right place, one of brotherly caring, because she was my mate.

Drager's concern was not the same.

"Lexie?" I asked.

He nodded. "She's being healed and is with her family. She'll meet up with us soon, I'm sure."

I was sure as well, because Lexie's real family was not the Lightsbringers.

Her family was Morgan.

My entire world.

Drager moved in closer, before noticing my expression, which had him backtracking to sit on the log farthest from me. Kellan, Tylan, and Emmen all took seats as well, watching the two of us warily. I didn't want to sit, too riled up, but if I could keep my focus on the upcoming battle I'd make it through this meeting.

Taking a seat, I let my gaze settle on Drager, who was framed by masses of red and green bushes, looking uncomfortable in a way I'd never noticed before. He met my gaze without any expression, and I shook my head and looked away. I was done with him for today.

"Okay, I know we're not in the best position at the moment," Kellan started. "Emotionally, I mean. The trust and bond between us have been damaged for a long time, and as we predicted back before we were all blasted apart, that's given them the advantage they need to infiltrate our world."

No one argued. How could we when all evidence suggested that in a large part this was our fault.

"I learned quite a lot when I was pretending to be on her side," Drager said shortly, staring at his feet. "Mother's side, that is. Turns out Xalifer is not what we remember. In fact, I don't think any of our memories were real."

I'd suggested this before, but at the time no one had cared enough to delve deeper into it. "There are no female dragon shifters," Drager continued, and since we were all aware of that as well, none of us reacted. "We can only breed with humans, and Mother is a fucking human. I can't believe it."

I bet that bastard couldn't, after the multitude of times he'd looked down on Morgan for her race.

"Why is she actually here?" Emmen asked, lacing his fingers behind his head as he sprawled back against a nearby tree trunk. "Is it to take this land and destroy any who fight her?"

Drager hesitated. "I don't know her entire plan, so a lot of this is guesswork from what I observed. Xalifer is a dying world. That memory is partially true. And to keep it functioning, they steal the energy from other planets. To make it easier on the process, they tend to wipe out or weaken the inhabitants first."

Finally, he was providing some new information.

"They're locusts, zapping around and finding rich fertile energy to take back to Xalifer, which they can move. Did I mention that already? Their fucking world moves."

He hadn't, but we'd heard the same from the guards. "Why did they not come here earlier?" Tylan asked. "We've controlled Eastern Risest for a couple of hundred years. More than enough time."

Drager, still staring at his feet, shrugged. "That part I'm not sure of, but considering I had to convince her to ally, I'm guessing she didn't send us here as a scouting mission. There's more to it than that."

I had my theory on the timing and Morgan, but I needed more evidence before I told my brothers. Jumping to conclusions could get us killed.

"Have we seen any human mates with them?" I asked.

Drager shook his head. "From what I heard, their mates are back on Xalifer, orbiting out there somewhere in the abyss of space like a giant fucking spaceship."

"Hence why we always had different guards," Emmen growled. "They can just switch out their fighters as needed."

Drager finally lifted his head as he replied. "Exactly that. They were reinforcing their warriors the entire time we were trying to take them down in the forest. Along with those fucking crystals, they have a huge advantage."

It was an advantage, but now we had the knowledge of their strengths, we could use that in future planning.

"I hate to point out the obvious," Kellan said with a

strained chuckle, "but even with our immense power, how the hell do five of us fight an entire world of shifters?"

"We need to take this new knowledge we have of them," I said softly. "Take it and use it against them. The warrior fae were figuring out a defense against the crystals, right?"

"Yes," Drager confirmed. "They said they can block the energy, but they won't be able to really counter it."

"I think I know a way we can," Emmen said, repeating what he'd told us in the cells. "We'll have to reinforce our bonds and connections, and practice working together though."

None of us argued, because deep down we always knew it would come to this. "When we figure it out, we start with Mother," I growled. Just the memory of her icy face had me wanting to burn her to cinders. "She's the ringleader here. Once she's taken out, the rest will falter."

Emmen shot to his feet and started pacing back and forth. "Yes, you're right. They were so deferential to her, as if she was a god herself."

Like mother like sons, apparently.

But we didn't use our power and control to indiscriminately destroy.

That was the difference.

Pushing up to stand as well, I decided I was done with this meeting for the night. I'd stayed away from Morgan as long as I could stand. Astra assured me that she slept peacefully still, but I needed to be at her side.

Protecting her. Protecting mine.

"Wait," Drager called as I turned to walk away. I paused but didn't glance back. "When should we meet up to practice fighting the crystal's power? We must figure that out, otherwise we don't stand a chance."

"In the morning," I shot back. "For now, I'm going to my mate."

Without another word I left the clearing and exited the forest, heading straight to the white house with yellow trim.

Back to Morgan.

Back to my peace.

At least for tonight.

CHAPTER 25

MORGAN

Heat surrounded me, and as I passed through the stage of pure exhaustion into a place of energy, I started to wake. Turning over, I went to kick off the bed sheets, only to find that there were no sheets. The heat that caressed every inch of my body *was not from a blanket*. It was a dragon shifter wrapped around me in the tiny bed.

The bed groaned beneath our weight. The only way he fit on here at all was that half of him hung off the side, and I was sprawled across his body… his naked body, if what I felt was correct.

I wasn't completely naked, glancing down to see a tank top, but since my tits had a tendency to go walking through the night, there wasn't much difference. Apparently, my right lady enjoyed hard muscles, because she was not in the fucking shirt.

Low laughter filtered into my frazzled, overheated mind.

Your tits are perfect, he said, outwardly still appearing sound asleep. *They know where they belong.*

And *damn* was it even hotter in here.

"Morning," I croaked.

His hold on me tightened as he rolled closer to the wall, pulling me with him. "We slept away the morning and half the afternoon," he said, voice deeper and huskier than usual. "Despite this fucking horrendous bed. I don't know how the fae deal with such tiny housing."

"Most fae aren't giants and don't need custom-made furniture." These Fallen gods were large in *all* aspects.

I didn't add the last part out loud, but he no doubt heard anyway. He was getting better at picking up my thoughts, or maybe I was just projecting them more naturally.

Both.

The way he switched between internal and external conversation didn't bother me in the slightest. I had the sense that if we lived long enough to truly establish a bond, I'd enjoy that part a lot.

His laughter this time was slower, sensual, and my toes curled as tingles raced across my skin. "It won't be what you enjoy the most, little mate," he drawled, tightening his hold again so there wasn't an inch of space between us.

"You didn't comment on us *living long enough*," I breathed, desperate for a distraction. If he didn't stop what he was doing, I was about to throw all caution to the wind and jump his fucking dragon bones.

Zahak stroked his hands over my stomach where my top had ridden up, burning a path across my skin. "I refuse to acknowledge that there's a future we don't survive in," he replied simply, and in my distracted state I'd already forgotten our previous conversation. "*We will* destroy those attempting to destroy us, and *we will* live happily ever after. The fucking end."

"You're a true poet," I said with a snort. "Have you considered writing romance novels?"

He rumbled beneath me. "I've considered living one. I'll leave the writing to others."

My heart did a little pitter-patter at the thought that he considered our relationship romance novel worthy.

I couldn't really disagree.

"Are you naked?" I asked suddenly. I could feel chest muscles and a hard thigh beneath me, but I hadn't looked to see if he wore pants.

Tightening his hold on my hip with one hand, the other stroked higher, brushing the underside of my breasts.

"Find out."

I almost missed those two words, but as soon as they registered I could think of nothing *except* finding out. I was definitely the woman for the job.

Shifting to my side, I ran my hand along his chest and down to find... bare skin. All the way. My panties and skimpy tank were all that separated us, and *no fucking wonder I'd woken up on figurative fire.*

"Z," I groaned, arching against him.

"Our claiming won't be like this," he said seriously. "We will seal our bond in the way of shifters, but that doesn't mean we can't have a little fun before."

I had questions.

A lot of questions.

Like... what did *seal our bond in the way of shifters* entail? And what sort of fun—?

My thoughts were cut off as both of his hands landed on my ass. He was so strong that even stretched out as we were, he dragged me up his body without any resistance, lifting me until my thighs settled on either side of his face.

By the time he got me into position, I was breathing heavily, and knew my panties were soaked. Falling forward, I used both hands to balance and brace myself against the wall, lifting a touch so I didn't suffocate him.

"Sit, sweetheart," he rumbled, the dragon peeking through.

It took all my control to lower myself until I felt his mouth brush against the cotton of my panties. That one touch sent a spasm of pleasure through me—my flesh was already so heated and overstimulated that I doubted it'd take more than a swipe of his tongue to send me over the edge.

Huge hands wrapped around my thighs. "You're still hovering. You don't have to fucking hover with me," he groaned, burying his face in my center. "Drop that delicious pussy my way and let me have breakfast."

He tugged once and I gave up the fight. If he wanted to go out this way, who was I to argue?

Letting my weight rest, I used my hands to keep myself balanced. Zahak's mouth was hot against me, and I expected him to remove my underwear using his energy, but instead he tightened his hold on my thighs until I couldn't move even if I wanted to.

His tongue was hot through the material as he stroked it over me slowly, taking his time, and even with the cotton barrier the pleasure was near unbelievable. I cried out when his tongue slid along the elastic side, as he drew out the pleasure in this slow, torturous build.

Rocking and crying, I was lost in the sensations of his mouth on my skin as he tasted me. It wasn't until I felt that first swipe against my clit, with no barrier at all, that I realized I was naked. At some point my clothes had vanished into the wind. Gone forever.

He opened his mouth and sucked my clit inside. "Fuck," he groaned, and that was when slow ended. Lifting me higher, he fucked me with his mouth, devouring as he went. There was no other way to describe it as his tongue stroked from the bottom of my pussy to the top, plunging inside as he ate me. My cries were just one long moan at this point, and I might have broken a few nails against the wall.

He had me in a chokehold, not literally, but in a way that I couldn't have left this room or the bed if my life depended on it. I was riding his mouth, and he was greedily taking it all. A spiraling in my lower half built and built until the world detonated and my vision wavered between dark and light. I threw my head back and screamed.

Zahak didn't stop there though, not even as I came so hard I saw stars. He caught every drop of my release and drank it down as if it were the lifeforce he needed to survive.

My body trembled as waves of pleasure continued to bowl me over, as if I was caught in orgasm ocean. It was almost too much to handle, but if he'd have stopped I might have died anyway.

The movement of his tongue eventually slowed, but it didn't halt, and all too soon I was writhing and arching against him. He held me in his grip, but not so tight that I couldn't ride his face. It was as if he knew I needed to move or I'd lose my mind.

I hear you, baby. My heart clenched hard, and I cried out his name.

Tingles raced through me as my breaths came out with more force. Through our mental connection, he sent images my way. Not just images, but feelings and... *Holy fuck.* He showed me exactly what he felt as he tasted me. It was the sweetest nectar to him, and already he was addicted to my scent and taste. *I will eat from you every day for the rest of my life,* he rumbled.

Feeling his pleasure with my own was too much, and this time when I came my entire body vibrated and jerked. My orgasm was more intense than before, which felt impossible, but here we were. Hard to believe that this was our first time together. I just knew Zahak was going to teach me pleasures I never even knew existed.

I couldn't wait.

Those rolling orgasms went on for a long time, and when I finally slumped forward, almost smashing my head on the wall, I let out a weak laugh.

Zahak lifted me, sliding me slowly down his body, and when we were face to face, I examined his darkly savage beauty, highlighted in slivers of light through the window.

Our gazes caught, and I couldn't help but lean over to kiss him.

Zahak let out a low sigh, the softest sound against my lips, and I wondered how long he'd waited for this kiss.

My entire existence.

My heart figuratively exploded in my chest, and I was drowning in the emotion of it all.

As our kiss deepened, I could taste myself, and I never expected to enjoy or be turned on by that, but there was no denying the way my center throbbed, my overstimulated clit screaming at me to fuck him.

There was no awkwardness between us as we kissed and touched as if we'd been intimate for years.

"We are true mates," he said simply. "It will always work. You can see the difference now."

I saw and felt it, without any doubt. Zahak had been trying to tell me from the start, even as he waited for me to wake up and realize it myself. I mourned that I hadn't known about my mate before coming here, because I'd wasted so much time with Drag—

The rumble in my head grew louder, and I decided now wasn't the time to delve into the past. Zahak had been patient and caring with me, but he was still a dragon, and that animalistic nature hovered close to the surface.

Clearing my mind, I leaned down to kiss him once more. He let me take the lead as I explored his mouth, until his taste had my head spinning. I wanted more. I wanted to devour him the same way he'd done for me.

He must have caught that thought as he groaned and deepened the kiss. "Morgan," he rumbled. "As I told you earlier, you never have to hesitate or ask permission to touch me. As soon as our bond is sealed, you'll understand the true depths of my need for you."

Sealing the bond better happen soon because I wasn't sure I had the patience to wait much longer. This human needed her dragon, and she needed him now.

CHAPTER 26

MORGAN

My plan to explore Zahak's cock, and those delicious ridges he sported, was interrupted by a loud knock against our door. Astra and Leo weren't in the room, but since they didn't knock, a fae was outside the door.

Or Drager.

I really hoped it wasn't Drager.

My panic faded as an image of Florentine floated through my mind, and I had a moment of wondering if I was suddenly psychic, before I realized the thought came from Zahak. We communicated mostly in words, so it was odd to receive an image from him.

It appeared that our mental connection was growing stronger.

Naturally.

Not in the forced way Drager used to infuse energy inside me.

"Florentine?" I called. Zahak made no move to shift our current *very naked* arrangement.

"Uh, yes. Sorry to disturb," she replied through the door. "But we're about to regroup and rework our battle plan. I thought you might want to be there for that."

I'd rather be here, naked, with a sexy dragon beast.

Zahak's laughter wasn't silent this time, and I found myself once again captivated by the rare times he laughed out loud. It was nice when he relaxed with me, letting his guard down in a way I hadn't realized these shifters could. I'd never seen this in the others, especially Drager, who'd made an artform of keeping me at arm's length.

"We're meeting at the field on the western perimeter," Florentine added through the door, and I had completely forgotten she was there.

"We'll be right out," I replied, resigned and a touch annoyed.

"Excellent," she said, "I've left clean clothes at the door."

We heard her walk away, and when I was about to push up and get off the bed, Zahak wrapped his arms around me and hugged me even closer. Every muscle in my body relaxed as I sank into him, and it was only when he let out a sigh and released me that I was able to pull myself together and get up.

I used the small washroom to clean up, since there was no time for the caves. Zahak threw the clothes from Florentine to the side, deciding to provide his own outfit, already waiting on the bed. Thankfully it was jeans and a simple white shirt, the underwear also simple and cotton. I liked comfortable clothes, and he gave me exactly what I needed.

"Why did Drager keep telling me that if he clothed me with his energy it would drain my own?" I asked Zahak as I finished dressing. "I mean, it was clearly untrue, because he ended up giving me clothes anyway and they never hurt me. But he still maintained that it would drain my energy."

"Because he's an asshole," Zahak said simply. "He didn't want to waste his energy, and he didn't want you to be able to absorb his power and grow stronger. If you were strong, you wouldn't need his constant infusion of power."

I recoiled, disgust curving my lips into thin lines. "Are you fucking serious? So, wearing clothes made from your energy allows me to absorb some of your power and be strong enough to stay here. So, it actually has the opposite effect of what he told me?"

Zahak nodded, examining my face as I fumed. *That motherfucker!* Drager… ugh. "Remind me to kick him in the balls when we see him today," I finally muttered, forcing myself to forget about the *asshole*.

"You got it, sweetheart," he said, and I swear that gleam in his eyes was pure excitement. I imagined that was how he looked when he cut off more than a dozen heads for me.

Zahak was scary, vicious, and deadly… just not with me. If he'd have been human, I'd have worried that eventually I'd do something to piss him off and he'd turn on me too. But he was a shifter. I mean, I'd already slept with his brother, so what more could I really do? He never treated me as less or made me feel bad for past decisions.

He just accepted me. It was insanely refreshing and still quite hard to believe.

"I'm in your corner, Morgan," he said softly as we left the house. "There's nothing that will change that. I'm sure we'll fight. I'll always be a fucking immovable object when it comes to your safety. And you're still an independent woman who will press against every boundary and rule I try to set in place. We'll battle, absolutely, and the makeup sex will near kill us both, but I will never not be on your side."

I was speechless. My feet stopped moving in the middle of the garden path as I stared at him. Just stared. Swallowing roughly, the burning behind my eyes increased, and with that, feelings burst from me. "From the first moment I arrived in this world, I've been half pretending it was a fantasy book. Living in a story explained away all the fantastical experiences I was having, but…" I swallowed roughly once more. "…I never saw you coming, Z. Not in all my wildest dreams and most fervent wishes for a partner in life. You're beyond my greatest fantasy story. I still struggle to accept that this is all real and won't be snatched away from me in a heartbeat."

From the first moment he told me we were true mates, a part of me had accepted it. Without question. The connection had been tangible, and so strong that even a human couldn't deny it.

"Our mates are only and always human," he told me, and I blinked at him, trying to understand what he was saying. "You are exactly what we need to complete our souls."

Humans? All of the shifters' mates were human? "Are you telling me there are no female shifters? Just human mates?"

He nodded. "Yep. Even our young are always male. Without humans, our race would die off."

Oh boy, I bet Drager fucking loved that. "Well, that makes my presence here a little more understandable. But… why humans? We're kind of weak and short-lived compared to you."

For a dragon his smile was very wolfish as he leaned down and pressed his lips to mine. I lost focus for a beat, opening my mouth and groaning when our tongues collided. "When we cement the bond, you'll have my strength and longevity," he said as he pulled away. "Mother is hundreds of years old, and powerful thanks to our father. You'll have the same."

"Where is your father?" I mumbled, a little dazed from the kiss.

"I don't know," he rumbled, stretching tall, his face once again impassive. "Until we unlock our memories, we only have fractured thoughts and shattered images in our minds. It's confusing and I can't tell what's real or not anymore."

When she had the crystal focused on me, the memories raced through my brain in tiny fragments. I just couldn't put them all together.

And now?

Now, the fragments are gone, and so are the memories.

It was frustrating, because I was afraid it was these memories we needed to defeat the infiltrators.

"We're going to keep digging away at the cracks," he said. "But in the end we may need to rely on instinct and our own path, without a connection to the past."

That I understood too, since I rarely looked back these days. Forward was the only way for me.

Astra and Leo raced up the path then, breaking up our intensity, and I gave them both a huge hug, relieved to see them.

"Is the meeting underway?" Zahak asked the larger sabre.

She rumbled a reply, and he nodded. "She said they're all gathered, and we should hurry."

Leo, who was at least twice as big again as he was yesterday, padded beside me, brushing against my legs. He offered the simplest and sweetest comfort, even if he was still a cub at heart, bounding off and chasing bugs.

"What are you going to do about Drager?" I asked Zahak as we walked. "Will you have to work with him in the final battle?"

His expression darkened. "Unfortunately, yes. It seemed that Emmen's plan to counter the crystal's energy will require us to join in a bond. I have no choice but to work with him until this is all over."

Drager, even without trying, had a way of making himself indispensable. My plans to kick him in the balls or drop him into a volcano would clearly have to wait. Zahak's laughter followed as he swept an arm around me and moved us faster along the path. "Volcanos won't work. We're born in a similar fire, but there are other means."

A snort escaped me. "You were born in fire? Of course you were born in fire. I mean, why not."

I didn't have to ask about other means, because I'd seen him tear that shifter in two like a piece of damn paper. I wasn't sure he could do that to Drager, because asshole or not, he was still his brother. But… the next time Drager pissed me off, I was going to imagine him as that guard.

"I'll destroy him in a heartbeat if he hurts you again," Zahak said casually.

He did not sound like he was kidding either.

"I'd never ask that of you," I said, reaching up to pat the arm he had draped over my shoulders. "I'm well read. Don't you worry, I'll figure out my own revenge."

"That I believe." He let out a contented rumble, and peace settled between us.

The early evening air was cooler than I'd felt in Risest for a while, but pressed against Zahak, I was warm. Heat roiled through my veins and into my center, and I enjoyed the sensation. It was almost as if I'd been born in flames with the shifters, and yet I was still human.

I felt the frailty of my race, while relishing in the truth that I might gain some of Zahak's longevity. I didn't want to leave him or Lexie, not for many decades, and it was a relief that my worries about aging and dying might actually be baseless.

If this were really a fantasy story, I'd be thanking the

author right about now, all the while knowing that soon I'd have to rage at them again, because there was still darkness on the horizon.

The battle wasn't won yet, but having Zahak back with me felt a hell of a lot closer.

The rest I'd deal with when it happened.

CHAPTER 27

ZAHAK

Her thoughts, so light and open, were refreshing. The jaded darkness in my mind eased up under the unwavering sweetness of my mate. She had fire, but they were baby flames, and I loved that about her. She brought me peace, and I finally understood what it meant to feel your soul settle. It grew harder to ignore the part of me that wanted to steal her away and ignore the death and destruction of this world.

When we arrived at the meeting place, a few dozen fae warriors and my brothers were already present. Keeping my hold on Morgan, we moved to stand beside Kellan, who shot us both a quick smile. "Now that we're all here," Emmen started. "Let's work out the next steps in our plan to take them down. We've already established that Xalifer, and their inhabitants—"

"They refer to themselves as galators," Drager added, interrupting quickly.

Emmen nodded. "The galators are a plague on the world. Already their presence has our skies darkening, and a disease spreading through the creatures of Risest." I'd told them about the disease in the trench when we were first captured. "Odds are, if their invasion goes on long enough, it will destroy us all. We must stop this now, once and for all."

Gazes lifted to the dark sky above, searching out Xalifer, before Florentine, the leader of Green Hollow, stepped forward. "We're running out of time. They have the advantage because they keep reinforcing their troops with more from Xalifer. We have no idea how many of them are on that world, but there's no denying that allowing them to continually add to their numbers and refresh their army, while we're beaten down and tired, is going to cost us in the end."

She was right. It was the reason Drager made the decision to withdraw our troops yesterday. He might be a disloyal bastard, but he was always strategic in battle.

"It's true," Drager said when she finished talking. "There's no winning if we don't stop them at the source." He gave a sideways glance to us, eyes lingering briefly on Morgan, before he drew his gaze back to the crowd. "We're debating the best path to take to destroy them. Maybe the five of us should head for Xalifer and take them down there."

Morgan flinched at my side, but I didn't visibly react. Drager had dropped that on all of us, but we were disciplined enough not to let it show.

Z! Morgan's voice in my mind was frantic. *Is Drager serious? You're going right into the fucking nest of shifters?*

I tightened my hold, before reminding myself of her fragility. It would be so easy to crush her in my need to keep her close, and with reluctance I loosened my grip. *He hasn't discussed that with any of us, but no doubt he has some stupid plan.*

"There's only five of you," Lexie said as she appeared

from the edge of the forest, looking much healthier than yesterday. Morgan stood straighter, her focus locked on her friend as she examined her for injuries. "How do you plan on taking them all down? You'll be captured or killed immediately. We already know they have sonar weapons and won't hesitate to use them."

The other Lightsbringers in the area nodded with their warrior daughter, and I expected Lexie to stand with her family, as would have been normal protocol, but she didn't. She made her way to Morgan, who wiggled out from under me to throw her arms around her best friend.

It was no surprise these two found each other on Earth. Neither followed the path of their race, and for that I was fucking thankful.

They hugged for a long time, and it was clear that Lightsbringers were upset—the energy in the area changed—even if they were too well trained to show it on their faces.

One of them chimed in after Lexie: "Our warrior daughter is correct. If you five get yourselves captured or killed, then we'll have no defense at all. There must be a way to bring them down here, to our territory, in larger numbers that we can ambush. We can call in more warriors from across the five lands, and together we can take them down."

"If we want them here in larger numbers," I said when there was a break in the chatter, "we have to take control of their leader. It's the only way. Then, when they exit their world en masse, we will have to be stocked up on those defense shields against the sonar weapons and have our own weapon to counter it."

"The sonar weapon has to be turned back on them," Morgan added.

The crowd grew silent, giving her their attention. No one dismissed her as a mere human, since they all knew what would happen if they did. Drager hadn't respected Morgan, which bled into the fae around him, but she was my entire world. They knew I'd kill them without a fucking thought.

"I agree with Morgan," Drager said.

Of course he did. Now that he had a reason to try to prove he was not a depthless asshole.

"Sounds like we have our plan of action over the next few days," Kellan said. "First, we call in all the warrior clans from across Eastern Risest. Second, those with energy manipulation skills work on the sonar shielding armor, since there's no point going into battle again without it. And third, we will figure out how to create a weapon of our own and use it to take their leader captive."

A sense of resolution washed over the crowd, each of us agreeing that this was the best chance of success against the galators.

Galators.

I hadn't heard that word before, not in the memories I had, but it felt familiar.

"You five will still be our best bets," one of the Lightsbringers said. "We'll be here to distract and disarm, but you'll have to do the actual capturing of the leader. You're stronger than the other galators."

"Why are you stronger?" Morgan asked suddenly. "Will there be any as strong as you five out there?"

Emmen shook his head. "There shouldn't be, because apparently we're the royal sons. Our parents are the rulers of the galators, and we were cast out for some reason. We don't know the full story, but our energy, especially when we use our unique royal bond, is not like any of theirs."

Drager met my gaze, and I let my hatred for him seep out, slowly. The knowledge that I'd have to open our bond again was irritating, but I'd do a lot worse to keep Morgan safe.

Dealing with his lazy, selfish ass would be nothing if we won this battle.

Tylan pushed himself up from where he'd been leaning against a tree. "Let's rest tonight. Tomorrow we get to work on our plan. We need to move quickly, because they'll be regrouping as well. If any of you have trouble working your side out, let us know, otherwise we can meet up again at the next darkening sky."

The fae warriors dispersed quickly, leaving just my brothers, Lexie, and Morgan. "Our bond is the most important part of this plan," Drager said without preamble. "It'll be the difference in this war. I can feel it."

"You probably *felt it* when you were betraying us," Kellan said, and there was no sunshine in his gaze for the *sun god*.

Drager pursed his lips, fire flashing in his eyes, before he took a few deep breaths to calm himself. "Look, I know I fucked up when I made my decisions, but I promise, at the time I thought it was the best way to save us all. What was the point of the five of us being in chains? Someone had to get you out."

"I got them out," Morgan sniped. "With *Mika*." Her voice choked over his name, and in her thoughts she wondered when we would give him his warrior farewell. "You weren't there, Drager. You're never there when we need you."

She said *we*, but it was more about the way he'd treated her, and the fundamental selfishness that shaped who he was as a shifter.

He took her criticism better than he would have from most of us. "I thought the best place for me was outside the academy, acting as a distraction, but I should have been there with you. I'm sorry about Mika." His expression almost appeared genuine. "But I'm here to do better, and I won't let you all down again. I'll stand at your side, even if it means a fight to the last breath."

The air simmered around us as he made that vow, and an iota of my fury toward him eased. It wasn't enough for forgiveness, but it was enough to work with him in the short term.

"I'll believe it when I see it," Morgan muttered, and despite the fact she owned my entire heart and soul, I loved her a little more in that moment.

You love me? Her shock was apparent as she turned to face me, eyes wide and lips trembling.

My adorable fucking mate.

Love, adore, cherish, and worship. These words convey a fraction of the way I feel about you, la moyar. A truth I intend to show you for the rest of our very, very long lives. If I must destroy their entire army with my bare hands to make that happen, I will, and not miss a night of sleep over it.

A tear escaped her right eye, tracing down her cheek, and I could feel how absolutely stunned she was. On shaky legs, she stumbled forward into me, and I wrapped my arms around her, cradling her against my body. I turned away so the others couldn't see her falling apart.

In our mental connection she was sobbing, and if I hadn't been able to feel how happy she was, I'd have lost my fucking mind.

Thank you, Z, she whispered, her mental voice husky. *You make me feel loved, and I love you in return. It broke me when we were separated, and I'll never forgive Drager for that, but I'm so thankful to have you back with me.*

My dragon raged, desperate to be free and claim our mate, but once again I managed to keep him contained. He wouldn't be patient for much longer though.

"Is she okay?" Lexie asked, her worried gaze on the side of Morgan's head.

"She's fine, but before we can do anything else, we need to lay Mika to rest in a warrior's ceremony. Morgan needs to grieve her friend."

Lexie didn't argue or question this, nodding resolutely. "Yes, that's our aim for tonight, and then tomorrow, you five will cement this bond. There's no point in heading back out there if we don't have the bond secure."

Lexical was well trained as a warrior, and one day I would thank her for keeping Morgan safe. For now, though, it could wait. Along with so much else.

Morgan was calmer now, and when she pulled away from me, her face was dry. Our hands found each other, and she laced her fingers through mine, her soothing energy calming my beast.

"We're going to send Mika off now," Lexie told her, reaching out to take the hand I wasn't holding.

Morgan swallowed hard. "I'm not ready, but he deserves this honor. He deserves so much more than this."

I led the way to where his body had been placed yesterday when we returned. It was a section of forest surrounded by ancient trees, and *junip* plants in full bloom, their large purple flowers scenting the area with sweetness.

"Honeysuckle," I heard Morgan murmur, looking around at the beauty of Mika's final resting place.

His body was already there, stretched out across a large pile of *yuan* sticks, plucked from the ancient trees blessed by long-ago fae leaders. He looked just as he had in life, only still now, without any animation. When Morgan moved closer, I heard her breaths catch in her chest as she struggled with her pain. Pain I could not shield her from, no matter how much I wanted to.

"He looks like he's sleeping," she whispered, staring at her friend, taking in the way his arms were crossed over his armor, eyes closed, as his hair flopped across his forehead exactly as it had done in life. The energy of the crystal had blasted him internally, but there was very little evidence on his body.

During the night, warriors had forged intricately carved wooden swords, which they'd plunged tip-first into the ground around his funeral pyre. The swords formed a barrier, and when they burned with Mika, they'd offer him strength and protection in the next life.

Morgan's eyes squeezed tightly shut, but she couldn't halt the tears seeping from beneath her lids. "He didn't deserve to die like this," she whispered. "He saved all of us, and I can't believe he's not here for me to thank."

"He knows," Lexie said hoarsely. "He did it for you, and for everyone in Risest, and he knows we're thankful. But for now, we need to send him on to the next life. He must join our ancestors in the Gardens of Eternity, and spend his days surrounded by the riches he earned in this life."

Morgan nodded, her face crumpled, and I stroked a hand up and down her spine, hoping to soothe a fraction of her sorrow. Grieving required you to express and feel the pain, since bottling it up could drive you mad, but allowing Morgan to feel pain went against every grain of my being.

"I'd like to say a few words," she croaked out. "Before you light the fires."

It wasn't the way of this world, our goodbyes usually silent, but no one argued. Her traditions would become part of our way now.

With a heavy breath, she released our hands and stepped closer to Mika. "From the moment I arrived in this world, I could feel the faes' disdain for me and my race," she started softly, voice wavering but she kept herself together. "Outside of Lexie and Zahak, the one fae who never treated me that way was Mika. I don't know the reason, I never got a chance to ask him, but whatever it was, he never acted as if I was lesser than him. He joked, and eased my way through obstacle courses that were so far beyond my ability it should have been impossible. And yet... with his help it wasn't. He had my back, even to the last second, and I can never thank or honor him enough for that."

Her upper half hunched in on itself for a beat, and that sadness in her head grew darker, filled with regret and desperate grief. It took every iota of control I'd developed over the past centuries to stop from going to her. She needed to feel this grief, and then release it to the world.

"I'm sorry, Mika," she cried. "You were a wonderful friend, and I'm so glad to have met you. Fly high, you are a true warrior, and I hope you find your peace in the Gardens of Eternity."

As she fell silent, the rest of us sent our energy into the warrior. When it was done, Lexie took Morgan's hand once more and pulled her away. My brothers and I moved around the body and drew fire from our center. We paused at even intervals and blasted at the same time, lighting his way to eternity.

In our lands, only the strongest of warriors were laid to rest via dragon flames, by the god of their area. To have all five of us was unheard of, but it was an honor Mika deserved.

Morgan's sobs grew, and when the fire raged, swords crumbling under the flames, I was finally able to gather her into my arms. "Thank you," she whispered against my chest. "Thank you for doing this."

"For you, anything."

I'd keep telling her that truth until she believed it.

CHAPTER 28

MORGAN

After we bid farewell to Mika, I felt both lighter and heavier. The pain settled, and while I knew I'd never forget him, I had released a fraction of the grief to move forward. He'd want all of us to keep living our lives. There was no point to his death if we didn't fight for life.

The Fallen Five remained in the clearing, Zahak holding me close to his side, and I was thankful for his support. Despite our vast power and strength difference, he never made me feel weak. I couldn't wait to see where we ended up in the next ten years. Or hundred.

Wow, wasn't that a thought.

My human brain wasn't quite ready to wrap around an eternity of life, so I focused on the now. "How long will it take for other warrior fae to arrive from everyone's lands?" I asked. "Is the plan to have your mother in our custody before they get here, or will we need their help to capture her?"

"We need to get that weapon under control first," Emmen said. "We can't enact the rest without that. Not when she can destroy us with one blast."

"I believe that crystal is what she used to destroy our memories when we fell from Xalifer," Drager said suddenly. "I overheard a conversation that didn't make sense at the time, but now I'm putting it together. We were young and that energy fractured our memories. I wonder if mastering the energy of the crystal would allow us to figure out how to reverse it, or maybe it would…"

"Break us worse," Kellan drawled. "I really don't care about my lack of memories from before Risest. This is our home now, and I'm cool just to forget the rest of that shit ever existed."

Through our bond, I could tell that Zahak didn't completely disagree with his brother. "It's only if our memories hold information that could be useful in defeating them," he said out loud. "Otherwise, I agree with Kell. My past life is a dead life. This is who I am now."

Shaking his head, Tylan let out a low laugh. "Who the fuck is this philosophical shifter?" His amused gaze met mine. "You're a little witch, Morgan. I'm getting my ass to Earth after this, and I'm finding my own witch."

I narrowed my eyes on him. "Women don't especially love being called witches."

Tylan shrugged. "She'll love it from me."

It was my turn to laugh now, my body shaking at the idiocy of what he'd just said. Though, in truth, he probably wasn't wrong. The Fallen Five were tall, ripped, gorgeous, and powerful. And just wait until she saw the ridges… though that might terrify her, at first.

"You're so fucked," Zahak said, his amusement internal so

only I could hear it. "I can't wait to see the rest of you crumble."

There was nothing crumbly about Zahak. His softness was for me and me alone, and I had to say, I never expected to be so turned on by the blatant masculinity of the dragon shifter. His strength, and protectiveness, and ability to take control, just plain did it for me.

If that meant I had to turn in my independent woman card, then so fucking be it.

I don't steal your strength or independence, Zahak added. *We are a balance, and we build together.*

He'd expanded on what I'd thought before. Zahak was obviously the stronger physically, but I had my own strengths in other ways. I'd known dominant men back on Earth, and they always struggled with the balance of protecting their women without crushing them in the process.

Zahak walked that line beautifully.

His chest rumbled as he held me, and I tried to ignore the throbbing low in my body. It was always this way around him, a desperate need for more, and to be closer, even when he was literally in my head.

The bond wants us to complete it. And we will soon.

That promise sent a surge of heat through my veins. I barely managed not to moan. No need to give his brothers ammunition to use in their ribbing against us.

Drager brought us all back to business. "To answer Morgan's questions from before, warriors should start arriving as early as tomorrow morning. If we use the portals. Better to risk the energy usage than get caught without enough warriors."

"That means we need to figure out a sonar weapon and capture Mother in a similar timeframe," Emmen said. "This is not going to be an easy task."

I racked my brain for an idea to help. Most of what I knew came from books, but I was a firm believer that was where the best ideas originated. "I think you need to set a trap, and draw her out," I said slowly, thinking of the last plot point I'd read in a story like this. "You're her sons, and there's a reason she chose this world to come to now. She wants you five, she's already tried to capture you, and I bet she's pissed you're free. We need to use that to our advantage."

Lexie remained silent, arms crossed over herself. She no longer bore physical injuries, but her soul seemed a touch weary, and I couldn't wait for this to all be over. She nodded at my suggestion, though, and it felt good having her back with me.

"I think laying the trap part will be easy enough," Zahak said. "Morgan is right, she's shown her obsession with taking us out, and now that we're free she'll be furious. But we also need to know how to counter her weapons. She thinks she has the upper hand because of that, and without a crystal to practice on, I don't know how we can be assured we've countered the effects."

Lexie stood taller. "Wait... I have an idea of how we can produce a similar weapon. It won't be as strong, but it should be enough. Let me check with them."

She was already spinning to leave, and I fought my instinct to stop her. The last time she'd been out of my sight, she almost died. "I'll go with her," Tylan said, sending relief through me. "Don't trap Mother without us."

Drager snorted. "If we don't do this together, we don't stand a chance. Mother must be ancient and powerful to control the galators as she does. I doubt there's much human DNA left in her system at this point."

It was clearly still hard for him to believe humans could be their mates. Drager needed to remember that without any power or abilities, humans overcame a lot. These powerful gods could learn life lessons from us, I was almost certain of it.

The smile Zahak leveled on me gave the distinct impression he thought I was cute, and I didn't know if I should be offended or not.

I enjoy your fire.

It was a simple statement, and one that made me stupid happy.

Lexie and Tylan took off then, and the other brothers decided there was nothing more the rest of us could do tonight. We'd reconvene in the morning when Lexie and Tylan returned. Drager was slower to leave though, and Zahak seemed to sense that his brother wanted a word. We remained in the clearing, even as Kellan shot me a worried glance.

A glance I understood, since there was an excellent chance these two were about to come to blows again. And there wasn't a single action I could take to stop them, outside of almost killing myself as a distraction. Hopefully it wouldn't come to that again.

When the three of us were alone, Drager closed the distance until he was only a few feet away. Zahak kept his arm around me, and I didn't make a move to leave his side.

"I guess you've made your decision," Drager said simply, and in all honesty, he didn't seem that torn up about it.

"There was no decision to make," I replied. "Zahak and I are bonded. You couldn't keep your energy within me even when you tried really hard. It's clear that these bonds cannot be manufactured."

"We knotted," he snarled.

I shook my head. "There's an explanation for that."

There is, right? I really fucking hoped Zahak had an explanation.

I got you, baby.

Holy heck. He sure did.

"On the night of the fertility ritual," Zahak started, "our brotherly bond was heightened due to the sheer energy of the event. It was my knot, and you received the remnants of its effect. That's why you never knotted again, because I shut that fucking connection down immediately, otherwise my dragon and I would have gone ballistic and destroyed everything."

Through our shared energy, I could feel that he'd had to shut more than just their bond down. He'd had to lock away his connection to me as well, and all I felt was intense guilt.

"I'm so sorry, Z," I said out loud, so Drager heard this as well. "I came into this world with no knowledge of anything, and I hate that learning the hard way has hurt you."

His growl ripped through the clearing, and it rumbled the ground briefly as he spun me into his body and lifted me off the ground into a hug. This shifter gave the best hugs, and I forgot my sadness as I all but morphed into him. "It wasn't your fault, and I don't blame you in any way," he rumbled near my ear.

I closed my eyes and just held on, the comfort top fucking level. I never got hugs like this as a kid, the sort where you were scooped up and wrapped tight until you knew everything would be okay.

Adults understand that everything is definitely not okay, no matter how solid the hug is, but kids don't. They're reassured and comforted, and Zahak was that comfort for me.

The longer his hold continued, the more I relaxed against him, even as parts of my body were the opposite of relaxed.

My legs felt weird just dangling, so I lifted them up and wrapped them around his body, settling firmer against him.

This positioning changed our comforting embrace into one where a throb returned to my center, my breaths coming a little faster.

"I've got my answer, and I'm just going to leave you two alone now," Drager said, and we both ignored him, wrapped up in the power surging between us. Surging and pulsing. Which originated in my vagina and ricocheted through the rest of me.

I had a freaking pussy pulse. *Wait, no.* I needed to never think that again.

Zahak's laughter surrounded me, and I relished making him laugh out loud. "I can't wait any longer to cement our bond," he told me, growing serious once more. "We will go into this battle bonded so you have my strength, and I can find you anywhere, even if they separate us somehow."

Fuuck.

Every nerve in my body stood at attention, and all I could think about now was *finally being with Zahak.* We'd waited a long time for this moment, and no one was going to wreck it for us.

Not while we retained any strength in our bodies to fight back.

CHAPTER 29

MORGAN

Zahak sent Astra and Leo to scout the area and ensure there was no one in the vicinity. My love for our sabres soared as I watched their glistening black coats disappear into the darkening forest.

"We won't have as much space as I'd like for this," Zahak said, his voice already deeper. "But we'll make do. I don't think I could hold out on the chase for long anyway."

He set me on my feet, and as his gaze lifted over my shoulder to peer into the darkness, a small smile tilted his full lips. "Astra said we're alone. You need to head in that direction."

He pointed down a small path, and my stomach flip flopped. We hadn't discussed the details of what this bonding entailed, but I had some ideas after he'd said *in the way of shifters*. I knew I was on the right track when scales spread across his arms and up his neck, his body growing larger too.

We were going to finish what Drager and his evil mother

had interrupted. The primal chase of mates. He wanted me to make him work for it, and I was determined to give it my best shot.

As he continued to shift into a hybrid form, it wasn't anything like the one the crystal had created in the cells. He was still—mostly—humanoid in shape, just larger and with scales. His eyes were a mixture of man and beast. His mind also took a different beat, with more energy and patterns emerging, along with a plethora of colors that I couldn't name. I'd never seen some of the shades that billowed through his mind.

Zahak took a step closer, and despite the heat he threw off I shivered, goosebumps crossing my arms. My skin felt sensitive, as if the very light breezes in Green Hollow were too much stimulation. Inside, heat roiled through my gut and into my limbs, burning through me with a throbbing that demanded to be sated.

Every part of me was ready for what came next, and even with the knowledge that my life was about to change irrevocably, I'd never been surer of a decision. Zahak was it for me.

Despite that, the energy of this hunt had tendrils of fear streaming through the heat of my body, as the urge to run grew stronger. Zahak reached for me and I dodged his grip, sprinting in the direction he'd pointed out earlier. The roar behind me shook the ground, and my heart skipped a beat even as I picked up speed.

Inside our bond, he shed the final façade of being humanoid and fully embraced the beast. I'd never fear Zahak, but there was a primality about this chase that had me trembling.

My clothes chafed at my heated skin, just as they'd done last time, and as I went to glance behind to see where Zahak was, my shirt got caught on a branch and all but jerked me to a halt. Wiggling, I was frantically trying to get free when I heard his dark laugh. A huge shadow washed over the already darkening path, and I was disappointed that Zahak had caught me so quickly. He stalked closer, and then in one swipe sliced through my shirt and bra.

My pants and panties were gone just as quickly, and I shivered once more as those gentle breezes brushed over sensitive skin. Need built inside me, and as I pressed my thighs together I wondered if I'd be able to run in this state. Wanting nothing on my skin, I kicked my boots off too, and decided I'd just deal with rocks and sticks.

Zahak rumbled. He was fucking huge, standing what felt like twenty feet taller than me. My hands lifted to touch him, to tear his clothes from his body as well, and he tilted his head back as if anticipating my touch.

Just as I was about to make contact, I let out a laugh of my own and took off once more. This was how it had been last time, naked and free, racing through the forest, knowing that the dragon shifter I loved was going to catch me. Catch and then fuck me until we were bonded forever.

You can run, la moyar, but I'll always catch you.

His voice was guttural.

With a little moan, I changed directions, heading down smaller paths, racing in and out of plants and narrowly avoiding *concors*. Those carnivorous piranhas had flashed their deceptive lights, and I only remembered *not to follow* at the last second.

Taking another left, this path looked darker than the others, and I realized I might have run too far. Just as I was deciding if I should backtrack, since we did not want to leave the protective barrier of Green Hollow, strong arms wrapped around me. I let out a shriek, but it was Zahak again, picking me up in a flash. He held me to his naked chest and my heated skin burned against his scales.

The thoughts and patterns in Zahak's mind were beyond my understanding, so I let go of trying to figure him out and just felt. I felt the vibrational connection between us. I felt his strength and energy as he lifted me higher, until our faces were closer. I felt the beat of our hearts, moving as a single sound.

I savored the beauty of this male.

"Mate," he growled.

His first kiss was a fierce slam of his mouth against mine, and I was moaning before our tongues even touched. He took control of the kiss, dominating it, so firmly that another ache settled low. The kiss continued for a long time, and I was lost in Zahak. He tasted like life and energy. Dark energy that invigorated me in a way I'd never felt. I'd have kissed him for an eternity if that were an option, just to feel this strength flowing through me. To feel his heat against me.

As a chick not born in fire, I was sure as hell addicted to it now.

The kiss never gentled as the tension between us built. Zahak wouldn't let me lift my legs, drawing out the torture. All the while my need grew. It grew until it was all-encompassing and had its own wings to fly.

He was stronger, setting the pace, and I just had to hope he'd catch me when I exploded.

Always.

A whisper. A promise.

His hands tightened on the back of my thighs as he drew me higher until our lips were forced to part because I was above his head now. "Z," I shrieked, reaching out to hold on to the tree branch above us. "What are you doing."

"Feasting," he rumbled.

He kept lifting, and his strength was so vast that for the first time in my life I felt small. Small and light, and no burden to anyone. When my stomach passed his face, his tongue darted out to taste my skin and I groaned at how good that one swipe felt.

The throbbing in my clit was almost unbearable, pleasure pain such as I'd never felt. I was half out of my mind, sobbing as he bit against my skin, softly, and then harder. I welcomed the pain. It balanced everything else.

He kept lifting, and as he breathed me in I wished briefly that I'd had a chance to shower. This wasn't the first time he'd tasted me, but the vulnerability remained.

"Fuck," he groaned. "Your scent. The singular most destructive scent in the world."

He held me like that, above his head, his face pressed against my pussy as he swiped his tongue and ate me like I was his last meal. I found myself settling, my legs over his shoulders as I held on to the branch above, and leaned back as far as I needed. Zahak's tongue swiped up and across my clit, circling that ball of nerves for a few seconds, before I screamed out his name, and would have come except he eased up at the last moment.

"Gah," I groaned. "Please, Z."

His breath was hot against my skin as he caressed lower, his tongue plunging inside me, over and over, his energy infusing with his touch, sinking inside and into my own essence.

My moans picked up, and as the spiraling in my stomach started to expand and expand, I felt like this time I might truly explode. Only to find Zahak's tongue easing out of me just as I went to tip over the edge.

"Why?" I cried, and groaned, and all but thrust my pussy into his face.

His laughter was low. *I need you ready. My beast is part of this tonight, and we can't be gentle.*

Nerves exploded just as fiercely, because I'd seen his cock, and I wasn't sure we'd survive what he had in store for us. It'd be a fun way to go out though, so I just settled in and let him dictate the pace.

His tongue swiped across my clit and then plunged inside once more, and I rode his face with complete abandon. His strokes slowed, the buildup starting in my very cells, as I lost my grasp on reality.

"Oh my gods," I choked out, hands aching from how hard I clutched the branch above. This time, as I panted and almost died from a lack of oxygen, Zahak did not stop. His tongue thrust into me faster and faster, and I was screaming as that spiraling pleasure exploded.

I came so hard that there were stars in my vision and I lost my grip on the branch. Not that it would have mattered, since Z's hold on me was more solid than anything I'd ever felt before. My pleasure was atomic, and Zahak took everything my body offered, relentless in his endeavor to feast, which sent me over the edge two more times.

Our mental connection grew stronger, and his dragon was roaring loudly. I felt the tension under his skin as he swiped his tongue from my ass up to my clit, until he'd consumed the last of my release, and that was when he slowly lowered me.

"Now," he rumbled, and I gasped as my legs wound around his body, the thick head of his cock pressed against my entrance.

A low moan fell from my lips, but with it a niggling thought at the back of my head screamed that Zahak was still trying to be gentle for me, which I didn't want tonight. If I was his true mate, then I would survive whatever he needed in this first claim, and with that, I shocked us both by pushing away.

He almost dropped me, and I took advantage of that, by wiggling down to the ground.

The giant dragon-man watched me closely, his chest heaving as he waited for my next move.

Leaning forward, I shot him a low smile. "Tag, you're it." I slammed my hand on his chest and then turned along the path and took off.

This time when he roared, there was no mistaking the shaking of the ground. I almost tripped as it rocketed under me, but managed to keep my footing. Maybe it was his energy, or my own desperate need, but I was fast enough that it took him many minutes to catch me.

This time, he wrapped his arms around me and took me to the ground. It should have hurt, but with his fiery energy burning up my body, I felt nothing except his weight behind me.

His hands curled under my hips and he lifted me onto all fours. The thick head of his cock pressed at my entrance, and he thrust once. The burning was intense, almost painful, but with the next thrust my body opened for his in a way that had never happened before.

Fire raged between us, and I was screaming by the third and fourth thrusts of his massive dick. The ridges scraped over sensitive nerve endings, and I was coming before a coherent thought could settle. Coming and screaming. Clawing at the ground as we sealed our bond in the way of shifters.

Understanding that there might be such a thing as too much pleasure, I let the stars dance across my vision without fighting the darkness around them.

"Hold on, mate," Zahak rumbled, as he pulled farther out

and slammed into me so hard that if he wasn't holding on to me, no doubt I'd have ended up in the trees.

If I hadn't been filled with his energy, and the mystical nature of our mate bond, I suspected his strength would be crushing me, but I felt none of that. It was just pleasure, and I prayed that he'd never stop fucking me like this.

Mewling cries escaped, as I sought traction on the dirt, gasping when he suddenly shifted our positions, turning me so that we were face to face. His cock was out of me for less than a second, and that was way too long as my hips surged up, needing to feel that drugging pleasure once more.

Zahak lifted my ass to thrust harder and faster, and I came so aggressively that I barely managed not to bite my tongue off. Leaning down, he kissed me as he fucked me in long hard thrusts, those delicious natural ridges scraping across *all* the pleasurable nerve endings.

At this point, it was as if I was in the midst of one continuous, intense orgasm. If I'd been fully human still, I'd have worried about my heart holding out, but Zahak's energy kept us safe.

"Never stop fucking me like this," I groaned, needing this to go on forever.

"La moyar," he rumbled, his thrusts slowing, and I felt his cock swell inside me.

That was when I remembered the knot.

For a split second I panicked that it might not happen, that in the end it had all been some sort of cosmic joke and we weren't true mates. His cock swelled further until I felt like I was about to burst, and as I was hit with my eleventy billionth orgasm tonight, he called my name, and jerked inside me.

Heat scorched us, along with a thick swelling at the base of his cock, when his power merged with my essence. The knot grew larger, filling me almost to the point of pain, until it hit a spot of pleasure inside. *Fucking hell.*

"Feel our bond, baby," he whispered, the dragon easing in his voice now that we were knotted, his seed spilling inside me. "This is our connection."

The knot swelled again, and as more of his release seeped into me, I knew that our bodies would remain locked until he had given me every part of himself.

The pleasure was too much. Orgasm after orgasm rolled through me, his knot pressing on a button of ecstasy that had opened the floodgates.

Darkness closed in, and I came again as everything went black.

CHAPTER 30

ZAHAK

The knot held us in place, our bodies joined as two parts of the same whole in a perfect connection. With each throb, my seed filled her. Claimed her.

If it were possible, I'd have stayed buried inside her for the rest of my life, pressed against soft curves, feeling her heat around me. My obsession with my woman had reached peak levels, and when she'd instinctively known that I should take her from behind for our first mating, she'd ripped my fucking heart out and claimed it as her own.

She was perfect, and I was one lucky asshole to have found a mate as strong and incredible as Morgan.

As the pleasure pushed her past her limits, I held her gently in my arms, and groaned at the sensation. Our bond was sealed now, our minds merging until it was near impossible to know whose thoughts were whose. It would calm eventually, but I was pleased that no one could keep her from my mind now.

Not even these fucking galators.

Sensing it would be hours before the throbbing knot eased, and my release was done, I decided to take her back to the house to rest in comfort. Her weight was nothing as I lifted her from the ground, and instinctively she wrapped her legs around my waist as we remained locked together.

I couldn't have separated our bodies even if I wanted to.

And I sure as fuck didn't want to.

Astra scouted ahead to ensure we remained alone, because Morgan was naked, and I'd have to murder anyone who saw her like this. Through our connection, she moaned with each throbbing release of my cock. The pleasure was too much for her to handle, and I had the sense that it'd never be quite this intense again. From now on, it'd be differently intense, as the first bonding was the strongest. This knowledge was based on pure instinct, not memories, but I trusted that part of myself. It was borne from the dragon side.

Morgan was mine forever, and while I knew humans had never really understood the concept of mated for life, she was handling it quite well. So far. Whatever happened when she woke, we'd deal with it together.

I groaned at the pulse in my cock and had to pause and close my eyes against the sensation. Morgan wouldn't get pregnant from our mating tonight, because I had deliberately chosen not to release the energy required to create life—another instinct ingrained into our essence, as we all knew the process of creating life with our mates.

Morgan was human, and I wanted to give her time to adjust to all the ways her life was about to change.

Human.

Without humans, our race would have died out. We needed them, and yet we hadn't made it to Earth during our mission to find mates. What the fuck had gone wrong? Where was the malfunction in our journey? The plan to capture Mother had multiple facets to it for me, because we needed answers. I might not require my full memories back to be happy, but there was information missing which would help me move into the future.

With Morgan.

Astra kept the fae away from the house, and when I entered, darkness surrounded us. *Stay alert*, I warned her. *They're not all friends here*.

She snarled playfully, and I knew she was reminding me of who and what she was. My greatest ally would never be taken by surprise by a regular fae.

When we reached the bedroom with its fucking miniscule bed, I stretched out on my back, Morgan straddling me. She finally stirred. "Z," she moaned again. "Oh, fuck. You're still inside me." She shifted her legs on either side, pushing up to see my face. "What is happ—" she cried out again as the next throb was particularly brutal.

"It's my knot, mate," I rumbled, mesmerized by the sight of her naked breasts. She had lush curves, and I was going to spend decades exploring every inch of her delectable body. The urge to thrust came over me, but the knot held us firmly in place. "We'll remain locked like this until all of my seed has been released."

Her eyes flew open and she stared down at me, before crying out again and leaning forward to drop her hands on my chest. I kept hold of her hips, flexing my fingers against her soft skin. "Seed. Am I going to get pregnant?" she moaned.

I couldn't tell from her tone if she was happy about that prospect or not, but in her mind, even amidst what felt like one continuous orgasm, there was a flicker of unease. As I'd suspected, she wasn't ready yet. She wanted more time where we could just be together and be selfish with each other. Our race, the galators, might focus on finding mates, breeding our mates, and becoming warriors to protect our world, but for Morgan I'd wait as long as she needed.

"Not yet," I told her. "I have to add my energy to create life."

She cried out, her head tilting back as nails dug into my skin. "Z, I don't know how much more I can take," she huffed. "Can I die from having one continuous orgasm?"

The thought of her death sent rage coursing through me, and she must have felt the tension in my body as her eyes opened wide once more, and she tried to breathe naturally. "I won't die," she hurried to say. "I'm just being dramatic."

"I will destroy anything and anyone that hurts you, la moyar," I managed to growl between my clenched jaw.

Her smile was gentle, her eyes filled with warmth as they shone a brighter blue than I'd ever seen. Her beauty was beyond anything I'd ever imagined, subtle and unique.

Another throb, and she moaned softer, going with the sensations. "I love you, Z," she whispered. I wasn't sure if she wanted me to hear that or not, she said it so quietly, but then she repeated it in our mental link.

I love you.

Fuck. A roar shook my chest, but I held it in, afraid that it would hurt her. *You're my fucking soul, Morgan. My heart and soul. I would not walk this world without you.*

Her smile was as beautiful as the rest of her, and she didn't wipe away the tears trailing down her cheeks, even as the pleasure took us both into another orgasm and we groaned with each pulse. "Drager has no fucking idea," she breathed.

Forcing myself not to react to the fact that we were joined in a mating knot and she was mentioning my brother, I waited for her to continue: "His knot lasted about two seconds and was clearly a result of our bond. This... this is unlike anything I could have imagined. Will it always be this way?" She threw her head back, tits popping out before her, and I couldn't answer because I had to taste her skin. Lifting my head, I ran my tongue up the side of her breast and captured her nipple, rolling it around my tongue until she was screaming and huffing.

Her body was sensitive from our mating bond, and I was hungry to taste more of her.

"Holy fucking hell."

Another throb, and I could feel it finally easing, our connection settling as the release ended. "I don't believe it will be this intense every time," I murmured against her body. "This is our first true mating connection, and from now on the knot will hold us, but in short increments. Until that time you decide you want my young, and then we'll have this plus more."

In her mind, images flashed of Morgan holding a baby in her arms, a perfect male shifter, and a feeling of warmth and love washed through her. "One day, Z," she promised. "I'd be honored."

The honor was all mine.

The throbbing eased again, and with that our bodies unlocked from each other. Morgan slumped forward, breathing heavily, a light layer of sweat covering her. "Is there a bucketload of cum in me right now?" she mumbled, and I couldn't help but laugh out loud.

I'd laughed more in the last few weeks with my mate than I had in the two hundred years before. She brought lightness and happiness into my world, and I was finding it hard to remember the miserable fuck I'd been before Morgan.

"Yes, little mate. There's a bucketload. You better get used to it though, because I have a new obsession."

"What's that?" Her voice was muffled against my chest.

"Keeping you filled with my seed, so that even as you walk all you can feel is my essence inside of you. Dripping from your pussy, and down your thighs."

She swallowed hard, and despite her countless orgasms I felt her arousal at the prospect of my seed filling her.

A dragon could grow fucking addicted to this feeling.

"You're in my head at all times now," she said, meeting my gaze. "So why am I not surprised you want your cock in me all day as well?"

She was teasing, but I was dead serious. "Don't tempt me, Morgan," I warned her. She had no idea how possessive I was, and I didn't want to freak her out just yet.

"I think I need some sleep, Z," she yawned, completely wrecked by our first mate bond sex. "Make sure you wake me when Lexie and Tylan get back with whatever is going to help you counter the sonar weapon."

Pressing my lips to her forehead, I ran my hands over her back. "I promise, sweetheart. Now sleep. I'll keep you safe."

She yawned and mumbled more words, but they were lost as her mind went soft and fuzzy and she drifted off to sleep.

I was tired as well, or as tired as our race got, but I couldn't bring myself to sleep just yet. This moment had been one I'd waited my very long existence for, and I wasn't ready to let it go. I needed a few more hours of holding her in my arms, our bodies semi-joined as she remained on top of me, our minds meshed so close I could see her dreams.

Finding my mate had never been on my priority list, but now I hated that I'd waited so many years. Whatever Mother did to us, it almost cost me my chance to know Morgan. To feel this love and contentment.

That had me angrier than the fact that she'd captured and tortured me.

She'd find out soon enough that fucking with my mate or our bond was the quickest way to her death. Mother or not, I'd destroy her in a heartbeat for Morgan.

CHAPTER 31

MORGAN

You know that feeling when you wake up the morning after overexerting your body? Where you have aches in places you didn't even know *could* ache, and you're half wondering if you'll even be able to walk when you get out of bed.

Yeah, I had that feeling.

Waking, bathed in morning light that was stained the crimson of the sky, I groaned at not only the heat surrounding me—I was apparently still sprawled across the broad and well-muscled chest of my dragon shifter mate—but the throbbing between my thighs.

As we'd both slept, his knot had released my body, but the aftereffects of that sex remained. It wasn't a bad throbbing, but it did remind me that he'd had to rearrange parts of me to fit, and then I'd orgasmed for approximately an hour or ten.

Low laughter filled my mind, and I relished how open and inclusive our mental connection felt now. It had changed with our bonding last night, bringing us closer, allowing me to immerse myself in this connection.

I'd never felt more secure and satisfied in my life.

Zahak's mind was open, and I could feel what he felt, and fuck… he felt a lot.

The most devastating part—in the best way—was how unconditional his love was. I'd never have to change or prove myself to be deserving of his feelings. He saw me, all of me, from my weird quirks and book loving nerdy tendencies to the lingering emotional damage my narcissistic mother left within me. He saw it all and accepted every part of me.

It was a touch harder for me to read his dragon side, which was animalistic, with less coherent thought and more instinctive reactions. But it was clear he would guard me as the most precious treasure in the world.

"You keep these thoughts up and I'm going to fuck you again, mate," he rumbled. "And I know you're sore."

Holy trinity of yes. I wasn't even sure I'd ever be too sore to be fucked by Zahak.

His rumble grew louder, and then I was lifted across his body, until my thighs, once again, settled on either side of his face.

"This is how I start my morning…" His words vibrated against my heated, sensitive flesh, and I rocked forward without thought. The first caress of his tongue was almost soothing, easing away the aches left behind from last night. The evidence of what we'd done was no doubt everywhere across our skin, but Zahak was unbothered as he indulged in his favorite breakfast.

All too soon I was crying out and riding his face, the spiraling in my stomach sending me over the edge as I jerked and came hard. Zahak's growl ripped through the room as he took in my pleasure. Resting my hands against the wall, I closed my eyes and sucked in ragged breaths, wondering how I'd lived without this in my life.

You never will again. Every fucking day, baby.

Yep, okay. I won the lotto.

When Zahak was done, he lifted me up and set me on my feet beside the bed. He was up in a flash, and there was literally no way I could move that fast, even if my ass was on fire. He dressed us both quickly, and then we set off for the bathing house.

Once again, any fae that were in there at the time cleared out as soon as Zahak and I entered. I'd never been a fan of this type of power move, but I also didn't want anyone to see him naked, so I decided to just go with it. We didn't linger long though, not wanting to keep the cave to ourselves when so many others needed it. *When this is over*, he said in our connection, *we will go to my home, and no one will interrupt us for as long as we want.*

The aching need in my center kicked in hard at the very thought of weeks alone with Zahak. Naked. "Yeah, we need to destroy your mother and the shifters immediately," I said in a rush, pulling on my clothes once again.

Standing tall, I pushed my hands through my hair, expecting it to be tangled and messy, but it felt smooth and soft. It had been a long time since I'd looked in a mirror, but there were reflective glasses near the back of these caves, so I wandered over while Zahak got dressed.

At first glance I let out a low gasp, and knew I had his attention as his mind melded into mine. "I look different," I whispered, blinking again and again, as if that would clear the reflection.

When Drager infused energy into me, there had been subtle changes, the sort of perfection I hadn't really loved, but then it had worn off, and I'd been okay with that.

Now, filled by the energy of a true bond, the changes were different again.

I didn't look perfect. My skin was smooth, yes, and my hair was without tangles, but it was the glow that really caught my eye. And how confident I stood.

"Your stamina and strength should have increased. Your longevity, too," Zahak said, standing behind me, showcasing how huge he was in comparison.

"I'd dominate the obstacle course…" I found myself unable to continue, my chest clenching hard. I'd never be able to see an obstacle course again without mourning Mika, and it was still too raw for me to think about his loss. My time last night with Zahak had been healing, and I'd needed that, but that didn't make the death of a friend any less real or painful.

"Come on, mate," Zahak said gently, drawing me closer to him and away from the glass. "The others have returned. We need to reconvene so we can end this once and for all."

Needing this distraction, I nodded and turned away from our reflections.

Striding to where I'd left my boots, I pulled them on over the black tights Zahak had created for me. The fact that he could whip up clothing from just the energy he controlled was fucking amazing. "The material comes from the world around us," he said, seemingly enjoying being in my thoughts. "And I know what you like to wear."

He sure did. Not a single pantsuit in sight.

Along with the black tights, I had an oversized purple shirt and comfortable underwear. My dream outfit.

As we left the caves, a dozen or so fae warriors were waiting at attention near the entrance. They nodded deferentially to Zahak as he passed. It was hard for me to remember that he was revered as a god in this land, when all I could feel was the warmth and comfort of his love and support.

Zahak allowed my thoughts to flow freely as we walked toward the large meadow on the edge of Green Hollow, where the warriors met to discuss their next plans. He didn't say anything, just held my hand, his mind a calming wash of energy. I realized that he didn't have a constant litany of thoughts and worries. He could just exist in a soothing blue sea.

It calmed me as well, and by the time we reached the main group I felt relaxed and at ease for what was to come next.

That was until Lexie and Tylan stepped out of the trees, and with them came the most unexpected sight. The calming wash of Zahak's mind sharpened as he took in the creatures following them out into the clearing.

All the fae stepped back until only Drager, Emmen, Kellan, Tylan, Zahak, me, and Lexie remained close. "Lex," I breathed, and as I spoke there was a screech at her side, and I focused on the creature there. "Cal!" I added, and I would have rushed forward, but Zahak edged in front of me protectively.

"It's okay," Lexie said softly. "Cal is quite fond of our little human."

Zahak bristled, and I'd have to tell Lexie not to use that particular terminology any longer. A rumble escaped him, but he didn't stop me again as I stepped forward to my bestie and her giant bird. "Hey, friend," I said cheerfully. "I was hoping we'd meet again."

Calendul, a yonter who could rip my head off with ease, squawked and leaned down until our eyes were even. She didn't touch me, but a moment of connection passed between us. As she pulled away, I observed the dozens and dozens of yonters behind her, most standing tall as they watched the fae.

"How did you convince them to help?" Emmen asked,

eyeing the creatures. "They're the most resistant to my rule in Santoia."

Lexie shrugged. "One, I grew up with most of these birds and I call a lot of them friend, and two, they kind of want to save the world they live in. It really wasn't hard to convince them."

Calendul released that vibrational hum that had sent fear through me the last time. Today, it was a mere brush against my energy, remaining surface level.

Her weapons will not work against you any longer, Zahak said, satisfaction in his tone. *You're too strong now.*

His energy and mine were bonded, and with that I'd inherited his strength and longevity. Not that I wanted to think too hard on living for centuries, focusing instead on all the time we'd eventually have together—once this world was returned to its rightful leaders.

Lexie stepped closer, spreading her arms out on either side. "The yonters have agreed to help us learn how to counter the sonar weapon. As you're all aware, they have a powerful weapon of their own that works in a similar manner. Individually, it won't be strong enough, but when they bond together as a whole, it will be almost as destructive."

She had Zahak's focus now, and with that, there was a glimmer of hope inside that this would work. Hope and darkness, as he knew that for this to happen, he had to open his bond with his brothers.

Well, with one of them in particular.

Drager's hard gaze met mine, as if he could also hear our internal thoughts. Returning that stare with an equally fucked off one, I told him with my eyes that there was nothing between us. And I didn't have a single regret about the path my life had taken.

Zahak's warmth surrounded me once more and I sank into his energy, feeling myself calm.

He has no power against us, he told me. *All he has is envy for what he could have had, and never appreciated. I hope he learns from his actions, especially if he plans on finding his true mate, because from what I've learned, humans won't just take his shit. And they shouldn't.*

The Fallen Five had the personality, power, and looks to steamroll even the toughest of women, but I believed, based on absolutely nothing except instinct, that the women designed to be their mates would be harder to flatten.

Drager would do well to learn from his mistakes with me, and consider himself lucky that I hadn't been his mate to lose. Our getting together was a colossal fuckup, but I'd never be angry about it because it brought me to Zahak—to my future and true happiness. For that, I would tolerate Drager's presence in our lives.

Tolerate and nothing more.

That's my mate, Zahak said, wrapping his arms around me and hugging me tightly.

Ah, yes, my new favorite place to exist.

In absolute fucking bliss.

CHAPTER 32

MORGAN

The presence of nearly a hundred yonters had the fae on edge. Warriors held their weapons close to them, and as more groups arrived from around Risest, there was a tension in the air that told me one small spark and everything would go up in flames.

I really hope this works, I said to Zahak. *If you can learn how to counter the weapon, you'll be able to take your mother by surprise, and that's the opportunity we need to capture her.*

He nodded. *Either way, I'm taking her down. I will be stronger when connected to my brothers. She won't get the drop on me again.*

She'd had to continually bring in reinforcements to take him down last time, but it was the weapon that gave her a true advantage. If the Fallen couldn't counter it, they would lose, no matter their strength. When Zahak didn't comment on that thought, I knew I was right.

"Okay, the rest of you need to bring the new warriors up

to date," Florentine called loudly, as more fae arrived. "I've rerouted the portals so that they're spitting everyone out over in the far reaches of Green Hollow."

I hadn't seen the leader of this gorgeous little village in some time and was surprised by how pale and tired she looked. Her armored clothes were disheveled and dusty, and I really shouldn't be surprised—she'd been frontline in the last battle and probably hadn't slept for days. Still, it was odd to see her not completely put together.

"We're going to run out of room pretty quickly," she continued. "As the groups arrive, we need to get them moved away from the portals so the next lot don't crash into them. Eventually, we'll be pushed out of the protective barriers, allowing the infiltrators to track our growing army. We must plan for a battle at this moment." There were nods from those around us. "Okay," Florentine said with a wave of her hand, "let's leave the Fallen Five to deal with the yonters, and we'll organize the army. Follow me."

She turned to cross over the river, heading toward the section of forest where I'd found Astra. Warriors fell in behind her, multiple races from multiple lands already here, and plenty more on their way apparently.

I caught sight of a few familiar faces as they left, including Chaple the satyr, and Jords, the asshole lieutenant in Drager's military. They really were bringing in every abled-bodied fae to fight. As much as I worried for these warriors, at least I knew they would battle as part of the strongest army of Risest.

In almost no time, the clearing was empty of all except for the Fallen Five, Lexie, Astra, Leo, me, and about a hundred yonters. We pushed back toward the river to allow more of the birds to step into the open, their huge eyes locked on the nine of us. Only Leo appeared unconcerned, alternating between snoozing and headbutting Astra. He was bigger again, already the size of a full-grown panther.

Finding him was meant to be, Zahak said. *He is your match as a soul-creature, just as Astra is mine.*

Leo rumbled and pounced on Astra, showing a lot more grace and co-ordination. He was no longer a cub and had apparently moved into the young adult stage of a sabre. He rubbed up against my leg, and I leaned down to run my hands over his fur that wasn't quite as velvety either.

Sabres looked super soft, but there was a coarse layer across their coats, which helped them in water and protected them from attack. Leo's layer was finally growing in.

How long does it take them to reach full growth? I asked, wondering if Zahak knew. I assumed he found Astra as a full-grown sabre, but maybe she'd told him about her time as a cub. If she remembered.

It varies depending on their circumstances. At this rate of growth, he'll be bigger than Astra in another week or two. As a male, she said he should be quite a lot larger than her, and way more temperamental around those he doesn't trust.

Great, I'd have to lay down some rules with this little guy. Wrapping my arms around Leo, I gave him a hug and kissed his head. "Stay with Astra, okay," I whispered. "I don't want you hurt by the sonar weapon."

"I'm sending Astra to observe the warrior's arrival and report back if there are any signs of the disease, as we bring in more fae from across the lands," Zahak said, allowing everyone into this part of our conversation. "I'm hoping it was contained in the trench, since that's the only parts of Eastern Risest below the surface, but we can't take any risks. If we see any signs, we need to deal with it immediately before it takes out our entire army."

"Good idea, bro," Kellan said. "I really don't want to see any of you assholes with your bones on display. Fuck that."

"Another reason for us to hurry the fuck up," Emmen rumbled. Scales flittered across his golden arms before fading out again. "We keep giving Mother time to fuck this world up, and we're risking all of our fae in the process."

It was the truth. The crimson sky above reminded us that the energy of this land was out of whack, and we were running on borrowed time to save it all.

"Let's get started, then," Drager said, face creased in deeper lines as he focused.

Astra and Leo took off, the smaller sabre running at her side, and I watched them until they jumped the river and disappeared behind the houses. Zahak's energy caressed my mind. *They'll be fine. I'll keep in mental touch with Astra.*

Thank you. I hoped to communicate and bond with Leo as he got bigger, but for now we had other priorities.

Zahak exhaled a drawn-out breath, his mind growing darker. *I need to join my brothers now. Stay in my mind, la moyar.*

I'm not going anywhere. I didn't even know how to go anywhere with our essences so intermingled. I enjoyed his warmth wrapped around my energy though, and while he'd assured me that we'd eventually be able to separate ourselves mentally, for now our closeness was comforting.

Zahak released his physical hold on me and crossed to stand with the other four shifters. Lexie moved to my side, and the yonters remained where they were, appearing as ancient and stable as the trees behind them.

"I'll do my best to protect you from the yonters' blast," she told me, reaching out and capturing my hand. The moment she did, she let out a shocked gasp and jumped about three feet in the air. "Holy banana balls, Morgs. You're —" She shook her head. "You're really frogging powerful."

My energy calmed at the familiarity of Lexie's fake curse words. "Maybe I'll have to protect you from the yonters' blast," I teased.

Lexie continued to shake her head, wide eyes locked on me. "I mean, you've been glowy for a while now, but it's really obvious today. You and Zahak are like *bonded* bonded now," she breathed. "What in the worlds...? Do you feel like Superwoman or something?"

I hadn't had a chance to really test out my new abilities, but there was no denying the strength coursing through my body. I was stronger. More comfortable in my own skin. My energy burned hotter as the swirl in my gut grew, changing my essence.

"I feel different," I admitted, and it didn't escape my notice that we had the attention of the five shifters; Lexie's gasp before had been loud. Zahak's smile was soft as he lingered in my mind, feeling my emotions.

"Zahak and I have full mental communication now," I told her, knowing they could all hear. "Our energies have mingled, and I'm stronger. I should live as long as he does and have strength against illnesses or injury that would normally kill a human."

Lexie's joy burst from her as rapidly as shock had. She threw her arms around me, burying her face against my neck, sniffles following. She was crying, which had my eyes welling up as well. "I don't have to lose you," she said, words muffled against my skin. "I have feared that for so long but told myself it was better to have loved you even for a short eighty years than to never have known you."

Holding on tightly, I wondered how I could feel so happy and content when we were still in so much danger. All the more reason for us to get our ducks in a row and make sure we had the upper hand.

Lexie must have had the same thought, pulling away a second later to wipe her eyes. Determination creased her features as she turned to Cal. "Okay, you five need to find harmony, and start your vibrational weapon."

"Turn away from the main town," Emmen said, addressing the yonters. "We don't want to injure any fae that get in the way."

As a single unit, the yonters shifted their position to face the forest. The Fallen Five moved together, crossing into the trees to reach the front of the flock. Lexie and I remained where we were, at the back, away from the direct blast of the weapon.

It didn't matter how far away Zahak traveled, his mind was as close to mine as when he stood at my side.

Well, hello, little human.

I jumped.

That was not Zahak's voice, but it was familiar: Kellan.

A beat later I heard, *Fucking hell, this mate thing is intense. Zahak is about to kill us all for just lingering near her mind. But also I like it in here.* That was Tylan, and as I pushed further into our bond, I found myself drifting between the brothers. Holy odd sensation.

A gentle shove from Zahak sent me back in my head, with his warmth surrounding me.

Mine, he grumbled. *I'm not sharing her.*

You're a greedy bastard, you know that, Kellan whined. *We don't have our own mates yet, and it's downright rude of you to keep her all to yourself.*

I could still hear their conversation, but I wasn't directly in any of their minds now, after my possessive mate had laid down the law.

He's not too bad at shari— Drager started, and I snapped.

Shut the fuck up, immediately. You were an annoyance and a distraction. Don't place more importance on it than it was.

The silence that followed was so loud it felt like screaming, and then four of the five cracked up as my head filled with a range of rumbly laughter. *Fucking gold. You deserve ever bit of her ire, brother.* I couldn't even tell which one of them said that to Drager, I just knew it wasn't Zahak.

Lexie's touch on my arm had me jumping again, and I pulled myself out of the Fallen Five's mental connection. "You okay?" she asked.

I nodded. "Oh yeah, there's just a few more voices than I'm used to in my head."

It was lucky that Zahak could shut off his brotherly connections when we were finished here, so that I wasn't permanently in my own personal harem of sexy shifters. As great as that sounded in books, my heart belonged to one, along with my soul. Not to mention that I was already waddle-walking this morning. I doubted I could take another four massive co—

Mine, Zahak repeated, and this time it was deeper and rumblier.

Always.

I was thankful when their focus shifted away from our bond and into their brotherly bond.

The other galators don't appear to have mental connections like this, Drager told them. *This is only between royals and those born in the same bloodline. It's especially strong for pod brothers.*

Which was Zahak and Drager. I hadn't known exactly what that meant, until I saw some images from Zahak. There was an egg looking shape, and flowing lava field, and…

Holy fuck. Was I going to have to lay eggs to have dragon babies?

Zahak's energy was soothing. *I'll explain it all later, sweet-heart. Nothing for you to worry about now.*

The brothers cut off the thoughts of eggs and pods, and I shoved those worries deep down inside. No matter the changes my energy and body were going through, my brain remained human, and it would take time for me to wrap my head around the more foreign aspects of being mated to an alien-dragon-shifter.

Well, if we won this war, it seemed I'd have all the time I needed. If we didn't, I'd be dead and it wouldn't matter.

Either way, we'd find out soon enough.

CHAPTER 33

ZAHAK

It had been decades since the five of us had joined together in a way where our minds were open, energy and thoughts free to flow between us. When we first landed in Risest, our bond was as easy as breathing, but today there was an adjustment period.

Maybe it was that Morgan was part of the connection now, through me, and I didn't appreciate all of them having access to her mind. I was a greedy bastard and wanted to keep her all to myself.

Completely understandable, brother, Emmen said, surprisingly calm. *She's… different to what I expected. She makes you different, but in a way that feels right. I'm curious now about the rest of our mates.*

Me fucking too! Kellan exclaimed. *I never thought I'd see the day, but I'm ready for some of that softer energy in my soul.*

They had no fucking idea. They'd felt tendrils through me but wouldn't understand until they experienced the bliss of their mate's energy infusing with theirs, and changing everything.

Of course, there was always one grumpy fuck in the equation. *The sooner we get this over with, the better,* Drager bit out. *I remember now why we stopped communicating this way in the first place.*

He remembered because it had been his idea. He'd wanted to plot and plan for more territory and he didn't want the rest of us to know what an untrustworthy, power-hungry shit he was. Like we hadn't already figured it out in the previous decades we'd been bonded.

Okay, well, let's do it, then, Tylan said, his expression calm. *The yonters are waiting for our signal to attempt to blast us, so give us this plan to counter them.*

In the spirit of bonding, we kept our conversation internal now.

We have to use our dragon energy, Emmen said. *When Morgan mentioned that it would take another sonar weapon to blast back, I was reminded that we have a rumble, which works in a similar manner to soundwaves. We never use it, because it requires all of us to work together.*

Should we be in a half-shift? I asked. The rumble was tied to our dragons. *Or full shift?*

Let's start with half, Tylan suggested. *See if it's strong enough. We have access to a lot of our dragon energy in half-shift, and it'll be much easier to grab Mother if we have opposable thumbs.*

He wasn't wrong.

Kellan pulled his dragon forward first, and with our connection open, that energy brought on all our hybrid forms. We grew larger, and scales covered our skins. The glow of our change filled the clearing briefly, and I felt Morgan's awe as she followed through the bond.

You can watch our shift now, I told her, attempting to keep my brothers out of our conversation.

Oh, yeah, Kellan hooted, *You can watch me shift any day, little human.*

I wanted to tear that nickname out of his mouth, but since I was reasonably fond of my brothers—three of them anyway—I refrained. *Little human* was a disgraceful name for someone as precious as Morgan, so they could have it.

I love you, she whispered, seemingly uncaring that the others could hear her.

That shut all those fuckers right up.

I love you too, la moyar.

I felt the desire then, from my brothers. Not for my mate, but to find their own. Morgan's presence had unlocked a need, and it would beat like a drum against their souls until they figured out who was wandering around in the human world, unprotected, and without her true mate.

Fear tasted bitter in our bond, and I understood it. To know that Morgan had been on Earth, vulnerable, and under the care of parents who didn't treat her as the valuable and precious human she was, had me raging. The only reason I wasn't tearing that fucking world apart was that she was here now, and I no longer had to trust her safety to anyone except myself.

Focus! Drager snapped, before he calmed himself, probably sensing I was about to remind him who he was talking to. *I mean, we need to get this done before Mother figures out our plan. Let's practice the dragon rumble together.*

Pushing my personal feelings aside, I focused on the task at hand. The five of us formed a line and faced the flock of yonters. These birds rarely congregated in such large groups, and it was fascinating to see them here today.

In our hybrid form, our hearts grew larger as well, with

extra side chambers of hollows and dips, where energy and blood flowed. It was from here that we could draw up flames, and it was also in these side chambers that we could send out a vibrational attack to disorientate and physically shoot back our prey.

The vibrations rattled my chest, and I built them inside for far longer than I would normally have. The other four did the same, and soon we found a level of connection which had our rumble moving as one frequency.

"Now," I heard Lexie shout to the yonters, sensing our energy.

We held the rumble inside, allowing its slow build. I'd had no idea it could feel like this, and it was soon clear that in battle we needed to build until we were at bursting point.

The yonters' humming grew louder and stronger as the ground trembled beneath my boots. They were starting slow, but soon found a singular resonance—a harmony—which they directed at us.

Having felt the effects of that sonar crystal not that long ago, my beast attempted to push free the moment the vibrations hit us, but I held the shift at bay.

"More intense!" Lexie shouted again. "Give them everything you've got."

Almost immediately the pressure on our bodies increased, but in our hybrid form we were already splicing and dicing our essence, which kept us stabilized.

The half-shifted form is the form we must face them in, I told the others. *Our cells are already split, so there's less impact.*

Yes, they called back.

It's amazing, Tylan added.

The rumble inside our bond grew stronger. It was time now to see if it countered the yonters' attack. We started slowly, a trickle leaving our bodies. *We'll go faster against,*

Mother, Emmen said. *But this will be a good indicator if it's going to work at all.*

The vibrations increased again, and the ground was shaking so intensely that leaves and twigs fell from the trees around us.

The yonters' energy was visible in the air, which was where I focused on sending our rumble. My brothers followed my lead, the waves of our energy set to crash into theirs.

This will work, Morgan said, sounding confident. *I can feel it.*

We all felt it, and when our rumble slammed against the yonters' weapon, there was an immediate relief on my body. The energy trying to tear my cells apart ceased, and we were able to move forward when previously we'd been stuck in place.

Our rumble was stronger than the yonters and soon pushed them back, so we shut it off immediately. The aim here wasn't to hurt them; it was to make sure our rumble would work on that style of weapon, and now we knew it could.

Mother will never see it coming, Tylan said with confidence. *She thinks that the five of us are separated from each other, enemies, and the fact that Drager turned his back on us only helped reiterate the distance between us. Our bond is her downfall, and I don't know how or why, but having Morgan as part of this already makes our connection stronger.*

I hated to admit it, because I didn't want her skipping around in their minds as she unintentionally did before, but Tylan was right. Her softer strength helped us cement the frazzled edges of our bond. Maybe, if the others found their mates, our connection would be near unstoppable.

I think that's why she decided to invade now, Drager said

suddenly. *It's Morgan. Us finding our mates does strengthen us, and for the first time there was a possible candidate in Risest. I feel like she's been keeping an eye on us for years, and when we were no threat she let us go. But with our mates at our sides, we will be a formidable power.*

Drager had finally tapped into our theory that Morgan's arrival and the timing of the invasion were too close to be a coincidence. My brother, for all his flaws and faults, did have one of the more strategic and analytical minds for battle. Not just battle, but conquering other lands, and taking them for his own. He knew how Mother thought because he thought the same way.

Definitely a plausible explanation, Tylan added. *Except for the part where we are a threat. In what way could we have ever been a threat to a world and people we couldn't remember.*

I thought about how my fractured memories were swirling around, and how Morgan's energy cemented some of those thoughts. Helped me remember. *Maybe if we find all our mates, our memories will no longer be locked away,* I suggested.

A double whammy to Mother, who clearly didn't want us stronger, mated, or with our memories.

I really hope she dies today, Kellan growled, his sunny personality fading under his rage. *I want her dead, and I don't care how it happens or who does it.*

Me too, little brother. Me too. Even though we couldn't kill her before she acted as bait, after that was done… well, who knew what would happen.

Lexie and Morgan wandered through the yonters to reach us. The five of us released our connection and returned to our normal bipedal forms. Once my brothers were out of my mind, I pulled Morgan's energy all the way back in so that we were once again mingling as one.

I like that hybrid form, she told me with a small smirk. *I like it a lot.*

Her mind went to last night and the way my hybrid form had fucked her hard on the ground. *Mate*, I warned her. Now was not the time, because there was only a sliver of control stopping me from stealing her away and keeping her in my cave.

Her thoughts sobered a touch. *I need you to promise that you're not going to die on me, Z. I won't survive it.*

Truthfully, I had no idea if she would literally survive it or not. There were my instincts about the bond, and then there was facts, and I didn't have the second to back up the first. *I'm very hard to kill, sweetheart*, I reassured her. *Don't worry about it, we've got this.*

As long as Drager doesn't betray you again, she shot back.

He wouldn't dare.

Connected as we'd been, he'd never have the chance to even think about it before the rest of us would know. Drager wasn't my worry. My concern was the unknown still. Was there a threat stronger than Mother that had been wiped from our memories when we were cast from Xalifer?

"Okay, so I'm guessing it worked as expected?" Lexie chimed in. "Are we ready to move on to the next part in this plan?"

We were more than ready. I was done with these galators infiltrating our world, and it was time to send them back to their own. Once and for all.

CHAPTER 34

MORGAN

As the yonters left Green Hollow with all our thanks, Cal lingered a moment longer, touching her beak and wing to Lexie's shoulder. To my surprise, she did the same to me, before she turned and rejoined the flock. I felt a real sense of pride and accomplishment in having her as a friend, akin to how I felt about Astra and Leo.

I didn't understand it, since I'd never considered myself as someone with an affinity for animals, but there was no denying the evidence. My life was richer having these creatures in it, and I wondered how I'd been so satisfied with my previous *empty* world.

Thank the gods for Lexie, or I wouldn't be the mate Zahak had now.

I'd have been useless.

You're perfect for me, Morgan. In all the phases of your life. Your strength is innate and can be owed to no one except yourself. I'm honored to have you as a mate.

Zahak was the cheer squad I could really get used to having in my life.

"The yonters will remain close," Lexie told everyone, and I stopped worrying about the *what ifs and maybes* of my existence. "Just in case we need their weapons again. They're also going to alert us to any galators approaching. A pre-warning system."

That made me feel better and worse, as the memory of Mika sprang to my mind. I appreciated every ally we had in this war, but I also feared who we would lose before this was all over.

"If we want to have a chance at taking out Mother," Drager started, "we need to get moving. Find a location and draw her to us. She won't come alone, and she won't even be the first to approach, so we need to prepare ourselves for a battle."

"What if one of us does get captured," Tylan said suddenly. "I don't know about you four, but the moment her goons captured me and Lex, she was there right after."

"It was the same for me," Emmen confirmed. "But was it just a way for her to reacquaint herself with her sons before throwing us into prison?"

Their eyes all turned to Drager. "As the only one of us who didn't get thrown into prison," Tylan said dryly, "what was your first meeting with her like?"

Drager had the sense to look uncomfortable. "I was captured, and she appeared about three minutes later. It was so fast that she either knows how to instantly transport where she wants to go, or she waits in the wings while others do her dirty work."

"That one," I said without hesitation. "She just screams of the type."

He shot me a long glance, before tearing his gaze away,

and I was relieved that there wasn't the slightest surge in my body for Drager. No twist of my energy. No ache in my chest… or lower. Nothing. Whatever had been connecting us was gone now, and I was sure that the reason was Zahak. He'd been the connection all along.

"She came right up to my face as she examined me, and then she said, *You're the son I find most of myself in.*" Drager shuddered, as if trying to shake off the feelings that had resulted from that. "She ran her hand over my chest," he continued, "and I could feel her energy sinking into my own. It was… disturbing."

Everyone looked disgusted now, and I really hoped that there was no rapey stuff about to be revealed from momma dragon. Creepy bitch.

"She told me that all but Zahak had been captured and that I'd soon be joining them. As she went to leave, I said to her, *You won't take Zahak without my help*, and that stopped her. She turned back, and I quickly added. *I'll help you, but in exchange I want the human he has with him. She might be his mate, but I found her first.*"

And there he went, admitting that all along he knew I wasn't his damn mate. A part of me was sad that he hadn't been more roughed up during his capture.

"She stared at me for a long time," he went on, "then smiled this really fucked-up smile. All smug and satisfied. She agreed with my plan, and I promise, all along I just wanted to remain free so I could figure out how to get you all out of her clutches. Mother stayed nearby until Zahak contacted me, and when we found out where he was heading we laid a trap. Mother used another energy charm, one different to the sonar weapon, and laced the air with enough mating energy that it was a mini version of the fertility ritual. I told her that would throw Z off his game and give us a chance to take him by surprise." Drager shrugged. "It worked as expected, and I freed you as expected, so we're even, right?"

Zahak's rumble was the most animalistic sound I'd heard in his human-ish form. "Not even fucking close, brother. We'll never be even for what you've done. But I can at least work with you on this and not need to kill you every time you open your mouth, so there's that."

Drager shrugged once more. "I'll take it."

Tylan interrupted the tension by bringing us back to his original point. "Okay, so that very fucking long explanation confirms that Mother hangs on the edges, so if one of us was to be captured again, the rest of us can wait in the wings and step out to take her down."

"What if the orders are to kill you now?" I suggested, panicked at any of them being used for bait. I could also feel that Zahak was about to volunteer, as the strongest of the five.

"We'll remain in our bond," Emmen said, lowering his voice in what he no doubt hoped was a reassuring manner. "Strengthening all of us."

I nodded, still unsure about this. "Okay, and how will the rest of you remain undetected. Even if these galators are weaker than you guys, they're still freaking strong. They're going to sense you there, waiting on the periphery, right?"

"Oh, I think I can help with that," Lexie piped up. "I'll create a pocket of energy for the others to hide within. Like a giant version of the energy pocket I use to keep my weapons."

"You won't be able to weave one large enough to house four of us," Zahak said. In our connection, it was clear that he thought her idea was solid, but he had to be practical. "You can't just keep us invisible. You have to contain our energy as well, and that would take—"

"My entire family." That shut him up, and Lexie nodded a few times, as if working it out in her mind. "Yes. Yes, that's it. They're all here, and they can help me knit the pocket together. It will probably take us the rest of the day though. Can we hold out that long?"

Zahak and Emmen exchanged a look, and then Emmen let out a harsh breath. "Not really, but I think this is our best option, and it's worth waiting longer to get it right."

I agreed. The stronger and more organized their plan was, the less chance any of them would get hurt. Or worse.

Lexie straightened, gave me a quick hug, and turned to leave. "We'll work as fast as we can," she called over her shoulder. "Rest up, we might be able to leave this evening if all goes according to plan." She disappeared a few seconds later and I tried not to panic at her being out there without me.

Not that I was much use in defending us, but I had a very badass mate who would have our backs, and that was a nice little weapon.

You think I'm a weapon, la moyar? Zahak's voice was lazy, drawling, but there was a spark of arousal in his tone as well.

Maybe. Definitely.

He laughed then, having heard both thoughts. *You can use me...* He paused. *...as a weapon whenever you need, mate. I'm at your disposal.*

A shiver traced down my spine and I swallowed my moan. We weren't in the company for outward signs of arousal—I'd never hear the end of it. Of course, Zahak chose that moment to bring forth the memory of my thighs wrapped around his face this morning.

Fucking hell. A harsh breath escaped, and any hope of hiding my arousal from the others was dashed when his brothers looked my way.

"Clearly we know how you two plan on resting," Kellan said with a laugh, and then a groan, before he ran his hand through his blond hair. "Fucking hell. I'm jealous. I'm going to jerk off now, thanks very much."

He started to leave, only pausing when Emmen yelled, "Don't go too fucking far. We need to be ready to leave at any given moment."

Kellan lifted a hand but didn't turn back, and then he too was gone from the forest.

I was just about to ask Tylan what he planned on doing for the next few hours, but I didn't even get the first word out before Zahak wrapped his huge hands around my hips, lifted me up, and threw me over his shoulder.

The quick movement took me completely by surprise, and I didn't manage to utter a single word until we were already back in the village, hopping over the river, and heading for Florentine's house. At this point we'd probably overstayed our welcome there, but so far she hadn't returned or commented, so hopefully she was expecting our continued use.

"Your mind is fascinating," Zahak said conversationally, as he ducked down and brought us in through the front door. "It's refreshing."

I huffed. "You can't just haul me around like a sack of potatoes," I said.

His laughter was in my mind once more. "Sure, sweetheart."

"You're not going to stop, are you?"

More laughter. "Never."

As his hands flexed against my thighs, I decided that I wasn't *that* mad about it. Having a mate who wanted me like this, and wasn't afraid to show others his need, was a bonus I never expected. Zahak was private, I'd seen that from the first time I learned about the scary god of the Isle of Denille. He might not want to share me, but he never hid how he felt for me.

He loved me, and he showed everyone that.

Yep, a really unexpected bonus. They were adding up fast, and even though I'd only ever been fluent in girl and romantasy math, I had some new numbers to enjoy.

It turned out that *mate math* was just as good as the other two.

CHAPTER 35

MORGAN

We didn't get a full day before the Lightsbringers were done forming a pocket of energy large and strong enough to hopefully hide the Fallen Five. Well, four of them at least.

Zahak made very good use of our time, and if I wasn't woken from every nap with an orgasm via his mouth from now on, I was rioting. Pleasure dragging me from sleep was the way I hoped to spend the rest of my life.

"Come on, mate," he rumbled, his eyes darkening. "Or I'll never leave this bed, and there are worlds to be saved and destroyed."

I could see in his mind that he was ready to blast Xalifer into a million pieces. He didn't care that it was his home planet, to him it was an abomination, stealing resources and destroying other worlds for energy, and he wanted no part in it.

When we stepped out of Florentine's house, noise

slammed into me, and I almost jumped at the sudden influx of stimuli after spending most of the day secluded away. If the noise they made as they trained and prepared was any indication, the number of warriors here had to be ten times what it was this morning.

"I hope this plan works," I murmured, looking around at all who had come to fight with their gods.

"It will." Zahak was confident, and it reminded me of an epic fantasy book I'd read a few years ago. It had this massive end of series battle, and just as they were preparing to head in, knowing that many of them would die that day, one of the protagonists said *If you go into battle without confidence, you've already lost. Never manifest your own defeat.*

Zahak knew the fantasy book way.

As we walked along the bank of the river, toward the meeting place, fae moved respectfully out of our way. Many of them bowed in greeting for Zahak, and to my utter fucking shock, me as well.

They know your worth and importance.

His words sent shivers down my spine, because I'd never been able to see my own worth. I knew most of this respect was due to my bond with Zahak, but I'd take it for now. Eventually I'd prove that I had my own strength.

Back in the clearing, Emmen, Kellan, and Tylan had already arrived, but there was no sign of Drager and Lexie. "Drager do a runner?" I said wryly. He still wasn't my favorite dragon. He only made top five because the galators didn't even count.

Zahak laughed darkly. "He's on his way. He got delayed with *someone.*"

His tone indicated that *someone* was most definitely female, and I waited for feelings about that to arise. But there were none. I honestly didn't care. If anything, I was glad that another kept him occupied so he didn't keep shooting lingering stares my way.

"Still hasn't learned his lesson about his true mate, I see," Tylan noted, leaning back against an ancient tree that had to stand two hundred feet in the air. The lowest branches were so far above, I almost couldn't see them.

Zahak regarded his brother closely. "You plan on remaining celibate until you find your mate?"

I knew from memories I'd seen, and what he'd chosen to share, that Zahak hadn't been with another fae in a very long time. Near a hundred years, and before that it had been only on rare occasions. He remained alone and in his cave during the fertility rituals and hadn't actively sought pleasure because it always felt empty to him.

Clearly Tylan was coming to the same conclusion. "Now that I see what you two have," he said softly, "I'd never risk my mate's happiness. I want her to know that the moment I realized that this was the true path for us, I stopped all the bullshit and gave her my full focus and respect." He shrugged as he ran a hand over his beard. "My determination to win this war has increased tenfold. I'm going to find my mate and the same happiness I see in Zahak."

Even Emmen nodded, looking less surly than usual. "It's true. Not even when we were younger and carefree was Zahak relaxed and calm. His soul was restless, and now it's not. Simple as that."

"Will you search for your mate as well?" Zahak asked him.

Emmen took a moment to answer. "I'm not sure. I don't know if this is the path for me, and I don't want to focus on anything except the next steps in our plan. We might all be planning for futures we don't even have."

Zahak and Tylan rumbled at the same time. "Never go

into battle expecting defeat," Zahak said, repeating my thoughts from earlier. "We're stronger than them, especially if we stick together. If we weren't a threat, Mother wouldn't have focused so much on taking us ou—"

His words were cut off by a screech that rose up from the forests beyond the Green Hollow borders. Loud and intense, it had my ears ringing, as shouts rang out from the warriors.

"That's the yonters," Kellan said quickly, glancing around. "The early warning system."

In Zahak's mind everything slowed down and he fell into warrior mode. "They've found us," he said shortly, and in the same instant I felt the snapping connection of the five brothers lock into place. It was faster than last time, and there was less dominance in the structure of their power.

I'm on my way, Drager said through the bond, and I felt his urgency as he hurried. He had Lexie with him, and for a moment I wondered if she was *the one* he was with, before I realized the impossibility of that. One, Lexie would never do that to me, even though I seriously didn't care. And two, she'd been with her family weaving that pocket all day.

Through Drager's eyes she looked tired and pale, as if she'd been drained of energy and was forcing herself to keep moving.

Meet near the river, Zahak said, mentally sending a location to Drager.

He grabbed my hand and we moved quickly, back into the throngs of fae who were assembling and preparing for battle. They held weapons, swords and crossbows most prominently.

"Listen up," Emmen shouted as we passed through the groups. "If they're in dragon form, under their wings is the most vulnerable area to hit them. We're fairly armored everywhere else. The eyes are another good spot to aim for. If they're in human form, never take them on alone. They're faster and stronger, so don't let them get their hands on you. Work in teams."

He repeated this message as we moved through the crowds, and most of the fae warriors bowed and saluted with a hand tapped on their armored chests.

We found Drager and Lexie two minutes later as they reached the far side of the river. This was the widest part, and not where anyone usually crossed, but they both leapt over with ease. I'd have landed right in the center, for sure.

Despite the tension within and around us, Zahak's amusement at my thoughts still filtered through. His brothers didn't notice, already gathering closer to map out their plan.

"Do you have the pocket ready?" Emmen asked Lexie.

She nodded. "Yes, we weaved it as large and strong as we could. Hopefully it will contain your energy. No one really knows the full strength of the five of you together, so it's all just hopes and dreams at this point."

The yonters' calls shut off dramatically, and there was a beat of silence before the noise within this hollow rose up. "They're inside," Drager bit out. "Who is going to be the one used at bait?"

"It should be two," I said suddenly, and the brothers all looked at me. They could have read my plan internally, since we were all connected, but they respectfully remained out of my mind. "I feel like just one of you seems an obvious trap, and your mom might remain hidden away. There's also more chance of Lexie's pocket holding three of your energies rather than four, and I don't really want any of you to face the galators alone, you know."

Tylan reached out and threw his arm around me, hugging me close, even as he ignored Zahak's rumbles. "She likes us, guys. She really likes us."

Shaking my head, I attempted to shove him away, but he was too strong to budge. Zahak reached out as well, but Tylan scampered off at that point. He wasn't messing with his big brother.

"It should be Zahak and me, then," Drager said, focusing on the plan once more. "We're the oldest and strongest."

"Debatable," Emmen muttered, but didn't argue further.

"I agree," Zahak said, and I wasn't surprised. Despite their feud and differences, he was protective of his brothers, and would not recover if anything happened to them.

I'll make an exception for Drager, he said bluntly.

Drager just snorted, and to my surprise all I felt was amusement from him. He hadn't taken offense to Zahak's jibe, and I had to assume that meant they were getting back to normal brotherly interactions, versus murderous ones.

"They're here," a shout rang out, and immediately the sound of weapons clashing rang out through the town. We were near the back, with hundreds of fae warriors standing between us and the galators.

"Let's get this plan in motion," Lexie said. She wiggled her hands around in front of her, playing with what looked like thin air, but at the same time she was dragging it.

"To make it large enough, it's heavy," she said, looking flustered. "You'll have to attach them to your armored plates —" She gestured to Zahak and Drager. "—to keep your hands free while you take your brothers."

The shifters nodded, seemingly unconcerned as the cacophony of noise increased around us. I glanced along the river to see what was happening, and by the time I looked back, Tylan, Emmen, and Kellan were gone.

I still felt their energy through the connected bond, but it was muted.

"Our connection isn't as strong with them in the pocket," Drager said to Lexie. "But it will have to do."

She nodded. "Yeah, unfortunately there's nothing that can be done to fix the thickness of the pocket, because once again, you guys are too frogging powerful to be contained in anything less."

Drager's eye twitched at her use of non-cursey words, but he didn't comment on it. "We should head out to the edges of the forest," he said to Zahak. "She'll be waiting on the fringes, hoping to draw us out."

Lexie had her swords in her hand in the next instant. "I'm going to fight on the frontline. I hope you catch her."

My gut roiled, and I fought my instinct to reach out and capture her so she couldn't leave. Lexie was my family, my best friend, and my fear at her getting hurt… or worse… was almost debilitating. She noticed my panic, and paused to double back and hug me, sword held in one hand while she used the other to wrap me up tight. "I wouldn't feel right leaving the warriors to fight without me," she whispered near my ear. "But I promise to come back. I'm not that easy to kill."

"Astra and Leo are out there," Zahak said, listening in. "Find them and stick together. They'll be great assets. Astra knows my weaknesses well."

Lexie eyeballed him for a beat, and then nodded. "Keep her safe," she said, voice lowering. "Or else."

With that open-ended threat, she blew me one last kiss, then took off into the crowds streaming toward the main fight. Leaving us with hopes and a plan that just might work.

CHAPTER 36

MORGAN

"**I** want you in the pocket." Zahak drew my attention away from the crowds, and I blinked at him, wondering if I'd misheard.

"Sorry, what?"

"In the pocket with the other three," he said forcibly. "You are important, and you are vulnerable in this situation. I won't be able to fight if I'm focused on you and not on the plan."

I wanted to huff and refuse, because it felt wrong to not be at his side, but I couldn't deny that I was vulnerable and near useless in a fight. As a human unskilled with weapons, I'd only get myself killed.

Not a fucking chance.

Zahak's growl was feral, and I had to pat his arm and remind him that I was perfectly fine.

"Okay," I agreed. "I'll remain in the pocket. You're going to have to show me how to get in there. I can't see it."

"None of us can," Drager replied with an eye roll. "That's the whole fucking point of it."

I flipped him off. With a smile of course.

His eyes darkened. I could tell I was annoying him.

Life mission accomplished.

Ignoring us, Zahak reached behind him until he found what he was looking for. Dragging *nothing* forward, he indicated I should move between his parting hands. "Step in," he said, and I ducked under his arms and moved through the gap of his arms. As I stepped forward, a tingling sensation brushed my cheeks, and by the time I blinked again I was inside. Which I only knew because three shifters were in there, watching me with amusement.

"You'll get used to it, little human," Emmen said, and I could have sworn a smile graced his face, before it vanished just as quickly.

"I highly, highly doubt it," I said, shaking off the odd sensation of walking into a pocket. Inside was nothing but white. It looked the way I imagined the inside of a hot air ballon would, as the epitome of sensory deprivation.

A beat later, the pocket jerked forward, and I would have fallen if Tylan hadn't caught my arm to keep my steady. The sensation of moving this way was beyond weird, and as we floated along, my stomach swirled, and I really hoped I wasn't about to get motion sickness.

Close your eyes, sweetheart.

Zahak's voice washed through my mind, and everything calmed. I didn't even have to close my eyes as his energy centered me. It was quite possible that a good portion of my initial disorientation had been from our muted bond. Nothing could sever our bond now, outside of death of course, but this pocket muted the connection. He'd found a way to push through when I needed him though, and holding on to his energy, I stopped trying to control the movement, trusting they were taking us where we needed to go.

———

ZAHAK

The Lightsbringers had weaved such a strong, complete energy pocket that for the first time since we cemented the bond, there was a muted feel to our connection. The second Morgan stepped inside, I wanted to tear it open and retrieve my mate.

"Come on, she's safe in there. We have a fucking job to do."

Drager, tapping into his death wish again, snarled at me as he moved to jump across the river. I had to follow closely, because the pocket was connected to both of us, and there wasn't a damn chance I was letting him drag me along as well.

It took some maneuvering for us to get over with the pocket, but we managed it quite easily in the end. As frustrating as it was, and even wanting to rip his fucking spine out through his mouth, there was no denying that Drager and I made a good team. We always had.

Morgan's unease reached me a beat later, as we ran through the village, the pocket streaming behind us. The warrior clans got out of our way to make it easier, but there was no way my brothers and Morgan weren't getting thrown around in there.

Sending calming energy toward Morgan, I was relieved that our connection remained solid enough to share power. Tylan had grabbed her before she fell as well, and I was relieved that she hadn't hurt herself.

Near the barrier of Green Hollow, the galators were lined up in both dragon and bipedal forms, attacking in groups. The fae were heeding our advice and not engaging them alone. Bodies already scattered the ground, but many of them were galators. The warriors had learned a lot from previous fights, and we had the numbers over them at the moment.

When we stepped out into the open, we drew the attention of a large group of galators. "There's got to be fifty of those fuckers," Drager snarled, staring across the long line. "The largest number she's sent so far."

"She sent enough that we'd be forced to react," I said shortly. "I think we should leave the barrier and step out into the open."

Drager didn't argue, and through our bond I felt his agreement that this was the right path. We were strong with our fae warriors beside us, and she'd never appear in those circumstances. It would only be when we were at the disadvantage.

As we closed in on the border of the hollow, the galators brought out their sonar crystals to blast the fae, and I braced for what might happen. As soon as they released the initial blast, the Lightsbringers, Goldenseels, and Turnchartens, the strongest warrior clans, hauled up huge silver shields they'd had stored in their own pockets of energy. The metal wasn't as intricately carved as it would normally be for a warrior clan, but it did the job they needed.

The sonar soundwaves slammed against their shields, reducing the crystals power to almost nothing. Just like that, the fighting field leveled out, and the galators were backpedaling to figure out their next move.

"That's why Lexie was a little later getting back," Drager said as we watched on. "She was ensuring they finalized these shields, with the help of a few yonters."

Our fae were more than holding their own, so we were able to step from the protective barriers of their land and out into the open. As if they'd known our plan as well, the moment we were in the clear, a dozen galators emerged from the trees.

"Ready, brother?" Drager said, smiling as excitement at finally getting to fight lit up inside him.

"Fuck yes," I snarled.

These bastards would die today. Every single one of them.

We struck first. I had already torn out two throats by the time the galators blinked. My hands shifted between normal and claws seamlessly. Since I'd rip through them easier in my hybrid form, I let that energy free, until I was filled with the dragon's strength.

Morgan stayed with me the entire time, never averting her focus, even as I raged. My mind turned darker, and I let myself go into the violence. The energy pocket kept Drager and I close, but that only helped us fight together.

You have to lose, remember?

Kellan's drawling reminder filtered into our heads, scratchy and faint. Another dozen galators appeared behind the first group, who were all dead. Resigned to the plan, I released my hold on my energy and hybrid form, returning to my weaker version. Weaker, but never weak.

"We have to go down," Drager muttered, and my lips curled involuntarily at the thought. But he was fucking right. If we wanted to capture Mother, we needed her to think she had us.

The second group of galators had energy crystals with them, and as we pretended to leap forward in an attack, they opened the boxes to blast us with soundwaves.

The sensation triggered me back to the cells, and even with the strength of our brotherly bond, it was strong enough to knock me to my knees. Drager landed heavily behind me, both of us determined to endure for as long as it took for Mother to appear.

The pain from the energy shattering our cells was intense, and I reserved most of my focus for blocking Morgan from the effects. She remained strong in our connection, sending me her support.

I was undeserving of her, but I sure as fuck wasn't letting her go.

I wasn't that altruistic. Not even if it was for her own good.

"How much fucking longer?" Drager grit out, scales covering his body.

He hadn't experienced this before, and therefore had no real concept of how bad it could get. I'd been blasted for hours and as a result, my body and cells were adapted to anticipate and reject fractions of the weapon's destructive power.

I had the sense that if I spent enough time being blasted, I'd figure out how to fully adapt and block all on my own.

Already trying to get rid of us, Tylan said, voice barely audible.

Zahak, you have to go down. That was Emmen, who had somehow figured out that I was the reason we were still being blasted and no sign of Mother.

Releasing my strength, I gave them what they wanted and let the weapon shift me into that bastardized version of my hybrid form. Scales covered me, my eyesight merged with the dragon, and heat built in my chest.

Submitting to this weapon went against every instinct I had, especially when my mate was close, but we had one chance to do this, and I couldn't fuck it up.

More galators arrived, and two more sonar weapons were

revealed. This time, when the blasts hit, they were too strong for me to fight, and I was no longer pretending to submit.

Build our rumble, brothers, Drager called. *We must be ready to take them down.*

As we were slammed against the ground, the very bitch we'd been waiting for stepped out of the trees. Dressed in a white cloak, she all but glided across the ground over to us, head held high as she looked down on us, the weapon not affecting her in any way.

Her cloak, I said through our bond. *It blocks the energy somehow.*

I hadn't paid attention to it last time, but she'd worn a cloak then too.

"Hello, my sons," she drawled, her words vibrating with power. "I've been most displeased since you all broke out and left me." Her gaze settled on Drager as he lurched back and forth on his hands and knees, parts of him dragon, and other parts bipedal. "Especially you, Drager. I thought we were alike, able to see the bigger picture, and know that sacrifices must be made for the greater good."

He snarled, managing to lift his head and meet her gaze. "We're nothing alike, you evil bitch. I can't wait for your blood to coat my claws."

She laughed, as if it were a joke. She wasn't the only one either as her galators bellowed; a few even shifted into their dragon forms as if this was so funny it brought on the change.

Pathetic. They were pathetic and weak, giving shifters a bad name.

Mother held a hand up and they all fell silent, allowing their puppet master to pull their strings.

"I'm sorry, my sons," she finally said when all attention was on her. "My plan was never to destroy you, but it's clear you'll keep fighting the inevitable. I can't have you and your fae destroying our people. You gave them our secrets." She tutted, pacing for the first time. "I thought I prevented that by scrambling your memories, but you know enough now to be a threat. And what do we do with threats?"

There was a chorus from behind her. "Eliminate them."

This time her smile held a hint of sadness, along with the standard insanity she presented at all times.

"Goodbye, boys," she whispered. "Your brothers will be joining you soon."

She had no fucking idea.

As she turned to leave, Drager and I cemented our connection and drew on the other three, only to find that the dampening of our bond was inhabiting the build of our rumble. It was there, but we couldn't completely access the power, especially not with the crystal weapons trained on us. But if the others sprang free, Mother would know she was outnumbered and vanish immediately.

Leaving us out of options and about to be destroyed.

CHAPTER 37

MORGAN

Feeling Zahak's pain and being unable to do anything except send support was akin to torture. He was protecting me from the brunt of it, but I felt enough to know that if the weapons were aimed at me, I'd be dead.

Like Mika.

It was only their dragon side that kept Zahak and Drager from being obliterated.

By the time their Mother finally appeared, I was silently sobbing as Tylan held my hand. "Zahak is strong," he said over and over. "This will not kill him. I promise."

I believed him, but it still killed me to feel his pain.

The arrival of the queen bitch herself was a distraction, and I found myself examining her closely through Zahak's thoughts. She was smaller than I expected, and while her face was partially hidden below a white cloak, I saw enough to notice her pale coloring, shaded in icy whites and blues. She looked very young, no older than twenty.

"She bonded with Father at a very young age," Tylan said, sensing my thoughts through Zahak. "She looks innocent, but the power has corrupted her."

Maybe it was the age she was taken, or maybe other factors were at play as well, but my hatred for her grew as she hurt and threatened my shifters. When she told them it was time to die and said her goodbyes, I barely managed not to scream.

"Okay, this is where we need to release our rumble and elevate the connection," Emmen warned. "Let go of Morgan so she doesn't get swept up in the energy, and focus on giving Drager and Zahak our power."

Tylan did as he was told, and I took another step back, determined not to interfere or cause this to go wrong. We had one chance, and we had to use it now because I wasn't sure how much longer Zahak and Drager could withstand the onslaught. The brothers had to fight back now.

Only the energy wasn't building as it had done with the yonters.

Emmen, face creasing as they attempted to build the bond, finally let out a snarl. "The pocket is interfering with the bond. We're still connected, but in our attempt to hide our essence, we're also weakening ourselves."

"Weakening but never weak," Kellan added, the catchphrase of sorts for these five.

"Still, we can't be even a fraction weakened if we want to take these weapons down," Emmen raged. Scales shot across his arms as the temperature rose within the pocket. "She's tearing them apart out there."

She was. Even as he tried to block me, Zahak's pain was burning my skin. I tasted blood, and I couldn't tell if it was mine or his, but even so, they were running out of time.

"We have to get out of the pocket," I said quickly. "It's the only option." The three exchanged a glance. "I know you're trying to keep yourselves hidden so your mother doesn't do a runner, but what's the point if you're going to get half of you killed?"

My voice reached hysterical levels, and in my desperation I clutched on to Tylan once more, unintendedly shooting my panic into him. Heat surged under my hold, and with a gasp I attempted to yank my hand away, because it was starting to burn.

But I couldn't pull it free.

This sensation was similar to when I'd touched Drager during the fertility ritual, and the energy held us in place.

"Fuck," I heard Kellan whisper, but I was too focused on the lava flowing under my hold to try and figure out what had shocked him.

"She's joined completely in our bond," Emmen added, answering the question anyway, "and… we're stronger."

There was literally no need for them to sound so freaking shocked by this. Yes, sure, I was a human and virtually useless when it came to sharing power, but I mean, if I could bond with Zahak and be a true mate, I certainly had some worth…

That thought must have registered with all five of them, because it was Zahak in my head now, sounding stronger as well. *Our mates make all of us stronger*, he huffed out. *Morgan will be the savior today.*

With that, the rumble built hard and fast, and I felt my own chest respond. I was no dragon, but for this moment I was as close as a human could get.

The heat under my hands faded, and built in my chest, and if my jaw wasn't locked against the vibrations shaking me apart, I might have screamed. I wasn't sure how much I could handle, but I wasn't about to tap out. Not when they needed me, not when we had an actual chance to follow through with the plan.

The plan was all we had, and even as we stood here, there were fae dying back in Green Hollow.

We had to end this. *Now.*

"Imagine," Kellan grit out, his words vibrating too, "how powerful the ten of us would be. Five shifters and five mates."

They were already blessed with immense power. I couldn't really imagine it increasing, but there was no denying what was happening here. Through the bond, we could feel Drager and Zahak releasing their rumble. It blasted through the weapons held by the dragons and knocked them all back.

Including their mother, who must have realized a beat too late, because she was a fraction slow in vanishing from the scene. Drager caught her, wrapping his long arms around her smaller form.

Zahak ripped through the infiltrators in the clearing, tearing heads from shoulders, and guts from bodies. He was without mercy, his mind dark and blank, and I doubted even I could have gotten through to him.

You will always get through to me. His words were deep and dragon-like, and it was comforting to know that even in pure rage he would never hurt me.

"I think we can exit the pocket now," Emmen said quickly. "Zahak's not leaving any fun for us."

Kellan let out an exaggerated sigh. "Well, we can console ourselves with the knowledge that they'll all come now we have Mother. No one will miss out."

They were scarily bloodthirsty, and I was here for it.

It grew more apparent, as I lived out a fantasy story, why I loved anti-heroes. No qualms with these five about ending these bastards where they stood. No worries about the greater good for planet Xalifer. They came to our land, and killed our people, and they had to die.

The end.

Don't ask me when I started to think of this as *my land and people*, but it was what it was. Not even the strangest happening for me this week.

Emmen left the pocket first, then Kellan, and I was third, with Ty right behind me. They were protecting me and we all knew it, but no one said a word. The warmth I'd felt when we'd all been connected no longer surged through my body, but a fraction remained behind my eyes as I blinked rapidly. These small acts of kindness hit me right in the feelings.

Outside the pocket, I blinked at the vibrancy of color and noise. There was also the stench of death, which I'd never really had to experience before. Not like this. It was one thing to read about a bloody massacre, and quite another to see and smell it.

My stomach roiled, and Zahak was before me in a heartbeat. So fast that I was pretty sure he appeared magically. He was responsible for much of this carnage, but thankfully only had a few spatters of blood on his cheek. "Are you okay?" he asked, voice still deeper as scales traced across his skin.

I nodded rapidly. "Right as fucking rain," I said in an overly high-pitched voice.

Tylan snorted laughter, but shut it off when Zahak turned in his slow predatory way and leveled him with a stare. I patted his chest. "I'm perfectly fine. What's the plan now?"

"We get Mother to a secluded place, ask the questions we have, and then pin her to a stick in the middle of a field and draw them out of the shadows."

Their mother looked dazed, but she was awake, secured in Drager's arms. She didn't struggle as her gaze shrewdly locked on me. I moved closer, and Zahak remained at my side, stopping me when we were about six feet from her.

I stared at her, noting the crystal-blue eyes, full pink lips, and eerily pale skin. Her beauty was undeniable, but then again, so was the manic glaze she wore. Momma dragon was a touch unhinged.

"You're going to regret this," she said, so calmly. "You have no idea what you're dealing with."

Before I could stop myself, I was the one snort-laughing, and then covering it up with a cough. She glared harder, and I pressed my lips together. "Sorry," I ended up saying around another escaped laugh, "it's just such a bad-guy cliché to do the whole *you will regret this* and *you have no idea what you're dealing with* line. I'm just really happy to know *it is* used in real life, and that all baddies read from the same handbook."

At this point I was babbling, and everyone was looking at me, and some of them totally thought it was cute. I could tell. Especially Emmen as he glared, eyed narrowed and lips curled.

You're fucking adorable, Zahak said through our bond.

"Come on." Emmen shook his head. "We need to question her and map out the rest of the plan before the full might of Xalifer descends on us."

Tylan let out a low whistle as he fell in line beside Drager, who continued to hold their mother. "I don't think we need any plan except to let Z loose on them."

I really didn't like the small smirk playing around their mother's lips as she stared at Tylan. She clearly didn't think Zahak was going to be enough to take them all on, and I hoped that in their questioning of her, they figured out what she was keeping from them.

The general galator was clearly no match for these five, but I guessed in large numbers they'd have a chance. Still, with the fae helping, there wouldn't just be *five* for this final battle.

There had to be another advantage she was holding close to her chest, and I wondered how much sharp prodding it would take to rip those secrets free.

Hopefully a lot of prodding.

Zahak hadn't had enough blood, he needed his pound of flesh from his mother as well.

He'd get no judgement from me. After everything she'd done, she deserved to lose that flesh and more. Betraying her children wasn't even the worst of her crimes.

She was a locust, a plague on the world, murdering people and stealing their land's energy. The sooner she was dead, the better for all the worlds.

CHAPTER 38

We registered the chaos in Green Hollow as we crossed back through the invisible energy shield that protected these lands. Expanding my senses, I was relieved that most of the energy we felt were fae. The galators sent in here had been a distraction to draw us out, and there were no reinforcements yet.

Most likely because we had their commander in hand, preventing her from calling in more of her soldiers. She hung like a doll in Drager's arms, quiet and compliant, and as soon as we had her in a position to question, we were going to find out the reasons for her confidence.

Morgan walked at my side as we crossed through the forest and into a clearing we'd used before. My mate was glowing, energy spilling from her skin as tendrils of light filtered through the canopy and highlighted the gold in her long brown hair, which she pushed off her heart-shaped face. The blue of her eyes was more vibrant and beautiful than ever, and I marveled at her increasing the dragon energy when we were all joined.

We knew so little about the mate bonds, a terrifying prospect when my driving urge was to keep her safe. Even from myself. For that reason, I'd would never have let her touch the bond as she did in the pocket, and for that we'd never have known the true power of the mate bond.

The connection between my brothers and I remained partially open now, and as I remembered the surge of power between us, I knew we'd been fucking idiots to ignore that strength for decades. Our lack of foresight was the reason we were weak enough to invade, and it was our job moving forward to ensure that never happened again.

In the clearing, Drager stripped fibers from nearby plants, and used his energy to weave ropes to bind Mother to the tree. He drew from our bond to strengthen their lengths and guarantee she couldn't pull herself free. Not that she'd get far if she did.

Keeping Morgan just a step behind me, I joined my brothers in a semi-circle around the bitch who gave us life and then tried to take it away.

We regarded her closely.

Her smile never wavered, and I got the sense that she was drawing this out for her own personal amusement. Or she was expecting a rescue, and for that we needed to hurry.

"Why did we leave Xalifer all those centuries ago?" Emmen asked her bluntly.

Her smile grew. "To find your mates, of course. Every male, when they reach the coming of age, must journey to Earth and seek out a human who is compatible. Your father did that for me five hundred years ago, and it was your time to do so."

Morgan's reaction to the fact that Mother was over five

hundred years old and looked like she was twenty was all internal. I felt her shock, but no one else would have known. My mate had grown skilled in schooling her features.

"Why didn't we make it to Earth, then?" Kellan asked, voice soft. "What went wrong?"

This was the first time the smirk vanished completely. "You wouldn't understand."

"I think we can keep up," Drager snarled. Our bond was limited, but even without it we all felt his anger and frustration.

"You were a mistake," she whispered, glancing between the five of us. "Too powerful. We would have lost our rule to you, and we weren't prepared to give it up."

I had no idea what I'd been expecting her answer to this question to be. Maybe along the lines of *There was a malfunction, we don't know why you ended up in Risest*. Instead, it sounded very much as if the fact we landed here had been the plan all along.

I wanted to confirm my suspicions: "You sent us here instead of Earth?"

Her laugh was low and bitter. "I sent you to your deaths, but somehow you survived. You, Zahak, stepped before your brothers and took the brunt of the blast, but the others were too close. They were hurt as well. Somehow, though, even injured, you five managed to bond tighter than ever, proving what I'd feared all along about your combined strength. You got yourselves to this pathetic little world all on your own."

Brunt of the blast. The tingling across my skin reminded me of the scars that littered my body. That had to be the moment I'd been marked, for very little else marred our skin.

Emmen closed in on her, right near her face, expression wreathed in hatred. "What happened to our memories?"

She examined him, swallowing roughly. "When the

energy hit it was supposed to destroy the five of you, but thanks to Zahak and your bond, you all resisted death. The hit was strong enough to rattle your brains though, and I saw your faces go blank as you vanished through the transport. I figured you'd eventually perish out there."

Morgan shifted at my side, and I heard her thought: *She couldn't have known her sons very well if she truly believed that.*

My mate had seen our strength from the beginning, which more than made up for our fucked-up parentage.

Tylan, who had been quiet up until now, relaxed his stance and let his arms fall to his sides. "How long was it before you realized we were alive? Was that the reason you decided to invade Risest?"

She wasn't looking at him as she answered. She stole a glance toward the sky, and I got that sense once more that she was preparing for her rescue. "It took a few dozen years before I found your energy trace," she murmured, distracted. "But it wasn't until *she* showed up at the library and I could sense the energy of a mate." Her focus was on Morgan now, and I stepped in front of her, blocking Mother's view. "I knew it was time to end this before you all figured out the strength in the mate bond."

Ironically, it might have been her showing up that forced us to discover that.

"So the moment she started to work at my library, you've been spying on us?" Drager drawled.

Her laughter this time was lighter. It was clear she switched between slightly deranged and completely deranged with ease. "Of course. I have always periodically checked in to make sure you weren't remembering or growing powerful enough to claim the throne. It might be our way for the children to ascend if they're more powerful than the parents, but it never sat right with me and your father."

It was clear that she enjoyed her power too much to ever want to give it up, and so she'd plotted to destroy us. A plot that failed, but as long as we were without memory and content in Risest, she was happy to let us be. Of course, when Drager's need for power brought the humans into the world, she had to pivot and change directions.

"You should have continued to ignore us," I told her, none of the anger and hatred I felt noticeable in those words. I didn't want her to think we gave a shit about her, even if it was painful to learn that your parents tried to kill you for power. "We weren't even looking for our memories. We already know that what we have here is far better than what we left. You are the maker of your own destruction, and you're about to learn what happens when our world and fae are threatened. All this power you've hoarded and sought will be for nothing when I destroy Xalifer."

Her smile vanished, and she looked at me differently, as if she'd been underestimating us up until this point, or maybe she assumed we'd never hurt our parents.

Both incorrect.

Turning away from her, because I was done staring into her crazy eyes, I found myself meeting another gaze: Drager's. He looked conflicted, and I had an idea of what worried him. He'd inherited her love of power, sacrificing relationships in the pursuit of it. If he didn't change his ways, he now stared into his future. Meeting Mother again was his wakeup call, and if that dumb bastard didn't take it, I'd have to kill him before he destroyed us all.

"I think I've heard enough," Tylan said, voice as inflectionless as mine had been. "Let's get her set out as bait and bring their fucking world to its knees."

A plan I was all in on.

Drager released her ropes from the tree, binding her

hands behind her instead. He lifted her small frame, holding her prisoner, but again she never made a single move to resist or escape. She remained a doll, hanging in his arms, that fucking smirk back on her face.

She noticed me glaring and smiled harder. "You've forgotten one very, *very* important factor in your plan." She chuckled. "It is a good plan, don't get me wrong. I didn't sense your brothers there, and I have no idea how you all had the strength to blast our Zen crystals as you did, but there's still an element that you can't control. Do you know what it is?"

None of us answered, we were done with her bullshit, and needed to focus on ensuring the next part of the plan went off without an issue.

Heading toward the fighting, we had to find one galator alive to send back to the mothership to pass on the message that their queen was captured and the entire fucking hive had better descend.

We've got motherships and hives. Are we ready for these alien bees?

Morgan's mind was calm on the surface, but even as she tried to joke I sensed her panic deep down.

It's going to be okay, sweetheart. Her warning is a tactic to throw our confidence so we start to second-guess this plan. She only needs time and an opportunity to escape, and she's working to ensure she has both.

Morgan was briefly silent, before she wrapped her tiny hand around my wrist, needing the physical connection. *I hope you're right, Z. Just… don't be too confident. Be prepared to pivot if needed because I don't trust she isn't cooking up a nasty plan B herself.*

Morgan thought we were too nonchalant in our dealings with the queen of the dragons, and I couldn't assure her that we would come out victors here today, but I had a lot to fight for.

My future and world were at stake, and I'd absolutely pivot if needed.

I want you in the pocket again when the battle starts, I told her. The energy remained attached to me, even though Drager had ditched his side earlier.

I prepared for her to refuse, but she gave it some solid thought first, working it all out in her mind. *Okay, I promise to use the pocket if the battle grows beyond our control. But until then, I want to be out in the open, able to see what's happening. I don't like the muted nature of our connection when I'm in there.*

Drager knocked on the blocks of our bond then, and I opened the connection. *Morgan should wait up at Lancourt while we fight it out*, he said suddenly. *I don't like the way Mother is reacting to this all. She's too confident. If Morgan waits in Lancourt, she can escape back to Earth if the worst happens.*

The fact that he was worried about her as well, and sought to protect her, pissed me right off. But in the end, the more powerful beings she had defending her, the safer she'd be. Just as long as he never touched her again.

I'll be able to stay in Lancourt now without issue? Morgan asked.

Of course, Drager said, arrogance on full display. *You're one of us now. You could go anywhere and survive.*

Morgan nodded, looking pleased by this truth. *I'm not doing that though*, she said.

Drager's energy drifted harder through the bond, and it was clear he was about to argue, but she got in first. *The worst is not going to happen*, she started, *and if it does, then I'm here with Z. We're a bonded pair, and where he goes, I fucking go. Even if that's the next life. While I appreciate you trying to keep me safe, Lancourt is not a suggestion I can get behind. Sorry.*

Part of me wanted to force her to leave. Force her to get to safety. But there was no way we could stand so much separation. Not newly bonded.

There was also the risk that a galator could infiltrate Lancourt—they'd be able to kill her in an instant. So, no, she was staying with me, where she was the safest.

Where I'd protect her with my life.

CHAPTER 39

MORGAN

"What's your name?"

I was sick of calling her the dragon mom. She wasn't really a *mom*; she was the *birther* and that was all.

"Queen Rose," she said, looking pleased with herself.

Queen Rose, the creepy bitch, hung in Drager's arms, always smiling but in a very unsettling way. "I was from a poor family," she said, as if I had cared enough to ask more questions. "Poor, pathetic, and lower than dirt. The sort where my mom was sent out to sell herself so we could eat, and my father… hurt me." She cleared her throat, the smile wavering. "When my Thorne came for me, it was the happiest day of my life. He stole me right out of my bed on my eighteenth birthday, brought me to Xalifer, and within a day we were mated. He saved me, and now I'm a queen. I never again had to worry about my terrible family, who are long dead anyway."

Her laughter was a tinkle of mirth, floating away on the breezes that had picked up the moment we left the forest. "You were only eighteen?" I asked softly. When this Thorne had sealed their mate bond, her aging stopped, so she was forever a teenager. "Eighteen and kidnapped?"

Her gaze was piercing, the blue turning even icier. "Do not pity me, child. I have lived a million lifetimes since then, and all of them wonderful."

Yeah, especially that one where you tried to murder your fucking children, you psychopath.

As a human with less-than-amazing parents—nothing like her, of course, so I counted myself lucky—I had no sympathy for a woman who would hurt her children.

"You should have learned from the mistakes of your parents," I told her shortly. "They hurt you, and then you hurt *your* children. You're no better than them, even as you look down on them as being *poor and pathetic*. They were a product of their times and what they needed to do to survive. You have no such excuse."

She wasn't smiling now. "You don't understand. This was about survival for us as well. I had too many babies. Normally we only have one, maybe two, but I had five. And despite two born first, and then the other three later, they're all bonded as if they'd been in the same pod. We created a power too strong to exi—"

I punched her.

I really couldn't explain what came over me, but as she was blathering on about killing her children, a red haze descended over my gaze, and I darted closer to Drager and slammed my fist into her fucking face.

Her head had nowhere to go, because she was held against Drager's solid chest, and it hurt way more than I expected when I made contact.

But it hurt her too.

She snarled, struggling against Drager's hold to try to get to me. A thin trickle of deep red blood oozed from her lip, but she couldn't break free.

"You're dead," she shouted. "You're all dead! And this time I'll make sure it's done right!"

Shooting her a smirk of my own, I strolled over to Zahak, who wrapped an arm around me and hugged me tight. *We need to end this now,* he growled, *because I need uninterrupted days with you, killer.*

Nervous laughter escaped from me, as I enjoyed the hug. "She's a nasty bitch. I honestly couldn't stand listening to her for one more second."

That was said out loud so she could hear it, and sure enough, she was once again struggling to escape.

"Don't fucking move," Kellan said, getting in her face while pointing his finger into her chest. "Or we'll let Morgan have another round with you. She's got a decent hit on her."

Having Zahak as my mate was everything I could have ever asked for, but to also get *brothers* with the deal was a very nice bonus. My family, always so small and limited, now felt vast and full of possibilities for the future.

If some crazy bitch didn't keep trying to take that away from us.

Flexing my fingers as we walked, the ache was already easing as we moved toward the battle. The roar of the warriors grew louder as the river came into view. "Astra said the galators' numbers have dwindled," Zahak told the group as we reached the western riverbank.

The fighting was about a hundred yards away, and I could see the fae, swords glinting in the eerie light of the crimson sky. An earthy scent lingered in the air, and I forced myself not to consider the cause of it, even as it reminded me of the carnage Zahak left behind outside the border.

"Is Lexie okay?" I asked Zahak. "Did Astra see her?"

He didn't get a chance to answer, before Astra bounded over to us, Leo at her side. I wasn't surprised this time to see him bigger again. I'd learned to expect anything from these mystical creatures. As I leaned over to pat his huge head, Lexie appeared on the edge of the fight, waving to let us know where she was. The relief I felt at seeing her had my knees wobbly.

"Enjoy your reunion, human," Rose snarled. "You'll all be dead soon. We've already started the process of corrupting your world. By the time this final battle is done, it'll be too late."

Forcing myself not to look at her, I focused on the sabres, who were jumping all over Zahak. He held them both in his arms, and then Leo turned and jumped on me, knocking me to the ground as he proceeded to lick across my face. "Leo," I laugh-gasped, "you're too heavy for me, buddy."

Air rushed back into my lungs when Zahak hauled him off. "Gentle with her, cub," he warned, dropping the enthusiastic sabre beside me. "She's precious cargo."

Leo rumbled, but when he approached me again, it was with a touch less enthusiasm. By this point, Lexie had reached us, and she was the one to haul me to my feet for a hug.

Covered in blood as she was, the hug was squishy and gross, but I didn't care. My best friend was alive, here, in my arms, and there was nothing more I could ask for.

"How's the battle going?" Kellan asked her.

She nodded as she released me. "Good. We have decimated their troops almost completely, and are regrouping for the next wave." Her eyes landed on the dragon mom, who was thankfully quiet again. "Good to see you are on track with your plan. Now it's time to work out the final logistics."

She fell in beside me and answered the rest of the shifters' questions.

"How many did we lose?" Emmen asked.

"No more than fifteen percent," she said. "Those deflection shields made all the difference. I mean, once they saw that their crystals wouldn't be effective, they did resort to brute strength, which got a few of us killed, until we fell back into formation. As you all warned us, we never took them on alone. We have a pretty good handle on how they fight now."

"We've given the fae the weapons they need to defeat us too," Drager said morbidly.

Lexie shot him a dark stare; she was less Team Drager these days. "We all know you're stronger than them, and that there's no reason for us to rebel against you. We accept your rule, and the freedoms we have. You bring calm to the chaos of this world. We're not going to attack you."

"Don't believe her son," Rose said. "Eventually, one of them will want what you have. It's always the way."

Lexie just stared at her, before whipping around to me. "She's missing a few branches in her tree, isn't she?"

I snorted, clearing my throat. "The whole top half, it seems."

I ran my fingers through Leo's fur, which held only a hint of baby softness now. *They grow up so quickly*, I joked to Zahak, feeling nostalgic over memories of his tiny body snuggled into me. I'd never have that again, and it just hadn't been long enough.

Their breed of sabre is very adaptive, he replied. *Leo was forced to grow up even faster than usual to keep himself and those he cares about safe, but he'll always be your baby. That's just how it works.*

Leo rumbled as if he'd heard those words, and I leaned in

to hug his massive head. "Love you, buddy," I said. I gave Astra a pat and told her the same, happy that they were safe and near us.

"Okay, let's get this fucking party started," Kellan said. "I have a mate to find."

We'd unlocked a new obsession for him, and I wasn't going to be the one to break it to him that there were more than eight billion people on our planet, and no guarantee his mate had even been born yet. I'd let him have his hope for as long as possible.

Surely, if they had just learned of their true mates, and fate was at work here, the timing would work out. If I were writing the story, that's what I'd do. Even if it was a ridiculous cliché.

As long as my characters got their happy endings, who cared about clichés?

We will have our happily ever after, Zahak said, and I should not have felt so freaking happy when we were on the brink of war and had no idea what crazy Rose had up her sleeve.

Which reminded me… We hadn't addressed the information she'd let slip before.

"Rose," I started, facing her again, "what did you mean when you said the process of corrupting this world would be too far gone to turn back?"

Her gaze found mine, but she didn't answer.

"Their world is poisoning this one," Lexie said, which we'd already surmised as much. "One of the soldiers was talking about it when I ripped his guts out. Said we could kill them all, but we'd still never win." She looked up toward the darker sky. "That's why it's crimson, and why disease is spreading. So even if we do defeat them, it'll be too late to save our world."

"She said by the time the battle is done," Drager growled.

"Which means there's still time now. So let's stop them before it goes any farther."

He stomped off with Rose in his arms and we all followed, heading into what remained of the battle. The fae moved aside when they saw us, and we got to the frontline in a matter of seconds. There were only a few galators still alive—three males to be exact, sprawled on the ground, about to be finished off.

"Wait!" Emmen bellowed, and the fae stilled their weapons, turning to their gods. "We need one alive," he added when we were closer. "We have a message to send."

The galators surged to their feet when they noticed their queen, each of them roaring as heat built in the clearing. "Go back to your planet and tell them to send every last shifter down here," Zahak told them, his words dripping with viciousness. "This is the final battle, and if you don't want your queen to die, you won't delay."

A galator with olive skin, deep brown eyes, and an expression of hatred, spat on the ground. "You wouldn't kill your own mother."

Zahak's claws appeared, and he swung around and stabbed Rose right in the side, sinking those lethal points in to the hilt. She screamed, writhing in Drager's hold, and two of the Fallen infiltrators surged forward, only to have their throats ripped out by Emmen and Tylan.

"We would kill her without blinking an eye," Zahak said, slowly removing his claws. "Every minute you delay in delivering this message is another hole I put in her side. How many can she sustain before it's too many?"

Rose's cries had halted almost immediately, but she was breathing heavily, that darker than normal blood staining Drager's arm on the side she'd been stabbed.

"Tick tock," Emmen said. "Time is running out."

The galator was shaken, his skin paling. With one last look at his queen, he spun on the spot and took off out of the barrier.

This was it. The final part of our plan was falling into place.

We just had to hope we weren't already too late.

MORGAN

After the galator raced off to deliver our message, Zahak and his brothers consulted with the leaders of the warrior clans. There were members from all five lands here, and while I was sure more than a few rivalries existed, today on the battlefield everyone worked together.

"We need to move the injured into the healing waters," Florentine shouted as she raced over to the Fallen.

I was immensely relieved to see her alive and well. Her brother arrived a few seconds later, diving straight in to help move the wounded. There were about twenty injured enough to require some assistance, which wasn't the worst result, but there were also at least double that dead. Which weighed heavily on me.

War was so senseless and destructive. I had no idea why anyone would intentionally inflict this on their people.

"What's the plan now?" one of the Lightsbringers asked, wiping their sword with a piece of cloth. "They'll be back with what could possibly be thousands, and then we'll be the outnumbered ones."

"We need to narrow their path to us," Emmen said decisively, "so they can't all charge us at once."

"Yes," someone shouted. Noise blew up, and maps were suddenly pulled out of energy pockets as the leaders crowded in to discuss a new location for this final fight.

With nothing useful to contribute, I remained quiet and observed the fae. Lexie stuck to my side, and I couldn't help but marvel at the changes in our lives. "How do you think the library is going?" I asked her, absentmindedly running my hand over Leo's head. Astra was with Zahak, a dozen feet away.

Lexie settled in closer to me. "Even in the midst of war, you're thinking about your library. Drager should really give that to you guys as a mating present."

My lips twitched, but I didn't laugh. "Drager doesn't seem the type to hand his things away, and I doubt he's getting ready to celebrate our mating." Especially not by gifting a few million dollars in real estate.

You want the library? He'll give us that library.

This time I had to laugh, all the while appreciating that even deep in conversation with someone, Zahak was always with me.

"Lord Zahak is talking to you, isn't he?" Lexie said with a gentle smile.

Focusing on her again, I returned her smile. "How'd you know?"

She hugged me around my shoulders. "Your energy softens when he's near you." She leaned in and whispered: "And I've never seen you like that before."

That lump returned to my throat as emotions overwhelmed me. "I can't explain it," I rasped. "It's magic, Lex. I know you said that doesn't really exist here, but these mate bonds have to be magic. I mean, I've read about them a million times, and I've rolled my eyes at the absurdity of how quickly some of them fell for their mate, but now that I've experienced it, I owe all those ladies an apology. It's beyond my control, and I don't even want to fight it. Why would anyone want to fight what feels so freaking good?"

"Maybe if he was a bad guy," Lexie shrugged, "you'd at least pretend to fight his pull. But everyone knows he'd get you in the end."

My eyes found Zahak. He wasn't watching me, but I felt his attention as strongly as if he had his gaze locked with mine. "To some he probably would be considered a bad guy. If you fuck with him, you'll absolutely regret it, and I don't see him as a *sacrifice his loved ones to save the world* sort of shifter, but I wouldn't do that either. Zahak puts me first, and all I feel is loved and accepted when I'm with him. Not to mention he can use his tongue in ways I didn't know were possible. I'm one lucky human."

I'm the lucky one, la moyar. I'd burn everyone and everything in the worlds to keep you safe. Sacrifice them all. Don't forget that.

Oh gods.

Lexie brought me back when she said, "Super frogging lucky."

Zahak laughed. *Your friend is interesting.*

She was that and more. She was my chosen sister, and I loved her more than I could ever express. "Why don't you swear?" I asked Lexie, my curiosity rearing up now that I knew who she truly was. "I'd always assumed it was your upbringing, but it's clear that fae curse as much as me, in your language equivalent anyway, so there has to be another reason."

Lexie was quiet, still holding me to her side as she stared

into the fae army milling around. "As you've probably noticed, my family is regimented," she finally said. "Growing up, we couldn't be individuals, you know. Everything matched. Everything was in line." She waved her hand toward some Lightsbringers. "Look at them. Even resting and recovering, they're still in formation. I just wanted individuality that they couldn't control. All the armed forces swear here. It's a way to let off steam, but not cursing didn't give me anything different either, so I went for oddball phrases that made everyone stare at me and wonder if I'd lost my mind. I think it's the reason Drager thought I was suitable for the Earth mission. Humans are odd, and I was too, so it fit."

"Thank fuck about that," I burst out. "Imagine if you hadn't been the one chosen, and we'd never met." I honestly couldn't even consider it. "You're my soulmate as well, you know, just in a different way to Zahak."

His rumble filtered to me, but it was light and without any real bite.

"You're mine too," Lexie sniffed, "and I refuse to have these conversations any longer. This is the whole *get all your feelings out because some of us might die* speech, and we are not flappin' here for it."

"Right! We're done."

No more maudlin end-of-world discussions. This was just the next step in the battle, and we wouldn't lose. Zahak said to have confidence going into a fight, and I was doing just that.

Leo rumbled, drawing my attention, and I placed my hand on his head, to find the word *hungry* drifting through my mind. Words in my head weren't unusual now, only this didn't come from Zahak or any of the Fallen Five.

It was Leo.

He's learning to communicate with his bonded one. Astra is hungry too, so they're going to feed and replenish their strength before the fight.

Joy flourished in my chest, and leaning forward I pressed a kiss to Leo's head. "You clever boy. Yes, go and eat, but don't be long. We're moving to a new location soon, I believe."

He rumbled and licked my cheek, before bounding away with Astra right beside him.

"The portal locations have been set," Zahak called a few minutes later. "We need to leave now if we want a chance to make it to the battlegrounds before they return."

The slightly relaxed atmosphere faded. There was a clank as weapons were drawn across the clearing. Lexie held her sword as well, and Zahak was at my side once more, keeping his bulk in front of me. We weren't amongst enemies yet, but he trusted no one.

"Sweetheart, don't forget the pocket of energy," he told me. "It's still attached to me, so you'll be able to access and hide if the battle rages beyond our control."

"Okay," I agreed, hoping it wouldn't come to that.

Drager lifted his bound mother once more, still carrying her around like a petulant child. We all moved to the front of the line, heading out of Green Hollow's territory and into the forests beyond. "Will our sabres be able to find us?" I asked, worried that they weren't back yet.

"They'll follow our energy," Zahak assured me. "They can use the portals as easily as we can."

That was good to know, and they really couldn't be too much longer, right?

Zahak picked up on that thought. "They're already on their way back. They fed rather quickly."

My sigh of relief was audible.

When we reached the transports that had been set up as

soon as the fae settled on a new location for the final battle, the warriors moved through quickly, and when it was our turn, I held on to Zahak.

"Come on," Kellan bellowed when we emerged on the other side—into another forest, with smaller and less dense foliage. Salt scented the air, and the ground we stomped across was both sandy and rocky. "We need to get to the Valley of Wardens before the galators descend."

The initial pace of our march was intense, and I was relieved when Astra and Leo joined us a few minutes later. Both growled and rumbled hello, before falling in line.

Far above, the first shadows of the dragons falling from Xalifer began to show. "How long until they're on the ground?" I asked.

"They'll have to change directions to find us, so we have at least an hour," Zahak bit out. "Just enough time for us to get into place."

"What land are we in?" I asked.

"This is part of Tylan's land, the Craters of Lastoa," Lexie said. "It'll get more rugged when we're out of Boulder Forest."

The pace picked up once more, and I hoped this Valley of Wardens was the advantage they were banking on. I hated the thought of losing more fae here today, but the truth was, they were not as important to me as my friends and family. Maybe I was the bad guy after all.

You could never be the bad guy, Zahak told me. *You just know your limits. And losing those you love is a hard limit.*

He was right. I'd never wish death on anyone here, but if it came down to choosing, I'd always choose those I loved.

With the increased pace, I started to fall behind, but Zahak remained at my side with Leo and Astra between us. Lexie and the other Fallen were a few steps ahead. The forest thinned out, and when we exited it was onto barren and rocky land. That briny scent increased, and a flash of blue off in the distance was the ocean.

The land dipped down, and that was when I caught sight of a set of cliffs rising from the rocks. The cliffs stood at least a hundred feet tall, with a wide gap at the base that narrowed near the top. "You can't fly in," Zahak said as we crossed toward the cliffs. "And the entrance is too narrow for more than a dozen to enter at one time. In the Valley of Wardens, we'll be trapped, which is a risk, but we'll also have the advantage."

"Fae don't usually visit these cliffs," Lexie said, listening in. "This is where one of our great wars took place. It was said that the wardens were our first guardians, and the fae revolted against them. They destroyed a thousand fae warriors to hold their rule, but in the end succumbed to their injuries, leaving our world desolate and dark. Like when the Fallen Five first found us. There are other stories as well, but this is the one that matters." She looked up at Zahak. "Another reason you all don't need to worry about us rising up against you. We learned our lessons, and unless you abuse your power, you're safe from us."

Zahak nodded, acknowledging her reassurances.

Inside the entrance to the valley, between those two intimidating cliffs, there was next to no illumination. A few fae threw up blobs of what looked like glow-in-the-dark slime, which stuck high to the cliff walls, giving off more light than I expected.

Everyone pushed through the mile or so of cliffs, and when we emerged on the other side, it was to find a valley the size of Green Hollow, surrounded on all sides by cliffs even higher than the pair we'd just passed between. Higher, and with a closed ceiling as well, as the rocks curved into each other. There were some cracks up high, letting in natural light, but it was still dim.

"Tie Rose to those rocks near the back," Kellan said to Drager as we crossed to where they waited. "Everyone else needs to get into formation." Fae continued pouring through the tunnels, filling the valley with their numbers. Nerves started to roil in my gut as I considered how dangerous this situation was. We did have the advantage, but they might have enough fighters to just keep coming through that tunnel until all of us were dead.

There was just no way to know how this was going to play out.

"Where will you stand?" I asked Zahak, needing a distraction.

He looked toward the one entrance and exit, then pointed to the side of it. "We're going to use the rumble to weaken them, so we'll help our frontline take them out as fast as possible."

I found my focus drifting to Rose as Drager secured her to the rocks. She still wore a look of great confidence. She wasn't worried even as the fae plotted, and thousands of them, armed to the teeth, filed into the valley.

Were we still missing an important aspect of this final battle? Was our plan about to backfire, until we were the mice trapped in the hole?

I glanced up to the rocky covering of the valley, with no way for even a dragon to escape, and hoped we'd done the right thing here today.

CHAPTER 41

ZAHAK

The bond with my brothers hovered just below the surface, ready to call on the moment we were under attack. We hadn't experienced war like this before, though many of the fae who stood here with us had. As I stared around at grim faces, still shaded in grime and blood from the last battle, I hoped that we'd made the right decision.

Once Drager had secured Rose to the back wall, digging his claws into the rocks and embedding the ropes deep, he made his way to stand with us. The queen of the galators was strong, thanks to her age and the bond with our father, but we were coming to see that she couldn't best us alone. She couldn't shift, or manipulate energy, instead she relied on the galators to fulfill her plans. She was waiting for a rescue, her confidence stemming from that, and possibly something else.

"I think it's Father," Kellan said, breaking our silence as

we watched the fae pour into the valley. "He must be alive still, right?"

"I assume he's alive," I said, my focus on Morgan, who chatted to Lexie a few feet from us. In our bond, she followed both conversations, having already grown adept at managing the internal and external. "But he's still only one versus five, and the fact that she threw us off our world all those years ago tells me he can't be powerful enough to keep us in line."

Logically speaking, this made sense to me. If Father was this big bad shifter who was able to take us out and save his crazy mate, she'd never have feared our power in the first place.

What if you're not powerful enough yet, Morgan said, and I opened the pathway between all of us so they could hear her too. *She didn't want you all to find your mates. That was when she attacked you, when you were about to head for Earth. And then again when I showed up as a potential mate. At this point, we're four mates down in the perfect power. Maybe your dad can still kick your ass today.*

None of us could argue with her logic. Until we'd felt the surge in power today, when Morgan was forced into our bond, we'd had no idea that our mates could elevate our energy. Our lack of knowledge was the advantage Rose still had over us.

"I think she's right," Drager said with a stiff nod. "Morgan has a way of looking at situations in a different light. A new perspective. I think being so widely read has helped her human brain develop further than most."

Morgan was at his side in a heartbeat, and when she jabbed him in the gut I reached out to snatch her away. But apparently she didn't need my help. She dodged his hands, and mine, and jabbed him again.

Darting away, with more speed than she should have

possessed, she dropped her hands on her hips and glared. "I'm done with your insults and snark," she snapped. "You're an asshole, and not as smart or powerful as you think. In fact, since I arrived in this world, I've seen you make *many* questionable decisions. So grow the fuck up. If humans are your mates, then we're your fucking equals, and you need to accept that and move on from your prejudices."

For a solid minute after she was done, there was only silence. Shock radiated from the fae nearby as they tried to comprehend what they were hearing. No one in this world would have dared to speak to their *gods* in such a manner, and the fact that a human had blew their minds.

Drager wore a look that indicated he was debating what way to handle this. His gaze briefly met mine, and I silently reminded him that Morgan came first. I'd killed for her before, and I'd do so again in a second.

"My apologies," Drager finally muttered. "It's a bad habit that I will endeavor to strip from my soul."

Morgan glanced over her shoulder at me, and I shot her what I hoped was a reassuring smile. She narrowed her gaze, no doubt wondering if I'd forced Drager's apology. In the end, she gave up worrying about it, and nodded stiffly in his direction. "I don't accept your apology just yet. I want actions to back up the words, but I'll refrain from punching you again. At least for today."

Kellan and Tylan stifled smiles of their own, and I tried to remember my life before Morgan came into it. So fucking dull, endless and boring.

Further conversation was cut off at a commotion near the mouth of the cave. "They're here!" a fae screamed, voice echoing off the walls of the valley.

Those warriors who were still entering hurried their movements, while all the others spread out in formation.

There were thousands of fae in here, limiting our movement, but the plan was to rotate our frontline so we wouldn't lose our advantage in taking out the galators as they entered the valley.

"We need to move into position now," I told Morgan. "You wait here, mate. Off to the side where you're safe."

She nodded, swallowing roughly. "Be careful, Z. I love you."

I loved this enigmatic and frankly mystical woman more than was sane or possible. Brushing my hand along her cheek, I gave myself one more second to stare into the deep blue of her eyes before I had to focus.

Moving with my brothers, we reached the wall near the entrance, preparing our rumble. The bond surged, and this time Morgan was part of it. She didn't have to move closer. It felt like she was right by our sides.

Lexie, sword drawn, remained with Morgan, and I checked the pocket was still attached to me. Without anyone inside, it was lighter, so it wasn't until I felt the join in my armor that I could confirm it remained attached.

Astra and Leo moved between our legs, tense as they tracked the energy of the galators heading toward us. There were a lot of them. They had brought their full force, and it was more than I'd anticipated. But our plan was set now, and we would see it all the way through.

"Mother is still fucking smirking," Emmen snarled, glancing behind to check she remained where Drager had secured her.

If anything, her smile had grown bigger and more confident, and I resisted the urge to just knock her out. *Maybe I should go and talk to her*, Morgan suggested. *I know you five have to stay here and do your rumble thing, but I'm still connected even over there, and I just feel like we need more information. I don't want anyone to get hurt here today because we overlooked something important.*

No, I snapped, fear shortening my tone. *I don't want you anywhere near her. She's toxic and powerful enough to hurt you if she gets free.*

But why the fuck is she so confident? Morgan pushed. *We need to know.*

There was no way Mother would reveal her advantage. She hadn't done so yet, outside of those few snarky comments. *What if all her bullshit is just to undermine our confidence?* Emmen suggested. *We don't even know if she has any advantage, but one way to throw your opponent off is to act like you've got a secret weapon up your sleeve. I say we ignore her once and for all and focus on the fight we know is coming.*

The first of the galators roared through the doorway. Tapping deeper into the energy of our bond, our rumble burst from us faster than ever. Our warriors knew to remain back from the entrance so they weren't hit, and when the first galators slammed to their knees, arrows and darts were shot with precision into their bodies.

We'd taught our fae to aim for the throat, avoiding the armor and stronger parts of our bodies.

Galators went down in a heap, only to be kicked aside as the next line followed. This went on for some while, until the entrance was littered with their dead. The opposition soon learned though, as the next group headed through with stones in their hands. Their sonar weapons crashed against our rumble, sending off fragmented pieces of the soundwaves.

Fae pulled out their shields and rushed forward to battle head-on.

We need to get closer, I told Morgan. *Do you want to use the pocket now?*

Leo purred harder than usual, taking off back to Morgan.

Lexie is heading in to fight, but I'll wait with Leo. Be safe.

You have my heart, I replied, *and my soul.*

With that, she sucked in a deep breath as I raced away from her. Leo had reached her, and even though he was young and inexperienced in fighting, he was still a weapon. Astra stayed at my side, and was already in the middle, tearing through galators.

Determined to return to Morgan as quickly as possible, I joined my brothers on the frontline.

Leaders don't let their warriors fight without them.

This was our battle, and it was time to end this fucking war once and for all.

CHAPTER 42

MORGAN

Standing to the side, watching Lexie—who hadn't been able to resist joining her family—and the Fallen Five fight without me, was harder than I expected. Not that I had any idea what I thought I could do, but it felt wrong to remain back here, watching.

Regarding the battle itself, in the beginning we did great. The fae were taking out the galators as soon as they entered the valley, but as we'd expected, their numbers kept arriving, thick and fast.

Wave after wave.

Eventually it grew too overwhelming. The bodies piled up, and the fae had to retreat farther back into the valley. Then our warriors started to go down too, and I found myself glancing back to Rose, wondering if this was where her confidence came from. The sheer quantity of galators under her control would eventually overwhelm the few thousand fae warriors we had.

Zahak and his brothers were a massive help to the front-line, slicing and dicing through their opponents, dropping bodies and kicking them to the side in a frenzied fervor.

Through the bond, there weren't a lot of coherent thoughts, just pure predatory rage. Their beasts had risen to give them additional strength in this fight.

I glanced at Rose again.

Still fucking smiling.

Her warriors were dying a dozen a second, and yet she wasn't worried.

This made no fucking sense to me.

Edging along the wall, Leo looked up at me, and growled low. *Stay*. He wasn't huge on sentences yet, but he got his point across.

"I know that Zahak said to stay," I replied, still edging along. "But he's also not the boss of me. We're mates, partners, and some might even say equals." No one would ever say that, not even me, but it was a great argument and I was sticking with it. "I just need to chat with momma dragon. She knows more than she's telling, and I swear this is the part in every great story where the bad guy needs to monologue to make us all aware of their ingenious plan."

She was due a monologue. No way would she keep holding out.

Picking up the pace, I kept my thoughts calm and concerned for the fight so as not to trigger Zahak's protective instincts.

Mate, you're going the right way for a punishment later, he growled in my head. I'd been fooling *absolutely no one* with my stealthy trip along the rock wall. *Get your ass back to the spot I left you.*

I'll be two minutes, I promised him, *I just want to question her once more. I'm still surrounded by warriors.*

Even rotating their frontline, and losing a few soldiers, there were thousands of fae around me and Rose. I'd never be alone with her.

I heard a long huff and then, *You have two minutes, sweetheart. If you're not back then, I'm coming for you.*

A promise and gentle threat, and I was fine with both. If I wasn't worried about distracting him for longer than two minutes while he was fighting, and leaving the frontline short one of the Fallen Five, I'd have tested his threat to its full extent.

Zahak's presence remained heavy in my mind as I picked up the pace, dodging and shoving my way through fae to get back to Rose. When the warriors realized who I was, they got out of the way for me, which I'd never get used to. Or maybe it was Leo who had them parting like a biblical sea, but whatever the case, the journey was easier and faster.

Rose's gaze found me when I was a dozen yards away, and she watched me closely as Leo and I crossed toward her. "What advantage do you have up your sleeve?" I demanded, not bothering to ease into it. We had no time left for pleasantries—not that she deserved any. "At this point, we can't do anything to counter it. It'll probably be worse for us to know what's coming for us, so just fucking spit it out."

She tilted her head, arms bound at her sides, the ropes lodged deep in the rocks, with the distinct impression of claw marks, pinning them in place. "You're an odd human," she said, voice throaty. "I was born to shine, to escape the mundane existence of my pathetic life, but you... you're different."

I waved her off. "Yeah, yeah, I'm not the typical mate for your shifters. I don't fucking care. I just want to make sure your sons live past today."

"They won't," she said simply. "If my mate hadn't had a

weakness for them when they were babies, I'd have killed them as soon as the second pod hatched." She *tsked*. "He's a fool, but he's also a fool in love and obsessed. You might have noticed that with our Zahak. His obsession is even more apparent than his father's, and that's saying something."

"Your mate would kill them for you now?" I guessed.

She nodded, showing her shiny and predatory teeth as she smiled broadly. "In a heartbeat. The years without his sons have hardened him, and since I'm all he has left, he will never risk me. You made a mistake in capturing me, because he will emerge for the first time in centuries. He will leave our home and tap into the power of his ancestors. He's not a normal shifter. Not even like my sons. He's the reason they're so powerful, but they can't best him today. Not while they're missing their mates."

At times, I wished I hadn't read so many books, so I wouldn't have an insight into the twist at the end. But I always saw it coming. As I'd predicted, daddy dragon was the big bad. He was going to be more powerful than the five of them, and they would be weakened and tired after battling thousands of soldiers. The threat of the Fallen Five had always been in their ability to find their mates and turn the power of five into the power of ten.

"This is why you never wanted them to find their mates," I whispered. "It's the ten that's the most powerful."

She nodded, no hesitation. "It's not that the humans add strength, it's that you bring out *their* strength. When a shifter is mated, he's at his peak. Relentless and powerful beyond belief. You're still going to be all but useless."

"Are you useless?" I shot back. That one stung a little, reminding me of the times my mother called me pathetic and useless because I wouldn't do what she wanted.

"I am," she said matter-of-factly. "I have power in what I control, and the respect my shifters have for me and my mate, but I'm no more powerful than I was as a pure human."

Hence the reason she hadn't attempted to escape.

In the end, she was a human with a powerful mate.

Just like me.

Was it frustrating that we were only vessels used to build up the man in our lives? Yeah, it kind of was, but the pure patriarchal side of the situation was simplifying a very complex bond.

I got a lot out of the arrangement as well.

I got the love of a powerful man who had already shown he would do anything for my happiness. I got support and protection, and the ability to live long enough to achieve everything I'd ever wanted in life.

I got Zahak.

Forever, sweetheart. Now get your ass away from her, and back here where I'm closer to you.

This time I was more than happy to follow his orders. Rose had given us the missing information. *Did you hear her warning about your father? He's the one you need to conserve your energy for.*

There was a pause where he focused on the new wave of shifters, before he returned to me. *It's too late to worry about it now. She's underestimated us before, and I have a feeling she's doing it again. Let us worry about dear old Dad.*

Some days I loved their confidence. Other days it absolutely terrified me.

Confidence was great. Overconfidence could be a death sentence.

When Leo and I returned to our waiting spot, the giant sabre positioned himself in front of me, and I didn't question why. There were more galators in the mix of fae now. The bottleneck at the doorway had worked great for a while, but the sheer numbers were overwhelming our frontline. The scent of death grew stronger, and I tried not to focus on the blood and bodies strewn across the ground. Even if they were now fighting in what looked like puddles of intestines…

No, no way could I keep the contents of my stomach in place if I examined the ground again.

Zahak came into view, and I focused on the beauty of him in fight mode. He was larger, nearly seven feet tall, as the dragon surged beneath his skin covered in a protective layer of black and gold scales. His dark hair fell perfectly across the rugged plains of his face as he slashed through two galators and tore out their throats.

Even if I'd attempted to write my own hero in a book, Zahak was so much better. But what if he was taken from me today? What if this was our last moments in the perfect bond I'd been gifted?

My gaze shot to Rose. That fucking bitch was watching me, reminding me with her unwavering stare that I was about to lose everything I loved.

There had to be another way to stop this. Even human and weak, as she'd pointed out, I had a brain, and I wasn't afraid to use it to save our world. I just had to figure out what I could do.

What strength did I have which she would have underestimated? She hadn't existed as a human for centuries. I'm sure she'd forgotten a lot from her short time on Earth.

I ran countless possibilities through my mind, dismissing most of them in an instant. Acting as a distraction was going to be top of the list, but why would I distract their father? He didn't care about me. I was only one of five mates—it might have been a different story if all of us were here.

For me to be a distraction, I needed to go big, but for the life of me I couldn't think of a way to make that happen.

Morgan, I'm about to march over there and remind you why it would be a very bad idea to act as a distraction, sacrifice, or come anywhere near this battle.

There was not an ounce of amusement or give in Zahak's tone, but there was a hint of fatigue, which sent me spiraling into panic mode once more.

I'll be doing whatever it takes so you survive, I warned him.

The rumble of a response I got in return sent shivers down my spine, which settled as heat in my gut. I'd gotten used to his power inside me, and the way I felt stronger and more capable than ever, but that single sound reminded me that Zahak was the god around here.

Last warning, mate. You will go in the pocket, and I will not let you out until this is over.

Over. Over could mean life or death. Win or lose.

End of my dreams.

Or just the beginning.

We were balanced on a precipice and one little push could send us either way.

The sound of battle picked up once more, and behind it there was a low-level thrumming that grew stronger over the clash of weapons and armor. A few galators turned into dragons, attempting to fly into the air, but the Fallen Five kept hauling them down before they could do any damage.

The thrumming grew stronger and stronger, until the ground started to vibrate, sending trickles of rocks down from above. The light grew a touch brighter in the valley, showcasing the carnage in long streams of illumination, filtering through the ever-growing cracks.

The thrumming was shaking the valley apart, and if I'd

been on Earth I'd have thought it was a huge burst of electricity. Here, though, I knew it was a far worse threat.

Daddy dragon was on his way, and he was not happy about it.

CHAPTER 43

ZAHAK

While Morgan was questioning our mother, I'd had twenty percent focus on the fight and the rest on her. My mate was my number one priority, and it wasn't as if I needed more than minimal focus to kill these galators. They were pathetic. *Mother must have killed off any shifters who were strong,* Drager said casually as he swiped through two more, dropping bodies onto an already crowded ground. *It's embarrassing for them and us, since this is our race.*

Such a fucking waste, Kellan huffed. *They're just shifters, like us, only way shittier. But they're dying for that crazy bitch who's grinning over there like she's watching a funny show.*

They had a choice, Emmen added. *We all have a choice. And the consequences of that choice arrive today.*

I agreed with him. It barely bothered me to destroy my race, because they'd been the ones to invade us. We didn't ask or seek out this battle, but we'd do whatever was needed to end it.

Do we need to discuss what Morgan just learned? Emmen added as he picked up a shifter and piledrove him headfirst into the ground. The shifter's claws glanced off his arm on the way down, leaving a shallow cut, but otherwise we had minimal injuries. So far.

Father is the weapon she's had up her cloak, Tylan snorted. *I just don't get it. How much stronger than the five of us could he be?*

I only had fractured memories of a giant beast who used to shift and wrap his tail around us when we were smaller.

I have the same memory, Kellan said quickly as he punched a shifter into the rock wall, before giving up his fun and slamming his claws into his chest to rip vital organs free.

I don't know what we can do to prepare outside of keep our link open, and elevate our energy when he arrives, I huffed, dealing with four shifters at once, ducking and dodging their strikes. *The five of us fighting together is our strongest offense, so when he arrives we should move away from the entrance and focus on the true threat.*

We couldn't leave the frontline yet, there were too many shifters pouring in, their sheer numbers starting to push us back. They kept attempting to shift, but as soon as I felt that swirl of energy, I got to them fast, and cut them down in a blink.

Attacked from above, the fae would be at a massive disadvantage, and I was having none of that. Up until this point, the fae hadn't fared too badly, but if we left the frontline, that would change very quickly. So the fight continued.

Astra dragged bodies away from the entrance to keep the path clear, swiping through galators as she went. As I lunged at another shifter, my dragon pushed against my skin, reacting to a low humming that filtered into the valley.

The fae warriors didn't react until it grew much stronger, but my brothers and I were on high alert. The vibrations rocketed down our spines, shaking at our beasts.

Tapping into the bond, we rumbled back to stop the attack, but there was no change to the increasing hum.

I don't think he's attacking, Tylan said suddenly. *I think that's just his energy.*

Fuck.

Mother's confidence had been borne from the truth as she knew it: our father was a scary, ancient, powerful shifter—one who controlled his world and had done so for hundreds of years.

Still, I hadn't been that worried. There were five of us, and only one of him, but as that thrum of power attempted to bury deep into my essence, and it wasn't even a direct attack, I knew we were about to enter the hardest fight of our lives.

We cannot let him split us up. I sent this warning to all my brothers. *Stick together, fight together, build up the energy. I'm about to let Morgan fully back in. Stay the fuck out of her mind.*

Kellan laughed, out loud and in our bond. *We're about to become dragon meat thanks to our parents, and you're worried that we'll catch a glimpse of your mate naked in a memory.* He paused. *Wait, is it possible to…?*

Drager growled, and I waited for him to say something insulting about the bond or Morgan. Instead, he snapped, "Focus, he's almost through the tunnel."

The thrashing of his energy increased and the fae closest to the entrance dropped to their knees, heads in their hands, as the power rattled their brains. The advance of galators was slowing, but there were still too many of them.

Fighting the disorientation, we tightened up our shielding and let loose the rumble to knock them back. The next few minutes were spent taking out every galator who entered the valley, until there was a pause, and they stopped appearing. For the first time since they'd arrived, the entrance was empty.

The valley rumbled with the increased thrumming, and an intense heat billowed out of the tunnel. My energy swelled with the heat, because it was ours… the one we'd been born into. It boosted our power and opened the mate bond as more of Morgan's energy seeped into our centers. All of us felt a power boost from it.

"Can't wait to find my mate," I heard Kellan mutter out loud. "Fuck me."

When you're already old and powerful, you don't expect to be shocked by an increase in energy, but we were.

A figure appeared in the dimly lit passageway to the valley, not in dragon form yet, just a bipedal about my height. When he stepped into the valley, I noted the dark hair and a familiar face void of all expression. His dark gaze locked on each of us. "Where is my mate?" he said, a whisper of power stabbing into us.

As he stood there, not attacking, he still exuded power to a degree that made my teeth ache.

Thorne is one scary daddy shifter. Morgan's thoughts were filtering through to us. *Looks just like Z and Drager.*

She wasn't wrong. He was a harder, older version of us. We still aged, even if it took thousands of years.

Drager surprised us as he spoke up: "If you want your mate, you and your galators will leave our world and never touch another fucking planet. That's what we're asking, and if you don't want us to keep tearing through your shifters, take this one-time offer and run."

We hadn't discussed a deal, but if they left now and we never saw them again, I'd be okay with it. As long as Earth wasn't their next target. But since they needed that world to repopulate Xalifer, I doubted it'd be in the line of fire.

Thorne stared at Drager for longer than was necessary to convey his annoyance. "I'll be taking my mate back," he finally rumbled, and the energy he exuded increased again, "and my galators. But first, I need to do what she set out all those decades ago. I need to kill you five to ensure our power and rule is undisturbed."

He sounded tired, resigned. No doubt his crazy-ass mate had been draining him of life for a very long time, but he clearly loved her, and was about to prove that by killing us.

Z… Morgan's voice was a tremble in my head. *I'm scared.*

I wanted to reassure her, but I wouldn't lie to her about the odds of us making it through this.

I'm sending Astra and Lexie to you. Don't go anywhere without them. If he's stronger than us, I want you to run back to Earth. I love you, la moyar.

Her sobs echoed through my mind, and I knew that tears would be falling freely down her face, but I couldn't focus on that. I had to give my all to this fight so that I'd be the one to take my mate home. Not to Earth. But to our *home.*

Here, in Risest.

Thorne's energy increased once more, and he started to shift. It didn't surprise me that our fight would take place in our strongest forms. My brothers immediately wrapped power around themselves to shift as well, but I took a risk and charged at our father, slamming into him and pushing him back into the cliff. My claws slashed across his chest, but that was the only injury I managed before he sent me flying away.

He was a dragon in the next heartbeat, and I would have been destroyed by his claws if my brothers didn't jump in front of me, already in their own dragon forms.

That gave me the few seconds I needed to call on the shift, and as my bones broke and my body reformed into a giant beast, I relished our renewed strength.

Thorne was a huge dragon, bigger than even my beast, and he was black as well, with the same fully gold wings as Drager.

I think the gold is a sign of royalty, Drager rumbled, voice of the dragon. *None of the others have them.*

It was true. Not a single shifter we'd seen or fought had the gold. Maybe it was just a symbol of our bloodline, but since that was apparently a royal one, it still stood to reason.

Thorne lifted from the ground, sending gusts of wind across the fae, pushing them back. From the entrance, the galators were once again entering the valley, so our warriors had to step up without us. We had to end this now, or it'd all be for nothing.

Drager and Emmen dove first, aiming for his wings. If they could hit him in that vulnerable joint between body and wing, his flying would be hindered. Of course, Thorne, centuries older than us, knew our weaknesses too, as he tucked his wings in tight and dove lower, out of the way of their strike.

He swung his tail at the last second, which was long and filled with lethal barbs, and struck Emmen in the side, sending him hurtling twenty feet toward the wall of the cliff. His next move was fast, crashing both sets of front claws down Drager's gut, ripping and tearing before Drager could pull away.

Tylan, Kellan, and my beast descended on him while he was occupied with attempting to disembowel Drager. I landed on his back and tore into the softer joins of his wings, managing to hit this time. Tylan slashed his face and Kellan flipped over and hit the underside of his tail. We needed to take out his weapons, and those spikes were even deadlier than I'd first thought.

Through our bond, Drager was bellowing in pain as Thorne dropped him heavily to the ground. His beast almost crushed a dozen fae, but they managed to get out of the way just in time.

Flapping my wings, I lifted quickly, and got out of Thorne's striking range. Kellan wasn't so lucky, only managing to snap off five of the dozen spikes before he was stabbed in the side with a heavy slam of his tail.

The dragon king was fast.

Beyond our abilities.

And it looked like the slashes I'd made in his wings were already healing.

We need to find a weakness, Emmen spat, recovered from his hit into the wall as he joined me. We circled the huge black beast, trying to work out the next attack. Kellan fell to join Drager, which meant two of our brothers were out of commission.

Tylan joined us in the air, and the three of us continued to circle him.

Anyone got a plan? Ty huffed.

We were running out of time. With two of our brothers bleeding on the ground, a weakness had to present itself fast, or we'd all be dead.

CHAPTER 44

MORGAN

In different circumstances, the sight of six majestic, terrifying, brightly colored dragons flying above us, their stunning gold wings glinting in the slivers of light, would be a core memory.

One I'd never forget and would love to recreate in a story, even though there were no words to accurately describe the beauty, grace, and lethal predatory vibes of the beasts. But it would have to be very different circumstances, since today, my mate and his brothers were being torn apart by one of those beasts.

The Fallen Five were strong, but Thorne was older and stronger. His brutality already had Drager and Kellan on the ground; the other three were circling as they attempted to figure out their next attack.

"They keep pouring in," Lexie snarled. "More and fucking more. We're going to lose here if the Fallen can't kill their father."

She was referring to the galators, who were once again pushing through the cave entrance, striking at our fae warriors. "Go to them," I said, nudging her. "I'm still over here in the corner, but none of us will be safe if they get through the entrance. Help your family."

Lexie didn't even remotely look torn. "You're my family," she shot back. "And I will protect you. The rest are holding their own."

They were—barely. This level of attack couldn't be sustained for much longer.

Zahak had me fully immersed in the bond, but there weren't any thoughts from their beast forms. It was rage, fire, and focus on their prey. They went in for another attack, and barely survived the swipe of claws, flames, and sheer bulk of Thorne. I heard a filtering of a thought from Emmen about finding his weakness, but I wasn't sure there was one.

"Do you know any weaknesses of these shifters?" I asked Lexie. "Have you learned of even one in all the time they've ruled this world."

She shook her head so rapidly that I knew there wasn't a hope of me discovering one. "No. There's none that we've ever seen. I mean, outside of their human mates. Now that we know about you, we'd cut off the doorways as an initial step in taking them down. No need to give them any extra power boos—"

I gasped loudly. It was so fucking obvious. We'd completely forgotten Thorne's greatest weakness. She'd been right there in front of us the entire time. Reaching out, I wrapped my hand around Lexie's hand on the hilt of her sword. "Can I borrow this?" I asked.

She blinked at me. "What for? You're not thinking of doing anything stupid like trying to fight dragons? You've had three fight classes, babe. You're not quite ready."

Zahak copped another hit above us, and I felt his pain deep in my chest, which had me panic-snapping at her. "Of course fucking not. Just… trust me. I have an idea."

She wavered for a few seconds, before she relaxed her grip on the blade and let the heavy weapon fall into my hands. "I trust you," she whispered, and I swallowed back another sob, nodding in return.

Knowing I had limited time and only one chance, I spun and raced through the crowd, heading for the back wall. Rose had her gaze lifted above, watching her mate, the smallest smile on her face. At first, I thought she was relaxed, but then I noticed her working at the binds holding her, hands lifting at her sides, and I picked up the pace.

If she escaped, all would be lost.

She pulled her focus from the dragon fight as I raced over with two sabres and a Lightsbringer warrior at my side. "You're too late," she shouted. Her eyes fell to the sword I had at my side. "You think to threaten me with a blade. My Thorne will rip you into a million piece—"

I stabbed her, right in the throat, without thought or hesitation. Swinging the blade to the side as I'd been taught in my *three fight classes*, it tore through her neck, until her head was held on by half a flap of skin.

"Fuck."

I swung around and stared at Lexie, who had *actually* cursed, her wide-eyed gaze on Rose. The queen of the shifters let out a final gurgling sound, slumping against her ropes. Ripping the sword free, I was about to stab her again, to ensure the job was done right, when a rumbling roar shook the valley.

Filled with pain and anguish, Thorne's roar knocked most of us to our knees, and a large clump of rocks landed on the ground beside me. With that, a new danger arose from my actions. I'd wanted to weaken him, since we'd overlooked that if I increased my mate's powers, then so did Rose. But now his grief was going to bring the entire cavern down on us.

Another roar, and I looked up through the falling debris to find Zahak and Emmen with their claws around Thorne's neck. The three fought for many seconds, and I held my breath as they finally drew wounds across his body. My plan had worked. The ancient king was weaker, and more than that, he was giving up.

Thorne's fight all but ceased, and if he hadn't been aiming to kill my family, I'd have felt sorry for him. Losing his mate, after hundreds of years, had broken him.

Zahak and Emmen took full advantage, and with a roar of their own they attached their claws to his neck again and flew in opposite directions. The crack was audible as the dragon king's head tore free, and a few seconds later his giant dragon body slammed into the ground, landing near Drager.

The second the king was dead, the shaking eased up, the final rocks tumbling down. "Morgan!" Lexie squealed, pulling me to my feet. "You frogging did it. You did what no one else thought to. You found his weakness."

My hands trembled. I'd lost Lexie's sword at some point, and since I couldn't see it on the ground, I hoped it was back in her pocket of energy. "It was the only way," I rasped, my throat burning. "We're their strength and their weakness. I figured that without her he'd not only be distracted, but weaker." It had been a guess, and a hope, and I'd murdered their mother without thought.

Turning, I dry-heaved but managed not to vomit, even as my stomach whirled. Planning murder was distasteful, but I'd do it again in a heartbeat if it meant saving my family. My mate.

I'm coming for you.

Zahak's voice in my head calmed me, and as his huge dragon landed a dozen feet away, the fae parted to let him through. The light increased as he shifted back, and everyone shielded their eyes. *Even me.* I still hadn't fully looked upon him in the shift, but I saw enough as energy washed across him, changing cells and reforming his body.

He reached me in the next second, and I was swept up into his arms, his lips pressing to mine. The kiss went on for days, weeks, months. I had no idea. Time and existence faded, and all I had was my dragon.

"You saved us," he whispered when he finally pulled away. One of his hands was under my ass and the other on my back as he held me against him. My legs had made their way home, around him, our bodies firmly aligned. "You saved me when you arrived here, and now you keep on fucking saving me. I'm supposed to protect you."

My chuckle was husky. "We protect each other. It's a team effort, and I'm proud of who we are together."

A loud clanging from behind reminded me that we were still in a battle, and I gestured for Zahak to put me down, but he didn't loosen his hold at all. "They're fleeing," he said simply. "The second their leaders fell, those weak bastards took off. Xalifer will be gone soon."

"And the negative effects of its influence?"

His smile faded. "We're about to find out."

Eventually, he set me on my feet, and we faced his all but decapitated mother. "We'll leave her here," he said. "As a reminder to never stand against us. Burning them is the way of the dragon, and neither deserve that." His parents were dead, by our hands, and yet I couldn't feel any pain about it from him.

"They haven't been our family for a long time," he said

simply, picking up my thoughts. "I doubt they ever really were. There's no mourning from me."

I squeezed his hand as we turned away, and I tried to push the image of Rose's body from my mind. I'd done what had to be done to save everyone, and I couldn't let that fester inside like an infected wound. They wouldn't win, not even that way.

We started toward the entrance with Lexie, Astra, and Leo. The fae cheered as we passed, and I was relieved to see that many had survived. "What about all the other bodies?" I said as we got closer to the exit. "Will they remain here as well."

"For now," Zahak said. "We have other issues to deal with first."

The fae warriors were leaving the valley, ready to return to their homes and lives. They carried our dead with them, and I knew there'd be a huge ceremony with all five dragons sending these brave warriors on to their next life.

My chest tightened when I thought about Mika, but he'd be in great company in whatever lay beyond this existence.

Standing off to the side, Emmen and Tylan held Drager and Kellan between them, I was relieved to see that while the pair looked beat up, they were starting to heal. As we closed in on them, the four locked me in their gazes, and damn... it was disconcerting to be their sole focus.

"We owe you our thanks," Emmen said formally, and then he shocked me by stepping forward and wrapping the arm not propping Kellan up around me. Getting a hug from *this* dragon was completely unexpected, and I kind of just stood there in shock, wondering what was happening.

"I think hell froze over," Kellan rasped, sounding pained. "But we're fucking thankful for you."

Zahak growled, and I was released from Emmen's hold.

"Get your own fucking mates," he snarled at them, pulling me tighter against his chest.

"Oh, we plan on it," Kellan added, a touch stronger. "Now that the battle is done, and our world will return to normal, it's my number one priority."

"We hope the world is normal," Lexie bit out. "Crazy-dragon-mom did mention that the negative energy from Xalifer would reach a point of no return."

Our group sobered, and we remained silent as we trekked along the tunnel once more, until we emerged from the cave into the land beyond, to find a beautiful bronze night sky above us.

No lie, a tear trickled down my cheek at the sight, and I knew it had all been worth it. Fighting for the beauty and freedom of Risest. We weren't the only ones just standing, staring up into a sky that was pure perfection. Every fae warrior took a moment to appreciate what we'd been fighting for.

It didn't make the losses any easier, but it gave them a purpose to keep moving forward. Those who had given their lives had done so that we might have this moment.

I almost can't believe it, I said to Zahak, glad that his brothers were no longer in our bond. I just needed him and his energy tonight. *To know that we won this fight. All of us working together.*

I know, sweetheart. We have to finish cleaning up what's left behind, and mourn our dead, but then you and I are due a few very long weeks on the isle. I've got plans.

My body shivered involuntarily as heat bloomed inside and out. Even Lexie noticed and reacted. "I don't know what you two are discussing," she said, "but leave it for when the rest of us without mates aren't around. I'm about to combust."

Zahak's smile was slow, and my stomach flipped just as slowly. This dragon... he could make me forget the days of battle and fear—and the fact that I'd just stabbed Lexie's sword through a woman's throat. He made me forget everything except him.

Him, us, and our future together.

A future as bright and beautiful as the night sky above.

Lexie said there was no magic here, but I had to disagree.

I'd found plenty of magic, and I was never letting it go.

CHAPTER 45

MORGAN

The next few days were some of the best and hardest I'd experienced in Risest. Hard because we lost over a hundred fae warriors during the battle. Florentine had been hurt, but she lived. Her brother was not so lucky.

Lexie and I held her hands as the Fallen Five sent all the warriors off to the next life, and we sobbed with her and every other fae who mourned here. Lexie had lost family as well. Almost no clan or race escaped this loss, and the sheer outpouring of grief broke me.

It was a mass farewell, in a space different to Mika's, because they needed to have open skies for the raging fires the dragons breathed across them.

They are honored, sweetheart. Zahak was comforting me, even as he performed the ceremony with his brothers. *We will not forget their sacrifices, and we will ensure that it's not in vain.*

They'd already started the process of that, as the five lands formed new alliances. No longer would Eastern Risest be a divided land, with plans to now have a combined warrior force, with *all* of the Fallen Five as their leaders.

Zahak and the others did offer the fae a chance of independence from their rule, but they declined. They trusted in their leaders and did not want any others. The Fallen fae gods remained as they had been since they fell. Gods both revered and powerful.

After the farewell ceremony for the warriors, Green Hollow emptied out, with the fae returning to their homes. The five lands were still under the rule of individual gods, but there were no more competition or divide between them. Especially not between the brothers who ruled them all.

They'd learned a powerful and devastating lesson here, and from it they decided the only way forward was as a strong, united front. There was no reason to believe they'd ever be invaded again, but the possibility would always be there. We had no idea what the future held, and preparing for it just made sense.

Zahak and I strolled along the river later that day, and a fraction of the heavy sadness that had been pressing on me since the ceremony lifted. My dusty pink sky had returned, my mate was safe, and the threat against us was no more.

The world of Xalifer was gone, and since we'd decimated their numbers and killed their leaders, the consensus was that they wouldn't be back.

Zahak had a theory of where they'd head now. "You still think they'll assimilate into Earth?" I asked him, tilting my head back as a cool breeze brushed over my face. Even Green Hollow's weather was calmer and less heated.

"Depends on if they decide to try and rebuild their race or not," he said. "Some of them would have mates already, but we were getting the impression that we weren't the only matings our mother attempted to prevent. Which explains why they were so much weaker than us. Mates increase power, and none of them had the chance to find theirs."

It was true, the shifters they faced hadn't had the Fallen Five's strength. Weak, robotic minions, blindly following the orders of their megalomaniac leader. This was their first chance at freedom, and I hoped they choose wisely.

"How are you holding up?" Zahak asked me as Astra and Leo bounded across the river toward us, done with their run and feeding. They'd found an entire field of their favorite plants and were indulging regularly. Leo was bigger than Astra now, the size of a freaking bear, and I adored his playful nature.

"I had a nightmare last night," I admitted. "But I was able to pull myself from it."

Zahak had been comforting but not intruding as I worked through the demons that lingered from the final battle. I had no regrets about what I'd chosen to do, but that didn't mean there weren't scars.

"I didn't want this path for you," he said, holding me close as he'd done a lot since we returned. The heat between us reared higher, a reminder that we hadn't had a chance for much alone time recently. As the pain in my chest eased up, the ache in my center deepened. "You should not know death in that way. That's my job as your mate."

Pressing into him, breathing in his rich, fiery scent, I let out a contented sigh. "I'm proud that I managed to do what was needed to save my friends and family. I know you told me to run if it all went to shit, but that was never an option. If you were lost to me, I would be lost to me as well. There'd be no running. So, in a huge way, I was saving myself along with everyone else."

It was odd that many fae viewed me as a hero when all I'd done was remember the trump card we'd been holding all along. A card we'd shoved to the side, used as bait, and then let her smirk her way through the battle. The fae and shifters, all warriors, had all their focus on fighting, but as the weakest link in the group, I'd had to think outside the battlefield.

I'd done what was needed, and I would do it again in a heartbeat.

Astra and Leo reached us, and we were distracted with pats and cuddles, before Zahak straightened. "I think it's time for us to return to the isle," he said. "We have work to do there as well. I've got to open the trench, even if all who had remained within was taken by the darkness, it should be opened for the nightmare creatures to return if they choose."

Astra and Leo both rumbled loudly, and I was proud of Zahak. "I think that's the right decision too. It looked like it would be beautiful down there, when it was open to the world above."

"Are you ready to leave now?" he asked me, and I nodded.

"How are we getting back?"

His smile was slow, predatory. "Dragon, of course. I'd like to take it all in and make sure there's no damage to our land."

Our land. Those words shivered down my spine and tingled through my body. Like a cloak of energy draped over me. I wondered if I'd ever get used to it.

"Okay, but I need to let Lexie know."

Zahak didn't argue. He accepted completely that she was my family and I wanted her as close as possible. Of course, I also wanted this time alone with my mate, so we'd compromise and make sure a meetup was organized for *after* our time on the isle.

We found Lexie and the other Fallen in the dining area of Florentine's house, drinks spread across the table. This was the celebration of life after the farewell of the bodies, and as soon as we walked in the door they found chairs for us to join.

Someone had lit a fire in the hearth, and soft music drifted through the air, giving everything a very pleasant and relaxing feel.

"I'm guessing we're losing you two for a few weeks," Lexie said when I settled in beside her. "You haven't even had your honeymoon yet."

Zahak's brothers laughed and joked with him, and I forced myself not to blush, even though everyone here clearly knew we were off to have a ton of sex.

"I'm going to miss you," I told her softly, leaning over to drop my head on her shoulder. "Let's organize a meetup at the library when Zahak and I are finished..." I paused and cleared my throat.

"Fucking?" Kellan added crudely.

Zahak smacked him in the back of the head, and I shot a narrowed glare at him. "Finished opening the trench, and ensuring his lands are safe."

Kellan held both hands up in front of him. "That was my second guess."

"We all need to get our lands into order, and work on this combined warrior force," Drager cut in, serious as always. Dude was back in his three-piece suits, looking like a scary bank manager. I preferred the more rugged, relaxed style of my mate, but there was no denying Drager had his own appeal. Just not for me. His poor mate better enjoy pantsuits, that was all I could say.

"Okay," Tylan chimed in, taking a swig of his drink, placing the glass cup on the table. "Let's all take a few weeks to get our lands in order, then meeting at the library is a great idea. I need some human lessons before heading out into the world."

The thought of returning to Dragerfield sent a thrill of anticipation and excitement through me. That building and the books within would always hold a significant place in my heart, even if I wasn't the biggest fan of its owner.

Zahak stood then, clearly having exhausted all his patience. "Okay, brothers, we'll see you in a few weeks. I'll be closing our bond while I'm on the isle, so don't get in touch unless it's an emergency."

"That's the Fallen version of a sock on the door," Lexie whispered loudly, and I couldn't help but snort out a response. It was true though. Zahak was prewarning them not to come knocking except if the world was burning down again.

Which was fine with me.

Lexie followed as I stood, wrapping her arms tightly around me. "I'll miss you, bestie," she said, and I tried not to bawl. I could love these changes in my life, while still mourning some of them. Lexie and I had spent every single day of the last few years together, but since I discovered Risest... well, it had been different.

"We'll find our new normal again," she whispered as she pulled away. "I'm building a compound near the academy where we can live with our own space, but close to each other."

"I'm in," Tylan said immediately. "I'm sure our mates are supposed to be best friends as well, and I'm ready for these gooey family feels. None of us were born into amazing families, so we'll make our fucking own."

"We are the actual family you were born into," Emmen said drily, "but I get what you're saying. I wouldn't mind a little company from time to time. It was getting lonely as the supreme ruler of the wilds."

They'd been lonely for a long time, and even though

they'd all come together under rather shitty circumstances, every one of the Fallen had grown from the experience.

We could feel the joy within them at having their brotherly bond back.

Gods might set themselves apart from the mere mortals, but that didn't mean they should.

"Come on, mate," Zahak growled. "We have plans."

He held out his hand, done with this conversation, and I barely managed not to express my excitement at weeks of uninterrupted time with my mate.

It was a dream come true. It was what we'd manifested through the battles and fear.

Then, when we returned, we'd get to visit the library.

After a final round of hugs from everyone—except Drager, who shook our hands, and gave a formal nod—we were out of the house and heading to an area where Zahak could shift. Astra and Leo remained with us of course, and when the three of us scrambled onto his back, I marveled at my new athletic prowess. No one had to help me reach his leg to climb up, and I wondered what I'd achieve with a little training.

Your power will only grow the longer we're together, dragon-Zahak rumbled through our bond. *You are the perfect match for me, la moyar.*

When he spoke like that, shivers raced up and down my spine, and I tried not to physically react. The voices of the Fallen had been tempting and seducing me since my first introduction to them, and I was fucking blessed to have that rumble in my life forever.

Forever.

Zahak agreed.

MORGAN

The Isle of Denille was even more stunning than it had been the last time, now bathed in the dusty pink sky during the day, and then the bronze and gold hues of the night. There was a rugged beauty to Zahak's land, as pockets of forest, rocky plains, and cliffs mixed seamlessly. He spent a long time flying over the landscape when we first arrived, and thankfully it appeared that his creatures were all fine.

The isle had many that were familiar, including fantines and dunedins, our favorite murder-bunnies, but there were also many I'd never seen before.

That's an ondor, Zahak said as we passed over the top of a dozen creatures. They lifted their scaled heads, and I couldn't get over how much they looked like miniature Komodo drag-ons. All of them watched the scaled beast above, who was a thousand times larger than them, before going back to feasting on the carcass of whatever they'd brought down and killed.

When we reached a section of the trench, Zahak hovered longer than he had anywhere else, observing. The negative energy seeping in from Xalifer had impacted those in that trench the hardest.

They're all gone, Zahak said with an undercurrent of rage. *The disease took the nightmare creatures who'd remained in there.*

Leaning down, I wrapped my arms around his neck, avoiding the spikes that protruded from his head. "I'm so sorry," I whispered. "I'm so angry that this happened, and I hope that when you open the trench, others will return."

Zahak was quiet for a few minutes, still just hovering above, his wings flapping steadily to keep us afloat. *I think it might be best to close it once and for all*, he said, and I was taken by surprise.

"Close it completely?" I questioned.

Yes, he murmured. *The disease is still there. I can scent it in the air, and if any return, they might be affected too. I can't take the risk. While it's a loss I didn't see coming, it's time to pivot once more. The trench is now, and forevermore, a mass grave of shadow creatures. I will let them all know.*

I had no idea what to say after that, so I just sat with him and the sabres as they mourned another loss to this world. If Rose were in front of me in this moment, I would have stabbed her again. Bitch invaded our world, sent her negative energy into it, and never gave a single damn of the lives she destroyed. They'd been doing this for fucking years, getting away with it, growing stronger.

Stabbing her in the throat had been too easy—she should have suffered first.

Laughter, low and subtle, echoed through my mind, and I

was relieved to feel a break in Zahak's mourning. *I like this side of you, sweetheart,* he said. *Let's go home.*

Home.

Holy shit.

I was finally going to see his cave. I wasn't sure what to expect, but I hoped it had a bed. And a bathroom. Not that I was really worried. Zahak always thought ahead and would never take me where I couldn't survive.

Banking to the left, he flew away from the trench, crossing what appeared to be the center of his land, with wide, open spaces expanding around us. I glimpsed a few villages in the distance, relieved to see fae mingling, looking safe and healthy. The disease had not spread from the trench, and in some ways the fact that it was still mostly closed off might have saved the rest of this world from being infected.

The scent of ocean grew stronger, brought in by swift winds, until we were soaring on the edge of the blue-green water. The color darkened farther from land, while remaining aquamarine near the stretch of sand.

This is our beach, he said as he changed directions once more and headed for a set of cliffs set high above the most perfect white-sand beach. It was immediately appealing, and I hoped we could paddle there. One day I might even learn to swim.

Expecting him to soar over the top of the cliff, I was surprised when he slowed about halfway up the face, and it was only when I noticed an opening, partially hidden by the shape of the surrounding rocks, that I realized where his cave was: a hundred feet in the air, and only accessible by dragons.

Well, we were certainly going to have privacy. As long as I didn't sleepwalk and find myself falling to my death.

Zahak laughed and grumbled at the same time. *Not a chance, sweetheart. Not a single chance.*

The opening wasn't huge, so he had to land on the edge, digging his claws in. *Climb over onto my nose and I'll lower you inside*, he told me.

I didn't hesitate, carefully maneuvering over the spikes on his head, until I was straddling his nose. The beast breathed deeply as I settled in, and I could feel his hunger rising. The man and dragon were the same being, and they both wanted to eat me.

In the best way, of course.

Wait until you shift back, Z, I said with a laugh. *The human body can only handle so much.*

I needed help to handle his bipedal form, as he called it, so the dragon was definitely out.

You smell delicious, mate, he said as he lowered me to the cave floor.

It had been more than a few hours since he'd stopped to give me a break, so my legs were wobbly until I figured out how to stand again. Astra and Leo bounded off soon after, and the light grew immensely bright as Zahak shifted back.

Only this time, he didn't bring any clothes with the change, standing there gloriously naked, his perfect form highlighted in the final light of a day fading into night.

"Astra, take Leo to your section and leave us be for some time," he rumbled, darkening eyes on me.

After nudging against my side affectionately, the pair took off, and I got a split second to wonder what her section was before Zahak was right in front of me. He moved like a ghost, so fast and quiet, that I let out a little squeak.

"Welcome home, mate," he said, voice deepening as he reached out and brushed a hand down my cheek. "Unfortunately, the tour is going to have to wait."

Pushing myself up on my toes, boots stretched to their full

limits, I pressed my hands against his chest. "Fine by me. My patience has run out for the day."

I was in his arms in a heartbeat, his firm hands gripping my thighs as he lifted me up and into him. Our mouths met frantically, the desire driving us nearly out of our minds, and I was desperate to strip my clothes away so I could feel his skin against me.

We needed this. The love and healing and bonding.

This celebration of life we were lucky enough to live.

Rumbles rocked through his chest as he tasted my mouth, demanding everything and more. He controlled the kiss, so dominant, and by the time he pulled away I was dizzy and sucking in the air my screaming lungs demanded.

"Fuck," I huffed. "That was only a kiss."

His grin was wicked and a little terrifying. "First of the million you'll get over the next few weeks, so prepare yourself."

"I've been prepared from the second I met you, Z," I whispered, throat thick with emotions. "I dreamed of you, and it's better than I could have ever imagined."

He kissed me again, over and over. We were at the edge of our restraint, needing to ease the aching inside, but he spent forever just kissing me, exploring my mouth and my throat, tasting across my skin and slowly stripping my clothes from my body.

Walking us through the cave, I managed a few glimpses, to find his home was surprisingly modern: lots of rugs to warm up the stone floors, fireplaces to ward off the chill of the ocean air, a stunning internal waterfall and hot springs, along with a huge bed that was definitely dragon-king.

When he lay me back on the bed, the scent of clean sheets and Zahak surrounded me, and I decided that this was my happy place. Zahak didn't say a word as his mind wrapped around my thoughts and feelings. He took his time, stroking my heated, sensitive skin, sending the swirls of desire in my gut hotter and higher.

I was writhing on the bed by the time he finished, clawing at the sheets, and he'd done little except caress my skin and kiss me.

As he shifted lower, between my legs, he breathed in my scent. Scales appeared across his arms as they wrapped around my thighs. "Delicious," he murmured, and then his tongue swiped to the top of my slit, taking in all the arousal that had been gathering there. He ran his tongue over me again and again, devouring. He took my pleasure and drowned in it.

I came in the first two seconds. Then again not even a minute later. The orgasms built slower after that, until I was screaming and crying in pure ecstasy. Zahak's mouth suctioned on to my clit, pulling the bundle of nerves deeper between his teeth, as one finger slowly entered me, curling up to hit that spot which always sent me over the edge.

He sucked harder, and a second finger joined the first, stretching me almost painfully. Pleasure-pain, and I was here for it.

"Oh my fucking fuck," I cried out, arching against him, my release so forceful that it squirted from me, soaking Zahak's face. He growled again, and when he lifted his head and wiped his fingers across the moisture on his chin, he licked up every drop.

My body was vibrating now, cells on fire, as the need between us grew.

He crawled along the bed, and using his arms to brace himself, he leaned down and kissed me roughly. My need built and built, and when he settled in between my thighs, I opened my legs and wrapped them around him.

The thick head of his cock pressed against my entrance, and I cried out, needing more. The heat roared as he adjusted my frame to make room for his size, and it was once again seamless as he thrust slowly inside me. It took time, even with his energy, but eventually I was able to take his full length.

He pulled out in a single movement before thrusting back in, and I clung to his shoulders, nails digging in as I tried not to explode. He continued with the long, slow thrusts that had me going crazy. Sobs and cries escaped as the swirls in my body expanded.

"Zahak, please," I begged. I needed him to finish. I needed to feel the thick knot of his cock pulsing inside me, sending my body into oblivion.

Shifting a hand under my ass, he changed our positions, and I gasped as he hauled me up on top of him as he dropped down onto his knees. We were still joined, my legs around his waist, but from this position, he held me higher to thrust with more speed.

I lost myself.

The slow building pleasure detonated, and I was left with fractured thoughts. When he came soon after, the knot thickened, and it locked our bodies in place, pressing into my g-spot, along with other pleasure zones.

Zahak groaned my name and whispered his love as the pulsing throb kept us both groaning and writhing.

The first time he'd knotted, it had lasted for hours, and I'd passed out from the pleasure. Every time since it lasted about half an hour, and I remained awake and conscious for every second of the intense experience.

Each pulse brought on a mini-orgasm, and I was sated as fuck when the knot finally released. Not that Zahak left my body, remaining inside, with me sprawled on top.

"How long until you can do that again?" I murmured, needy for more.

My body shook as he laughed beneath me, and I groaned as his cock, still hard, thrust inside again. Unable to help myself, I pushed up on him, moving my hips as I chased my next high.

Zahak, no longer laughing, stared up at me, and his expression looked a lot like awe. Riding harder, I leaned over and kissed him. "I love you," I said, breathless, the edge of an orgasm already building.

"La moyar," he returned. "You are the greatest gift in my life, and I will cherish you for eternity. You will never want or need for anything, and I will destroy any threat that comes your way."

He let me continue to control the pace for a few minutes, before his hands settled on my hips as he held me in place and thrust faster. "You are mine," he continued, speaking each word with each thrust. "Today and for eternity."

Eternity was just enough time for me.

Zahak's love language was the same as mine, and I'd never felt more certain that we were perfect for each other. Cosmically designed to be together.

I couldn't wait for our eternity.

EPILOGUE

MORGAN

"**W**ell, well, well," Lexie said with a huge smile. "Don't you look like a glowing, sated woman."

I was back in the library, back with my bestie, and life had never been better.

She pulled me into a fierce hug, and I breathed deeply at the pure happiness I felt. What an amazing few weeks it had been, holed up in Zahak's cave, and now back in the library.

"You really do look amazing," she added, pulling away to look me over. "Mated life agrees with you."

I couldn't deny it, my happiness and the energy from Zahak had resulted in a glow I'd never worn before. And I wasn't pregnant, because we'd decided it still wasn't time for that step in our journey. There was no rush, and we were content to enjoy these days alone.

Zahak had explained the whole process to me: a combination of energy, a gestation period of five months, then I would birth our son, and he'd arrive still in the embryonic sack. Zahak called it a pod, but I had mentally renamed it to a more human term. No need to freak out my brain yet. After I gave birth, *the sack* needed to finish gestating in lava, and then we'd have ourselves a baby shifter.

Terrifying, glorious, and miraculous all at the same time.

"I'm so freaking happy to see you," I told Lexie, focusing back on her. "What have you been up to?"

She smiled. "Oh, so flippin' much. I have to tell you everything. Come on."

She dragged me into the deeper shelves, where we'd hung out during work and hidden from Simon, the caretaker. Zahak was off chatting with his brothers, giving me time to catch up with my bestie.

"We managed to create a compound for all of us near the academy," she said when we reached our spot.

I moved to a nearby shelf, running my hands over my books. "You built houses and everything in a few weeks?"

Lexie shrugged, taking a seat at the table. "Well, unlike you, the rest of us don't have mates keeping us occupied. We had some help from the students as well, so it moved forward rather quickly."

It was exciting to know that Zahak and I could split our time between our cave home and the compound we'd share with our family. Such a picture-perfect ending to our story. Or, really, it was the beginning of the next story for us.

"Zahak got the trench closed before we left," I told her, my voice lowering. "And he found another section of the isle to set up as a sanctuary for the shadow creatures who want to return home."

"That's great," she said, her expression softening. "It makes all the difference to them, you know, having their needs acknowledged and cared about. They're used to being relegated to shadows and sidelines, forgotten."

I agreed. The few we'd spoken with had expressed their gratitude. The sanctuary already had fifty or more inhabitants, along with hundreds of others who visited when they needed the energy of fellow shadow creatures. Astra and Leo were there right now, helping to keep it running smoothly during this initial setup period.

"Drager has a surprise for all of us too," Lexie said suddenly, as I pulled out a book I hadn't seen before, wondering if it was new or if I'd somehow missed it when I worked here.

Placing it back on the shelf, I turned to face her, leaning against the shelves. "A surprise. This should be interesting."

Her lips twitched. "Very interesting. I think I'm the only one who knows, since he asked my opinion on it, but I'm pretty sure you're going to like it."

I was more than a little curious now, and as I stared harder at her, reminding her that besties don't keep secrets from each other, she let out a sweet laugh. Her delicate features, that I now knew were elfin, softened as she stood. "Come on, I'll let him tell you. It's part of his path to making amends, and I won't ruin his surprise. We can finish catching up later." Her eyebrows waggled. "I'm going to need more deets on these sex sessions you've been having."

My cheeks burned, but it wasn't from embarrassment. Just thinking about Zahak, the way he touched me, how I woke every freaking morning with his tongue inside me, was enough to send my temperature skyrocketing.

"That good, hey?" Lexie said, shaking her head. "Not going to lie, I'm jealous. I wonder if I can turn myself into a human and find a Fallen god to worship me as well."

Crossing over to her, I wrapped my arms around her in another hug. "We'll find your perfect mate, don't worry. He's out there."

When I pulled back, her smile was rueful. "I'm not so sure, but at least I can live vicariously through you. So, details. Later."

"You got it," I said.

We linked arms and made our way downstairs to find the guys. Through Zahak's mind, I knew the five of them were on the main floor: the ballroom, where it had started for me all those months ago. They stood close, and I could feel that they were happy to see each other again as well.

There was a comfort when they were all together, and I was relieved that there would never be distance between them again. They'd learned the same hard and valuable lesson as the fae of Risest. Their strength was in their bond.

"Hello, little human," Kellan said, bounding over to sweep me up into a hug. "We've missed your pretty face."

Zahak's growl had less bite than usual, but Kellan still released me just as quickly.

I got hugs from the others, and even Drager this time, though his was very quick and almost clinical. He wasn't taking any chances that Zahak would decide to once again rip his throat out.

"It's great to see you all," I said, looking around. "And the library is exactly the same. I've missed this place so much."

Tylan took a second to look around, as if he hadn't really seen it before now. "It's nice," he agreed. "I don't know why I expected the human world to be primitive. Parts of it are actually more luxurious than Risest."

The technology here did make our lives easier, but in many ways it was far behind Risest. "It has its benefits," I agreed, "but I prefer home."

It had taken almost no time to start thinking of Risest as my home, the fae as my people, and the Fallen Five and Lexie as my family. Along with Astra and Leo.

My parents, by now, had probably declared me dead, and I figured it might be easier to leave it at that, since I couldn't exist with them in this world any longer. There was nothing left for me here.

You can decide what you want to do later, Zahak said. *You have plenty of time.*

He was right. I pushed the unpleasantness aside and said, "Drager has a surprise for us. I'm not feeling very patient, so can you tell us now."

Zahak crossed his arms. "This surprise better not involve my mate, or we're going to have an issue."

Again, there was no true anger in the threat, and Drager laughed, seemingly without taking any offence. "I wouldn't dream of it. I've learned my lesson, and I'm trying to be less of an asshole. It's a long process, but step one for me is to announce that the library is no longer mine."

I just stared at him, my heart beating fast. If he'd sold it to a human, I'd be devastated. At least while it was Drager's, I'd have been able to visit it whenever I wanted.

"Well, who the fuck does it belong to?" Zahak rumbled, reacting to the sadness that spiked through me.

"It belongs to all of us," Drager said simply. "I changed the legal documents in the human world, and now we all have rights to it. I was thinking..." He paused briefly. "...that maybe it could work as a base for everyone to stay when they search for their mates, and for Morgan to get her fix of the human world. I've even commissioned a wing of rooms to be added, so we all have our own space. Construction is to start this spring."

I blinked at him, feeling the heat burning my eyes. "It's mine too," I choked out. I didn't even care that I had to share it with the others. They were family, and this was another family home.

One here, two in Risest. I had never felt so full of happiness.

It was too much. I had to press my hand to my chest to try to ease the ache there.

"Thank you," Zahak said, shocking everyone into silence. "We appreciate this gesture."

I nodded rapidly, lips trembling as I fought for words. To know I'd be here as the Fallen searched for their mates, and I'd help them assimilate into the human world while they did so. I'd have my books, and we could add more to them, and then one day when Zahak and I decided to have a baby, he got to grow up here.

It was too much.

"She's going to cry," Tylan whispered. "I hate when she cries."

Emmen reached out to shove Zahak, but he was already moving toward me. "She's happy," he told them, his voice raspier than usual as he wrapped his arms around me. He held me tight, and I allowed all my joy to flow out in tears, soaked up by his shirt and the comfort of my mate's arms. My eternity was going to be perfect, and I couldn't wait to get started.

———

Thank you for being part of this journey with Morgan! If you'd like to stay up to date on more releases, you can join my   FB   group: www.facebook.com/groups/jayminevenerdherd

my   FB   group: www.facebook.com/groups/
jayminevenerdherd

WHAT TO READ NEXT!

I've had a lot of readers contacting me asking for what to read next. My recommendation for after the Fallen Fae Gods is the Shadow Beast Shifters series. Rejected- Book 1

My father made a terrible mistake. One I'm left paying for.

As a wolf shifter growing up in a strong pack, I should be living my best life. But after my father tried to kill our leader, I'm labelled an outcast, traitor, less than dirt.

When I can't take pack life any longer, I run, but apparently they don't like losing their punching bag. Torin, the leader's son, drags me back before my first shift... a shift that will reveal my true mate. I never could have predicted who mine would be, but the moment my wolf looks upon him, I'm filled with hope for a brighter future.

Afterall, no one ever rejects their true mate, right?

Wrong. Very wrong.

When the wolves attack, my soul screams for vengeance, and somehow I touch the shadow world.

Somehow I bring him to our lands.

The Shadow Beast. Our shifter god. The devil himself.

Turns out being rejected by my mate was only the beginning.

*If you like sexy, dark paranormal romances, with humor, steam, action, a tough heroine and an antihero, this is for you. Rejected is full length (100k) words, is book one of three in Shadow Beast Shifters series, and ends on a cliffhanger. It's recommended for 18+ due to language and sexual situations.

ALSO BY JAYMIN EVE

JAYMIN EVE

Fallen Fae Gods (Dark Romantasy dragon shifter/fae 18+) (complete)

Book One: Gilded Wings

Book Two: Crimson Skies

Shadow Beast Shifters (Dark and Sexy wolf shifter/ god Romantasy 18+) (complete)

Book One: Rejected

Book Two: Reclaimed

Book Three: Reborn

Book Four: Deserted

Book Five: Compelled

Book Six: Glamoured

Boys of Bellerose (Dark, RH rock star romance 18+)(complete)

Book One: Poison Roses

Book Two: Dirty Truths

Book Three: Shattered Dreams

Book Four: Beautiful Thorns

Demon Pack (PNR/Urban Fantasy 18+) (Complete)

Book One: Demon Pack

Book Two: Demon Pack Elimination

Book Three: Demon Pack Eternal

Supernatural Prison Trilogy (Complete UF series 17+)

Book One: Dragon Marked

Book Two: Dragon Mystics

Book Three: Dragon Mated

Book Four: Broken Compass

Book Five: Magical Compass

Book Six: Louis

Book Seven: Elemental Compass

Supernatural Academy (Complete Urban Fantasy/PNR 18+)

Year One

Year Two

Year Three

Royals of Arbon Academy (Dark, complete Contemporary Romance 18+)

Book One: Princess Ballot

Book Two: Playboy Princes

Book Three: Poison Throne

Titan's Saga (PNR/UF. Sexy and humorous 18+)

Book One: Releasing the Gods

Book Two: Wrath of the Gods

Book Three: Revenge of the Gods

Dark Legacy (Complete Dark Contemporary high school romance 18+)

Book One: Broken Wings

Book One: First World

Book Two: Spurn

Book Three: Crais

Book Four: Regali

Book Five: Nephilius

Book Six: Dronish

Book Seven: Earth

Hive Trilogy (Complete UF/PNR series)

Book One: Ash

Book Two: Anarchy

Book Three: Annihilate

Sinclair Stories (Standalone Contemporary Romance 18+)

Songbird

9 781925 876376